PRAISE FOR REMAINS

"The best hard sf stuff is built around a soft core of humanity, and Mark Tiedemann's *Remains* is no exception...That the hero and his compatriots are all too human gives him a chance to show off his understanding of the conflicted heart."
SHARON SHINN

"An intricate tale of love, loss and betrayal played out amid a complex and fascinating techno-industrial setting."
KRISTINE SMITH

PRAISE FOR MARK W. TIEDEMANN

"Mark Tiedemann is a writer of genuine talent and ability, who explores his cosmos with verve and a sense of wonder."
DAVID BRIN

"one of science fiction's great world-builders"
JOHN SNIDER, SCIFIDIMENSIONS

"Mark Tiedemann writes with an engaging energy, gritty realism, and a genuine concern for his characters."
JEFFREY CARVER

REMAINS

ALSO BY MARK W. TIEDEMANN

Compass Reach
Metal of Night
Peace & Memory

MARK W. TIEDEMANN

REMAINS

BENBELLA BOOKS
Dallas, Texas

BenBella Books
6440 N. Central Expressway
Suite 617
Dallas, TX 75206

PUBLISHER: Glenn Yeffeth
SENIOR EDITOR: Shanna Caughey
ASSOCIATE EDITOR: Leah Wilson
DIRECTOR OF MARKETING/PR: Laura Watkins

Send feedback to feedback@benbellabooks.com
www.benbellabooks.com

Printed in the United States of America

10 9 8 7 6 5 4 3 2 1

Library of Congress Cataloging-in-publication data

Tiedemann, Mark W.
    Remains / Mark W. Tiedemann.—BenBella Books ed.
        p.cm.
    ISBN 1-932100-49-0
    I. Title.
PS3620.I33R46 2005
813'.6—DC22

2004024649

Cover illustration copyright © J.P. Targete
Cover design by Melody Cadungog
Design and composition by John Reinhardt Book Design

Distributed by Independent Publishers Group
To order call (800) 888-4741
www.ipgbook.com
For special sales contact Laura Watkins at laura@benbellabooks.com

For Kelley Eskridge and Nicola Griffith,
for innumerable kindnesses and excellent friendship

ONE

MARS, 2115

MACE PRESTON BRUSHED REDDISH SAND off the dented and scarred recorder, tucked it under his arm and started the long trudge up the slope to the rim of the excavation. Like most of the debris found so far, the dark box showed signs of having been ripped from its moorings and tossed around by the hurricane-force winds that then buried the site beneath nearly seven million cubic meters of Martian dust.

As he reached the edge and stepped onto the solid ground of Hellas Planitia, Mace looked back at the ruin below. Diggers moved methodically, pumping and sifting sand, lowering the level of the burial, and concentrated extra effort at the far wall where the magline tunnel entered the site. Snaking tubes draped up over the rim at intervals, clouds of reddish dust shooting from their maws. Equipment jutted from the drifts below like toys abandoned in a playground. Eighty-nine bodies had been tangled up with broken habitats, tools, chemical wastes, food, clothes and construction material. Many had been uncovered already, but the excavation went slowly so as not to miss anything that might provide a clue about what had happened. Mace's patience wore thin. One of those corpses might be his wife.

Around the edge of the rectangular trough stood huge stanchions, three meters wide and two high, at thirty-meter intervals. Wispy black threads clung to their bases, part of what remained of the molifiber sheeting that had covered the trough. The stanchions held the fabric

1

tight over the volume, keeping an atmosphere in and the Martian winds out. At least, it had. No one yet knew exactly when that failure had occurred, only that during the recent sandstorm that had blown with 300 to 350 kilometer-per-hour strength across Hellas Planitia for nearly forty-five days the interlocking molecules somehow unlocked, the sheet tore, letting out the pressurized atmosphere within the site, immediately followed by the sand that had killed everyone and then filled the manmade hole. Mace guessed that the disaster had occurred during the past seven days. He had talked to Helen eight days ago. Then communications went down.

Mace seethed. So far all the recorders that had been found had been disconnected prior to the catastrophe. Not one had contained a recoverable record of the incident. No one had used the word "sabotage" yet, but Mace doubted anyone believed this had been an accident.

"Mr. Preston," a voice spoke through his earpiece. "Someone here to see you."

Mace turned toward the carryall squatting a few dozen meters away. Just beyond its hulking mass, Mace saw a three-passenger dusthopper that had not been there when he had left the carryall earlier.

"I'm coming in," he said. "I have another recovery."

No response. He made his way to the carryall with his find. The airlock was near the forward section of the twenty-meter-long vehicle emblazoned with the stylized star-and-fullerene logo of PolyCarb Intra-Solar, the main contractor on the site. His employers. A few more carryalls stood at intervals around the outside of the dig.

Mace stomped his feet just inside the hatch, raising small clouds of wispy red dust. Cyclers sucked it in, clearing it from the air before he went through to the inner lock.

He entered the cramped prep chamber and pulled his breather mask off. The cooler air tasted of plastic and metal. He had been outside for six and a half hours.

The specialist on duty accepted the recorder from Mace to log in. Then he took Mace's breather pack and hooked it into a recharger on the wall. Mace carefully peeled out of his overskin, mindful of the pendant hanging from his neck, while the specialist busied himself behind his small desk.

"Pushing it a bit," the man said. "Regs say never less than an hour's supply."

"Anybody else bring anything in?"

"No, sir. Mr. Cavery's still out, though."

Winston Cavery had been head of on-site security here before Mace arrived three days ago. Mace had assumed his position, demoting Cavery to his second.

"Who's waiting to see me?" Mace asked, annoyed at being reminded of safety regulations.

"Company brass, out of Burroughs. Just got in a couple hours ago. Didn't catch the name. She's with Overseer Oxmire, forward in ops."

Mace felt tired now that he was in normal air with normal pressure. He was ready to clean up and sleep. Instead, he slipped into a soft one-piece utility and went past the specialist into the main lounge. The smell of coffee and cocoa filled the air, drawing him to the dispenser. He drew a cup of hot cocoa, then went forward into main ops.

"—shouldn't even be here. He had no authorization—"

Mace stepped over the threshold. Cliff Oxmire, the recovery site manager, leaned against a console on the opposite side of the elliptical space, heavy arms folded over a wide chest. He looked up at Mace with a skeptical smirk.

Hobs, the ops cyberlink, reclined in his couch, a cable plugged into the socket at the base of his skull, plugging him into the database. His fingers twitched, a byproduct of whatever direct stimulation his brain received from the data flow. He was deep into the link, oblivious to anything else in the room.

The woman talking to Oxmire had her back to Mace when he entered. She turned now. Tall, olive-skinned, with thick black hair and wide-set dark brown eyes, she looked displeased to see Mace.

"Mace Preston," Oxmire said. He lowered his arms. "This is Cambel Guerrera. Corporate liaison."

"You asked to see me?" Mace asked.

"My request," she said. "Yes. Can we go somewhere private?"

"Use my cabin," Oxmire said.

Mace led the way back through the lounge, down a narrow corridor lined with sleeping berths stacked three high, some with curtains drawn. Oxmire's cabin was a cubicle just outside the equipment stores, a space barely long enough for a bunk bed, just wide enough for a fold-down desk and a commlink.

Guerrera closed the narrow door behind her.

"Just what do you think you're doing here, Mr. Preston?"

"I—"

She held up a hand. "Before you start making excuses, let me tell you what *I'm* doing here. Among other things, I've been sent to evaluate your conduct in relation to this incident. You were in Burroughs, 500 kilometers from here, four days ago, running security for Director Listrom's tour. You abandoned that assignment to come here. Right now that looks like dereliction and failure to follow procedure. You just took off, talked your way onto a transport full of rescue workers, and came here. Since arriving here you have replaced the head of security and run his operations as your own. You did this with no authorization from the company at any point, from any level. That's breach of contract. Cavery complained to Oxmire, Oxmire filed an official protest, which you ignored. Insubordination. Have I missed anything?"

Mace hesitated. He felt his anger rise. Calm down, he told himself. "No. Not yet."

"We can expect more?"

"Depends what we find here."

She crossed her arms. The fingers of her right hand drummed briefly on her left bicep. "Why did you abandon your assignment in Burroughs?"

"My wife is here."

Cambel Guerrera blinked, her entire posture changing. "Oh. I didn't know that. Who—?"

"Her name is Helen. Helen Croslo. She's a special projects consultant. Troubleshooter."

Guerrera's arms fell. "I see. That—I can understand your being upset, then, but—"

"Cavery's good, but I needed to be here. I needed to do this myself."

Cambel Guerrera frowned. Clearly she had expected something else, something for which a reprimand or worse might be not only required, but justified. Action was still likely—he *had* walked off a job to come here—but circumstances might lessen the severity. She nodded slowly. "You haven't done yourself any favors, Mr. Preston. Director Listrom is rather upset."

"I left him in good hands."

"That's not the point. You shouldn't have 'left him' in anybody's hands. I can understand the impulse, but there are rules."

"What would you have done?"

"That's also beside the point." She pursed her lips, regarding him. "I'm going to spend the next couple of days here. I'm to make a report on progress and on you. This is a very important contract for PolyCarb. We need to know what happened here, sooner rather than later. How did you know about the accident, by the way? It's been kept off the open media."

"Helen and I had been talking every other day. She missed two calls, then I found out the link was down to the site."

"And?"

"And what? I'm a security specialist, Ms. Guerrera. I found out what happened."

"From whom?"

"I'm not getting anybody else in trouble. This was my decision to come out here."

"You pulled rank, in other words."

"What else is it for?"

"You're a Martian, aren't you?"

"Originally. I'm Aean now."

"And your wife?"

"Aean by birth."

"Is that how you became Aean? Through marriage?"

"Do you have a point to make?"

Guerrera's arms came back up, refolded. "I would suggest you stop giving me attitude. You're the one in violation of company rules, Mr. Preston. I can either help you or hurt you."

"Which would you rather do?"

"I'm inclined to help you. Stop pushing me in the other direction."

Mace caught himself before provoking her again. He was tired and, he admitted, frightened. He had been plunging forward for three days now on adrenaline and hope. Both were fading.

"I'm sorry," he said finally. "What do you need to know?"

Cambel herself seemed to be fighting impatience. She sighed heavily. "Do you understand how important this project was? Is? This was the first leg of the CircumAres Underground entirely run by PolyCarb. Up till now we've been consultants and subcontractors."

"I read all the press material, Ms. Guerrera. That's what Listrom's doing in Burroughs, making nice with the Martian elite."

"So you have a sense how bad this makes us look."

"I admit I haven't given a lot of thought to PolyCarb's image since I've been here."

"Do. It's not just PolyCarb. To Mars, we're Aea. A lot of them don't believe we know how to do anything on a planet."

Mace understood what she meant. He had grown up hearing jokes about the orbitals, about people living in airless space, not knowing which end was up because there was no ground beneath their feet. Aea was the oldest and largest of the orbital communities. Mars was fast becoming the largest surface-bound colony, catching up to Lunase on the moon. Over decades competition had evolved between the orbitals and the planetaries. Despite their joint membership in the Trans System Congress—what was known as Signatory Space—it threatened to create serious divisions. Aea's work on the Jovian moons and now on Mars promised to head off such splits before they became endemic.

Martians admired good engineering. But it had to be surface engineering, planetbound, for them to trust the engineers. The Maglev underground project would go a long way toward convincing Martians that Aeans could be trusted.

"In a couple more days," he said, "Helen would've been done. We had it scheduled to meet at the Burroughs Grand Mariner and spend a couple days before catching a liner back to Aea."

His vision fragmented suddenly, the light shimmering. He blinked, wiped at his eyes. A convulsion threatened to take him over. He sniffed.

"I'm sorry, Mr. Preston. I would like a full report on what you've found here. I'll be getting reports from others as well."

He could not speak without losing control. He nodded, raising a hand in assent.

"Have they...have they found her yet?"

Mace shook his head, not looking up. Cambel Guerrera left the cabin.

Mace sat down on Oxmire's bunk to wait for the spell to pass. So far, since arriving on the site, he had managed to be alone when these episodes overtook him. Usually, he was tired when it happened. If he just waited it out, self-control returned.

He managed to suppress his tears. He went back to ops. Hobs was still there, plugged in and effectively absent. Mace sat down at the security console. He entered his code, waited for the clearance, then connected to Burroughs. A personnel file came up on the screen and he touched the icon for his second. He put the earpiece on as the link opened.

"Hey, boss."

"How did it go?" Mace asked.

"Mr. Listrom is extremely upset. The company sent someone to check you out."

"I know, she's here. What can you tell me about her?"

"Cambel Guerrera, been with PolyCarb about five years, moving up fast, but not exceptionally so. She has a reputation for fairness and thoroughness. She didn't go alone. There's an adjuster from the company with her, guy named Piers Hawthorne. Upper-mid-level type, standard clearance."

"An adjuster. Why? Isn't it a bit soon?"

"There's a security cordon around the site now. Martian authorities agreed to the request from the company. We want to find out what happened before anything goes public. Hawthorne needed to get there to do his job, theirs was the last scheduled flight."

"That'll be great for morale. I haven't seen him yet."

"Boss, you may have done me a favor, but this might cost you."

"I'll handle that. I just needed to know what kind of bureaucrat they sent me."

"Uh...have you found anything yet?"

"No."

"Well, look. Good luck, boss."

He closed the link and removed the earpiece. When he turned around, Cliff Oxmire was sitting at his own board. Mace stood and Oxmire looked up.

"Cavery just reported uncovering another cluster of bodies," Oxmire said. "Just north of the tunnel entrance."

Mace felt his pulse pick up. "And?"

"And I just checked your duty log. You're pushing your limit on surface work, Mace. Maybe you should get some sleep." When Mace hesitated, Oxmire added, "I suggest you do it voluntarily. I can order it, but that goes on your record."

"How am I supposed to relax after what you just told me?"

"Take a pill. I will tell you when we have ID on the bodies or if anything else turns up that you need to know about."

"I'm supposed to determine that."

Oxmire said nothing. Mace knew he was right, that it was within his authority to make Mace stay in the carryall for a number of hours.

"I sympathize, Mace," Oxmire said. "I won't let anything important go by without telling you. But I have enough to worry about without anyone, including the head of security, doing something stupid and getting hurt."

"I understand there's been a communications cordon put around us."

"That's right. I got the word when Ms. Guerrera came in."

"Let me know if that changes."

Oxmire nodded, still watching him. Mace headed back for the bunks. He picked an empty berth and climbed in.

Staring at the ceiling half a meter away, he tried to will his mind to stop working. He should sleep, he knew, but questions kept prodding at him.

The fabric that gave out had a near-perfect history of service. Molifiber was a light, deceptively strong material, the carbonile molecules bound more tightly together than anything found in nature outside degenerate matter. The stuff did not simply tear. But Mace knew of nothing that could do what had apparently been done. Unless the sheeting used had been defective.

He wondered what Helen had been doing here. As always, Mace had little idea what exactly she was doing. So much of her work she kept from him; most of it was sensitive, and the stuff she had told him about had been years old. He held security clearances one level below hers. She told him a lot more than she should, he suspected, which satisfied him that what she did had to do with experimental projects, or projects with substantial financial risk to the company, but nothing imminently life-threatening. Troubleshooting was a vague label for indeterminate functions. She had spoken to him about some of her jobs, showed him a few things she had done. From what he could tell, Helen was good at what she did. He wondered what she had found, if anything.

This had been a last-minute assignment, but at least she had been able to let him know about it. She had been on her way home, back to Aea from a long tour at Ganymede, when she was diverted to Mars. She had spent three days in Burroughs, then had headed for the new site. By the time Mace arrived on Mars, Helen had been there about two months, most of her stay spent at the new site. Mace himself had pulled strings and called in favors to get the assignment for security for Director Oswald Listrom's trip to Mars. Listrom was one of the board members of Aea, as well as upper management in PolyCarb. Very important. He had given final approval for Mace to head up his security team for the Martian visit. Listrom and his party had arrived on Mars nearly thirty-two days ago.

Once Mace had contacted Helen, he felt relieved. Routine, she told him, nothing to worry about, just some pesky details no one on the site had the expertise or authority to deal with. The sandstorm kept connecting traffic grounded, so they would just have to wait, but she knew a good hotel....

Mace tried to add up how much time they had spent together since they met. He kept adding wrong. All he remembered clearly was that they had met on Mars, almost seven years ago—Aean years, which were close to Earth standard—and had married almost a year after that. Actual time in each others' presence: less than two years total. No, he thought, that can't be right. I must be missing some days here and there. I must be—

"You don't really love me," she told him.

"Of course I do. I married you."

"To get Aean citizenship. You can't stand Mars. No, it's all right, I don't blame you. Nice place to visit, I can see that, but...."

"Helen."

"It's all right, I said. I like it this way. I know exactly what you want from me and I know exactly what I want from you. And I like you: I really like you."

"I love you."

"Maybe you do. But that won't save our butts if anything goes wrong. Being friends might. Don't look so worried. I asked you to marry me. I know what I'm getting and I like it."

He opened his eyes, shocked at the memory. She had told him that during their honeymoon in Helium, up near the north pole, a few days before she took him back to Aea and he became a citizen. He had felt small and embarrassed afterward, because he suspected she was right. He knew she was partly—he had always wanted to get off Mars—but he wondered about the rest.

The last few days convinced him she was wrong.

He wanted to see her, touch her.

He checked the time. To his surprise, nearly two hours had passed. He must have slept after all.

Two raps outside the berth startled him.

"Mace," Oxmire said. "They're bringing up more bodies. And we're close to the main bore."

Mace entered ops and the conversation stopped. Oxmire, Cambel Guerrera, Winston Cavery, and another man Mace did not recognize stood at the main board. They all looked at him when he came in. Cavery barely suppressed a scowl. Mace knew he would have to do something to make up the last three days to Cavery; he had bulled his way in here, wresting control of security from the younger man for no good reason.

He walked up to the group. On the large screen that dominated the console, a grid of the site showed the location of the excavation teams. Two teams worked on the entrance to the magline shaft on the northwest wall. Red markers showed where bodies had been located. Most of them now had green checkmarks as well, indicating recovery.

Initial deep scans had located all but three bodies.

"Any IDs yet?" Mace asked.

"That process is just starting," Cavery said. "Sir."

"Are they into the tunnel yet?"

"Be opening it up in another half hour," Oxmire said.

"How come you haven't used the surface accesses?" the stranger asked then. He was slim, almost slight, with wavy brown hair and a thin, aquiline nose. He reached to the screen and tapped at points along the tunnel. "The emergency accesses."

Mace felt momentarily surprised. Along the tunnel, at half-kilometer intervals, a series of shafts would be sunk from the surface down to the base for use in case of shut-downs or other unforeseen problems with the line. He had known about them, but he had neglected to ask.

"They're not opened yet," Oxmire said. "The shafts are bored, but they aren't cut through."

"None of them?" the stranger wondered, frowning.

"Half hour you said?" Mace asked.

"We've recovered sixty-eight bodies so far," Cavery said. "Several were clustered near the mouth of the tunnel."

"You think they were trying to get in there?"

"Possibly," Cavery said. "Or they just got blown in that direction until sand filled the hole."

They would never know exactly what had happened, but their models suggested that when the molifiber ripped open, the trough funneled the winds for a short time, increasing intensity and velocity. The habitats in which workers sought refuge had been torn loose. Rescue workers had found many bodies beaten to death inside the prefab structures.

As sand poured in, the turbulence faded. Survivors suffocated because air supplies had been separated from habitats or because people were caught in the open and buried.

Mace noticed then that Oxmire wore an overskin. "You're preparing to go out?"

Oxmire nodded. "I want to be there when they break through."

"I'll come with you."

"You go see the pathologist first," Oxmire said. "Check your fatigue toxins. I don't need any casualties on this."

Mace resented the suggestion, but nodded anyway.

"Doc clears you, you can join us at the hole."

Oxmire moved away, then, followed by Cavery, who still wore his overskin.

"Mr. Preston," Guerrera said. "Before you go out, I want to speak to you. Privately."

"Sure."

Cambel Guerrera followed Oxmire and Cavery. She wore soft, loose utilities.

Mace leaned over the console, studying the grid. He tried to imagine the amount of debris, the strength of the winds, the chaos that must have exploded when the sheeting peeled away. Scraps of the molifiber had been collected and sent back to Burroughs for study, but no word had come back from the lab yet.

"Specialist Preston?" the stranger asked.

"Yes?"

"We haven't met. I'm Piers Hawthorne. I'm the adjuster—"

"Uh-huh. I was told you hitched a ride with Ms. Guerrera."

"It was the last available transport here."

"Was it so important that you couldn't wait till everything was secured?"

"I believe it's best to see things as soon after an accident as possible. Tidying up tends to obscure certain aspects."

"Hmm."

"I wondered," Hawthorne continued, "if you might spare me some time for a talk. I understand that you suffered a loss here. I don't intend—"

"Have you seen the site, Mr. Hawthorne?"

"—to be—excuse me? No. I mean, I did when I arrived, but only briefly. I've been...remanded to the confines of a carryall since. No one will take me. I'm not familiar with the protocols, or I'd just do it myself, but there are regulations—"

"Come on, then."

Mace headed for the prep chamber. When he stepped in, the indicator above the lock showed that it had cycled less than a minute before. He went to a locker and pulled out two overskins. Wordlessly, he showed Hawthorne how to wear it, helping the man into the protective sheathe, then putting on his own.

"Ms. Guerrara requested that you see her," Hawthorne said. "Don't you think—?"

"Do you want to see the site?"

"Well, yes, of course."

"Then let me worry about Ms. Guerrera."

"Mace?"

Dr. Leong, the resident pathologist, leaned into the room, frowning.

"Mr. Hawthorne has requested a tour of the site," Mace said, beginning a checklist on the breathers. "Everyone else is busy, so I'm taking him out. Would you care to monitor the lock for us?"

"Cliff wanted me to do an exam on you," she said.

"You can do that when we get back in. I need to be there when they open the main tunnel." He looked at her. "You can monitor or I'll just set it on automatic."

Scowling, she held up a finger and disappeared. A minute later she returned with a tray containing a syringe and cotton swab.

"What's this for?" Mace asked.

"Don't argue. You want to leave now, you'll humor me. Give me your arm." He shrugged out of one arm of the overskin and offered the bare bicep. She drew blood, pressed the swab to the puncture, and went to the console. "Cliff will still have my hide if anything goes wrong, but at least we're both following his instructions."

"Have a little confidence in me. Nothing will go wrong." Mace helped Hawthorne with his breather. "Make sure the seal is tight here and here. A leak won't kill you, only make your excursion time shorter. Try your comm. Can you hear me?"

Hawthorne nodded. "Stat check."

"What?"

"Stat check. My link is fine."

Mace gave Hawthorne a raised a thumb, then went to the lock. The part of his mind that concerned itself with rules, disciplines, logics, and limits seemed to stutter. He was not really violating orders, only Oxmire's expectations. He knew how to live on Mars better than all these Aeans, knew what his own capabilities allowed. He could sleep when they found Helen. Alive or...

The change in pressure sounded like a hollow whistle that faded to nothing just before the outer door slid aside. Then he stood at the top of the ramp, staring at the Martian landscape. Mace had never been able to find the beauty most Martians professed to see in it. To Mace, the reds, yellows, ochers, oranges, and bloody shadows comprised a singular idea: lifeless pride. It frightened him growing up with it and it intimidated him now. He had been overjoyed to get away from the scarred deserts.

He had seen images from the early days of human settlement. The sky was a different color now, different even from his childhood memory, bluer, the clouds a bit muddier. Manufacturing, agriculture, the presence of a few million humans spilling gases, all combined over time to thicken the atmosphere. Then it had been an average of only eight millibars, less than one one-hundredth of a standard atmosphere. Now it averaged nearly thirty-five millibars. What that meant to Mace now, standing here above the ruins, was that fifty years ago the air lacked the carrying capacity to cause a disaster like this. The sandstorms of legend had been thin veils much more visible from orbit than on the ground. Now a few of them held real force.

"It's really something," Hawthorne said.

Mace glanced at him. "You're not a Martian."

"No, no. I'm from Aea."

"And before that?"

"Why do you think there was a before?"

"An impression."

"Hmm. As a matter of fact, I was born on Brasa, but my parents emigrated when I was three. I don't remember very much. And you, Specialist?"

"Born and raised here."

"But you live on Aea now?"

"Aea's home, yes."

Mace descended the ramp. Below, the siphon pumps stood idle. Sand no longer spewed from their ends, jutting above the lip of the trough. Diggers worked at clearing away the mounds of accumulation. Nearly a kilometer away, against the opposite wall, he made out a haze of reddish dust at the base of the now visible primary tunnel.

He followed one of the ersatz roadways left by the path of the diggers. Spurs and crossroads shot off at irregular intervals, trails leading to forage sites where debris or bodies had been uncovered.

The entire volume under the canopy had been pressurized. Not that difficult to maintain in the Martian atmosphere anymore, not nearly as difficult as on Earth's moon where the seals had to be complete, the shells hardened against the occasional meteorite that still, after all these billions of years, fell from the residual debris of formation. The stanchions around the edge of the trough had held the canopy against a partially buried lintel, stretched tight, while the air pooled in the bottom of the trough, rising to billow the molifiber ever so slightly. Some leaked, but minutely and leisurely. The sheet was more than enough to keep the worksite viable while construction proceeded. Eventually, a harder ceiling would have replaced the sheet. Piece by piece, the trough would have become a buried town. When the canopy was finally rolled away and carted off to be used elsewhere, it would leave behind a complicated roof with built-in solar collectors, windmills and windstills, communications antennae, telescopes, and ventilators to outgas CO_2, CH_3, and other byproducts of mining and manufacturing. Below this roof a town large enough for a few tens of thousands would eventually exist, one more stop along the CircumAres Transit, the planned transportation system that would one day circumnavigate the planet, with spur lines to every inhabited area.

Safety regulations required overskins worn at all times at such a site, but Mace knew better than to expect full compliance. Martians were obsessively conscientious people and understood the many ways death can come upon the unprepared. But less than half the personnel here had been Martian. Many had come from the orbitals, where the precaution of an overskin made little difference in a major accident.

"Specialist..."

Mace looked back to see Hawthorne lagging behind, working hard to keep pace, boots sinking to the ankles in the powdery drift. Despite the low g, walking on Mars took practice. Mace waited impatiently for the smaller man to catch up, then strode off at his normal gait, long Martian legs slicing scissors-like, overmuscled now after the adaptation treatments he had undergone for life in Aea. For life with Helen.

"Odd, it doesn't look so deep from here," Hawthorne said.

Mace looked to the right, at the rim of the eastern wall, nearly a hundred meters high. "Never does. Optical illusion."

"Of course..."

Diggers kicked up reddish clouds around the mouth of the tunnel. Another siphon took the deposits from the insect-like machines and shoved it out somewhere over the western wall.

"Mace?" a voice snapped over his comm. "What are you doing out here? I thought—"

Oxmire broke off and Mace checked his comm display. The conversation would have gone out over the shared link. He saw the numbers change just before Oxmire spoke again, to a private channel.

"Did Leong clear you?"

"Mr. Hawthorne wanted to come down and see the site. Nobody else was available." He looked at Hawthorne, but the man was not privy to this exchange.

"I didn't particularly want him here. Last thing we need right now is an insurance adjuster making estimates around corpses."

Mace did not reply.

"Well, as long as you're here," Oxmire said finally, "come on. We're almost to the tunnel. They've broken through."

Mace made his way among the big diggers. The machines moved, oblivious to his presence. The heat from their ventilators distorted the air and dramatically increased the temperature around them. Their treads had pounded the soil into a hard surface that only their considerable weight disturbed, keeping a mist of fine particulate constantly airborne. Walking became easier for Hawthorne on ground that did not yield fifteen to twenty centimeters with each step and he managed now to keep abreast of Mace. They covered the distance quickly.

Comm babble chattered in his ear, updates on digger timetables, crew reports worried over sifting the loads of dirt before dumping them into the siphon hoppers, and a foreman giving instructions to a crew erecting lights in the tunnel, the maw of which still seemed like a half-buried cave, so close now that the curve was less apparent. The smooth walls soaked up light and gave nothing back. Within, halogens glared like a jagged row of stars, leading into blackness.

"I understand this was to be the main anchor for the Elysium Planitia leg," Hawthorne said.

"Will be." Mace glanced at Hawthorne. "You don't think it'll be shut down, do you?"

"I wouldn't know," Hawthorne said. "A loss like this...hard to say what management will decide. Too expensive to clean up and start over, too much invested to let it go. If I were to guess..."

"If you were to guess?"

"I'd say they'll finish it. We're already halfway around the globe, from Helium to Lowell to Sagan to Burroughs to whatever mythic name they'll pick for the next station. Halfway. Too far to go back, not far enough to stop."

"Spoken like a true booster."

"Answered like a true cynic."

Mace increased his pace to move ahead of Hawthorne.

The harsh halogen light made the scattered drifts burn brightly, like pools of molten sulphur. Faintly through the tenuous air came the grind and whir of the diggers, sounding as though they were far away even while they rolled right beside him. Nearly half a kilometer in, well beyond the point where sand had reached, Mace saw the unsteady flicker and track of handheld lamps.

Several rescue workers gathered in a rough circle, lamps aimed at the ground where two of them knelt on either side of a disconcerting shape. Their stillness and attention, enclosed by the cathedral vastness around them, seemed almost ritual and solemn. Mace walked around the perimeter till he found an opening.

The shape resolved into a body. It lay on its back, arms spread, one leg outstretched, the other folded sharply with the foot tucked under the buttocks. The head was cocked at an odd angle, neck broken. Mace squatted by one of the two kneeling people studying it.

"Has it been moved?" he asked.

"This is how we found it, Mace," Oxmire said. "We're a 180, 190 meters from the edge of the drift we dug out...say, 500 meters in from the entrance, give or take."

Mace carefully eased his hand beneath the broken neck, feeling along the ground for something hard and sharp that might have caused the injury in a fall. Nothing. He studied the surrounding floor. The original drilling had left a solid, nearly smooth surface. He saw a scattering of footprints—mostly those of the rescue workers—too few complete enough to form a readable pattern.

"Imaging?" he asked.

"We're waiting for the recorders. Mace, you don't have to do this personally."

"Yes, I do."

Oxmire sighed and nodded. "Where's Hawthorne? I thought you brought him with you?"

Mace stood and scanned the circle of workers. "Damn."

"Clanton, Lors, go find Mr. Hawthorne. And when you find him, escort him back to ops."

Two people left.

"Any other bodies?" Mace asked.

"A few caught in the drift near the entrance. This is the first one in this deep. We're still looking for more."

The circle opened then to admit the technicians with their recording equipment. Mace watched anxiously as they extended the imaging frame out above the corpse. Everyone stood back a little further when they signaled. Lights glowed around the rim of the frame.

"Okay."

Mace knelt beside the body and worked the mask loose. Its neck resisted, stiff with morbidity. His pulse quickened until the mask came free and he saw that it was not Helen. Not Helen. The eyes were locked open in surprise. Mace shined his lamp close and saw the ugly purple and green around the neck. He turned the body slowly, conscious of the ongoing imaging.

The bruising on the neck darkened as it crossed the very back, except for one clear circle of skin about four centimeters in diameter, directly center below the base of the skull.

"Shit," someone hissed.

Mace looked around at the crew, but none of them spoke again. He examined the clear disc, pressing the livid, unpliant flesh.

"An implant," he said.

"A ramhead," another voice said, answered by a smattering of soft laughter.

Ignoring them, Mace found the release, a centimeter out on either side of the small nodule. The dead, unyielding tissue made it difficult to operate, but he managed to pop the button out. He dropped it into a pouch on his belt and stood.

"Finish the imaging, then have a med team pick it up." He looked from masked face to masked face. "Are we ready now to continue on in a professional manner?"

Most of the crew nodded silently.

Several meters further on Mace and the crew came to a surface access. None of the accesses had yet been fitted with airlocks up top—in fact, a meter or so cap of rock had been left intact—only down here, in the tunnel. The pressure door stood open. A narrow, rough-hewn passage ran about fifteen meters straight into the rock to open onto a wide platform in a circular chamber. Directly opposite, another passage led to the stairs that ascended all the way to the surface, a hundred meters above.

Another body lay sprawled face down in the center of the platform, feet aimed at the stairs. In the sharp light of their lamps, Mace saw that it wore no mask and that its hair was pale and thick. Before he thought, ignoring Oxmire's order to wait, Mace knelt beside it and turned it over.

For several seconds all he saw was a tatoo on the left cheek, an ornate mandala that said very clearly "Not Helen." He swallowed hard and let out a heavy breath that sounded close to a sob. Carefully, he lowered it back down, stood, and stepped away. He began to feel embarrassed at his loss of control, of damaging the site before imaging could record it.

Oxmire patted his arm briefly, then went to examine the body.

"Neck's broken on this one, too," he said.

"Is it normal?" someone asked.

Mace glared at the workers huddled by the entrance. "Meaning?"

"Not a ramhead," Oxmire said.

"Since when," Mace asked slowly, "have we had a roster of bigots working for us?"

"Mace—"

"I don't care, Cliff. These people were coworkers. You *will* talk about them respectfully."

The silence stretched until a few of the workers retreated. Oxmire cleared his throat.

"Mace," he called. "Look."

"What?"

"Footprints. Someone went out this way."

Mace stared at the clear prints. Two sets, heading for the stairs.

"I thought none of these had been drilled through to the surface yet," he said.

"None should've been. But—"

Mace took Oxmire's handlamp and followed the footprints, heading up the stairs.

"Mace, wait—"

He took the steps three at a time. The passage was tight, almost claustrophobic, and the treads cut steeply in the Martian fashion. His lamp danced over the rock, giving him quick, broken impressions, one side to the other, up and down. He came to the first landing expecting to find another body, but it was empty. Without pausing, he bounded up the next flight.

At the second landing he slowed, the lamplight bouncing off details that seemed out of place. The wall to this left was scarred near the floor. The footprints, nearly gone, suggested that they had paused here, worked on something, their angle and direction all wrong for a continuous ascent. But he hurried on. He wanted to make sure Helen was not lying on any of these stairs or at the opening to the surface, even though surface survey already would have told him that and had shown nothing.

A wire, maybe, or something less substantial, or even a set of rocks placed just right—there were so many ways to set a booby trap. His foot slid, stuttered, caught, and he became aware that the wall to his left moved. He only *heard* it move for an instant before seeing the flash and bending to take the impact that sent him tumbling back down the stairs, the lamp clattering and spinning before him, the light strobing frantically end over end as he followed, end over end, until the light, along with all feeling, was cut off.

TWO

MARS, 2115

"*I HAVE A PRESENT FOR YOU.*"

"*I've got what I want.*"

"*Yes, I'm sure you do. But you don't have what I want you to have.*"

"*What's that?*"

"*Me.*"

Mace watched Helen open a small case, silk-lined, and take out a pendant. Five or six centimeters in diameter, the silvery disc bore an engraved HC, and hung on a delicate chain.

"*What's this?*" *Mace asked as she handed it to him.*

"*Me. From now on you'll have me with you even when I'm gone.*"

"*You're leaving again?*"

She nodded, snapping the case closed. "Long trip. Ganymede. About fourteen months. That is my persona encoding. Recently updated."

"*I promise not to open it till you get back.*"

"*Just promise to open it if I don't.*"

"How do you feel, Mr. Preston?"

"Where am I?" Light stabbed through a gummy film that obscured his vision, so he kept his eyes closed. The dream receded into a confusing melange of memory.

"On a transport back to Burroughs."

The voice was familiar, but he could not place it yet. "Burroughs . . . well, turn us around. I'm not finished."

"Four broken ribs, a cracked femur, sprained left wrist, bruises over most of what isn't broken. Remarkably, no concussion, but Oxmire attributed that to a thickened Martian skull and an evident lack of damageable brain."

Mace felt himself begin to laugh. His chest constricted and the ribs hurt just enough to stop him. "So put me in a body brace and turn the transport around."

"Can't do that, Mr. Preston."

Mace forced his eyes open. He blinked vigorously and the haze broke apart. Smooth blue-grey arched overhead. To his right he saw monitors glowing dimly. Beneath everything came the rumble and vibration of the transport engines and the whisper of circulating air. His mouth felt cottony and he breathed in the tepid-water smell of sterile sheets. A woman sat near his left hip. He stared at her for several seconds.

"Ms. Guerrera."

"And your memory seems intact. Is there anything I can get for you?"

"I wasn't finished." He worked his tongue against the inside of his mouth. "Water."

Cambel Guerrera leaned forward and pulled a tube down and inserted it into his mouth. He drew on it automatically and cool liquid flowed.

"There's nothing left for you to do, Mr. Preston. No other bodies were found, the tunnel is being recorded in excruciating detail, and your second, Specialist Cavery, has everything securely in hand. With your injuries, any further work you have to do can be done at a workstation."

"Did they—?" He stopped. He wanted to know but he wanted to see for himself.

"We'll be in Burroughs in less than two hours," she said, standing. "You should sleep. I'll be nearby."

"How did I—what happened to me?"

"You tripped a mine. Damn near sealed the shaft, it took nearly three hours to get you unburied."

"A mine."

"Sleep, Mr. Preston."

The proteins, pseudoviruses, aminosteroids, and other therapies the pathic facility at Burroughs administered to him were all variations on the adapt treatments that had enabled him to walk and breathe normally on Aea with its one standard g. The anæsthetic worked only so well, though, as if unable to keep pace with the pain from the accelerated healing. Mace tolerated it because it meant less time in pathic.

By the fifth day of treatment he could walk unsupported and sit up without his ribs driving him back down. He ordered a slate and a connection to the Hellas site database.

ACCESS DENIED scrolled across the screen. He reentered his code and watched the words appear again. Calmly, he began entering other codes, but with each new string of digits, access remained denied. He started contacting people, asking, then demanding explanations, until abruptly the only thing he could call up on the slate were public access posts. PolyCarb had shut him out.

He walked out of pathic on the eighth day to find Cambel Guerrera waiting for him at reception. She wore a plain blue suit, collar sealed high against her throat. Mace studied her while he went through all the releases. She seemed on edge, the sharp angles of her face even more pronounced by the tension in her eyes.

"Ms. Guerrera," he said quietly.

"Cambel, please." She tried to smile. "We—I—have things to discuss with you. Can we walk?"

"So the pathologists tell me."

Mace kept his pace restrained, though he wanted to stride along to dispel pent up energy. Cambel clasped her hands behind her back and leaned slightly forward, as if walking up an incline. The corridor curved to the left, then began a gradual descent.

"You're curious," she said finally, "why your access has been closed."

"Putting it mildly, yes."

"The...irregularities...of the recovery operation have precipitated questions regarding your performance and possible connection to the incident."

"Connection...?"

"There's been a conference of the principle management and oversight, field oversite, engineering, security—"

"I'm security."

"Winston Cavery represented security."

Mace thought about that. Cavery had been thoroughly resentful at being displaced as head of site security. "All right."

"There were lapses in procedure—"

"Any operation of that size, there will be lapses, Ms. Guerrera."

"—which compromised the final integrity of the rescue operation."

They emerged from the corridor into a crowded interchange. The round chamber contained kiosks and patches of plant life, benches and public access terminals. The thick smell of cooking and chlorophyll mingled heavily with the odor of people and ozone in the chill air beneath the low dome. Eight other interchanges like this tied Burroughs together with its thirty-five thousand residents and the turnover of visitors—small compared with Helium and its quarter million inhabitants or Lowell with nearly two hundred thousand. People lived in the open here, under the ground. Habitable space was expensive, it had to be dug out and modified; privacy was found in small, closeted places.

Mace let Cambel lead him around the rim of the chamber and into another, quiet, artery.

"So what's gone missing?" he asked abruptly, gratified by her startled look.

"Three items. A recorder salvaged from the southeast corner which you personally took to ops. And a cyberlink augment that was found on one of the bodies in the primary tunnel. I'm told you secured that as well."

"I turned the recorder over in prep. In fact, I did that just before I met you."

"The record indicates you brought it in. The recorder itself is missing."

"A carryall isn't that big. Space is allocated very efficiently, there's nowhere to hide something like that."

"It wasn't found."

"The augment—"

She stopped and turned to face him. "Mr. Preston, it doesn't matter what you tell me. You violated several protocols. You were not assigned duty to that site, you came in and took over from the properly assigned officer, you flouted safety regulations, you openly questioned everyone's performance, and you disregarded a strong suggestion from the site supervisor. You injected yourself into the midst of an ongoing recovery operation for personal reasons and consequently failed to perform a job that wasn't yours to begin with in a professional and competent manner."

Mace felt his hands curl into fists. "And what specifically am I being charged with? Dereliction of duty? Sloppiness? Sentimentality?"

"Sarcasm is hardly the response—"

"I did my job as competently as any other assignment. If things are missing someone else took them."

"If that was a demonstration of your competence, you would have been dismissed long ago."

Mace glared at her.

She raised a hand. "First, this wasn't your assignment. You broke regulations to go there. Secondly, the data trail for the missing items ends with you."

"So? It often does end at one point, only to reappear somewhere else."

"Mr. Preston, it is beside the point."

"There's something else, isn't there?" He studied her. "You said three items."

Cambel hesitated. "There is some question concerning the circumstances of your wife's disappearance."

"Not her death?"

"Not now. According to the company, she was never there."

"What?"

"Helen Croslo never went to that site."

Mace turned away from Cambel Guerrera, his breath coming quick and irregular for a few seconds.

"She's not dead."

"She hasn't been declared so, no. Not yet."

He looked at her. "What do yo mean, 'not yet'?"

"There are irregularities—"

"You like that word, don't you? What do you mean? I spoke to her, there's bound to be a log of the call. She sent word to me on Aea that she'd been diverted here. If she hadn't been sent—" He stopped. "Oh, I see. The alternative is that she's the saboteur?"

"We're not really prepared—"

"I've worked for PolyCarb long enough to know that a suspicion like that might as well be an accusation. You're looking at the wrong possibility—"

"Mr. Preston."

"Someone is working to falsify the log—"

"Exactly, Mr. Preston."

"Then—" He studied her narrowly. "Me."

Cambel tilted her head. "The evidence is inconclusive. Your record with the company has been excellent and nothing in your history suggests any connection that might be taken advantage of by an enemy. People have argued in your favor."

Mace grunted. "That's reassuring. You said I tripped a mine?"

"That's right."

"Why was a mine placed in a shaft that wasn't bored all the way through?"

"It had been. A stone cap had been placed over the surface opening."

"Any evidence of someone leaving by that route?"

"No, but the storm would have covered anything up. Since we have incomplete records, we have no way to tell who might have been missing. We're going through personnel logs, but..."

"I'm not going to be allowed to investigate."

"What do you think?"

"So what happens next?"

She resumed walking and he automatically kept pace. "Two options. The first, presuming that you *are* connected to those missing items, you can make a good faith gesture by returning them."

"That assumes I can get my hands on them."

"Can you?"

"No."

"So much for the first option. The second... there is a strong conviction that your wife had something to do with the incident."

"You said she wasn't there."

"Officially, no. But your claim that she was has raised questions. She wasn't officially there. She should have been back on Aea seventy days ago. She hasn't been found, alive or dead."

"That's... incredible."

Cambel Guerrera shrugged. "Personally, I don't think much of the idea. Helen Croslo also has an exemplary record with the company, much longer than yours. There simply isn't anything in her jacket to suggest anything like this. But the fact remains, we need an explanation for the shareholders, and in the absence of anything more credible, this will serve."

"But—"

"Which leads to the second option for you. As spouse, you can legally declare her deceased."

"To what end?"

"A declaration of death would invalidate any and all of her ID throughout Signatory Space. If she *did* survive, she could not return to Aea or gain admission to any Signatory community as Helen Croslo. She would be a pariah. If she is indeed involved, that would serve as punishment and a safety measure to limit her free movement and access."

"You don't need me to do that."

"No. It would be simpler, but we could arrange it ourselves. However, this would ameliorate your own position."

"Why would you be worried about that? Fire me and leave me on Mars. Easy solution."

"PolyCarb isn't that cavalier with valued personnel—"

"Valued hell! I'm a security specialist; we come cheaper by the dozen."

"You underestimate your worth. And PolyCarb's investment in you."

Mace grunted. "I'm already being shut out. Keeping me employed, of course, would be an easy way to keep me under scrutiny, wouldn't it? If you cut me loose I might start turning over all kinds of rocks PolyCarb doesn't want disturbed."

"You can always quit. These are the options the company has instructed me to offer. If Helen is dead, then what difference does a legal declaration on your part make?"

"What if she isn't?"

"Then the only reasonable explanation is that she's involved."

"And if she isn't?"

"That's not a possible view. If you refuse, we can only assume that you're involved as well."

"But I'm not. So if neither of us—"

"You're not listening. Nothing else fits what we know. We have no other viable possibilities."

"Then you haven't looked hard enough! What you have is an insurance problem and a possible shareholder crisis. You want to use us to cover the company's butt."

"I won't say you're wrong."

"You can't."

"But I can say that if you compromise us in this you will remain on Mars, Aean citizenship permanently revoked. You know that much already. But they'll also claim you were working for Lunase. You'll find it very hard to get work. In time, a case will be built and you'll be prosecuted. Think about your options, Mr. Preston."

"You're overlooking the obvious."

"Oh?"

"Do this—use us as scapegoats to pacify the shareholders—and the real perpetrators remain at large. You can't justify the expense of a continuing investigation if you claim it's already solved."

"I should escort you to your rooms now. You need to get off your feet."

"Damnit—"

"I strongly urge you to think about yourself. Your wife is probably dead. In fact, I'm almost certain. Even if she got out of there alive, she had no way of getting to shelter before her breatherpack gave out. She could have stayed on the site, but we didn't find her. She ran. Or she's dead and we simply haven't found the body. In any case, this is just a formality for you. A formality that can save you a lot of grief. This is a reasonable course of action. You accomplish nothing by going counter to it. That would only jeopardize any future chances you might have." She came close to him. "Do you understand me, Mr. Preston?"

He thought he did now. She was linked, this walk was being recorded, the formality was already in process. She could not admit any of that, though, without compromising the company and the validity of anything he might say. But she was trying to give him a chance. He wondered why and thought, for a moment, that perhaps she hated doing this as much as he did.

"I think I'd like those rooms now, Ms. Guerrera."

"And you'll think about what we've discussed?"

"Yes."

"Good. I'm sure you'll make the right decision."

He thought he understood the byzantine thinking behind the way Poly-Carb was handling this. By declaring Helen dead and allowing him to keep his job, the company did not have to acknowledge a plot to the shareholders. There was nothing for them to see that suggested a lack of confidence in PolyCarb's employees or employers in the company. It was perverse, but it seemed consistent with the way corporations solved dilemmas. Admit anything, admit nothing, act or not, but above all, preserve the value of the shares.

And Helen?

Helen had kept things from him. He always understood this and had accepted it. From time to time he sensed how much she withheld, but it did not matter. It was her job; he was only her husband, and they had agreed not to let it be an issue. But now he felt handicapped by not knowing. What had she done for PolyCarb? The company did not acknowledge her presence at Hellas Planitia. But they had sent her there, diverted her return flight from Ganymede. Mace's policeman mind could find only one explanation that made sense—her troubleshooting for PolyCarb included high-level security matters. In her own fashion, she was as much a cop as he. Was. Had been.

So what was going on at Hellas Planitia that brought Helen into it? And had now cost her her life....

He sat in the dark, drinking whiskey, and traced the Minoan maze of his own thoughts. If he fought company wishes now they could dismiss him, strand him on Mars, and put a blight on his record that would keep him from getting another decent security position. Without that, he would lose complete access, and without access, he could never find out what happened. He could do nothing outside Aea. He had to decide what was more important—finding Helen, assuming she lived, or finding out what had happened to her, alive or dead. If she was on Mars and alive, he might find her under any circumstances. But if she was in trouble or off planet...or dead...his ability to find anything out would be virtually nonexistent without his PolyCarb position. Or at least without the resources Aea could provide. Or was that a rationalization? Because, he morbidly and guiltily thought, he could not abide the thought of being stranded on Mars. Particularly not now, not after this. He needed to be on Aea. It was not clear that he needed PolyCarb as much.

Who had drilled that emergency shaft all the way through? That would require special equipment and time. Someone on site, in a management position most likely, would have to have known. If someone escaped through that shaft, it followed that they would not be running into the desert with no hope of rescue. Someone had picked them up. How many? Did Helen know?

He discounted any local involvement. Martians distrusted orbitals, but they would not go this far. The benefits to Mars outweighed most other considerations. It made less sense that it was someone from within the company. One of the other orbital communities? Midline? Brasa? Also unlikely.

Lunase. The moon harbored grudges, resentments, most of them baseless, but they were an insular people. Mace wondered if a Lunessa company had bid on the CircumAres project and been beat out by Aea.

Helen....

Believing finally that he had no choice, Mace sobered up long enough to sign the documents and went back to his suite of rooms with a bottle of whiskey. He distrusted inebriation but he could think of no good reason not to indulge it this time, especially with good product. Mars produced a variety of vodkas—the potato did remarkably well here—but Mace had never developed a taste for it. Another reason to get back to Aea. Better liquor. He poured three fingers of expensive single malt and raised the glass in toast to his phantom wife.

Forgive me, he thought. If she was dead, there was nothing to forgive. If she was alive...then she had lied to him, too, because the only way for her to have survived was for her to be part of the incident. Had she been a good enough actor to hide it from him? Evidently, if true. But he did not believe it. There had to be some third answer that could satisfy everyone and give him back his wife.

"I've signed you away, though," he muttered, staring at the pendant on the dressing table by the bed. The disc contained her ROM encoding. Helen's persona, downloaded before she had left for Ganymede. He could access it, run it through a hired cyberlink, and find out—

Find out what? The persona, run through the medium of another person, would be Helen. She could still refuse to tell him anything and it would embarrass them both.

Besides, he did not think he could bear to talk to her as a ghost.

He grunted. He thought he loved her. He did. But then why betray her?

After two days alone in the expensive rooms PolyCarb had put him in he realized that he was waiting for Helen to walk out of the desert and make everything right. He knew better. If she had gotten to the surface and started walking, she had walked to her death. There was no way around it.

Still, he felt the guilt like a pain he could not locate.

Through the gummy murk of his stupor he could not say with certainty that he had not married Helen to get off Mars. Her death, it seemed, now served the same end.

He vaguely expected everything to return to normal after his act of private treason, that in a few days he would be given his position, authority, and access, and be allowed to go back to work. What he did not expect was to be ignored. He made calls which no one returned, tried to tap into the data he had been closed out of to find that he was still barred. He fenced with a few company mouthpieces and in a moment of rage he contacted a lawyer. But he gave that up and continued drinking, waiting to be evicted from the suite. He formed a vague plan of taking the eviction before the Martian Bench himself and forcing PolyCarb to disclose—publicly—why they had placed him in such circumstances. According to Martian law they would be obliged to show just cause or return him to his prior status.

No one evicted him. One day Cambel Guerrera showed up to fetch him. It did not occur to him to wonder why someone of her corporate rank would be sent to do this. He was too amused watching her control her disapproval at his condition. She and the two orderlies packed his few possessions and escorted him, bottle in hand, to the nearest subsurface rail station.

Martians glared at him. He glared back, enjoying their discomfort. He was an affront to their oft-denied fastidiousness. They claimed to abhor weakness, but Mace, who knew them from their nurture, believed they had lost the ability to distinguish strength from discipline and responsibility from habit. He returned their disdain by flouting his disregard for Martian tradition—the one thing they never admitted to hating but hated above any moral lapse.

Once Guerrera and her pair of helpers boarded a bullet for Helium, they had a compartment to themselves, even though the trip only took three hours. Mace huddled in a corner, sipping from his bottle, and stared at his knees.

He was grateful that Guerrera did not talk to him. All he could have given her then was a surly attitude or worse. He had lost control of his situation. It seemed that keeping this knowledge to himself stole back a fraction of the loss. He could not manage the circumstances, but at least he might keep them from managing him.

At Helium the balances changed again when he realized where they were taking him. The orderlies escorted him to a hygiene facility where they relieved him of his bottle, now nearly empty, and gave him an injection that brought clarity and vomiting with cruel efficiency. Shakily, he walked alongside Cambel Guerrera through spaceport customs and stayed awake during the blood test and interrogatory before heading up a ramp to a shuttle car. He stood, holding onto a ring overhead, for the short ride out to the orbiter. Once he lay back in the acceleration couch he could not keep his eyes open. Lift-off compressed his already abused stomach, but he held his dignity and made orbit without heaving.

The orderlies helped him aboard the big company transport and to his cabin—a chamber the size of an overlarge closet dominated by the bed—and left to return downwell, to Mars. Cambel Guerrera remained.

"We leave orbit in two hours," she said. "Can I get you anything?"

She stood in his cabin door, arms folded, unwilling to enter all the way. Mace saw the stress around her eyes, the set of her mouth, the way she stood, feet apart, as if preparing to defend herself, or run.

"Is she really dead?" he asked.

She frowned. "You'll have leave time. You can be alone, do what you like. Acclimate yourself."

"Why are you doing this? Why is the company going through all this if Helen's really dead?"

"I really don't know, Mr. Preston." Cambel stepped back, into the passageway. "The ship's lounge is fully stocked. I'm told they have a good bar. There's plenty to keep you occupied during the trip."

"Where are we going?"

"Home, Mr. Preston. Aea."

THREE

LUNASE, 2116

"DOLLARD."

Nemily looked ceilingward. The woman beside her stopped talking and tugged at her lower lip with her teeth.

"That's me," Nemily said, rising from the narrow bench.

The woman—Katya or Kanya or something—gazed up at her with a look of anxiety and concern and drew the icon hanging around her neck closer to her face, touching its rounded top with her fingertips. The container shone dully, polished by years of fondling. Nemily wondered what she kept inside, but it was impolite to ask.

"You've been nice," Nemily said and turned away.

About twenty other people occupied the inadequate benches in the waiting room, most of them holding their own icons. A few—like Nemily—did not have one. Now they watched her as she headed for the door to the advisors' cubicles, expressions varying from awe to envy.

"Remember what I told you," Katya—or Kanya—called after her.

"You've been helpful," Nemily said over her shoulder, and hurried through the door. The woman had told her a cautionary tale about her son who had been applying for a travel permit for years, finally achieved his goal and left Lunase only to die in an accident on one of the processing platforms out near the Belt. Safer to stay home, she implied, beneath meters and tons of regolith. The risks of leaving, to wander among the artificial stations, or even to Mars or one of the asteroids, outweighed the perceived benefits. A sensible Lunessa put such ambitions aside and settled down to the responsible life of making Lunase a better hab. Look at what happened to that man's wife when she received permission to go to Brasa to visit relatives and contracted a virus no one in Lunase could even pronounce, much less cure. She was marooned now on Brasa, unable to leave, barely tolerated by the Brasans, her life miserable, and there sat her husband trying to obtain permission to go to the same diseased place just to be with her. Most requests were turned down for medical reasons, and everyone knew the best biotech in the system was on Aea and they never shared and certainly never let Lunessa in, so why even bother to apply for an access visa? Travel was dangerous, unpredictable, unhealthy and unsatisfying. Better to stay. Better to work in the warrens. Better to never go onto the surface to see the perpetual sky. Better to forget there were other places. Dreams of leaving were like dreams of Earth—fruitless and irresponsible.

Yet Kanya was here, as were they all, chasing after a way off the moon, away from Lunase.

Nemily crossed the threshold, into the advisory area. She paused before the large display to locate her name and the cubicle to which she was to report. Bett Rolan had advised her the last three times and she hoped to see her again. The board directed her to Cubicle Twelve.

She rapped sharply on the door and pushed through. The advisor behind the desk looked up.

Not Bett.

"Dollard?" he asked.

"Nemily."

"Sit."

Nemily squatted on the low stool in front of the desk and waited while he made notes on his slate. When he looked up he seemed upset.

"You work for SetNetComb."

"Yes."

"Doing?"

"Traffic monitor. We—"

"Performance?"

"Adequate. Eighty-nine percentile."

"Explain what you do."

"I monitor the hydrogen byproduct from the fusion reactors. Helium$_3$

goes into the reaction chambers, hydrogen, helium$_4$ and a proton come out. I funnel the hydrogen into water production. I—"

"How long have you worked that station?"

"Three years."

"Before that?"

"Halide production, electron separation."

"Reprimands?"

"None."

That startled him. He blinked as if a bright light had suddenly struck him in the face. He checked his slate, then nodded once.

"Your loss could affect morale. Do you realize that?"

"Yes."

"You're prepared to accept the weight?"

"Yes." In truth there would be no weight, no burden of guilt. If she left her cadre, morale would rise. She possessed the highest performance ranking and management constantly reminded everyone else that they fell short. No one there—except management—could be unhappy with her loss.

"Are you taking a restructure regime?"

"A preliminary series."

"You look it. Stand up."

Of course, she thought as she rose, he could mean that management would suffer a drop in morale. That had never occurred to her before. If so, though, why would she carry weight from that?

"Turn around. Stop."

She faced the exit. Symbolic, she thought wryly. No permit this time, this is the portal through which you came seeking, this is the portal by which you will leave, denied.

"Take off your overshirt."

She peeled the loose, thigh-length garment over her head and held it dangling from her fingertips.

"Turn around."

He drummed his fingers on the edge of his desk. "Do you have trouble with all those new muscles? People look at you?"

"I haven't noticed."

"Which?"

"Neither."

"Are you usually so unobservant?"

"Sir?"

"Un-ob-serv-ant," he pronounced slowly. "So. Usually. Are you? An interesting word. To be not observant, a failure to observe. To not pay attention. Not give passive service. Service is central. You do not serve when you fail to notice those around you. Old word, rich meaning, several functions, all of which indicate a lapse."

"Pardon, but usually I am too occupied serving in other ways to pay attention to the shortfalls in others. May I put my overshirt back on?"

He nodded, adding a desultory flick of his fingers.

"You know," he said, "they don't like our kind in Aea. They especially don't like your variety of our kind."

Nemily tugged the neckline till the shirt settled correctly, then sat down.

"Sir?"

"Cyberlinks. You know, outside Lunase people call you ramheads."

Just like they do inside Lunase, Nemily thought, among other things even less polite. Lunase possessed a higher than average population of Cerebro-Augmented-Persons. Lunase produced more than anyone else. The best facilities for installing the implants could be found here and Lunase boasted about that. For the best CAPs, Signatory Space came to Lunase.

"I'm aware of that, sir," she said.

"Aeans are arrogant, elitist, judgmental. You won't like it. It would really be best if you simply went back to your cadre and did your service. Why do you want to leave anyway?"

"Personal reasons."

He pursed his lips again and Nemily waited for the next sermon. She hoped he was not one of the faithful, a true devotee of the Temple. The Temple taught endless lessons about the drawbacks of the personal.

But the interest seemed to drain out of his face. He sat back and folded his hands across his lap.

"You have a sponsor, Dollard. Somebody on Aea wants you."

"I—"

"Your permit is approved, Dollard. Understand? You've been accepted. Normally this would never happen, but you have a sponsor. I assure you that without that we would not be so cruel as to allow you to go. But the protocols are satisfied and you have no blemish. Approval has been given to step up your adaptation regime. You'll need it to survive among the mutants." His mouth twitched toward a smile. "Perhaps you'll fit in after all."

Suddenly he moved quickly and efficiently, punching his slate, drawing discs from hoppers, and shuffling together a packet of material. He pushed it across the desk.

"Study. Immigration law, admission protocols, an overview of custom. Away from here you will be a representative of Lunase. We expect you to conduct yourself accordingly. The rest of your docs will be forwarded pending medical assessment."

Her hand trembled slightly as she reached for the packet. She tucked it into her waistband, nodded slightly, and stepped toward the door.

"Dollard."

"Sir?"

"You'll miss us."

"Of course."

She left before he could say another word, another challenge to try her patience. Nemily knew her patience to be long and resilient, but this one—she paused at the board again to find the cubicle and the name: Pisquol—seemed to enjoy a gift for undoing her restraint. Why do I want to go to Aea? To be away from you. All of you.

She walked into the waiting room and immediately the worried eyes locked onto her. She strode through their invisible lures and nets toward the main access. Near the door, she glanced over to Kanya—or Katya—and saw the woman staring at her, hands white-knuckled around her icon. Nemily raised a thumb, the gesture of success. The woman's mouth dropped open in an expression of shock and anguish. She ducked out of the room before anyone spoke.

I am leaving all of you, she thought as she joined the flow of people, her hidden permission giving her confidence. She looked at the Lunessa directly and enjoyed their evasive glances. I am leaving. . . .

Nemily had applied for emigration six times. Application was free, as long as you agreed to see a counselor who wanted to know why you wished to leave. Nemily always told them that she intended to trace her family and Lunase lacked the facilities and inclinations to help her do that. They understood the impulse of the orphaned to find their progenitors—it was at the heart of Temple philosophy—and it tended to bypass the usual objections. Still, they urged her to stop thinking about it; that in her case the search more than likely would turn up nothing; assured her that she would find only frustration—all of which she knew to be true and none of which made the least difference. In fact Nemily cared nothing for the Belt family that had sold her to Lunase as an infant, indenturing her to the Combine, and dusting its hands of her. It was only an excuse to find a way out.

A score of lesser reasons drove her decision. She did not like her roommate, Clare, and especially disliked Toler, Clare's lover. Toler dealt in vacuum—not uncommon in itself; everyone knew someone who trafficked in contraband, but Toler did not even try to hide it, meaning he either did not care or was protected—and gave Clare all sorts of niceties. Scent organs, silk loungers for off-shift wear, alternate wavelength lights, flavor tabs to add to food, access codes for higher-level datastores, a variety of pharmocopiates of which Clare had become nervously fond, and music, definitely the hardest to leave. It was all vacuum, black market, contraband, and Nemily worried about being discovered and disciplined. Toler was often gone for long stretches of time and Clare was careless sometimes about who she showed off Toler's gifts to. The entire situation kept Nemily constantly anxious.

She delayed informing Clare about her pending emigration because she told everything to Toler. He already knew Nemily had been applying and that was unsettling enough. But not telling Clare anything was nearly as revealing as telling her everything. Especially after the increased adapt treatments began swelling Nemily's joints and muscles. In the confines of their shared apartment, it was impossible. Nemily compromised, telling Clare that she was undergoing preparatory treatments in case she got accepted.

"If you weren't so short," Clare observed one evening, "you'd be almost Lunessa Standard by now. Is that normal?"

"Mmm."

"What'd the pathologist say? Maybe you're having an abnormal reaction. That could cause trouble if you start in earnest. A friend of mine's brother had trouble with that and developed acromegaly, then he couldn't go anywhere."

"Mmm."

"You ought to check."

"There's no problem."

"I don't know, you're looking awfully big for prep stage."

Nemily looked up from the slate in her lap and watched Clare as she restitched a blouse to conform to the latest cut. Nemily envied Clare's ability to remake her clothes. Clare had worked in a garment shop once but claimed that dealing with customers pushed her too close to breakdown. Now Clare did what Nemily had gotten away from, working for the Combine in halogens, herding molecules for the alchemists.

Clare's body conformed to the coming Lunessa norm, tall and thin, over two meters and nearly gaunt. Projections claimed that in two or three more generations, the average height would top three meters. Already new warrens were being planned to accommodate the need for head room. At one point six meters, Nemily was already markedly behind any Lunessa body norm, with no hope of ever catching up. The adapt treatments only made her seem shorter.

Suddenly Clare stopped working and stared at Nemily. Nemily usually avoided Clare's gaze when the mood turned serious, but now she met her roomy's stare evenly. She was surprised when Clare, wordlessly, put away her stitching and left the room. A few moments later Clare's door slammed shut, leaving behind a thick stillness.

She puzzled at Clare's reaction through her next shift. Coworkers stared at her in the shower. She finished quickly, self-conscious of her body. She had begun wearing looser clothes to hide the changes. It was becoming harder to walk normally, both because of the increased strength and the pain. She stepped carefully, afraid of launching herself into the now-too-near roof of the corridors.

Toler waited in her space, sitting in Nemily's favorite chair, long legs stretched out and crossed at the ankles, fingers laced over his stomach.

"Nem, sweet," he said, smiling.

Nemily immediately wanted to turn around and leave, but she forced herself to stay. This was still her space, Toler was the intruder.

"I hear you're leaving us."

"Clare say so?"

"Would she be wrong?"

"She didn't get that from me."

"That's not a denial."

"Stat check, Toler."

"I need a favor. I assume you're going to Aea? I want you to deliver something."

"I don't do vacuum, Toler. I've told you that."

"Yes, but this is different. You're going to a strange place, a new world, different costs. You need resources. This will help."

"Is Clare here?"

"Do you hear, Nem?"

"I do, you don't. I said I don't do vacuum."

Toler stood. "There's an easy way and a hard way—"

"Should I call civic maintenance?"

"Look, ramhead, don't play at misunderstanding me. All those wires don't deceive; you think clearly, you understand. We can do this so you leave clean, make a little extra when you arrive, everybody's happy. Or we can abort you. I know people, delay is no problem. Too much delay, your adapt treatment goes past its optima, complications arise. I'm not asking, I'm instructing, are we clear?"

"You can't abort me. I have a sponsor."

"How do you think that happened? Eh? You're going because someone on Aea wants something." He reached out to grab her wrist.

Quickly, she snagged his hand and twisted it, startled at how easily he nearly went down. Toler had always been so strong, and Nemily often suspected he had gone through adapt treatments. But now his mouth stretched wide with pain and Nemily could feel the fragility of the bone and cartilage in her grasp.

"You don't listen, Toler," she said, her voice trembling slightly. "I don't do vacuum." She released him and he stumbled back, cradling his injured wrist. "Is Clare here?"

Toler went to the hygiene. A moment later Nemily heard water running. Her entire body quivered in response to her heightened pulse and she felt bright, delicate and hard at once, tingly the way she did in the minutes before sex began. She flexed her fingers and decided that she would miss this new power.

"Thanks for telling Toler."

Clare stopped pushing her food around with her chops and frowned at Nemily. "Telling Toler what?"

"About me leaving."

The quality of Clare's frown changed, from puzzlement to unwelcome understanding.

"I didn't," she said.

"He said—"

"I *didn't*."

"Then how did he know?"

Clare resumed stirring the ceramic sticks in her bowl, staring into the mixture of rice and lentils and spinach as if it held profound secrets.

"Clare?"

"Toler drifts with some peculiar people. Stay away from him."

"I intend to anyway."

"So you really got a permit?"

"Yes."

"Were you going to tell me?"

"Yes. Eventually. Before I left anyway."

"Why not before now? It must've been weeks ago, judging by your adapt progress."

"Pathic says I'm reacting faster than norm."

"Still—"

"Three weeks ago. And a few days. They say I have a sponsor."

"You're really going?"

"Of course."

Clare's eyes flickered up briefly, leaving an impression of mistrust and pain. It startled Nemily.

"Does it hurt?" Clare asked.

"What? The adapt? Sometimes. I wake up with cramps occasionally."

"I wondered. I hear you wandering the space at night, sometimes. I thought about doing it for trend, filling out my frame a little, but it's too expensive just on a whim."

"The exercise regime isn't fun."

Nemily broke off a piece of the hard rye bread and chewed on it, waiting. Clare had not taken a bite of her food since she had sat down at the table. Nemily considered taking her empty bowl to the cleaner, but Clare's attitude seemed to demand her attention.

"Aea?"

"Hmm?"

"Aea. You're going to Aea."

"Yes—"

"You are a thoughtless cleft, you know that?"

"Clare—"

"You weren't going to tell me. You were just going to not be here and let me run around trying to figure out what happened. It wouldn't matter to you if *I* left like that, so why should it matter to me? It never crossed your...mind...that not everybody sees things the way you do and maybe some of us actually get hurt by things that never touch you at all."

"Clare, I don't understand why you're upset. You've never been fond of me as a roommate. After I'm gone you can get someone in here that you prefer. Maybe even Toler."

Clare's shocked look preceded the bowl of food across the table. Nemily jerked to one side but the bowl caught her shoulder and rice and lentils and spinach sprayed explosively around her, following her slowly down. She heard the bowl crack off the wall then hit floor nearly a second later. The food still rained on her as she twisted around to get to her feet.

Clare stood away from the table with her arms pressed to her sides, fists tightly balled. Her face burned vivid red and tears gathered heavily around her eyes, just beginning to ooze down her cheeks.

"Is *that* why you're leaving? Because you think I want *Toler* in here? Damnit, Nem! *Why don't you ever ask?*"

"That's not—"

"Damn damn damn damn!"

Nemily took a step toward Clare, not really certain what she intended to do. Perhaps hold her, perhaps slap her; she felt capable of either. But Clare backed away quickly and Nemily recognized the expression on her face—fear. Clare was terrified and now she seemed to realize that Nemily knew it. She backed up to the door to the kitchen, came against the jamb and let out a high keening wail.

Nemily understood now. Toler frightened Clare. She could not stay away from him; he fascinated her, held her somehow, but she wanted him kept at a distance, the distance of separate space. Nemily was the excuse, the shield, the reason Toler could not move in with Clare, and Clare depended on her presence to control her own obsessive fascination. It did not make sense, but it defined Clare.

"I'll clean up later," she said, turning away from Clare. "I have something to do. Just leave it."

She went to her bedroom and locked the door.

She kept her augments in a small, cloth-lined case. Since taking the position on the hydrogen conduit, there had been no need to use any but the one she usually wore. This line did not even have the special inserts the alchemists required. The specialized capacities of the small implants were wasted on something so simple. Besides, her pathologist had cautioned her against switching capacities while the adapt treatments continued.

But she needed to sort things out and to do that she needed to dream. Her implant did not permit normal REM sleep, so she had to use an augment to facilitate her dreams. She opened the box and selected the one that did, the collator. She reached to the back of her neck and found the hard node in the shallow trough below the base of her skull and pressed her fingers in around it. She felt the delicate click of the augment releasing, the small button extruding from the socket...and the colors she saw dimmed, almost leaching completely out of the walls and the covers on her bed. A distant ringing started as she placed the augment in its spot in the case and took out the new one. She pushed it into place until it clicked. For a few seconds the colors poured back into her surroundings, too rich, too deep. She closed the case and returned it to her bureau, then stretched out on the bed. By then, everything looked flat. That was the external, it was unimportant now. What mattered were the almost physical sensations of connection happening inside.

She closed her eyes and watched images dance.

She came partly awake, aware of being very afraid, but locked in place, unable to move. Dreamstate could do this, she knew, and she tried to convince herself that she was only collating. But the impressions layering over her semi-conscious mind made no sense and her dreams always made sense.

"—don't, please, leave her alone—"

"Shut up, will you? Damn."

"See here, she hasn't used the math augment in months."

"So?"

"Toler, don't—"

Heavy footsteps seemed to rattle the flooring and she heard breath sucked sharply, a brief cry, and scuffling. She wanted to wake up, to turn around, to see, to stop. The door closed.

"—basically an algorithm anyway, so it's the perfect place to hide it.

This is even better than the other ones. We have to cram it in somewhere that *maybe* won't be accessed, but this—"

"—hurry up, will you? Maintenance is on its way, the eyes won't be
shut down that long."

"I thought you said you'd permanently shut them down here?"

"Just hurry."

"...another minute..."

"You're sure—?"

"You've hidden the vacuum in her things?"

"Of course—"

"Then there's no problem. Customs will find that, the appropriate
contact will be notified, and part of the new code keeps her from finding
the vacuum before it's delivered. Simple. There. Done."

"Good. Let's—"

"Wait wait wait, don't be so impatient. What does she have in now?
Let...me...see...recorder-collator, good."

"Now what the hell are you doing?"

"Cyberlinks don't sleep the same way we do, there's less buffer between waking and dreaming. You don't want her remembering this, do
you?"

"But you said this thing—"

"This immobilizes, it doesn't lobotomize. A simple adjustment—"

The procession of senseless sounds and dim images crumbled into
fragments and dispersed, leaving behind, upon waking, only a crawling
unease that she could not quite ignore.

Clare avoided her. Nemily put it down to embarrassment over her out-
burst. She did not know how to reassure Clare, tell her that she did not
take it personally, so she tried to ignore the new awkwardness between
them. At least Toler had stopped coming around. When Nemily asked
about him, Clare told her he had a new position on fourth shift. Nemily
sensed Clare's reluctance to discuss it. Not that it mattered, as long as
Toler stayed away. Nemily wanted nothing to jeopardize her permit.

She went through her work distracted, unable to concentrate. Under
the alchemists she would have been making explanations constantly,
racking up a table of reprimands for minor oversights. On hydrogen the
errors were virtually meaningless, but Nemily knew her performance

was low. She attributed it to her pending emigration and all the attached concerns and tried not to let it bother her.

Five times she checked her personals and each time she forgot to go through one of her bags. She considered running a full diagnostic on her system, but the idea that something might be wrong scared her. Not now, then. Later, when she got to Aea, when it would not be a reason to prevent her from emigrating. If she had an error her permit could be frozen until it was repaired. If it could not be economically repaired, she could lose her chance to leave. She was not required to undergo a diagnostic before she left. Best to leave things undisturbed until she was off the moon.

She kept a picture of Aea tucked against one of her bags. Like a talisman, she regarded it as good luck for her, and she intended to carry it on board the transport in her jacket instead of packing it away.

Aea was the largest—and oldest—orbital, one of the three founding communities of the System Congress, including Mars and Lunase, an anchor of Signatory Space. It was an O'Neill colony, a giant shaft capped on both ends with docks and communications aparatus, enfolded by three enormous wings that functioned both as solar collectors and as blinds, opening and closing against the windows running the length of the tube to give the interior a day-night cycle. Built originally from several smaller orbitals in the years after the Exclusion, when Earth had closed itself off from the orbitals in response to their declared political independence, Aea had grown, piece by piece, into an enormous artifact hovering far out in space beyond the orbit of the moon, at the L4 libration point.

Beyond Aea other orbitals formed a stepping-stone chain throughout the inner system. Midline was between Earth and Mars. Brasa midway between Earth and Venus. Others, scattered about, interconnected by constant in-system traffic. Aea was building new habitats out among the Jovian moons and there was talk of going to Saturn soon.

Out of the mass of unasked-for cautionary advice she had been given, the only warning that seemed to have any substance was the one she had paid the least attention—departure anxiety. When the day came, Nemily experienced wave after wave of unfocused fear. She kept dropping things, rushed through routines and made mistakes, and worried constantly about nothing in particular.

Unexpectedly, Clare came with her to see her off. After the last month of almost unbearable tension, when every conversation they had tried to have turned into an argument about Nemily leaving, it surprised Nemily when Clare met her at the door to their space to escort her to Lunar Egress.

"It's crowded," she commented.

About forty people waited in the large room, all perched on the flimsy-looking plastic benches, arms and hands protectively around their belongings. A long counter dominated one wall, the window shuttered.

"It's cold, too," Clare added, folding her arms against her ribs. "Is there anything you left that you want me to do anything with?"

"No. If I forgot something you can keep it."

"You? Forget something?"

"Have you talked to anyone about sharing space?"

Clare shrugged elaborately. "I thought of Ruann, the one who works for that wildcatter. But I might see if I can't make it alone."

"What about—?"

"I haven't seen Toler in three weeks." Clare's head pivoted quickly, searching the room. She sighed. "I never knew so many people left."

"From what I've heard, most come back."

"I hear that, too, but you know, I've never talked to anyone who has."

The metal blinds behind the counter rolled up loudly, revealing four people at consoles. One of them spoke into a microphone, his voice crackling through the room, unnecessarily loud.

"*We'll begin processing you through now for transfer to the freighter* Colfax. *Please have your permits, health chits, and Lunase IDs ready. Any delay in processing your exit visas may result in fine, prosecution, cancellation of permit, or all of the above.*"

Nemily sorted her bags so that she could carry them easily in one hand. All her muscles ached from the adapt treatments, but nothing seemed much of an effort. Her gear seemed to weigh almost nothing now. She took her time arranging the straps and handles, aware of Clare's intense stare.

"*—after receiving your exit visas, proceed through the access to your left. There you will be issued your shipboard necessaries, which you will be responsible for and must return to the quartermaster of the* Colfax *when requested—*"

Nemily stood. Clare reached out as if to touch her.

"I heard there's an opening in oversight on the proton line down in section D-3. I thought maybe—"

"Clare."

"—the space is so big, it might be more than I need. Maybe I can trade for smaller if it gets too much, but—"

"Clare."

"—*you need to piss, there's a siphon on the foot end of your berth. Do not defecate. Aea wants your stool. It's only a twenty-eight hour transit, you can hold it. If not, you'll be scraping it off*—"

"—doesn't make a lot of sense to run all the way out to some tin can in space just to find a better position. You've ruined your body and I don't know what I'm supposed to do—"

"Clare!"

"—*three lines, here, here, and here. Keep hold of your personal belongings. Once through processing, Lunase denies all responsibility for property*—"

"What?"

Nemily stood directly in front of Clare, looking down at her. Clare's face showed a cascade of emotions, shifting slightly as each one claimed momentary supremacy.

"Why did it take you so long to say?"

"I don't—"

"—*if everyone cooperates, this won't take very long at all and you'll be on your way in no time.*"

"Why now? You could have said any of this over the last three years."

Clare winced. "I didn't know what it meant."

Three lines began to move, one body at a time, toward the desk. Nemily hoisted her gear.

"Nem," Clare said, reaching out. She stopped short of touching Nemily. "If I'd said something sooner, would it have made a difference?"

"I don't know."

Clare stepped forward suddenly and hugged her. Nemily returned the embrace uncertainly.

"Thanks," she said and stepped away from Clare to the far line.

A cleric from the Temple of Homo ReImaginoratus waited at the end of the counter, dressed in the drab earth tones of his order, waving a small blue chasuble, and mumbling incomprehensibly as each person passed through, imparting a sense of overwhelming sadness at their leaving. The clerks worked steadily, processing each traveler, looking no less dour in their grey utilities, but far less threatening.

Nemily's data cleared without a problem and she moved through the access, into a cramped hallway. More personnel worked another desk at the right handing out the items necessary for the flight. A water bottle, emergency breather mask, and a safety harness and tether. From there, the hallway became a long tube that connected to the well-worn interior of the orbiter.

She wandered through the labyrinth of steerage-class berths, unable to find the slot assigned her. She recognized the first signs of panic. Without a berth they would put her off. A woman taller than Clare, dressed in a stained but bright red utility, helped her locate the assignment. Nemily slid her gear beneath the wide, thick-mattressed bed and pulled herself into the tube-like berth.

There was a fifteen-minute delay. She pulled out the picture of Aea to gaze at while she waited. The entire room lurched when the engines started, droning deeply through the hull. The degree of relief upon departure surprised her. The orbiter rattled and shook, and all the way to the big freighter Nemily kept looking nervously at the warning icons, waiting for the machine to turn around and head back. She did not relax until she collected her belongings and stepped aboard the bigger ship, to find another berth amid a maze of berths.

An hour into the initial flight the engines kicked on a second time and she nearly cried out, afraid the ship was heading back to Lunase.

Lying in her berth, held in place by mesh, she began going over all the warnings she had ever heard, especially those in the last weeks, when everyone who knew she was leaving insisted on telling her stories of people who had left and returned discontented with life outside Lunase. She recalled each one and replayed it with the perfect clarity her augments enabled. She then noticed another common thread, obvious now that she knew what to look for. The anxiety had been real for each speaker, but it was not the anxiety the words described.

It was not a fear of leaving but a fear of being unable to leave, that Lunase, no matter how far away one got, always held onto its own and dragged them back in the end.

"I'm not going back," she whispered aloud. The bottom of the next berth was less than fifty centimeters away. She had no slate, no screen, no view of any other passenger. Steerage meant being hauled as much like cargo as possible without risking their lives. "I'm not going back." Louder this time, with more conviction. "I'm not going back."

She spoke quickly, a long string of assertion that took on the numbing drone of a mantra. As a child she used to go to the Temple of Homo ReImaginoratus and listened to the sycophants intone their litanies. In adolescence, the hypnotic quality of the cadences frightened her, and she stopped going. Now she spoke her declaration with the same monotone rhythm she had heard then. For a few moments she felt as if she were in the Temple. The air was cold and the chanting faint and insistent. She opened her eyes, her heart hammering, and saw the scratched bottom of the next berth.

But the chanting continued.

She listened.

All the passengers in steerage chanted. The words varied, but they all said, over and over, the same thing.

New places never make sense upon arrival.

"—g gradually increases toward the outer circumference. Where we are docking, g is minimal, less than a tenth standard. Therefore pay attention to safety instructions, do not bunch up in the access conduits, move slowly—"

There were no viewscreens in steerage. Aea remained an unseen place, somewhere "out there." She gazed at her picture as the intercom droned on.

"—remain in your berths until you hear the claxon. Shifting g can cause injury in the confines of the passenger areas. When you hear the claxon—"

Aea's shaft extended twenty-three kilometers. From a distance it seemed smooth enough, but up close the external constructs formed small forests of columns and poles and towers, patches of metal and composite barnacles that clung to the outer skin, and toward one end a larger ring that fit over the six-and-a-half-kilometer-in-diameter tube. It rotated once every two point seven minutes, which gave the interior almost a full g of gravity. Tiny service craft flitted about the exterior like bees.

"—deposit your water bottles, emergency breathers, and harnesses in the hopper marked in bright red as you leave. These are the property of the shipper and will be reissued. Failure to return company property—"

Aea had been sewn together from several separate torus stations. The project to bind the rings into one construct had taken less than fifteen years, but each ring represented anywhere from five to twenty-five years of time and effort.

"—no fatalities on this voyage, for which we are proud and grateful. It has been a pleasure serving you. May your stay on Aea be a fruitful one—"

The claxon sounded and Nemily, who had become aware over the last half an hour of having weight, eased out of the berth and climbed *down* to the deck. She drew her baggage from the locker at the base of her berth, third one up from the deck, then looked back up at the stack and counted seven slots. Ladders now extruded from the dividing walls. People higher up leaned over the edge and wrestled their belongings out of the storage space beneath them. Nemily was able to reach her own easily enough, but several people seemed to be having difficulty. Everything looked different, felt different with an up-down orientation and no way to float in place. It surprised her how quickly she had grown acclimated to weightlessness.

People crowded in the narrow aisles, gazes shifting from one meaningless detail to another, pausing on the faces around them, perhaps looking for someone who did not seem afraid. Nemily did not know what her own expression looked like but several people gave her brief hopeful smiles.

The light g deceived. People moved too quickly, bounded in the air, collided with others or with the emptying berths. Nemily concentrated on imitating a careful stride. Another queue, a crowded warren, people waiting for resources or trying to get through a jam to get home. She hoped not all the data lied. Aea was supposed to be spacious inside, plenty of room, and limited its population to keep crowding down. She did not want to spend the rest of her life standing in lines waiting for permission to breathe. She tightened her grip on her gear and put one foot before the other, another half meter gone by.

The data also claimed that Aea had never been finished on the inside, that life was lived amid open strutwork under the glare of constant sunlight and vertigo from the rotation of the orbital itself. Nemily had decided not to believe that part. The exterior construction had been finished for almost thirty years now, it seemed reasonable that in three decades the interior would be just as finished. Perhaps reality lay between the two assumptions. What would it be like walking across a girder with the stars visible below you?

No one talked. Between the ugly snorts of the signal all she heard was the shuffle and scrape of feet and fabric, an occasional flurry of curses as someone fell or rammed another. The claxon ended, the queue moved forward; chill air blew through the vents.

She looked up just as she passed through the hatch into the connecting umbilical. The red lettering around the rim had been scuffed to illegibility. The surface of the umbilical was a dull grey except for a path almost two meters wide beneath their feet which shone brightly, buffed to a high finish. It was an old ship.

As she emerged from the umbilical into a bright, clean chamber, Nemily searched for labels to identify the level. The docking bays formed four concentric rings around the hub. Within, she imagined, lay a maze of tunnels and chambers and factories and warehouses and corridors. What she saw here resembled the lounge back in Lunase, which gave her a brief fright till she noticed the differences—colors, signs, subtly different shapes. A low-ceilinged room with plastic chairs attached to the walls, and everything seemed to direct attention to the pair of desks at the far end through which everyone must pass, one at a time, overseen by several people in dark green suits who looked as efficient as Lunessa workers in the same job. She gripped her bags tighter, startled by a sudden anxiety. She looked around quickly for another exit, but the only way out lay behind her, back aboard the aging freighter. The line funneled down toward the desks; people shuffled along, tired and probably as nervous as she.

Closer, she saw people placing their belongings on a platen below the right-hand desk. The platen withdrew through a flap and a new one took its place, ready for the next load. The left-hand desk directed each person through another door on the other side. She chewed at her lower lip. Only five people between her and the desks and she realized that she did not want to surrender her gear. It was all she had. To give it up—

"Please place your belongings on the platen and step to the opposite counter."

She looked up at the woman giving the instruction. There was no malice in her narrow, dark face, just polite concern that what she must do be done well. Nemily hesitated. The woman pointed.

"Please place your things here. Step to the opposite counter."

Nemily drew a lungful of air. She felt a shudder as she set down her bags. For a moment she felt certain that her hands would not open. She did not want the woman to repeat the instruction a third time, that would be a very bad way to start life on Aea. She closed her eyes and opened her fingers and turned quickly away.

"Here is your temporary ID chit. Please do not lose this. Your belongings have been tagged with an identifying code that matches this one. You'll need it to retrieve your property. Please step through that door for your initial interview."

Blood throbbed in her ears. She glanced back at the platen, but someone else's luggage now occupied the space. There was nothing more she could do. She stepped through the door.

She was on Aea.

She wondered why they called it steerage.

"Please step this way. We have questions."

The office reminded her of the advisor cubicles. What had been the name of that last officious ass? Pisquol. Somehow the sound of it seemed appropriate.

The desk here was larger, though, and the slate sat up at an angle, and the walls were brighter. But it still—

She blinked. The man behind the desk had asked her something but she had stopped listening at some point several seconds or minutes before. On the desk before him lay five thin square cases. Pictures, faded but obviously at one time very bright and colorful, lay beneath the yellowed plastic surfaces. He opened one and within she saw an old, old data disc.

"I'm sorry," she said, "would you repeat that?"

"I asked if you were aware of the restrictions on smuggling," he said.

"Those aren't mine."

"Of course they're not. They belong to someone who expects to take delivery from you."

"No."

"Then they are yours?"

"No. I don't know where they came from."

The man—he was thick-faced, pale skin, with a wide mouth that seemed capable of twisting into any emotion imaginable—sneered and shook his head.

"We can't help you if you don't tell the truth."

"I—"

He drummed his fingers. "Yes?"

"I am telling the truth. You can—you can prove it. I—"

"Yes?"

"I'm a cyberlink. You can do a scan—"

"That could take days. Explain to me why you're valuable enough to spend days on the dubious effort of sifting through your codes to find something you may very well have simply erased."

"I don't—we don't—"

It was all falling apart. She felt angry and scared as she had never felt before. Toler had done this, she knew, Toler had asked for a favor and she had turned him down and now he was ruining everything for her. She understood little enough about normal people, but the one thing that she doubted would ever make sense was the way they felt compelled to destroy what they could not affect. He could have walked away, found someone else who would have done what he wanted willingly, but no, his pride had been hurt, and for that a dream must die. And there was no way to tell this man here, he simply would not understand. He did not know Toler, very likely knew nothing about the vacuum in Lunase, the way it worked, the prices exacted for the smallest show of dignity. She could only sit here, humiliated and terrified, and try to wrap her hope around the growing center of despair and make it feel...less.

"You don't what? Lie? I've heard all the stories about CAPs and I know better. You're human, just like the rest of us."

That shocked her. Half of it made her feel unexpectedly good, the casual way in which he accepted their basic commonality. The rest...she lied like everyone, broke the law like everyone, deceived like everyone.

He picked one of the cases up, turned it over. His face turned speculative.

"This is just music?"

"I told you—"

"Sure," he waved her silent. Suddenly, he tapped keys on his console. A few seconds later he looked at the screen. "Hey," he spoke to someone

Nemily could not see. "Got time to look at something? You'll be interested."

"Sure," a new voice said, a male voice.

"You really don't know who this is for?" the man asked.

"No. I don't know anything about it. I told you, someone put it in
my gear—"

"And you didn't check it and Lunase security didn't check it."

"Lunase... we were leaving... they don't care..."

The door opened behind her. She resisted the urge to look around,
afraid to show her fear to anyone else. She listened to his tread as he
came around the desk.

"Look at this, Mace."

The newcomer leaned over the desk and stared down at the cases.
Nemily looked up at his profile. His nose appeared slightly crooked and
he wore a beard salted with white. His high forehead did not crease,
though it gave the impression of concentration. He was tall, almost as
tall as a Lunessa, but much broader, his frame substantial. He lifted
one of the cases and held it carefully with his fingertips. He glanced at
Nemily and she immediately looked away.

"Contents clean?" he asked, his voice much quieter than she expected.

"Don't know. She claims not to know who they're for or where they
come from."

"Why show them to me?"

"You're interested?"

"Maybe." After a pause, he said, "Coltrane, Gershwin, Montgom-
ery...."

"Mean anything to you?"

"Greatness." He sighed. "Mind if I use the next room?"

"Go ahead. We're not going anywhere."

He scooped the cases up and left the room.

"What—will happen now?" she asked.

"That depends on what my friend finds on those discs."

She did not trust herself to say anything more. In Lunase it would
have been simple. Harassment came in definable shapes and to each
there was an appropriate response. She did not know the shapes here.
Not knowing, no response seemed best.

The door opened again and the tall man returned.

"As far as I can tell, just music," he said. "I might find something deeper if I had more time, but it doesn't look like anything else has been added. They're what they seem."

"Well, that's something anyway. Still, contraband—"

"Disappears all the time."

Nemily risked another look. The two men regarded each other in unspoken negotiation. Finally, the official shrugged.

"Let's talk, my friend," he said and stood. He pointed a finger at Nemily. "You stay here. I'll be back."

They left the office together then. Nemily became aware of her breath, loud and ragged. She searched the walls for the eyes and ears she knew must be present, as they were everywhere in Lunase. She began to imagine life as a series of small rooms connected by tunnels. There had been no intervening space, no empty void through which the *Colfax* traveled. The freighter had been just a slightly bigger room containing slightly smaller rooms, the whole of which had shifted a few meters over a day or so to connect to another set of tunnels and a new set of rooms. She could map it, trace the paths, and felt certain she could find a way to fit it all inside an even larger though not inconceivably big room.

The door opened and the official returned to his chair behind the small desk. He worked busily at his console for a few minutes, his brow creasing. Finally he sat back and smiled at her, his attitude changed utterly.

"So. Welcome to Aea. You're a cyberlink, did you say?"

FOUR

AEA, 2118

"ARE YOU GOING TO THE PARTY, MACE?"

Helen's voice echoed slightly in the greenhouse. It brought Mace unpleasantly out of a near-selfless reverie, the closest he ever came to the negation of conscious awareness bonsai reputedly enabled. In the three years since his return to Aea, he had become quite good at the art, though he had yet to achieve complete obliteration. He set the small pruning shears down and studied the plant before him. *Celtis chinensis*, a Chinese nettle-tree, its silvery trunk slanting gracefully in *shakan* style.

He cleared his throat; it always became dry when he worked out here, in spite of the moist air. His mouth tasted of bark, and his raw sinuses filled with a burnt odor.

"I wasn't planning on it," he said.

"I think you should."

Condensation tunneled the windows all around him, scattering the light and obscuring detail from outside, giving the impression of a wide, airy world beyond. Racks ran along one wall supporting his collection of philodendrons, ferns, ficus, rubber trees and the other bonsai.

"Why?" he asked.

"Do you want a list? Other people will be there."

Mace lifted the long-neck can from the floor and liberally soaked the loam in the shallow tray.

"Do you have the last update on my traces?"

"Yes. Completed half an hour ago. Don't change the subject. You need human contact as much as privacy."

"I have plenty of human contact."

"You do business with people. It's not the same. You spend too much time alone."

"By whose estimate?"

"Would you like me to cite the references? The standard psych vectors—"

"No." He set the can down, cleaned his tools by the sink, switched on the lamps that hovered above each tree, then made his way to the exit. At the door he pressed a panel and the walls darkened till only a dusky level of outside light seeped through. "Besides, I'm not alone. I have you."

"I'm hardly a substitute for the company of other people. You promised to start normalizing your life, Mace. This is a good step in that direction."

He could not argue. He had promised, though he wondered sometimes how valid was an oath made to a machine. He had taken steps to comply. He had been to a few parties in the last couple of months, small affairs he had gone to with someone else who had been invited. This was the first one to which *he* had been the recipient of an invitation and his reticence enfolded him like a blanket.

"Give me the update, Helen."

There was a moment's pause—for Mace's benefit, to let him know, subliminally, that the system was changing priorities—before Helen continued.

"Oxmire is still sequestered on the Titan platform. I have been unable to find an avenue into any data that might explain that. He is several months overdue for rotation. Cavery has been given a change-of-status on Midline."

"To what?"

"Unknown. All I have is a C.O.S. notice."

Odd, Mace thought, unless he was being moved into a secure position like Oxmire, removed from all outside access by a posting as site manager on Aea's Titan project. Cavery, though, had been shunted here and there through Signatory Space over the last few years, filling inconsequential security postings wherever PolyCarb had an office. If not for his PolyCarb employment, one might think he was a vacuum dealer. Mace wondered, not for the first time, about how that word came to be used for contraband. Vacuum. Nothing. It did not exist, therefore. . . .

The thought faded and he returned his attention to Cavery. He had been on Midline longest—six months.

"All right," he said. "When you find out, let me know."

"Of course."

The third man he had kept track of after Mars—Hobs, the cyber-link—was dead. He had been on a small station, Cassidy, when it had simply fallen apart. A year after Mace's return to Aea, Cassidy's structural integrity had dissolved over a few days, spilling its contents out into hard vacuum. The few ships that had gotten away later suffered the same fate. The cause was still unknown.

Similar things had happened to other people who had worked at the Hellas Planitia recovery site. He could not get to them, either because of inconvenient postings or because they were dead. He had fenced with the various bureaucracies and data systems since resigning from PolyCarb and had been effectively kept out. He had never been able to learn why Helen's presence at the Martian site was denied by Poly-Carb. Where had she died then? He had been forced to declare her deceased, but no corpse had ever been found, and all his attempts to extract information from PolyCarb about her location at time of death—like most of his attempts to discover details of her career with the company—had come to nothing. Paradox. She had died on Mars. But she had never been there.

He could always download the contents of her persona encoding and hire a cyberlink to run it. It was doable. Except he could not do it. The closest he had ever come to opening the encoding had been when he had programmed the domestic personality, the "Helen" that now conspired with his acquaintances to maneuver him out of his shell. That had not been a deep probe—barely enough to configure the major personality features, not enough to learn any secrets—and he had felt profoundly unsettled afterward, so much so that he waited nearly a month before running the new d.p. program.

No, what lay within the pendant would likely stay within it. He wanted to exhaust all other possibilities before resorting to such necromancy.

He had learned enough to know that Helen had been much more

than she ever told him. Her security clearance, for one thing, had not been a mere one level above his, but five levels. That was as inner circle as one could get inside PolyCarb without actually sitting on the Board. Troubleshooter indeed, he thought wryly.

But it had become apparent that he would probably never find answers to the questions he wanted to ask and that he had to make the decisions he had delayed making for three years—to keep digging at it or let it go. Friends, pathologists, psychiatrists, even his domestic personality, Helen, had convinced him to come out of his shell more, stop obsessing, and try to get back to something like a normal life. For the most part, he agreed with them. He only wished his reluctance would obligingly diminish.

The door let him into a brief hallway where he removed the multipocketed vest and hung it in a narrow closet. He ascended the short flight of steps at the end of the passage.

His house was a series of chambers attached to a central shaft that rose twenty meters to a domed skylight. A stair wound, colubrine, between inner and outer walls, up to a parapet around the dome.

He stepped into the open space of the turret—

"Mace."

—and glanced toward the skylight high above. "What aren't you telling me about tonight's party, Helen?"

The question was unfair. The system could not refuse a direct query and its context-response protocols kept it from dissimulating by actually proceeding to tell Mace everything it was not telling him. The result was a hint of hesitation while the system attempted—futilely—to find a way around Mace's programming. He wondered how it experienced frustration.

"You will disappoint a lot of people. I'm not supposed to tell you, but it *is* a party for you."

"Me?"

"Your birthday. A surprise."

"Not anymore."

"That is no excuse not to go."

"Do I need an excuse?"

"Mace...."

He crossed the floor to an archway that led into his kitchen. He pushed his sleeves up to his elbows and washed his hands in the sink.

He had received the invitation three days ago. The party was at Piers Hawthorne's dom and that alone blunted his enthusiasm. Normally he recycled such invitations, but this one had uncharacteristically come directly through Helen's system, so she knew about it.

"Mace."

"I have plenty to do tonight. The Influx reports alone ought to keep me busy for hours and I want to go over those updates—"

"I can do the Influx reports. There is nothing in those updates you can do anything about. You're simply trying to get out of something you know would be good for you."

Mace turned off the water and dried his hands. He sniffed at himself; his clothes smelled of earth and water-soaked leaves.

"Mace..."

He could shut the system interface down. The rest of the evening would be quiet then. But that was cheating. He had programmed her to do this kind of thing. Her nag factor, he called it.

"Mace..."

"If it will make you happy."

"I don't have a limbic system, Mace. Happy isn't something you can make me. You might consider mollification sufficient."

"You're going to get morbid on me now?"

"Whatever it takes to prevent you from becoming a hermit. You weren't a recluse when I met you."

And even though you're dead, he thought, you won't let me turn into one. His hand went to the pendant hanging from his neck. He rubbed it absently. "I did too good a job constructing you."

"Don't boast, it's immodest. Are you going?"

"I'll go. What time is it?"

"Eighteen-twenty. You have time."

"I'd better shower. Scrape off some of my reclusive odor."

"The water is already up to temperature."

He left the kitchen and went up the winding staircase. The outside wall was transpared and he looked across the grassy slope, past the copse of dwarf elms, to the ascending plain of parkland that ended sharply at the edge of one of the solar traps. The mirrored lid attached to the outer surface of the world was open and light came through the orbital-length window, scattered by the prismatic crystalline structure of the glass to spread and mingle with the light admitted by the other traps. On the far side of the bright ribbon Mace could make out collections of houses, roads, parks, lakes, and a few wispy clouds.

At the landing, Mace touched a contact just above his other *shakan*-shaped Chinese nettle and the wall opaqued to a milky translucency. He liked the pearly glow; it seemed to make the oval leaves of the miniature tree shimmer.

In his bedroom he removed the pendant and set it on a velvet square on his nightstand, then stripped out of his clothes. He slapped his stomach and kneaded the layer of fat that was beginning to hide the still-hard muscle. He tried to remember how long it had been since his last good workout. His joints ached a little more often lately. The most physical activity he indulged in anymore were his visits to courtesans, the ghosts, the ones who offered a buffet of downloaded personae, becoming any type, any one he might want.

Spending too much time with the ghosts, he thought. Too much time, too much money....

The water in the shower came on when he stepped into the booth. It stung at first, a degree or so too hot. The water shut off when he reached for the towel draped over the door.

I'm forty-six, forty-seven in five more days...I was forty-three when she died....

He pulled on a cobalt blue shirt and black pants, soft moccasins, then went downstairs to his den. The small room contained a high-backed chair, a display panel, and his sensorem. "Elgar," he said. "Cello Concerto in E minor."

He sat down as the sound of massed strings moved over him from the walls like a massage. He steepled his fingers beneath his chin and stared into nothing. The somberness of the opening sections gave way to an unexpected playfulness.

When it ended he closed his eyes and tried to hold the memory of the sensations, as if they were objects he might cradle in his hands. He hoped, every time, that the transformations in the music would stay with him. It was the joy and frustration of music that the experience remained vivid only during the performance. The memory served only to draw him back to listen again.

"Time?"

"You have fifteen minutes to get there," Helen said.

"You're sure I have to go through with this?"

"Don't press your luck."

Mace laughed. It felt natural, sincere. Maybe he would stay in a fairly good mood.

A short path led from his front door, between a pair of dwarf elms, to an aluminum postern gate. Mace's dom stood just off the curve of a wide pedistry that ran through the enclave, past several other houses, all set back from the walkway on sizeable plots of grass. Lights illuminated windows or glowed through translucent walls, pushing against the onset of nightcycle. Above, the section of one of the light traps visible to Mace still shone faintly, the external mirrors pivoting now to deflect sunlight.

Since taking retirement, things had gone well. The house he lived in was in a more exclusive area than the slightly more modest dom he had shared with Helen—the few times they had shared it, when she had actually been in Aea, free of assignments. He had never expected to have an upshaft address, at the moneyed end of Aea's interior. Piers Hawthorne had handled the insurance claims and had done well by him. He had thought little of the man after the incident on Mars until Mace decided to leave PolyCarb. Hawthorne remembered him, though, and took a personal interest in seeing to it Mace received everything he deserved. During the process, they had developed a kind of friendship. Mace had been bemused by Hawthorne's evident concern, but after the settlement he did not question it. Mace no longer had to worry about money thanks to Hawthorne's efforts. Hawthorne had even helped get him space on which to build his dom in this district.

Given more time, Mace would prefer to walk the three kilometers to Hawthorne's even more exclusive address. He lived spinward and further upshaft, in a more exclusive enclave. Instead, Mace walked briskly spinward to the tube station just outside his own enclave gate.

He descended the stairs to the shunt platform. He recognized a few of the waiting people and gave a polite nod. He considered descending one more level to the downshaft platform and finding a nightclub or theater, wandering the entertainment districts at the opposite end of Aea. He knew where he would end up and he knew that Helen would find out. Tonight he was more willing to put up with the party than another of Helen's lectures about bought companionship.

The public newsfeed, displayed on a large screen mounted above them on the wall, showed the latest about the new rounds of trade talks. Mace scanned them briefly while he waited. Lunase was upset about Aea's announcement that PolyCarb would begin large-scale manufacture of certain exotic materials previously made only on the moon and in the three orbital factories owned by Lunase. They considered this encroachment and demanded sanctions through the Trans System Congress. More of the same; Lunase had been complaining about orbital "encroachments" on their markets since the Exclusion.

The spinward shunt arrived and he took a seat toward the back of the car. It moved forward smoothly on its maglev. The ride lasted less than three minutes. Mace was the only one to get off at the PolyCarb CLUB STANDARD stop.

The enclave occupied lightly forested land, each dom surrounded by one to one and a half hectares. Compressed-earth pedestries wound throughout the thirty-five hectares of private grounds, marked by lights shining warmly along the edges.

Hawthorne's dom sprawled lazily, a jumble of differently shaped boxes. It was a child's idea of a house, Mace thought, grown large and ridiculous. Private flitters littered the lawn.

Mace felt his mood slipping even before he reached the porticoed entrance. He hesitated, his finger centimeters from the may-I-come-in, trying to find a graceful way and a legitimate excuse to walk away now.

Before he could press the mici, the door opened and Piers Hawthorne grinned at him. "Mace! I'm flattered! Come in, come in."

"Good evening, Piers."

Piers took Mace's arm and brought him inside the foyer. The door snapped shut and Piers waved him further into the dom. "This is special," Piers said.

The short hallway led into a reception area off which opened three wide doorways and a stair leading up. Piers guided Mace to the right, into a large room filled with people.

"Everybody!" Piers called out, silencing the babble of conversation. "The surprise has occurred. Mace showed up."

The number of people startled Mace. He tried to steel himself in the insufficient half-second before the cascade of well-wishing washed over him in a loud, meaningless froth.

"Mace—"

"—good to see you, it's been—"

"—very well, you've taken care of yourself—"

"—how are you?"

"—stranger anymore! I hardly knew it was you—"

"—damn, you haven't changed a bit—"

"—when did you get rid of the beard?"

Piers placed a hand on his back and guided him forward. Faces rolled past. The crowd parted to reveal a long table bearing a large chocolate cake forested with unlit candles. Even through the dense melange of colognes he smelled the chocolate. He had always liked the scent better than the taste.

Piers stepped past him, touched his shoulder lightly in reassurance, and lifted a glass of champagne from the table. He handed it to Mace and took another for himself, raising it above his head. A trail of liquid escaped the rim and snaked between Piers' index and middle fingers.

"Happy birthday, Macefield Preston," he said. He touched a small pin on his shirt and the candles lit simultaneously. "Your friends wish you many, many more."

A fresh ripple of birthday wishes coursed around him. Glasses were raised and Mace extended his own, turning in place so everyone could see it. He blinked, momentarily watering his vision. Feeling foolish, he faced Piers and took a drink.

"Make your wish and do your duty," Piers said, "I only have a two-minute permit for open flame."

Laughter behind him, Mace stepped up to the cake. He inhaled deeply—no wish occurred to him, only a kind of amorphous hope that all would be well—and, with an exaggerated show, blew out the candles. Even those he knew he had missed went out. He straightened, laughing, and for the moment he felt glad to be here. Piers handed him a cake knife. He moved it over the surface of the chocolate expanse, miming profoundly considered precision, and finally chopped downward. First cut made, he handed the knife to someone else and backed away.

"It was decided," Piers announced, "in committee, even, not to torture you or ourselves by singing 'Happy Birthday.' There are professionals present and I don't want them insulted. But you do have gifts to acknowledge."

A separate table stood by the far end of the main one that held all the food. Mace advanced on it with mock gravity. Piles of envelopes rimmed a collection of wrapped parcels in the middle.

"This is too much," he said.

"You could give them back," someone suggested.

"It's not *that* too much."

More laughter. Mace grabbed a handful of envelopes and sorted through them, holding each one up. No names scarred the surface of the variously colored and patterned paper. He stopped counting at twenty-five. He lifted each parcel and made a show of guessing its weight. By custom, nothing indicated from whom each gift had come. By custom, he left them unopened—that was a private ritual, to be done in his dom, alone. All he did now was touch each one, so the person or persons who gave them might see that he accepted it.

When he finished, a low robot carryall rolled up and he placed all the presents in its car. The machine trundled off and Mace offered a general thank you to the gathering. People crowded in and he suffered through more murmured good wishes and touching.

Music swelled over the room speakers, an insistent pulse beat overlaid by chord clusters that seemed to give birth to each other, and the attention of the partiers began to drift. Mace felt himself begin to relax as people wandered off, the whole fragmenting into small clusters.

"Are you still doing private security, Mace?"

"Of course. Business is slow lately, though, so mostly I do bad bonsai."

"Then you should fit right in with the *Pen-ching* Society. I hear they've given up on tradition and have started giving awards for freefall displays. Some of those poor things look like stiff octopi."

Laughter and faces swirled around him.

"Have you seen what Jar-lin is doing these days, Mace? She's using conductive sleeves and small currents instead of wire and hard work. Intriguing results, but they lack...something...."

"I never see you at any of the shows, Mace."

"I don't like to be depressed. It's bad enough my neighbors are better at it than I am."

"That's not true, Mace, I've seen some of your trees. Speaking of shows, Fogart is sponsoring a new one. Supposedly, he's inviting outside growers—Brasa, Elfor, Trinida."

"Is that legal? I thought Structural Authority forbade outside biologi-cals—"

"Then there'd be no immigration, dear. What do you think people are if not biologicals?"

"I just meant—"

"I think it's a challenge. He's suggesting that perhaps local masters have gotten complacent. For all I know, he's right. I certainly feel complacent."

"—even people have to go through decon and be certified. Put a tree through that and you'd kill it."

"Put some people through it and you kill them." White teeth showed in a cruel grin.

"It's what I heard anyway."

"Happy birthday, Mace. Is he seeing anyone these days? I didn't want to ask just right out like that, but—"

"Mace, you better get a piece of your cake before it's all gone."

"Thanks, Piers."

"No problem. Listen, I'm glad you came."

"I...thank you, Piers. It seems—"

A new hand closed on his arm, light and relentless.

"Mace, darling, I wanted to tell you how good it is to see you. It's been so long. Wonderful idea, Piers. How did you draw him out?"

"I told him you'd be here, Geri. He got all tongue-tied and tumescent but promised to show up."

"Nice to see you, Geri." He turned, breaking her hold.

"You look well. So, how many is this? Thirty?"

"Ha! Mace is the old man here. I couldn't fit all the candles on the cake. Next year I just do decades. Maybe I'll use votive candles, give it all a more nostalgic flavor."

"Cryptic flavor, you mean."

"I'll be forty-seven. Piers, as usual, is too soon with too much."

"Sorry, Mace. Couldn't put it *on* your birthday, you'd have figured it out."

"I hate to tell you, Piers, but he probably did anyway. Mace is very good at finding things out."

"That's true, he found you out, didn't he?"

"Go away, Piers, the adults have things to say. Mace, I wanted to call you anyway. Ravtec is thinking of doing a new showing, flat art, acrylic and oil and all that handmade stuff, and we wondered—"

"You should talk to Cambel. It depends on my schedule, but I personally don't have any problem doing security."

"Security? No no no, I wanted you to sit on the bench, be a judge."

"I—"

"I already have my people doing security, but I doubt it will be necessary, no one gives a damn these days for art."

"I'm flattered, Geri—"

"Happy birthday, Mace. You look good. Hello, Geri."

"Could you give us a minute, Van?"

"Maybe tomorrow. I understand your company is doing the refurbishing on the drainage system on the soy rings?"

"Van, no business, please. Call tomorrow, when you have that minute. Now, Mace—"

"Excuse me, I—"

"Mace, where've you been the last two months? I've been dying to show you my new Klein and you never return my messages."

"Paul, I—"

"Man's been busy, Paul, don't shear him now."

"Busy doing what?"

"For one thing, turning forty-seven. Mace, I saw his Klein, it's not much, the label's even gone—"

"Happy birthday, Mace, I wanted to tell you how good it is to see you. Stel and Jasper and Ku-yan and I are thinking of doing a new game. I'd like to invite you to join us."

"Game of what?"

"Bridge."

"You only need four for that."

"We're revising the rules. I said a *new* game."

"Excuse me, I'd better get some cake before it's all—"

"Mace, congratulations. I talked to Michel a few weeks ago. Very pleased with the job you did for his in-house spec, he says the system hasn't been breached since."

"His system has never been breached. It was purely prophylactic."

"I glanced at the code myself. Impressive. Very. I'd like to renew my offer. I think you're one of the best and I'd like you on my staff—"

"Is this a birthday present, Mishi?"

"No, this is extra. Besides, it would be a present for me."

"We've talked about this before—"

"I understand independence, Mace, and I respect your wish to remain...unattached...but truthfully, you're wasting your talents on small contracts. I—"

"Do you ever do any work for PolyCarb?"

"Of course not. They have their own staff, you know that—"

"Then I have to decline. If you ever get a PolyCarb contract, let me know."

"Mace—"

"Whatever this thief is offering you, Mace, I'll double it. Standing offer."

"Hello, Andre."

"Happy birthday. You aren't looking for steady employment, are you?"

"No, just steady distraction."

"Structural Authority contracted us to do satellite recovery."

"That sounds interesting."

"I wish I'd have gotten it ten years ago. There's not much left down there, but we dredge up some intriguing leftovers from time to time."

"Did you hear Brasa claims to have found one of the original deep-space research platforms?"

"I *heard;* I didn't *believe.*"

"In working order, they say, though the signals have been going god knows where."

"I don't know what Brasa intends to do with it."

"Oh, they'll lease it to us, of course. The neighborly thing to do."

"Mace, I want you to come over here and meet someone—evening, Andre...Mishio...."

"Good evening, Piers—"

"Come on, you haven't even got cake yet."

"Call me, Mace."

"Yes, I—"

"Over here, Mace, I'd like to introduce you to Delia. Delia, the guest of honor, may I present Macefield Preston—"

"Thank you for a lovely party."

"Oh, it's Piers' party—"

"But you're the excuse; you get the credit."

"Let me get you some cake, Mace. Be right back—"

"Are you enjoying it?"

"I haven't caught my breath yet. To be truthful, I'm not much of a party-goer."

"Nor I. Piers asked so sincerely, though I couldn't refuse."

"I—"

"Piers says you do security."

"I do some, yes—"

"What kind?"

"Personal, institutional. Mostly I design systems prophylaxis, data secures, things like that."

"But you do the real kind as well?"

"'Real' kind?"

"Body guarding?"

"Well, not so much anymore. There's not much demand."

"Are you partnered, Mace?"

"Um..."

"I don't mind, I just think it's polite to know—"

"Would you excuse me? I—"

"But—"

"Pleasant meeting you, Delia..."

"Maybe—"

Mace lost sight of Delia within four strides. He reached the table and placed his hands on it, reassured by its immobility, as if it could anchor him.

"So, what did you wish for?"

He closed his eyes briefly, then turned toward the woman who had spoken, ready to give a sarcastic answer. But in the near second it took to turn, he saw her and felt a faint rush of familiarity, the kind he had always heard called *déjà vu*, spoken as if an exotic name explained it.

She stood several centimeters shorter than he, with long, dark brown hair. Hazel eyes, though by their intensity they should, he thought, be bright blue. Incongruously pale eyebrows. Thin face, chin almost too long, wide mouth poised to smile, a small nose that seemed almost an afterthought. She looked at him directly and intently. Despite the unlikely combination of features, Mace was attracted.

"Excuse me?" he said.

"I asked what did you wish for. When you blew out the candles."

She meant it. Mace glanced back at the still-dispersing mob of partiers, all of them drifting away in small groups, mouths operating, expressing thoughts that did not seem to originate anywhere or impact anyone. Against that, she surprised him by being sincere.

He felt giddy for a moment, a bit foolish at his excessive reaction. He laughed. "I thought it was a tradition to keep that secret."

"It is. It's also a tradition for everyone to ask anyway."

"Is it?"

She grinned.

"Well—"

"Don't tell me. It's bad luck. You can only tell your true love."

"Oh. Well, then I suppose the secret will die with me."

Her expression changed instantly, humor banished.

"I'm sorry—"

"Forgive me, I'm being morbid—"

"—is it that bad?"

Mace felt himself step back from her as if physically shoved. "Um…"

"If you could do it again, what would you wish for?" she asked.

"I suppose…well, I suppose I would wish that I'd find something very important."

She smiled, but without her initial enthusiasm. The skin at the corner of her eyes crinkled. "Do you like parties?"

"Not one of my favorite things, no. I always end up in a corner, watching it go on, and wondering why everyone's having so much fun."

"I always come thinking one of these times I'll figure it all out."

Freckles spattered across her nose and cheeks. A fine tracery of lines on her forehead dispelled the initial impression of youth. She wore a plain white chitin, belted at the waist.

"I'm Mace Preston," he said, extending a hand.

"The victim—I mean, guest of honor—I know. Nemily Dollard."

"I—"

"Mace," Piers laid a hand on his back. In his other he held a small dish with a mound of cake. "Your piece. Oh, and I packed up all the candles and put them with your gifts, I thought you'd like to have them…ah, Nem, have you…?"

"Just now," she said.

"I hate to steal you away," Piers said, "but I want to talk to you briefly. Nem, would you excuse us?"

"Of course. Uh, maybe we'll see each other later?"

"That would be—" Piers dragged him away. "—nice…"

They reached the hallway and for the moment it was empty except for them.

"Mace, I wanted to explain about tonight—"

"Explain what? We've talked about this before, I don't care for surprises. But you never listen."

"People worry about you, Mace. We don't want to see you turn into a hermit."

"Thank you, Piers. And actually—this one is pretty good so far."

Piers smiled hesitantly. "Wonderful. In that case, enjoy yourself. I just wanted—"

"You succeeded. I'm grateful. Can I eat my cake now?"

Grinning, Piers walked away. Mace thought it often seemed too easy to validate the man's existence. Hawthorne had taken it upon himself to watch over Mace since representing him during the claims process, and at times Mace suspected Piers' motives, but he had put it down to a kind of assumed guilt—he had been there when Mace's life had changed and felt partly responsible. Much the same as Cambel Guerrera, though Piers still worked for PolyCarb.

He wanted to eat his cake in peace, away from the insistent well-wishing and socializing. The dish in his hand held no fork. He looked from the cake to the party and weighed the benefit of braving the gauntlet against the messy inconvenience of eating his cake with his fingers.

Then he glimpsed Delia. He turned sharply and strode down the hall, to the small toilet half hidden beneath the stairs. He knocked and heard no reply. He stepped inside and locked the door.

In darkness, he listened. No one walked by.

The only illumination—unless he switched on the main light—came from a small orange nightlight above the sink. Mace's eyes adjusted quickly. He sat down on the stool and propped the plate on his knees.

Gradually he picked up the muffled sounds of the party. By now people would be spread through most of Piers' meandering house. Of the few he might genuinely wish to see, none had shown up. At least not yet. Though he hoped to find Nemily Dollard again....

Nemily Dollard did not seem like Piers' usual coterie of guests, who used parties like a stage, all actors performing for each other, trying out their masks, new and old. That was the main reason Mace tended to dislike parties—he never knew, in this context, where the act ended and the actor began.

Not a problem he had in his occupation. In that context, he expected people to lie and hide. When the point was to unmask the actors, he felt confident, in control, but when the point was to simply appreciate the act and accept it as momentarily real, he experienced mainly distrust. It came automatically and he had to work to suppress it.

He had not felt that from Nemily.

Of course, it could have been a very, very good mask.

Mace pulled a few sheets of paper from the dispenser and, in the dim light, ate his cake.

FIVE

AEA, 2118

PIERS KEPT ALL HIS DOMICILE EXPANSION PERMITS in a frame at the top of the main staircase, proof of permission and display of ego to anyone who might question his possession of so much space. Mace noted the tiny eye of the recorder set in the center of the mount board; it counted the number of people who stopped to look at the array. The fact that Piers' house stood in an exclusive section of Aea where ostentatious use of cubic volume was expected and that the most likely people to visit his citadel couldn't have cared less how much room he took up only made the display inexplicable except as vanity.

At the far end of the hallway, someone stood pressed to the jamb, peering through a barely opened door. Music, partly obscured by the babble of voices, emanated from the room beyond. The man did not seem interested in the sound, but strained as if to get a better look at something or someone within. As Mace approached, treading quietly, the man stepped back, turned sharply, and disappeared down the adjacent hallway.

The stranger had moved so smoothly that Mace could not tell if he had been ready to leave on his own or had left because of Mace's presence. Curious, Mace went to the door and looked in. He saw no one he knew very well. He followed after the stranger, who had walked with the slightly hunched posture of a Lunessa. At the end of the shorter hall, stairs descended.

Near the bottom, Mace stopped.

"—told you not to—"

The voice was faint, but it sounded like Piers.

"She's up there. She's here." A different voice. Accented. Mace had heard that accent often enough working for InFlux. Definitely from Lunase.

"I don't care, that's no concern of yours. Now get your butt back—"

A door slammed and the voices became unintelligible. Mace felt torn between satisfying his curiosity and being a polite guest.

Before he could decide, a door below opened, casting light at the foot of the stairs, and heavy footsteps sounded. The stranger appeared at the bottom of the stairs. He stopped and glanced up at Mace, scowling, features half lit from the open door behind him. Then he was gone, the door closed, and Mace was left in silence.

Mace backed up the stairs.

He paused by the door to the music, his ears warm, and tried to sort out his impressions. There had been a familiarity about the stranger. Just a glimpse, not enough to be sure he could identify him later, but nevertheless he had felt a strong sense of recognition.

And who was "she"?

"Happy birthday," Mace murmured sardonically. He made himself shrug as if to leave his misgivings on the floor behind him, and went to the music.

Three guitarists played interlacing lines through the conversational noise. Curiously, the music came clearly through the clutter, and as Mace stood in the door listening he began to notice a rhythm to the talk, as if the audience were structuring their rudeness to counterpoint the melodies. But no one seemed to be talking. Of the twenty or so people present, all of them appeared intent on the performance.

The piece ended with a flourish of chords and the conversation blent into a short gush of white noise. The audience applauded. The musicians nodded, grinning with appreciation.

Nemily Dollard was on the floor, back against a sofa, clapping enthusiastically. She sat with her legs stretched out, crossed at the ankles, and her chitin had ridden up to her hips. She had taken off her slippers. She reached for the glass on the floor beside her and looked up at him.

"Oh, the birthday victim."

"May I?"

She patted the floor. "Absolutely."

He eased down, arm draped on the sofa seat. "I came in here expecting to see everyone being impolite to good music."

"Instead the musicians are impolite."

"What, uh...?"

"They have a sampler midied to their guitars. The music is designed to be played through chatter. They make the chatter compliment the music. It's annoying at first, but it makes sense after a while."

"Do they do anything without the talk?"

"Oh, yes, I've heard them elsewhere. Did you ever get to eat your cake?"

"Yes. Fine cake. Life is good."

She smiled. "What do you do, Mace?"

"You mean as in career? I'm retired."

"At forty-six? I'm jealous."

"Don't be. It hasn't got a lot to recommend it. Too much time and not enough to fill it."

"You live alone, then."

The inference surprised him. "More or less. I have a domestic personality in my house system. Among other things, she makes me go to parties."

"I don't even have a house system. Do you like them?"

"House systems?"

"Domestic personalities. Do you like them? You don't find them a little...alien?"

"I...no, not at all."

"You called it 'she.' A female template?"

"Yes. What do you do, Nemily Dollard?"

"Oh. I guess I'm prying. Sorry. Actually, I work for Piers. In his department, anyway."

"PolyCarb. Do you like it?"

"I—"

The guitarists began a new piece, the first measures a strong set of chords that seemed to ricochet off each other, surrounding the main theme before actually attacking it. Nemily's attention shifted immediately back to the music. Mace almost repeated his question, but Nemily Dollard's entire focus centered now on the musicians and their work. He knew that if he touched her she would react with surprise, that for the moment he was forgotten.

Her hands pressed flat against the floor, causing the muscles all along her arms to tense and reveal the definition achieved by long hours of exercise. Her fingers were short and slightly thick. Her legs were also muscular, making them appear shorter than they actually were. A faint trace of scar followed the line of her knees and Mace recognized the operation: adapt reconstruction. Her knees had given out and had been replaced. Nemily Dollard was an immigrant.

He might have seen her coming through InFlux. For all he knew, he might have been her first councilor, though he felt certain he would remember. As he thought about it he recognized that his attraction to her had less to do with her sincerity, as he had imagined, and more to do with a muzzy familiarity. He had seen her, he was sure of that, but it might have been only once in the last three years. If it had been during his first six months of volunteer service, he might never recall it; he had kept himself half numbed by alcohol, leaf, or any other intoxicant that came to hand. She may well have changed since then, too. He looked more closely now at the fine lines around her eyes and mouth for signs of other surgery. The fact that she appeared to wear her own face at one of Piers' gatherings, where the rule by which these people lived and breathed was to arrest aging at all costs (and the costs afforded on average were considerable), had also attracted him, but he wondered now if it might be an affectation, as meticulous in its own ends as the smooth obscurity of experience common among nearly everyone else here. He could not tell. The best remodelers could manage to hide their work from anything less than a professional examination. But the best were expensive and those who could afford it could afford it all. Why remake a face to appear naturally contoured by laughter and tears and worry and pleasure and leave unaltered the crude scars of an earlier, cheaper operation to replace overstressed and broken knees?

Her lips opened and her head swayed ever so slightly in time to the music. Mace caught the intricate melody now. They played major off of minor, weaving the relative keys in and out and around a long repetitive whole-tone arpeggio. The piece suggested the feeling that comes with the near understanding of a long-desired truth. Nemily Dollard listened with enviable attention.

As it ended, she closed her mouth and eyes and let her head fall back onto the sofa seat. Mace stared at her neck and wanted to touch it. Startled by his own impulse, he looked at the musicians. They were bright with perspiration, smiling the way lovers do after sex, exhausted and refreshed at the same time. People applauded and one of the guitarists ran his hand along the neck of his instrument, fingers teasing out a playful line as if to say thank you.

"So," Nemily said. "May I get you a drink, Mace Preston? Maybe another piece of cake?"

Piers' house emptied by twos and threes and even a few individuals, gradually revealing the debris of revelry. Partly empty cups, smeared dishes, lost bits of clothing, scraps of unidentifiable paper and droppings of food littered the floors, chairs, tables, stairs and any other horizontal surface available. Only a handful of people seemed to remember the reason for the party and, as they left, gave Mace a last wish for a good year to come. He wondered if he had missed the Lunessa; he did not see him leave. But there were others he had missed that he could call in the next few days to thank for being at the party.

Nemily wandered from room to room, chasing last fragments, a brief conversation or a drunken musician still attempting to hold an audience. Mace followed, at first at a distance, but more closely when she kept returning to find him, wondering what she sought, half hoping it would turn out to be him. .

Piers emerged from the direction of his kitchen, grinning broadly.

"Leaving so soon? But there are still people! Passed out here and there, but if they were awake I know they'd be disappointed."

"Give them my apologies. Thank you, Piers. I really enjoyed it."

Piers gave him a dubious look.

"No, I really did," Mace insisted.

"Then the surprise is complete. I'm glad you came."

"So am I." He gestured at the debris. "You need to clean up. I'm sure your houseguests don't need to wallow in aftermath."

Piers frowned. "Houseguests? I don't—oh! You mean the passed-out and semiconscious? I'll send them home by morning; they'll never know the difference."

Mace nodded, carefully controlling his reaction. "I have to go before I turn into a squash."

"Hmm? You mean a pumpkin."

"I mean I'm tired. Thanks again."

Nemily waited outside on the pedistry.

"I live in segment three, arc ninety," she said as they strolled down the path from Piers' house.

Mace automatically looked downshaft, about a quarter of the way up the curve of Aea, along a line of glittering lights that sprawled over most of eight arcs of circumference. CLUB STANDARD occupied most of twelve arcs, from one hundred thirty to one hundred eighteen.

"I'm...over there," he said, waving his left hand in the general direction of his dom, nearly sixty arcs away.

"Are you going there now?"

"I don't have to."

"I didn't think so. May I hold your hand?"

Mace spread his fingers. A moment later he felt her touch, interlacing his own.

"We could go—"

"I'd feel better in my own place," she said. "If you don't mind."

He wanted to ask why, then wondered why he did not. It surprised him that he might want something too much to question it, especially when he knew so little about it.

Even in the spent hours before morning returned through Aea's jalousied windows, people rode the shunts, as if pursuing final truths or last chances. Nightcycle was a pattern biological systems could not dispense with, but humans found it equally impossible to conform to its intended limits. Instead of cessation and rest, darkness only brought a different suite of activities. Five other people occupied the car they entered. At each stop, one or two would get off, only to be replaced by two or three new commuters. With each shuffle of occupants, Mace's anticipation increased. When Nemily stood, his nerves seemed to skip, jolting him to his feet. They ran up the steps to the spinward shunt.

"Here," Nemily said at her stop and took Mace by the hand.

They emerged in the middle of the strip of doms. All Mace saw, all he recognized clearly, was a collection of apartments, preformed assemblages, lights in some windows, most dark, the variously hued walls lit by bright halogens mounted on the upper corners of the structures. Nemily dragged him along the straight pedistry till she selected a doorway and led him inside.

He hurried after her up the stairs to the third floor, imagining as he ascended that he could feel the falling away of gravity. She inserted a key disc in a scanner and the apartment door slid aside.

He stepped through after her and stopped in the dark hallway, his shadow stretched ahead from the corridor light. The door closed, obliterating the shadow and leaving him abruptly motionless. Momentum lost, he stood still, agitated by unspent haste and uncertainty.

He sensed her close, then caught the whisper of breathing. Something approached his face, hesitated, and he flinched.

"Should I leave it dark?" she asked.

"Do you...I mean—"

"Either way. It—"

He caught her hand, surprised to find it so near. He tugged lightly and she came against him. He missed her mouth and kissed her chin, then dragged his lips up to hers.

"Dark is fine," he said when he broke away.

Mace sat up in darkness, disoriented. He stared out the open doors of a balcony. Beyond the railing, the lights of a township glowed up to the edge of farmland. The fields rose like a tsunami, flash-frozen at the horizon line of one of the light traps.

The panic passed in seconds. He drew a deep breath and reached for the nightstand. He found his pendant and held it, remembering everything in a rush.

"Mace? Are you okay?"

Nemily sat up beside him. The sheets fell into her lap. She did not touch him, only waited, which he appreciated. He swallowed and nodded.

Her apartment, her bed. Details of the room emerged—chair over there, bureau with mirror just inside the balcony doors, closet, dresser—even as the dream images that had waked him faded from memory, tucked back into the corners from which they crept in sleep.

"Yes, sorry. Forgot where I was for a second."

"Hmm. So soon? It's not even the morning after yet."

He gave a short laugh. She began rubbing his neck. Strong fingers. He groaned and pushed himself back against the wall. Nemily pulled him forward and stuffed a pillow behind him, then straddled his lap and worked at his shoulders.

He put the pendant back on the nightstand.

"Is that your good luck charm?" she asked.

"My wife."

She hesitated, then continued the massage. Mace felt foolish. He had long ago stopped hiding what the pendant was from people—if Poly-Carb or Structural Authority had wanted it back they would have found out what it was and taken it—but here the admission seemed awkward. He wanted to let the subject drop, and it seemed Nemily would let him, but the growing silence left behind nagged at him.

"It's a ROM. Helen died over—well, a little over three years ago. An accident on Mars. She worked for PolyCarb, too. For certain personnel they keep persona imprints."

"I know. They're hard to get hold of, though."

"It was a gift." Her hands moved down onto his chest. "Mmm. Where did you learn to do that?"

"Here and there. Isn't it a little morbid, carrying your wife's persona around on a chain?"

Mace's fingers curled up involuntarily. She took her hands away an instant before he felt the tautness in himself.

"Sorry...." she said and started to move away.

He caught her shoulder. "No. Don't worry about it." She resisted slightly. He laughed self-consciously. "I'm sorry. You have a point."

She relaxed and settled back onto his thighs. "Do you wear it all the time?"

"No...but I don't leave my house without it. It's a kind of pen-dance."

She laughed. "'Pendance'?"

"I said—"

"You said pendance."

"I meant penance."

"Why?"

"It's—we weren't together when she...well...." Mace shifted uncom-fortably. The dreams chittered from their corners.

"It's okay. You don't have to explain." Her hands came back to his shoulders and worked at the tension.

He concentrated on the sensations of her fingers, the stretch of pres-sure against his legs, the sound of her breathing, and his own response. He moved against the sheets and Nemily shifted one hand to his stomach. She scraped her fingernails lightly through the tufts of hair around his navel. His unease changed by degrees to arousal. He ran his hands along her thighs, first outside, then on top, then inside. She worked her hand beneath the sheet. He traced the outline of her hip, spread his hand across her stomach, and slipped his thumb into her hair.

Nemily raised herself up enough to pull the sheet from his lap. She leaned close to his ear. "By the way, happy birthday."

In the morning, Mace opened his eyes with no disorientation; he knew where he was. Gauzy light from the open balcony filled the room. He took a deep breath: the smell of strong coffee mingled with subdued muskiness. He rolled onto his stomach and pressed his face into the pillow.

Within the darkness behind his eyes he played for himself images of last night's events, from the first moments of pleasure at the party to the frantic grappling with Nemily. Her smell suffused the pillow and he felt himself thicken against the sheets. Amid the recollected impressions, a single feeling was prominent by its absence. His usual evenings out ended at Everest, Aea's finest brothel, with the ghosts, a selection of personalities augmenting a body to respond the way he wanted. He would leave hours before morning and slip home, sulking and apologetic, even though there was no one but himself to whom he might explain anything. It came closest to embarrassment. Nothing real ever happened with the ghosts, it was only physical, never a connection, so all he could keep were approximate feelings, and not even shame filled the gap where regret or fulfillment ought to be. That absence was gone, the "nothing" was missing. It would have made him laugh at its absurdity except for what seemed to be there.

A breeze rippled the sheets around his legs. He turned onto his side and looked out the open balcony doors. Nemily stood by the railing, brushing her hair. She wore a short yellow robe; light set it aglow around her body. She stepped back into the room and Mace slitted his eyes. He wanted to watch her for a few minutes, to see how she moved, what she did this early in the morning.

She placed the brush on her table and sat down. For several seconds she stared at her reflection, but with a distracted look as if seeing something other than her own face.

She opened a compact box. With her left hand, she pulled her hair away from the back of her neck, and with her right hand she extracted a small object from the base of her skull. For a few moments Mace stared at a dark hole at the edge of her hairline. Nemily placed the object in the box and took another one out, which she deftly inserted in the slot. Mace saw the dull white change color to match her skin the instant before she let her hair fall, once more covering her neck. She snapped the box closed.

Mace pushed himself up on an elbow. Her eyes flickered to the mirror, across her face, then to the right and locked. Slowly, then, she turned around.

"Good morning," she said.

"Good morning. Is that coffee I smell?"

Nemily nodded hesitantly. Then she left the bedroom. Mace scooted up against the headboard and picked up his pendant.

"What do we have here, Helen?" he asked in a whisper. "A ghost? Is that why she looks familiar?" He closed his fist around the pendant, suddenly self-conscious, remembering then that he had told Nemily about Helen.

Nemily returned and set a cup on the nightstand beside him. She went back to her dressing table and sat down. She folded her arms across her breasts.

"I guess you saw a lot."

Mace sipped his coffee. "Augments?"

"Uh-huh." Her eyes narrowed. "Some people don't like them. They don't care for the idea. They think they make us less human. If you're one of those, we can part now on pleasant terms."

"You're a cyberlink."

"Yes."

Mace set the cup aside and leaned forward. He wanted to ask, were you ever a ghost? did you ever work at Everest? Instead, he said, "If you don't want to talk about it, fine. But are you going to be disappointed if I *don't* leave?"

"You don't know me. You could learn all sorts of things about me that you don't like."

"I've had all my vaccinations and I'm not fresh out of the nursery." He shrugged. "What wouldn't I like?"

"I used to rent brain space."

Ah. She *was* a ghost. But.... "And what do you do now?"

"I work for Hawthorne."

"So which do you consider a social handicap?"

She started, blinked, and laughed, a sharp, harsh monosyllable very unlike the softer laugh Mace remembered from the previous night. She nodded and leaned back against the table.

"Right now," she said, "neither one."

The apartment was smaller than it had seemed the night before. Three rooms and a bathroom—bedroom, kitchen, and main room. Mace felt large and clumsy at the small kitchen table.

Nemily opened the box. "The augments are all specialized," she said. The velvet-lined interior made it look like a jewelry case. She pointed to each of the four mushroom-shaped buttons.

"This one is mathematics, this one is sensual-aesthetics, and this one is abstract reason. Each one taps into a different area of the brain relating to those processes."

"Last night you wore the sensualist?"

"Mmm-hmm."

Mace tapped the fourth augment. "And that one?"

"Recorder-collator. My journal, sort of. I don't remember the same things from one augment to the next unless I sort it all out properly. My brain is more compartmentalized than a normal brain. The various areas that have to do with different abilities or functions are isolated from each other. My short-term memory doesn't download, except for a permanent spool that gives me five or six minutes of RAM after I remove an augment. Not very much. So when I finish with one I insert the recorder. It stores the memories and helps me sort of rearrange them in my head so that when I'm using my synthesist"—she tapped her neck to indicate the one now in place—"I can remember. I can't duplicate the processes of the specialized inserts, but I have total recall of what I did." She paused, then laughed. "Except sometimes I get in a hurry and don't use the recorder. I've forgotten things for days before I used a particular augment and the recorder again. It can be embarrassing."

Mace understood how augments worked and this seemed unnecessarily complicated. Why, he wondered, couldn't they have cross-wired the implant so the different functions weren't isolated like this?

"So memory is selective."

She nodded. "I'll remember exactly what happened the last time I used that augment once I reinsert it. And the time before that and so on. Most of the memory is stored in my brain, but I need the augment to access it, to run the routine, if you know what I mean. There's a general continuity through the recorder and synthesist, but not through the others. They're too specialized. For instance, I have no memory of anything I did with the math augment while I'm in sensualist. I *could* use the synthesist all the time and get along quite well. The others are just extras."

"Job-related?"

"Mmm."

"You've done secure data work."

"I did, on Lunase."

"Is that where you got the implants? Lunase?"

When she nodded, he thought he understood the complications. The Lunessa had a reputation for a higher-than-average paranoia. If they could create a worker who might not remember what she did during her job, they would compromise the brain's ability to process information and store memory properly. The result might be something as byzantine as this.

"And what do they all augment?"

Nemily's smile vanished. "I have a permanent augment that keeps me from drooling and soiling myself."

Mace felt himself wince.

She blushed slightly. "I'm sorry, I—" She drew a deep breath. "I didn't have this installed voluntarily, okay? My brain doesn't—I'm—"

"Hey. It's okay. Sorry I pried."

"I suffered from PKU when I was a baby. The augments—I've had them since I was three."

"If you're uncomfortable with this you don't have to tell me anymore."

She nodded. "Anyway, I can also directly interface with any system that supports a standard IBM-Syntheco jack."

"I'm impressed." He watched her avoid looking at him. "And flattered. Thank you."

She gave him an uncertain smile.

"Will you still be disappointed if I don't leave?" he asked.

"No. Surprised? Yes. Disappointed...no."

Mace slapped a hand on the table. "I'm hungry. Want to go somewhere for lunch?"

Nemily studied him for a time, then removed her synthesist augment and replaced it with another.

"Sensualist?" he asked.

She nodded. Subtle changes in her features transformed her expression. A brightness entered her eyes, the same intensity Mace remembered from the party and afterward. The slight tension in her shoulders and neck changed, her posture shifting from anxiety to expectation. It was like watching her exchange herself for a different her, a putting on of a mood, an attitude, after taking another off. Mace had seen this before, at Everest, with the ghosts, but it never looked real with them. Perhaps because the fake personalities they used were just that, fake, and this, with Nemily, was real. Each of her augments, whatever changes they prompted, still left Nemily inhabiting herself.

"No," she said, taking his hand, "I'm not hungry. Yet."

SIX

AEA, 2118

AFTER HE LEFT, Nemily spent the night replaying Mace. Macefield Preston, 210 centimeters; 140 kilograms; grey-dusted brown hair; eyes the indeterminate color people called hazel; large hands; long legs; a fine tracery of hair falling from his navel in both directions, expanding like a waterdrop into the pool of curls on his chest and above his penis. His skin felt papery in some places, lightly dappled with fine bumps in others, and oily smooth everywhere else, except when he sweated and the smoothness spread everywhere, obscuring all other surface distinctions.

He seemed to like to arrange penetration so that as little else of their bodies as possible came into contact. It made for an interesting counterpoint to her own preference of pressing as much of herself as closely as she could to his body.

She resisted the temptation to edit the spool. The perfection of market-ready experiences left her uneasy afterward, even while the loops themselves seemed more than satisfactory, as if with the bought event the absence of earning the pleasure subverted the desired result. Clumsy moments, awkwardnesses, minor discomforts, hesitations, and the underlying uncertainty of adequacy, combined into a kind of validation. Two bodies fumbling toward bliss lost truth in a too-refined choreography, when the dance discards the dancers.

Her buffer interrupted after the fourth time, separating her from the impulses that drove the machinery of sensation. She opened her eyes reluctantly. Other sensations intruded: the sheets tangled around her legs, the dull ache in her neck from the angle at which her head lay, the thick odor of residual sweat and sex. She rolled over and propped herself on her elbows. A distant anxiety worked at her until she sat up, reached back, and unplugged the temporary augment. Her mind spun lazily in almost-vertigo until she inserted the synthesist augment.

Impressions continued. Her skin felt cool from evaporating perspiration; the lights were dimmed for nightcycle; her pelvis ached like an overused muscle; her head throbbed. She glanced at the time—twenty-three—and heard herself moan.

She stretched, discovering a score of smaller pains, then changed the sheets on the bed. Her pulse was up. She opened a drawer in her dressing table and took out the compact monitor, propped it against the mirror, then pulled a thin cable from its base. She opened her augment case and pried open the chameleon-skin surface on the recorder-collator and inserted the cable into the jack. The device ran through a self-diagnostic. When the screen gave her a nominal reading, she popped out her synthesist.

For a few seconds her vision changed—color went flat, almost disappearing, and shadows seemed murky, detail indistinct—until she inserted the collator. With a clear transition, the world resumed its normal intensity. Nemily blinked, then touched the start icon on the monitor.

The network of implants scattered throughout her nervous system registered on the small readouts. The main line that ran through the reticular structure, up into the branching connections to each major area, showed its rate of conductivity. Then, through that trunk, each node flared briefly as the program activated it. Her hands felt warm, then her face. A cold tingle coursed up her spine; her left knee itched.

The anxiety over Mace disappeared for several seconds and she experienced a sudden ambivalence about him. She remembered every action, every touch, every sensation from her arrival at Piers Hawthorne's party until Mace left at seventeen that afternoon, but they seemed like the actions of someone else, alien and peculiar. Just as suddenly, she tallied the BTUs and caloric intake for the last two days. Numbers shifted on the readouts. She felt momentarily hungry. Then the hunger seemed to move, lower down and higher up, and she remembered the last two days differently. She closed her eyes and shuddered.

She wondered sometimes what it was like to think unaugmented. The hyperawareness she experienced when plugged into one of the specialist augments gave her a feeling of power, diluted when she sorted the memories out into something like a normal experience. The truncated neuronal paths of her brain fed into synthetic pathways laid in to feed through the permanent implant and from there into the augment, where processing was facilitated and enhanced—essentially, she wore a CPU all the time to enable her to think and comprehend. The entire thing fed back into her organic tissue to be stored in the odd way her damaged brain allowed.

She had heard that full integration implants existed which would free her from the need to artificially sort memory, but she doubted at this stage she could be refitted.

The entire diagnostic took two minutes. She felt mildly exhausted as she removed the recorder-collator and replaced it with the synthesist.

Serotonin levels were slightly elevated and she noted a residue of adrenalin, but everything else was well within acceptable limits. She stored the analysis and returned the monitor to its drawer. She stripped off her shirt and went to shower.

She sat by her terminal, toweling her hair dry, and went through her messages. Advertisements for various products, an invitation to another party, and one from the Temple of Homo ReImaginoratus. She opened it and the aged, kindly face of the local rector, Patri Simity, appeared.

"You haven't been to Temple since you arrived on Aea," Patri Simity chided her gently. "It isn't good to completely lose touch with your origins, your sources. Besides, I personally would very much like to see you. We have services every three days...."

The message prattled on. Patri Simity had contacted Nemily shortly after she made it through InFlux. The rector had helped her find a dom, find her way around, put her in touch with potential employers. But Nemily had no intention of going to Temple ever again, though Patri Simity was a kind rector—especially compared to those Nemily had known in Lunase—and sometimes it seemed cruel to ignore her monthly invitations.

The message ended and Nemily dumped the advertisements. She decided to answer the other invitation later.

The next message surprised her. It was from Clare, back in Lunase. Nemily opened it, a bit dismayed at how eager she was to hear from her old roommate. Clare had been promoted twice since Nemily left. She had moved into somewhat larger quarters, though she still had trouble living within her stipend.

"Glim is gone. Has been for, oh, nearly two years. In fact, he left shortly after you did. I've asked around, but no one knows what happened to him. I'm hoping I won't ever see him again."

Nemily read the rest of the note apprehensively. Clare wanted to hear from her, learn how she was doing, and hoped everything was as Nemily had dreamed it would be.

"CAPs don't dream, Clare," she whispered.

She closed her terminal down then and finished drying her hair. So Toler had left Clare again. Nemily thought she ought to be used to it by now, he had always disappeared for long periods of time, only to return unexpectedly with no explanations other than vague inferrences to important work. But two years was far longer than any of the other times. Perhaps he had left her for good. Somehow, though, knowing that Toler was gone from Clare, possibly gone from Lunase again, disturbed her. She was tempted to try to replay Mace once more, give her mood an extra jolt.

She had expected Mace to make excuses and leave after his discovery of her modification. When he did not, she found herself mawkishly willing to share with him every detail of it. He seemed genuinely interested but she did not want to get her hopes up. She had always assumed there were people who did not find her augments repulsive. Most of her coworkers accepted them. But this was another level of intimacy, where otherwise untried tolerances often crumbled. After Mace had found out—after her cook's tour of how her brain worked—she had paid attention to how he touched her, trying to compare it to the previous night. If anything, he had been more open and generous. It became impossible to remain detached, but his hands had not gone to the back of her neck more or less often than before, the way they might had he been one of those fetishistically excited.

He had made love to her.

Too soon to tell, she thought, drying herself. For the moment he seemed to be a normal man—well, a somewhat better than normal man, kinder and more sympathetic—who found her attractive and treated her as a normal woman.

Normal...was it normal, she wondered, to carry one's dead wife around in a ROM, hanging from the neck?

She glanced at the time—twenty-three-fifty. Not long from now she would have to go to work. Feeling relaxed, she sprawled across the clean sheets and closed her eyes.

PolyCarb's campus occupied a couple of square kilometers at the base of the northern cap, upshaft, in segment one. As Nemily stepped out of the shunt, she saw a man in the pale blue worktogs of Aea Structural Authority Maintenance cleaning a poster off one of the platform walls. From the tatters that remained, she recognized it as a political tag from the Post InFlux Cooperative. Propaganda. She was amazed that anyone had managed to post it here.

She passed beneath banners bearing the bright azure, silver, and scarlet PolyCarb IntraSolar logo; they shifted slightly and the light rippled as if reflected off a pool of water. She queued up with several others at the security booth. One by one, people moved through the arch.

The man just ahead of her stepped under the arch. The alarm claxon went off. Nemily jerked back, bumping the person behind her. Thin bars snapped across both openings of the arch, trapping the man within. A pair of security guards hurried forward. One of them touched something on the arch and the grating bleat ended. The bars on the inside slid away and they gestured the man to come with them.

Nemily's pulse raced. She had never heard this alarm go off. In Lunase it was a common enough sound. Often some Lunessa would be singled out as an example, an alarm sounding and security grabbing him or her for no reason. Nemily had gotten used to not hearing them.

A plaque set in the right-hand leg of the arch caught her attention. "This security device is licensed and inspected by Structural Authority under provision 119 of the Internal Caretaker Mandate of C.E. 2062. Any unregulated use, tampering, or damage constitutes an actionable offense under the Public Safety Protocols of C.E. 2059."

The man was released. Nemily saw him striding unaccompanied, shoulders set, toward the main entrance. The bars on her side of the arch slid back and she passed through, half expecting the alarm to go off again. The security guards gave her distracted smiles and waved her through.

She took stairs to her workstation on the third floor. John and Tara stood by the samovar opposite their supervisor's office. Nemily went directly to her desk and put her augment case in the top drawer. The message light glowed on her monitor. She touched it and the screen brightened.

"Your presence is requested in Human Resources at your earliest convenience."

Below that was appended a task list.

"Where did *you* disappear after Piers' party?" Tara asked as Nemily reached the samovar. "We went to Raifa's but I didn't see you."

"The alarm went off on the platform this morning," Nemily said. She set a cup under the spigot and tapped in the code for hot chocolate.

"There've been a few of those," John said. "They upgraded the scans for profiles and frontals."

"Anyone in particular?"

"According to Emilio," Tara said, rolling her eyes in exaggerated disgust; Emilio worked one level up and kept the entire block current with gossip. "According to him, it's because of the PIF."

"What?" The samovar gurgled and liquid spilled into Nemily's cup.

John snorted. "That's what I admire about you, Nem. You're so unaffected by the world. You didn't hear the new Post InFlux Manifesto?"

"Oh. Them."

"Apparently," Tara said, "they've increased the percentage by threatening action against corporate spaces. When I got here this morning the shunt platform was covered with PIF posts."

"They were cleaning them off when I got here. And this is supposed to accomplish what?" Nemily sipped her chocolate.

Tara shrugged. "They think like Gaians."

"Their complaint isn't all that invalid," John said. "They say the new domicile construction is in violation of both Structural Authority protocols and immigrant rights."

"Really," Tara drawled.

"For one thing," John continued, "there aren't any decompression capsules in any of the units."

"There aren't any in my apartment either," Tara said. "So?"

"There should be."

"Anyway," Tara said, "security is being a bigger nuisance than usual. They searched my pack yesterday."

"Reactionaries," John pronounced and headed for his workstation.

Tara shook her head and tapped the samovar for another cup of coffee. "By the way, there's a Last Day party on two for—oh, what's his name? The one from Elfor in code—"

"Torem?" Nemily asked.

"Him. Plans are it continues at Raifa's all night."

"I'll see."

"You have to tell me where you went after Piers', but later. Tenure to secure." She took her cup and went to her own desk.

Nemily returned to her desk and sat down before her screen. She touched icons to organize her schedule for the day. The desktop blossomed into touch-sensitive screens and she began moving data around in preparation for interface.

Melissa came in. Small and intensely pale, she always seemed much younger than she was until she began to speak. Her voice came out low and evenly modulated and elicited confidence in her people. She stopped at the samovar, then spoke to Tara, then came to Nemily.

"Morning, Nem. Piers has a meeting at fourteen, he'll need a collation from the status files on the Diomedes works, an overview—stats, current condition, midlevel reports."

"Working on it already."

"Good. Did you see the message about Human Resource?"

"Yes, I'll—"

"When you get this Diomedes ready, go. You want to see a man named Koeln. I'll remind you."

"All right...."

Melissa patted Nemily's arm. "No problems, just routine updates. Anything else you need? I'll be unavailable for the next few hours."

"Um...no, I have everything."

"Good."

Melissa entered her own office space, separated from the main room by a transparent partition which now opaqued.

Nemily's console signaled that her prep work was complete and ready for her. She reached under the right-hand side of the desk and drew out a long, thin cable, then opened the drawer and took out her augment case. She connected the cable to her collator and extracted the synthesist from her neck. She inserted the collator and pressed the interface icon on the desk. Numbers shifted on one of the displays; she felt them, dim echoes in the back of her awareness. A blue light winked on and she touched the icon to boot—

—and stepped into the aisle of polished mahogany card files. A pleasant breeze passed through, scented with alfalfa and decay, tugging at the drawstring on the sunhat she wore hanging from her silk-collared neck. Nemily glanced up at the pristine blue sky and saw the sliver of a crescent moon, pale as a cloud.

The labels on the drawers glowed softly. As she moved from one to the next, per the list on the sheet of heavy vellum in her hand, they changed from pale yellow to red. She pulled open each drawer in turn and took from each a single folder.

At the end of the aisle, she emerged onto ankle-high grass. At the top of a gentle rise, a long table stretched beneath the shade of a pair of black-and-white striped umbrellas. She spread the folders out and began sorting through their contents, moving documents to a new folder she found already open on the table.

Halfway through, she hesitated, listening carefully. All she heard was the rustling of wind through grass and leaves, a slight flutter of fabric along the edges of the umbrellas. Nemily turned slowly and surveyed the distant, hazy horizon-line, then the rows of file cabinets that stretched from one horizon to the opposite. From where she stood she could see clearly down six rows. Empty.

As she turned back to the folders, something caught her attention in the sky, but when she looked directly she could not see anything. In moments the feeling of being watched evaporated.

She finished extracting information from the folders and set the stack aside. She spent a few minutes sorting the sheets in the new folder—chronologically, by subject, and by department, each sorting creating a new sheaf of papers, which presented itself on top depending on which tab along the folder's edge was used to open it—then sealed it with Piers Hawthorne's sigil and moved it to the far end of the table. Hawthorne's department dealt with site loss, claims for damage due to accident or, occasionally, sabotage and disaster. Each needed to be assessed and validated, costs estimated, and recommendations made. Usually, only other PolyCarb divisions were involved. Nemily had seen the flurry of bitter messages and countercharges that followed a denial, but since she had been here she had never seen one of his decisions successfully contested. Since reputations and careers depended on many of these decisions, Nemily felt tenuously proud to work for Hawthorne.

She replaced the source files in their drawers. When she returned to the table, the new folder was gone, exchanged for an elegantly written note.

"Please forward the following information to—"

Nemily carried the note back down the aisles. This was a simple pull-and-send request, though time-consuming because the files were scattered. It could more easily have been done by an electronic agent, but egents, as they were called, were not nearly as secure as a cyberlink. She wrote a checkmark alongside each item as she found it, then placed the documents along with the note on the table where the first folder had been. In a moment it was all gone.

The moon had become a clock face. She was ahead of schedule.

She pulled files and assembled data for the rest of her morning shift. Tasks completed, she returned to the table to sit down in the campaign chair that now waited beneath a broad umbrella. She had considered changing the quasi-Edwardian motif to something more efficiency-inspiring, but the surround was too relaxing for her to give it up. She laid a hand against her throat and found her collar open.

She sat up anxiously. She did not remember opening it. She surveyed the diorama again. Something on the horizon drew her attention and now, taking the time to examine it carefully, she could make out a faint puckering in the sky, like the stress lines in a sheet of heated plastic. As she watched, the damage faded, the blue resuming its smooth, pristine surface.

Her brooch lay on the table beside her. She snatched it up and pressed it between both hands—

—and extracted the jack. She noticed vaguely that her pulse was elevated. Her hands trembled slightly as she pulled the cable from her collator and let it snake back into its receptacle. With exaggerated care, she took out her case and exchanged the collator for her synthesist. When she reinserted the augment, color snapped back into normal register, but she also felt the full intensity of her unease. She was tempted to take the synthesist back out and wait while her internal system calmed her down, but that always left her feeling the rest of the day like she had missed something important. Instead, she sat back and waited for the wave of distress to wash away.

Across the room, Tara and John seemed busy with their own work, eyes fixed on their monitors, hands moving occasionally over icons, neither of them paying any attention to her. Nemily brushed her fingers over her mouth, but she had long ago learned how to keep herself from drooling while interfaced. Some cyberlinks never acquired that skill and spent the entire time uploaded sprawled like a rag doll, mouth hanging open.

She drew a deep breath. The tremors stopped. She surveyed her desk, then initiated a full diagnostic, even though she expected to find nothing. The flaw in the diorama looked familiar, though she had not seen anything like it since leaving Lunase.

It was a large system and took nearly two minutes for a full self examination. As she thought, it showed clear.

"Nem."

Melissa leaned out the door to her office.

"Yes?"

"Time."

Nemily checked her clock: thirteen-forty. She locked her desk down and stepped into Melissa's office. "I finished. Piers' data is in his hopper, the minders for the shareholder conference are out, and the analysis of—"

"I saw," Melissa said. She smiled shortly.

"Um...has a new program been installed recently? An oversight routine or something?"

"No. Why?"

"It just—a glitch I noticed, I thought perhaps it might be something new."

Melissa shook her head. "Not that I'm aware. I can check."

"I just ran a diagnostic and everything shows fine. I can do a more thorough check later. I'm sure it's nothing."

"Good. You'd better go."

Nemily backed out of Melissa's space, feeling better having reported the glitch. She waved at John and Tara as she headed for the door. Tara smiled, but John did not seem to notice.

Nemily rode the lift up two levels to the company mall. She stepped between two of a long line of thick columns that reached up to a balcony, which held another line of similar columns offering symbolic support to an arched skylight. Ivory-hued light fell to the imitation marble floor. The mall's design, she recalled from an orientation tour, was based on an ancient structure called Trajan's Forum, which had once existed in a place called Rome. The mall was a replica of the Basilica Ulpia, one section of the original building, which existed now only as a data template.

Human Resource occupied all of the antispinward balcony. Desks, widely separated, were scattered across the floor, some of them invisible behind privacy screens that shone dully like graphite in strong light. Nemily slid her ID into the reader at the top of the stairs and the screen indicated the desk to which she should report. She found it near the wall farthest from the edge. A man sat there, a carafe and two cups to one side of the flatscreen raised on the near corner of the desktop. He stood when he saw her.

"Ms. Dollard?"

"Yes."

"I'm Linder Koeln. Please." He gestured to the guest chair and sat back down. "Coffee?"

"No, thank you."

"Anything? Juice? Water?"

"I'm fine, thank you."

He nodded, a thin smile dimpling his plain face. He was a compact man whose head seemed slightly large for his body. His hands were wide and angular, strong looking. He poured himself a cup.

"You've been with us for nineteen months now?"

"Almost twenty."

"Mmm, and you've found the work satisfactory?"

"Entirely."

He glanced at his screen. "Three merit increases in stipend, full pathic and an educational allowance. How long have you been in Mr. Hawthorne's department?"

"I transferred to audit ten months ago and moved to my current position in adjusters five months after that."

"And before?"

"I started with PolyCarb in organics, on a comatulid line, doing oversight on mutation. From there I went to inspection of exotic metals, monitoring production of super stable alloys—"

"And ended up manager of quality control there."

"Yes."

"Impressive. Had you had any prior experience when you were brought into audit?"

"No."

"Were you approached by Mr. Hawthorne himself?"

"Directly? No, Melissa Car—"

"Melissa Cartol, his immediate assistant?"

"Yes."

"And what are your exact duties?"

"I'm a collator. I assemble requested data, trace peripheral material, and develop—"

"You assemble Mr. Hawthorne's reports."

"Um—I wouldn't—"

"It's what you do, even if the profile doesn't so indicate." He smiled. "This is confidential."

Nemily hesitated. Linder Koeln, though very good at masking it, seemed to be threatening her. He reminded her of the periodic morale interviews she underwent most of her life on the moon. For an instant she felt enclosed, part again of the warrens of Lunase. She glanced left and right reflexively, expecting to find cubicle walls instead of open space. The expanse of the balcony reassured her.

"Oh," Koeln said, leaning toward his screen, "forgive me. I can be thoughtless sometimes." He touched something and the reassuring space vanished, replaced by graphite-colored wall. "No one eavesdrops anyway, but this does provide a sense of privacy. Better?"

Nemily wanted to say no, but she did not want to upset Koeln. She nodded shortly and made herself ignore the walls.

"You're originally from Lunase, aren't you?"

Nemily stared at him for a long moment, comprehension opening with a chill. "You're security."

Koeln gave her a measured look which lasted a second too long for him to then make a convincing denial. He must have decided the same thing. He nodded.

"Then," she said, "this isn't routine at all, is it?"

"No." He shook his head in mock dismay. "I must remember that not everyone is as trusting as Aeans." He touched his screen and read: "Dollard, Nemily, InFlux number Nine-Five-Zed-El-One-Two-Dee-Eight-One. InFlux advisor Malcolm, Jeter Lowry. Point of origin, Lunase. Applicable skills, cyberlink. What did you do in Lunase?"

"My last position was on a splitter line attached to a fusion generator, water production. Before that I worked on a similar line for the alchemists."

"Did you know a man named Glim Toler?"

Nemily hesitated. Koeln leaned forward.

"Do not lie to me, Ms. Dollard. You have made no errors in judgment since you've been on Aea. In fact, you have an admirable record. You've adapted well. Most people from Lunase have a very difficult time shedding certain habits of coversion. Understandable, given the circumstances from which they come. We tend to overlook most of it, but occasionally it refuses to be overlooked." He sat back. "Let me ask a different question, then, before you compromise such a superb record. Had you ever been invited to one of Piers Hawthorne's parties?"

"I went to one two nights ago."

"Before that."

"No."

"He never invited you before?"

"No."

"Why did he invite you this time?"

"I don't know."

"Did he introduce you to anyone specifically?"

"No. Other people in my department were there, they introduced me around."

"Hawthorne himself did not?"

"No."

"Did you meet someone?"

"Several someones."

Koeln sighed. "I deserved that, I suppose. Let me be direct. You took someone home with you from the party. Who?"

"If you know I took him home then you already know who."

"True, but a great deal rests on your willingness to cooperate."

"Mace Preston. He was the—it was a party for him. His birthday."

"Had you ever met him before?"

"Not that I recall."

"He does volunteer work for InFlux. Are you sure you never met him?"

"I'm—it's not my nature to forget things, Mr. Koeln."

Koeln stared at her for a long time, then smiled again. "I'm told Mr.

Hawthorne spins a good time. Several years ago he was reprimanded by Structural Authority for one that nearly devolved into a riot. I wasn't with the company at the time, so all I know for certain is that the reprimand was issued."

"This one stayed civilized."

"I'm certain. Now, to my previous question—"

"I knew a Glim Toler. He was my roommate's lover. I didn't like him so I had as little as possible to do with him."

"Why didn't you like him?"

"He was—it's hard to say exactly—he was working vacuum—"

"Lots of people do that, contraband is almost a sacred calling to some. It doesn't mean they aren't decent people."

"He wasn't. Decent. He hurt Clare. I expect him to do badly, if he hasn't already."

"Mmm. Have you heard from him since coming here?"

She almost laughed. "No! He was one of the reasons I left Lunase."

"A necessary question, Ms. Dollard. I apologize. In fact, I apologize for this whole thing. I required information, you've provided...not all, but enough. My thanks." He touched the screen and the privacy field vanished. "You were sponsored here, did you know that?"

"Yes."

"Do you know by whom?"

"No. I thought that was a confidential matter—"

"It is, it is. Like anything else here, it's up to the citizen if he or she wants the subject to know. It's a gift and the custom of anonymity applies. Sometimes though there's a specific reason a sponsorship is made and revelation is made. I wondered if perhaps you knew."

"No, I was never told."

"I see. I may wish to ask you a few more questions. Please don't discuss any of this with your coworkers or supervisors."

"May I go?"

"Of course. Oh, by the way, I'm originally from Lunase myself. It's been some time since I've had any chance to speak with someone...from there. I wondered if—"

"Um...I really don't...."

"Unless, of course, your schedule doesn't permit it."

"Are we finished, Mr. Koeln?"

"Of course."

Nemily walked away, trying not to move too swiftly, trying not to attract notice. She managed to keep her stride normal despite a sudden, long-forgotten urge to run.

Everyone was gone when Nemily walked back into her office. She stood just within the door, heart racing, trying to understand why. Then she remembered the Last Day party for Torem on two and she heard herself laugh, sharply. She went to her desk and checked the time. Fourteen-ten.

She sat down, now glad to be alone. She had not been so frightened since her InFlux interview, the first one when she had been convinced they would send her back for importing vacuum. It surprised her a little that Koeln had not brought that up. But perhaps he did not know about it. She still found it difficult to believe security could be ignorant; she had come to assume that here they simply did not care about certain things the way they did in Lunase.

She tapped for an outside comm, then did a residence search. She found the number and made the connection.

"Preston dom, may I help you?"

The female voice distracted Nemily for a moment, until she recalled that Mace used a domestic personality. She wondered what kind of person owned such a voice.

"I'd like to speak to Mace, please."

"May I say who is calling?"

"Nemily Dollard."

"Please wait."

The trembling in her legs moved into her abdomen briefly, then faded. "Yes."

"Mace, hi. I hope I didn't wake you." She felt herself flush at the remark, wishing to call it back and put another, preferably more intelligent comment, in its place. Too late.

"No, not at all. I've been up—oh, at least five minutes."

She laughed loudly, embarrassing herself again. She drew a breath. This was getting worse. "I'm sorry, I can call later—"

"I'm kidding. I have a normal circadian, well, usually. Really, I'm glad you called. What can I do for you?"

Tell me I'm welcome, tell me I can stay on Aea, tell me I have no reason to fear... "Well..." She cast anxiously around for a reason, realizing that she had called him on impulse. "Um...we never did get that lunch."

"We didn't?"

She remembered the conversation, remembered lunch mentioned, then she replaced the synthesist with the sensualist. Paradoxically, she forgot sometimes, even after so many years, that the unmodified did not have the same precision of memory.

"No."

"I didn't notice. Well, lunch is past. How about dinner?"

"If you prefer—" she began, prepared to give him a polite way out, as if he had not really meant the invitation.

"Dinner, then. I'll be there at nineteen."

"Oh. That would be great."

"I'll make reservations. See you then. Bye."

The connection broke and she stared at the dead light.

Calmed by the concrete sense of an evening's plans, she checked her itinerary for any new tasks Melissa might have posted for her. The buffer was empty. She closed down her station and went home.

SEVEN

AEA, 2118

Mace liked Aea best during nightcycle. For him, the shimmer of light down its length, suspended like scattered jewels, looked like music, if it could be seen. He felt safe inside Aea, safer at night when the lights brought everything closer.

He walked the entire distance to segment two before catching a shunt. His path took him near one of the third-ring spokes that stretched from "ground" to the central shaft that ran from endcap to endcap, upshaft to downshaft. He craned his neck to watch a gondola rise toward its zero-g track along the spine.

On the shunt he closed his eyes, pretending to nap, revisiting his newly made memories. He had not sweated so much with a woman in months.

Frantic leisure.

Nemily accepted what was given, took a little more, and played with it, aggressively, athletically. . . .

He straightened in his seat, the pressure in his pants pleasantly uncomfortable, and glanced at the other passengers. None of them seemed to be paying him any attention. He got off at the station before his stop and walked the rest of the way to his dom, burning residual energy. As he turned down his path, he recognized another sensation: wonder.

"Welcome home," Helen said as he walked through the front door. "It must have been some party."

"It was, it was. Remind me to let you badger me into those more often."

"Obviously you aren't just now getting back from Piers Hawthorne's."

"No."

He walked into the kitchen and took a bottle of wine from the refrigerator.

"When will you learn to drink red wine at the proper temperature?"

Helen had always teased him about his barbaric taste in wine, lamenting that after all his time in Aea he had failed to cultivate civilized habits. He wondered if he continued to drink red wine cold just to honor that small difference between them.

"I prefer it cold," he said.

"Are you going to tell me where you've been?"

Mace pushed the corkscrew down into the fake cork and gave a deft, quick twist, extracting both with a delicate pop. He poured half a glass of dark red liquid and took a drink.

"Maybe," he said. "Do I have any messages?"

"You've been away for nearly twenty-three hours. You have several messages in the queue. Cambel Guerrera has been trying to get you since 0100 this morning. Philip Huxley has called twice today, Piers Hawthorne once. Officer Stat from Structural Authority would appreciate a return call, directory five-nine-five. And a Linder Koeln called at fourteen, requesting that you return his call as soon as convenient."

"Structural Authority...." Mace swirled the wine thoughtfully. Officer Stat was a departmental front; there was no such person, so it was a general call, but directory five-nine-five was the section of SA security that dealt with immigration. "Probably concerns InFlux. Who was that last?"

"Linder Koeln."

"Kellin?"

"Koeln. Linder."

"I don't know him."

"The call originated at PolyCarb. He did not say what he wanted."

Mace groaned. "More forms. Remind me never to sue a large corporation again. At least not for data. Money would have been easier to get."

After resigning from PolyCarb, he had pressed a suit to open the company files on Hellas Planitia. The last judicial ruling had been in

PolyCarb's favor, which had made him decide to stop the search. Poly-Carb had thrown money at him—bribes, for the most part, all couched in perfectly legal insurance settlements—but they had raised the stakes this last time and threatened countersuit and citizenship review. He had ceased his efforts to force PolyCarb to open its files. He was tired. The passive searches continued, but more and more he found himself less and less willing to tear at the curtains surrounding Helen's death. Safer to wait, perhaps, and let the data come to him. He told himself it would, and often he believed it. In any event, he desisted from attacking Poly-Carb anymore.

After yesterday he wondered how much longer he would care even about the passive searches....

He paused in the center of his turret, listening to the quiet of his dom. Perhaps this Koeln's call was related to the Officer Stat call. Perhaps PolyCarb had proceeded with its suit anyway. Either way, the intrusions were unwelcome. He did not yet want to shed the feelings from the past day.

"Mace?"

He sighed. "Connect to Cambel, please."

"Her house informs me that she is not home at present."

She never called for anything trivial, he knew. "Continue attempt till I'm asleep. Did she leave a message?"

"No. Philip Huxley did and so did Piers Hawthorne."

"Play Philip's."

A rich male voice filled the space. "Macefield, it's Philip. I have some new pieces. These you should see. The engraving, the quality—and they're pristine. Maybe this weekend? Call."

"Piers."

"Mace, Delia's heart is broken. I thought I saw you leave without her. I thought perhaps you intended to connect with her later, but she says not. Did I misjudge your taste or were you playing with me? Seriously, though, I'm glad you came—to the party and afterward, whoever you ended up going home with. If you live, give me a call, we can compare notes."

"He hasn't lost his sense of humor, I see," Helen said.

"How do you lose what you never had?" He started across the floor, to his music room, then stopped. "Connect to Piers."

"Must I?"

"Yes, Helen."

Presently, Piers' voice echoed. "Mace? What time is it—?"

"It's nighttime, Piers. I'm just returning the call."

"About time—where—?"

"Give my apologies to Delia, would you? I'm sure she was well intentioned. I appreciate the gesture."

"I'll pass that along. Maybe you and she could—"

"I don't think so. I have a favor to ask, Piers."

"That party I threw for you wasn't enough? Midlife greed, coming to surface at last?"

"The party was fine, Piers, really. I did appreciate it. Reminded me how much there is I don't pay any attention to anymore."

"Well . . . like what?"

"Some busybody from PolyCarb called me to make an appointment. It's probably more nonsense about the disposition of Helen's investments and follow-up on the suit. In case they didn't notice, the court ruled in their favor. I'm not resuing. And I think I've filled out enough forms and answered enough questions for one lifetime. I don't even work for them anymore."

"You *are* a shareholder, though."

"I'll divest if they don't leave me alone."

"You don't want to do that, Mace, it could tangle up your pension and then they really might countersue."

"Fuck my pension. I don't need it that badly."

"All right, be an idiot. How can I help you in your life's pursuit?"

"Ask around and see if you can find out what this may be about."

"Who called?"

"New name, I never heard of him before. Linder Koeln."

"I don't know him. All right, Mace, I'll look into it and see what's going on."

"I appreciate it, Piers."

"So . . . did you go home with anyone?"

"Is that really any of your business?"

"You're asking me to get you information on the people I work for on your behalf. Quid pro quo."

"Okay, then next time I have an opportunity I'll spy on the people you work for on your behalf. Let me know what you find out, Piers. And please tell them to get over me. I'm going to get over them. End."

Helen shut the link at the last word. Mace, feeling himself grin with self-satisfied mischief, continued on to the music room.

"Who *did* you go home with?" Helen asked.

"Is it any of your business, either?"

"Of course it is. I can't see that the vultures don't get you if I don't know where the bodies are buried."

Mace laughed. "My, we *are* getting morbid."

"Name, Mace?"

"Nemily Dollard."

"She works for Piers."

"So she claims."

"Data collation and retrieval. She's a cyberlink."

"I know."

"Immigrant, originally from Lunase—"

"Helen."

"Yes, Mace?"

"Enough."

"I don't understand."

"I seriously doubt that. I went home with her last night and spent the day with her. I enjoyed it."

"Will you see her again?"

"Probably."

"You didn't make a date?"

"Not as such. Why? I thought this was what you wanted me to do."

"Certainly. I'd like to see you do this every other nightcycle. Go to a party and spend the next day with a woman you don't know."

"You never do this when I go to Everest."

"They're ghosts. Both of us know all there is to know about them."

"You're interrogating me."

"You wrote the code, Mace. Part of my program is as caretaker. It's my job to caution you and see that you do not take unnecessary risks."

"That doesn't mean nattering."

"I'm hardly in a position to be confrontational."

"Hmm."

"Would you like me to finish running a background on Nemily Dollard?"

Mace opened his mouth to snap, but caught himself before he spoke. He *had* written Helen's parameters and this was indeed one of its functions. The system was programmed to proceed to the next logical question after a prolonged silence during an unresolved dialogue. That, at any rate, would be how he might describe it to a prospective client. It was simply doing its job, unable to alter its program so much as to accommodate a new emotional paradigm.

"All right," he said at last. "But don't tell me anything unless I request it."

"Within defensive protocols?"

"If she's that dangerous, certainly. But short of that, wait for me to ask."

"Understood."

He gazed up. Through the skylight, the opposite side of the world glittered faintly. His mood was not completely ruined.

"I'll be unavailable to anyone but Cambel till morning," he said.

"Of course."

He stepped into the chamber. "Stravinsky," he said. "'Dumbarton Oaks.'" He sat down and swallowed cold wine as the first measures filled the room. He did not want to think now, he wanted only to imagine. He traced in memory the ride back to Nemily's apartment, the eagerness with which he had followed her up the stairs, the taste of her mouth, the faltering steps to a sofa, and the adolescent fumbling with clothes that made them both laugh uncontrollably, the first touch of her nipple rising under his thumb, the quick breathing and sudden need to touch every part of her and to let her touch every part of him. He had not felt so consumed in years.

Perhaps he misremembered, but it had seemed that they had made no mistakes. No false caresses, no clumsiness, no technical difficulties...yes, that had to be the lie of pleasant memory. But he had slid inside her with an ease of familiarity that ought to have come only with time and practice.

She had moved him deftly, contoured herself to him....

He did not want to think, but he opened his eyes, uneasy at the incipient recognitions of things not as they should be. He had been with ghosts easily that skilled, that pleasant. But this had not been a transaction. He had not been buying a service. Nemily had made love to him, with him. It was different. He drank his wine and listened to the music and avoided the questions. Tomorrow, he thought, tomorrow I can think about it. Right now, I just want to enjoy....

Then he remembered his reaction to the augments, that something about them did not seem quite right. He did not know a lot about interface protocols—Nemily had been right about the prejudices cyberlinks provoked and there were few such systems on Aea, other than ghosts—but it seemed to him that her arrangement was unnecessarily...complicated....

He filled his glass again. And again. When the bottle was empty and the music long over, he went up to bed, groggy and slightly discontented.

His normal morning routine dictated coffee, vitamins, a short workout, and a shower. This morning he went straight to the shower. He came downstairs still dripping, a luxury he indulged since returning from Mars and learning to live alone. Water was no longer scarce on Mars but Martians still treated it with near-sacred regard. He had grown up taking dry showers in a cloud of tailored talc that left his body feeling rough and thirsty, wet showers a once-every-ten-days treat, withheld as a form of discipline. He enjoyed flouting his birthworld's traditions.

In the kitchen he poured a cup of strong coffee and perched on a stool. He drank half of it down.

"Good morning, Helen," he said.

"Good morning, Mace. Shall I connect to Cambel Guerrera?"

"Yes."

A few seconds later, Cambel's voice filled the kitchen.

"Where've—what time is it? Oh. Damn, Mace, where've you been?"

"Out. Piers gave a party."

"You went? Sorry I missed it. Um...I need to see you. Soonest."

"A problem?"

"I think so. Have you eaten yet?"

"No. Would you—?"

"Pete's Terrace in—what? An hour?"

"Hour and a half."

"See you there."

He noticed then the delivery light shining above the front door. Mace pressed the ACCEPT button and a panel next to the door slid aside, allowing a dolly to roll forward, laden with boxes and envelopes—his presents from Hawthorne's party.

"How long have they been in there, Helen?"

"Since yesterday midcycle."

He squatted by the stack. "Is it scanned?"

"Of course. No dangerous volatiles or suspect configurations detected."

He hoped none of it had been spoilable, either.

The wrapping paper varied from shimmery silver and blue to plain white to dark red. Most of the packages were small, less than twenty-five centimeters on a side. One thin rectangle looked to be about a hundred by eighty.

"I don't have time right now. Helen, would you store this? I'll go through them when I get back."

He watched the dolly roll off to slide into a closet by the door to his greenhouse. He went upstairs to dress.

Pete's Terrace looked out over a long decline toward a narrow stream that flowed spinward through a strip of parkland. The restaurant was not one but four terraces, each at a different level. Mace found Cambel at a table on the uppermost, a whiskey sour half gone.

"Sometimes," she said as he sat down, "punctuality is a curse."

"Yours or mine?"

She made a sound half-grunt, half-laugh. In the three years he had known her since Mars, Cambel had worn. She always seemed sleep deprived, and the vertical line between her eyebrows grew deeper by the month. Judging her on that basis was a mistake, though; she could be frighteningly perceptive. "I had a talk last night with PolyCarb security," she said.

"Oh no," he said with mock horror. "They've found out about all the padding in your old expense account. Don't worry, though. I think it's only a felony if you took too little."

"Very funny. As a matter of fact they were interested in our business."

"I take it you mean the vacuum."

She nodded and swallowed a mouthful of her drink. "Specifically, who our—my—contacts are. They're looking for someone."

"Anyone we know?"

"Not by the name they gave. Glim Toler. Sound familiar?"

"No."

"I didn't think so. I asked for an image, maybe I know him by another name. No image."

"They wouldn't let you see it or they didn't have it?"

Cambel frowned. "I'm not sure. My interrogator was the most stone-cold poker-faced professional I've ever seen. Gave absolutely nothing away."

"You didn't know him, either, then?"

"I've been out of the company nearly as long as you have. They're bound to hire new people. No, I didn't know him. A man named Koeln."

"Linder Koeln?"

"*You* know him?"

"He called yesterday. I assumed it was more nonsense about the suit. He's security?"

"Yes. You haven't spoken to him yet?"

"No, I was out late."

"I noticed."

"Why is PolyCarb security asking us about someone we don't know?"

"We do business with a lot of people, most of whom don't use their real names. I'd wager they're asking all the vacuum dealers of any weight."

"Why would PolyCarb be interested in him, though? If he's a vacuum dealer, then. . . ."

"He wouldn't say. But I *am* being followed now."

"Here?"

"About five tables away, just behind you and to your left. He spent the night outside my dom."

"May I take your order?"

Mace flinched at the finely modulated robot voice and stared at the short, columnar device that now stood beside their table. Mace could not, for a few moments, comprehend what the thing wanted.

"Um...yes. Coffee, croissant, oranges. Did you—?"

Cambel rattled the ice in her drink. "I'm fine."

The robot rolled away and Mace watched it, turning till he could glance over his shoulder to the table Cambel had mentioned. He saw one lone man, reading a slate over coffee. Short, ordinary brown hair, a squared face, large hands. Unremarkable. A perfect security agent. Mace turned back toward Cambel.

"Is that Koeln?"

"Oh, no. That's just a know-nothing shadow."

"All right. If PolyCarb security is asking about our vacuum trade in relation to this Glim Toler, we can assume he's not Aean. They'd know who he is already." He drummed his fingers on the edge of the table. "I got a call from SA, too. Officer Stat, immigration directory."

"Immigration?" She took an ice cube in her mouth and sucked at it for a few seconds, then spat it back in her glass. "Related calls?"

"Possibly. Hell of a coincidence, in any case."

"So Toler is an immigrant."

"If not, he may soon be."

"Which means there'd be an InFlux report on him. Or will be."

"I can find that out easily enough. For the rest, they must expect him to bring something in, something they assume would interest us."

"In that case, I think we should take an interest in Mr. Toler."

"Agreed."

The server trundled back with Mace's order, then rolled off. Mace methodically peeled an orange, thinking. He had asked Piers to find out what Koeln wanted. He hoped he had not brought trouble to Piers' life.

Of all the people he had known in PolyCarb, Piers and Cambel surprised him with their loyalty. He did not pretend, even to himself, that he understood it in either case. Cambel resigned after Mace did, her reasons as complex as they were clear. PolyCarb wanted her to spy on Mace. She had always felt he had been unfairly shut out of the investigation into Hellas Planitia; she believed him that Helen had been there, which meant the company was lying to its employees—not a surprise, but Cambel thought her position cleared her for that kind of information. When she refused to conduct surveillance on Mace, they began transferring her from place to place the way they had done most of the senior staff involved with the recovery operation. Insulted, she quit. She had been working with Mace since.

Piers had been the only one immune to PolyCarb's security games, at least so far. Mace wondered in the beginning if Piers had accepted the assignment Cambel had refused, but if so Piers had proved incredibly bad at it. No, Mace had decided, Piers simply knew too little about too much. He was an insurance adjuster. He was good at that.

"Toler could be a decoy, just to see if we do look," Cambel said abruptly.

"To see who we'd contact to find him, where it would lead? Don't credit them with more imagination than they have."

She smiled, then reached across the table to grab his croissant.

Or, he thought, they really want to know where he is, who he is, and don't want to be directly involved in finding him....

"Unless Structural Authority shows up with charges," he said, "we go on. PolyCarb can't make arrests, can't expel anyone, can't legally do much at all."

"PolyCarb security can obtain a judicial mandate."

"Until they do—"

Cambel rattled the ice in her glass. "So where were you so late? Have yourself a ghost after the party?"

Mace winced. "As a matter of fact, no. I didn't expect to be out so late. Helen said you called at one yesterday morning. A little early. What time did Koeln talk to you?"

"An hour before."

"An odd hour for him, too. At your dom?"

"No, I was out, too. He found me...there."

"At Reese's."

She nodded. Reese owned a club called 5555 down in the Heavy, "underground" in the outer circumference of ring five. Mace and Cambel had done security work on their commlines; over the last year and half, Reese had retained them to run security checks on employees and a few guests and recently they had done a large amount of work vetting guests for an upcoming private party. The place was more reputation than substance, but a great deal of illicit activity, especially vacuum dealing, went on in and around it. Cambel, to Mace's dismay, had developed a taste for it, despite the possible consequences to her reputation and conflict-of-interest problems. Mace had never questioned it too closely, though, because she had also developed other clientele and useful sources of information through Reese's.

"He wouldn't come into the club," she said. "Sent a request that I meet him nearby, at a coffee kiosk."

"Does Koeln know what we're looking for, then?" he asked.

She smiled wryly. "Do we?" She shook her head. "I want to say no, but I'm not entirely sure. Linder Koeln is an import. He's Lunessa, apparently worked security in Lunase."

"And we all know how thorough Lunase security is supposed to be. Hmm. Interesting." Mace finished his coffee. "I'm going to see Philip."

"What do you want me to do meanwhile?"

"Business as usual. But start asking about Toler. And if Mr. Koeln has contacted any of our sources. Who knows, you might have some of the same acquaintances." He stood. "I'll have a talk to him myself. Do you have only one tag?"

"As far as I've been able to tell."

"Good. In a few moments you can leave without him."

"What—?"

Mace walked away from her and made his way between the forest of tables to the lone man with a newssheet. Before the tag could react, Mace had sat down across from him.

"Good morning. My name is Mace Preston, I don't believe we've met. Have you tried the yams here? They're excellent. Allow me to treat you—"

The man began to rise. Mace stood.

"Don't make a scene," Mace said. "We'll both end up detained by SA, I guarantee it, and then you'll have to explain more than simply losing your target. Unless, of course, you *are* SA?"

The man scowled, glanced over Mace's shoulder, and tried to move around him. Mace blocked him.

"I didn't think so," Mace said. "Sit down and have some yams. We should talk anyway. Or at least, I should talk, though probably not to you." The man made one more move and Mace placed two fingers on his sternum. "I will put you in pathic if you don't sit down."

By the expression on the man's face it was clear he was weighing options. But suddenly he looked sullenly resigned and Mace knew Cambel was gone.

"Good, good," Mace said. "I want you to tell your supervisor—Koeln, is it?—tell him that I want to speak with him. I'll be at my dom later, but if I'm not, he can leave his code with my house and I'll get back to him. Now, really, let me buy you lunch. It's the least I can do after fouling up your assignment."

Mace went to the nearest shunt station and descended to the platform. As he expected, the shadow followed at a discreet distance. Mace boarded a shunt downshaft, toward the "south" cap of Aea's twenty-three kilometer length.

A map of Aea's tube routes covered the ceiling of the car, a bright red dot indicating their position within the nine hundred thirty-eight square kilometers of surface area. Elaborately geometric, the system broke the five segments down into quadrants and octants, station by station, the lines multiplying thickly toward the downshaft cap where industrial districts required short spur lines and inter-manufactory connections. The red dot moved from the lip of the second segment into the third, slowing at one of its two stops on the way to the fourth segment. Mace got off at the second stop.

Law forbade electronic surveillance in public on Aea, a rule many in Mace's profession found a nuisance. But Mace preferred it this way. If you wanted to follow someone you had to do it yourself. Structural Authority had tried to implement public surveillance once and had narrowly avoided a riot downshaft and strikes in the mid- to upshaft segments. Worries over crime or possible terrorism failed to persuade independence-minded Aeans to adopt thinking that made such practices necessary and normal. Aea was not Lunase, with its constant surveillance and intrusive security, and sometimes seemed to impair its own ability to operate to guarantee the distinction. Mace approved. In its own way, Mars had been as bad as Lunase.

The shadow followed him to Philip's, having already lost Cambel. The man was actually very good—Mace lost sight of him a couple of times—but it did seem a waste of skills. Mace did not worry about being followed to Philip's since he was a known customer of Philip Huxley.

Philip's shop occupied the center section of a long strip of shops that formed one wall of a broad plaza in arc one-seventeen. From here, some of the construction work in segment four was visible. People dotted the plaza; by midcycle it would be crowded and noisy.

Most of the shops had been decorated over time, some elaborately, others—like Philip's—with small details, like the three neon tubes that outlined the door and the anodized aluminum radiators extruding just below the roof line. A neatly lettered plaque to the right of the entrance announced "P. Huxley, Minuscule Rarities." Mace pressed the mici.

The door slid aside and Mace, with a last backward glance at his shadow, entered the shop.

Glass cases rose above heavy banks of drawers. Behind the glass stood rows of small objects. Toys, trading cards, mounted prints, ancient bound books. Toward the rear of the room a counter separated the brightly lit work area from the front. In its own wall niche, back by a panel that resembled waxed paper that gave off a gentle light, was a maidenhair tree, perhaps thirty centimeters tall, gracefully shaped in *Moyogi* fashion, the trunk curved ever so slightly. It was an elegant tree and Mace always felt a twinge of envy when he saw it. Philip had taught him the art and, as far as Mace was concerned, would always be the superior.

As Mace reached the counter, Philip looked up from the broad table at which he sat.

"Macefield." He grinned. "You're early, but welcome."

"I got your message," Mace said, leaning on the counter. A half-size chessboard lay beside his elbow, the tiny pieces intricately-carved orbital vehicles done in pyrite and corundum. He whistled appreciatively.

Philip stood gracefully. He was extremely tall, born and raised on one of the conversions, an asteroid hollowed out and filled with an environment. The low g explained his height to some extent, but his full two-point-three meters was the result of the adapt treatments he had undergone in order to live in the higher gravity of Aea. The only part of the treatments that had worked, Mace knew. A small number of people reacted badly. In Philip's case, his bones and musculature failed to respond properly. As a result, he wore a fine mesh of exoskeleton over his legs, torso, and arms. Without it, he could not walk, might even have trouble breathing.

"Happy birthday, Macefield. I apologize for not attending the party. I'm frankly surprised you went."

"It proved worth the trouble." He tapped the chessboard. "This is lovely. Is this what you called about?"

"No. I've recently acquired something from an acquaintance in Lunase that I thought you might be interested in. Come."

Mace stepped around the counter. He paused at the worktable. Precision knives, straightedges and brushes surrounded a sheet of brightly colored stamps. A monitor displayed an expanded image of the fine drawing of a man with thick black hair and florid lips.

"Macefield?"

Mace followed Philip through a narrow doorway into a pleasantly lit space. Four comfortable chairs faced each other across a low, round white table. Philip gestured for him to sit, then went to a bar and fussed with a tray. He set the tea service on the table and poured. Mace waited patiently. Rituals were important to Philip; he collected them as he collected everything.

He offered a smooth, handleless cup, then took his own and sat down. Mace held the cup on the palm of his left hand and with thumb and forefinger turned it, then drank.

"Very good," he said, and finished the tea. He placed the cup on the tray. "I hate to rush business, Philip, but there's a small problem. We've been contacted by PolyCarb security. Cambel was followed and so was I."

"Have they a mandate from SA?"

"I'm assuming not. So far it's only questions. But I was also called by Officer Stat, immigration directory."

"Regarding...?"

"The SA call, I have no idea yet. The PolyCarb inquiry concerns someone named Glim Toler."

Philip looked thoughtful, then shook his head. "I don't know that name. And the PolyCarb agent?"

"Linder Koeln."

"That name is familiar. He's Lunessa, I think. So are you going to suspend operations?"

"I don't see why. Koeln found Cambel, I'm expecting another call from him, I'm sure he knows about our business. If he doesn't, then I don't see any point, and if he does then it's a little late to pretend innocence. Of course, it could be a sincere request for assistance in finding someone."

"Then why annoy you by following you?" Philip mused. "I'll see what I can find out about Glim Toler, then." Philip waved a hand then, as if clearing the air of smoke. "I know your interests don't run to the quaint, but I have, as I said, acquired something unique."

"I'm always interested in what you find, Philip."

"You flatter me unnecessarily, but thank you." He laced his fingers over his chest and pushed out his lower lip. "The interdicts shut us off from more than we imagined—or more than we remembered. Little things, like linen and silk, not so little things, like music and art. Being barred from even communicating directly with Earth has been costly. Now that we're finally working through some of the difficulties, it appears there won't be all that much left."

Mace felt his interest swell. Philip's Earth watching intrigued him, though never enough to draw him into the company of Aean enthusiasts. Most people professed ambivalence toward Earth, pretending Gaia no longer mattered to them. After all, Earth had shut them out, unwilling to tolerate another independent state off the planet. Mace always thought it was economic—Signatory Space had access to virtually unlimited raw material, and over time they developed the technology to exploit it, creating a genuine threat to the market hegemony of the Earthbound polities—but no one cause could explain the complete rejection the off-Earth communities had suffered by their homeworld. But any news that came directly up drew instant attention, and the same people who claimed disinterest quickly learned every detail. Mace did not understand the fascination with a homeworld that had turned its back on its progeny—he lacked any such attachment to Mars—but he had developed a taste for Gaian artifacts.

"There've been rumors," Mace said.

"I get better data. Where possible, I have confirmation. There are still contacts on the moon that have access to Earth. Not strictly legal, true, but reliable nevertheless. Things are falling apart downwell and it's not a gentle fall. China is entering the eighteenth year of its civil war. We already knew someone had set off nukes down there."

"China?"

"They had divided their arsenal according to armies. Several generals always did have direct control over their warheads, and the generalships have been hereditary at least since the Twenties. Of course, they *could* have come from outside China, but...."

"My god."

"Yours, theirs...it's all the same to me. It's the information base that's the real loss. We haven't recovered a fraction of that stockpile. By the time we manage to lower the tariffs and get exemptions to the proscriptions, there may be nothing worth having."

"It's in the Archive."

Philip made a derisive sound. "The Archive is worse than a myth. People really believe that there's a satellite floating somewhere containing the accumulated database of Gaia. What started out as a witty remark is becoming an article of faith. How will they feel when they realize that it doesn't exist?"

Philip's vehemence startled Mace. He was used to seeing Philip in control, unflappable.

"It's not like stuff hasn't been coming up," Mace said.

"True, but a black market is viable mainly because of the scarcity of its product. Dealers can't survive an open exchange primarily because it would undercut their profits. There are terabytes of material still not retrieved. The doors are finally opening, but we may find the room empty. I've recently heard—and this is rumor—that strikes are being made against the governments and corporations at the vanguard of reestablishing ties with us. That the strikes are in the form of data destruction. There've been reports of entire libraries disappearing. Physically disappearing. Some sort of molecular disassembler seems to be ravaging synthetics."

Mace stared at him. "You mean like what happened to—?"

"We still don't know what happened to Cassidy. Or on Mars, at Hellas Planitia. But I wouldn't be surprised if they were connected events and similar to what I'm hearing about what's happening on Earth. Some data that comes up ought not." Philip shook his head, his expression intensely sad. "I can understand destroying people, but...."

Philip slapped his knees. "But we do what we can. Sometimes an unexpected treasure works its way up and I find myself fortunate enough to get hold of it."

He leaned toward the table and pulled open a drawer beneath it. He took a pair of objects out and set them near the edge, closed the drawer, and turned the tabletop till the objects were in front of Mace.

Less than fifteen centimeters high, the thin figures wore gaudy ancient costumes—knee-length boots, loose pants, short jackets and hats with plumes—and held broad, unfurled flags. The coloring seemed to shimmer—brilliant blues and deep reds, exaggerated flesh tones—and they struck bold poses, proud and arrogant. Mace reached for one, then looked at Philip, who nodded. Mace picked it up. It was perhaps half a centimeter thick, mounted on a flat base. Close up, he saw the fine engraving that went into the texture of the clothes and the facial features.

"What is it?"

Philip smiled. "Interested?"

"I'm—yes, of course. But I thought you said—"

"I don't entirely trust the security of our comm system, I don't care what guarantees are in the Charter. I'm known to deal in paper—stamps, currency, old documents, things like that. These are new. I prefer not to commit the acquisition to writing of any kind." He pointed at the model. "An engraved tin figurine. Made by a master miniaturist, Ludwig Frank, in Nuremberg, some time in the early Twentieth Century. The particulars are uncertain, but not the pedigree."

"Tin...."

"This, of course, is cast aluminum. The originals are, I'm told, still on Earth in a private collection and they *are* tin. My source obtained the digitized template and from that I made the molds. Very time-consuming, but fascinating work. This is what I mean about losing so much. I had no idea this sort of thing even existed until my source stumbled onto it and passed the information to me. Cast-tin miniatures like this were at one time enormously popular throughout Europe and America."

Mace set the piece down. "You can get more?"

"Possibly. Probably. It depends on whether it will be worth my while."

"What would make it worth your while?"

"Oh...two hundred a piece, with a promise to take more."

Mace considered. He preferred flat art and music—though he had never developed the taste in ancient postage stamps Philip had—but these *were* sort of flat. And exquisite. He could not imagine the motives of the craftsman to imagine and create such things.

Besides, he wanted something else from Philip.

"These," Mace said slowly, "look like they belong to a set."

"As a matter of fact..."

"Do you know how many there are in the set?"

"Fifteen pieces."

"Tell you what. Get me the complete set and I'll give you twenty-five hundred."

Philip barely reacted—a slight twitch in his face. "That might take some time."

"As long as I'm not senile before I get them."

Philip smiled. "As you wish. Do you mind if I keep these? I would want to make sure the coloring matches."

"Of course."

Philip rotated the table back and replaced the figurines in the drawer.

"I enjoy dealing with you, Macefield. You have taste."

"I've never been disappointed coming here."

Philip poured another round of tea and they repeated the small ritual. When the cups were empty, Philip carried the service back to the bar.

"Is there anything else I can do for you today, Macefield? After all, I owe you a birthday present."

"That would be a breach of custom, to know the benefactor of a present."

"Customs are not laws. What good are they if occasionally they aren't broken?"

"Then...yes, there is something else you can do for me. What do you know about cyberlinks?"

"Phenylketonuria," Philip pronounced carefully. He set his chopsticks down, his noodles half-eaten. "A perfectly treatable disease, but one must know how." He scowled. "Another example of lost knowledge. A gene turns off, an enzyme that should be made, isn't. Suddenly you have an infant that can't metabolize phenylalanine, which proceeds to warp brain development. It can be fixed. We didn't know."

"You didn't know?"

"Fifty years is a long time, Macefield. Out in the Belt there were communities that had been out of touch not only with Earth but with the established orbitals and Lunase. We grew up, went to work shipping rock back in-system, just as our parents and grandparents had done, and the only time any communications happened was when the banks talked to each other or an order changed. PKU was one of the rarer problems, but not so rare that it didn't cause us grief before we found out just how important old data can be."

"Was it common to give them augments?"

"Not at all. It was common to expose them."

"You're kidding."

"No. A lot of that went on. Resources were limited, defectives had to go." He raised his arms. "Some of us were lucky to be adults before problems manifested and we shipped them in-system."

"*All* of them?"

"No, not in the end. There was a clearing house set up to send them back here. Many were turned over to Lunase. They were starting their population push then. New bodies—even defective ones—were welcome. They have the doctors, after all. Your friend is probably one of those who ended up with augments, leasing brain space. I can make inquiries if you like."

"Not yet. I'm curious about the augment itself. I don't understand why one would have to be compartmentalized the way this one is. Specialized augments for specific functions, sure, but there could easily be memory overlap without the need of a separate collator, couldn't there?"

"Unless the user doesn't want it. Some companies that use brain-share insist on the added security of memorative isolation. Patents and copyrights. One of those compartments, I guarantee, contains a subroutine that allows for an external memory cache that bypasses the built-in cache. The cyberlink hooks in, gets work done, and at the end of the day remembers nothing, even with the use of a personal collator. It wouldn't be there to collate. If you don't want the people working for you to know what it is they're doing on your behalf, it's ideal."

"That's perverse."

"It is, isn't it? It gets stranger, though, when you understand that when the implants are initially installed, the system is arranged so even emotions can be controlled—isolating responses, programming in the ability to feel and recognize certain things you and I take for granted. Loyalty can be controlled and enhanced or distractions reduced or elliminated. But they were refugees, technically wards of the state. Lunase likes to talk about its political heritage as a republic and a free state, but much of that got left back on Earth, too." He shrugged. "They aren't slaves, though. After a certain period of time their contracts are fulfilled and they're free to go. Of course, most of them elect to stay there and continue working at the same job."

"So it's a security arrangement, the way she's constructed."

"Basically."

"Would there be a way to correct that, so she'd have full overlap?"

"Perhaps. Probably. You're a programmer, don't you know?"

"Only as part of my job, Philip. A security programmer. This is a hardware problem—hardware and wetware. I can do code, even some hard systems, but I'm not at all knowledgeable about brains and the actual physical interface."

"The sad thing is, the people who gave her that augment probably couldn't answer your question, either. They're technicians. Pop the top, insert the wiring, close it up, test the feed, put them to work. Agh! I'm becoming morose. I'll think about the problem, Macefield, and let you know what I come up with."

Mace stood. "Thanks, Philip. I appreciate your help."

"Not at all. Whatever I can do for one of my better clients on his birthday."

Mace returned to the main shop. He paused to gaze at the chess set on the counter.

"You do excellent work, Philip."

"Thank you. Do you know, those are all real ships?"

"Really?"

"Absolutely. The pawns are Mercurys on Atlas boosters. The castles are Geminis, the bishops are early shuttles, the knights are Kamirov-Foster Ares transports, and queens are Earthcorps Deep System Explorers, and the kings are—"

"Pegasus Interstellars."

"Yes...."

"I wonder if they ever made it."

Philip remained silent. Finally, Mace straightened, slightly embarrassed.

"Thanks, Philip."

The tall man nodded and Mace walked out of the shop.

It was past midcycle and the plaza was, as he had expected, crowded. Mace ignored the throngs. They were only masses on trajectories that he had to miss on his way back to the tube station.

He could not find his shadow.

EIGHT

AEA, 2118

NEMILY FELT MILDLY GUILTY not attending the Last Day party, but she did not know the man for whom it was given very well, and Koeln's interview had soured her mood. She left work early and stopped at a shopping plaza just across the ring in segment two.

As she wandered the shops she thought absently about buying a new dress for tonight, but Mace had given her no hint about where he intended to take her. Reservations, he had said, which to her always meant expensive. On the other hand, perhaps saving her money would be more sensible, especially if she ended up in trouble with management or Structural Authority. She might need it for—

For what? If they expelled her, they would provide transportation elsewhere. She would be starting all over. Extra funds might help, but not very much. What she wanted was to stay on Aea. If she could not do that, what difference did it make how much money she took with her elsewhere? It could never compensate for the loss of her home.

Home. She wondered when Aea had become home in her imagination. It felt comforting and dangerous at the same time, the potential loss greater.

She made herself stop and think it through. She was overreacting, old responses coming to the surface after long dormancy. She had done nothing wrong by Aean law (that she knew), they had no cause to expel her. A past association with a known vacuum dealer did not, in itself, constitute grounds for punishment.

A splash of shimmering blue caught her eye in a shop window and she crossed the pedistry to look closer. The dress was cut in an older style with broad shoulders that came to points and a skirt that folded over the back of the legs like the wings of an elegant insect. The fabric broke light up in small motes of rainbow pinpoints that floated on the dark blue like oil on water.

She entered the shop. The air was crisp with the scent of various fabrics, a kind of lush dryness. Nemily's fingers brushed over sleeves and skirts and pants; had she been wearing the sensualist augment she would have spent everything she had here.

The dress in the window was more expensive than she was accustomed to, but when she tried it on she knew she would buy it. The swoop of the skirt seemed to make her taller and the color against her skin contrasted appealingly. She turned on one foot, flaring the skirt, and laughed at the effect of light cascading down the insect wings. She caught the eye of a man peering through the window. He smiled briefly and looked away.

A reckless extravagance, but Nemily could see no down side to the expense. She left the shop feeling oddly invulnerable to failure—she was an Aean, she had just bought an expensive dress in an Aean shop, she was seeing a well-off Aean this evening. How could anything be wrong?

She followed the pedistry out of the mall and down along a stream that paralleled the way to the shunt station. A long strip of dwarf conifers lined the walkway. She looked up, at the opposite side of Aea, hazed by over six kilometers' distance, and felt secure, enveloped by the world.

She bumped into someone and stepped back, instantly apologetic. The man gave her an odd look, but shrugged and said it was all right, and continued on. Nemily, embarrassed, watched him walk on in the direction from which she had come.

As she was about to turn away, she saw something. For a moment she was not sure what had caught her attention. But then she noticed the man who had been looking at her through the shop window. He stood at the edge of the pedistry, hands in pockets, admiring the view downshaft.

Nemily resumed her path to the shunt station. After a dozen strides, she turned again, glancing over her shoulder. The man from the shop window was trailing after her. He turned his head a bit too sharply, then wandered toward the grassy border of the walkway. In a moment he looked as if he had been standing there like that all along.

All sense of security left her. She tucked her package under her arm and walked directly to the station. As she reached the stairs she looked back and saw him coming toward the station entrance.

Nemily joined a crowd on the platform waiting for the next car. A tingle cascaded over her shoulders and down her spine; she gave a start when the shunt slid up with a heavy rush of air. The doors opened and passengers shuffled on board, quietly finding seats. Nemily took one just inside the door and watched the rest file past. Her shadow was one of the last five to come aboard. He did not appear to even glance at her, but made his way toward a seat at the rear of the car.

She considered getting off just as the doors closed. In Lunase, she knew, there might be two or three shadows, backups just in case she might try to slip one. Here she was not sure. Security on Aea was so much less obtrusive than in Lunase, so much so that until today she had forgotten about it. But to Nemily, now that she thought about it, that only meant that they were better.

Perhaps she was mistaken. He might well be no more than a fellow Aean and she had taken his otherwise innocent movements as signs of intent.

The doors closed and the shunt moved on.

She did not get off in segment three. Passengers left, new ones came aboard, but her shadow remained in his seat, seeming to pay no attention to her. The shunt moved into segment four. He did not get off at the first stop.

At the second stop she exited. Few people got off here. She hurried across the sparsely peopled platform toward the stairs.

Mounds of dirt heaped around the station entrance gave the impression of ongoing construction. A small sign announced a new park under development, but Nemily saw no equipment. People sprawled against the piles of earth, talking, eating, treating the landscape with the evident familiarity of long use. The boundary of the proposed park separated it from clusters of prefab general housing units called assemblages. Nemily threaded her way along use-created paths and into the collection. People gathered in small groups near the entrances to several of the housing assemblages or sat on benches that lined the pedistries.

She had lived in one of these units during her first months on Aea. They were little more than large boxes attached to smaller boxes containing the plumbing and service attachments connected to Aea's general utility systems. Cheap housing, Aea exported them throughout the solar system. Ideal for orbitals. Nemily had even seen them in Lunase and had heard of them being used on Mars. On the moon they were called air holes; on Mars, shanties.

She found a vacant bench and sat down. She looked back in the direction of the shunt station, half expecting to see her shadow strolling toward her. Distant laughter ruffled the stillness. She saw no one approaching. She decided to wait a bit, till she was calmer.

The whir of approaching tractors drew her attention. From antispinward came a column of three machines, all painted in the blue and white of Structural Authority. Workers clung to them, riding on the running boards.

"Shit!" someone shouted.

Across the pedistry from her, Nemily saw a woman in a doorway, glaring at the tractors. After a moment she ducked inside. Nemily heard more shouting from within the assemblage.

A group of people burst from the assemblage and headed toward the vehicles. It looked for a moment like neither would stop, but the vehicles slowed to a halt, the whine of the motors spinning down to a low hum. People in Structural Authority uniforms climbed from the lead cab and met the group of residents.

Up and down the length of the pedistry, people came out to watch.

The two groups spoke in quiet tones for a time. Then, suddenly, one of the residents threw his arms out in an exasperated gesture.

"No! Damnit, those are people's *homes!*"

Nemily automatically looked up at the roof of the assemblage, suddenly understanding. Nesters.

Abruptly, the SA people returned to their vehicles, leaving the resident group to watch as the tractors moved toward the nearest assemblage.

The tractors extruded heavy arms that clamped onto the walls. Then, like improbable insects, they began to climb. When they reached the roofline, four stories up, they disappeared from sight. In a minute she heard more shouts and a few screams, mingled with the snap and metallic pop of destruction. People appeared at the edge of the roof. Some climbed down to the balconies around the lower level.

Construction of new domiciles never kept up with need. Often people built their own living spaces on the roofs of the assemblages, against SA regulations. From time to time, Structural Authority was forced to clear away the substandard and dangerous structures.

People converged on the lead SA vehicle. Nemily searched the crowd anxiously but could not see her shadow. She slid off the bench and hurried in the direction from which the SA column had come.

It was a long walk to the next shunt station. She was sweating and exhausted as she slumped to her seat on an upshaft-bound car. She squeezed her package to her breast, as if it were an icon that proved somehow that she belonged here. She had not been so frightened in a long time.

Nemily let herself into her apartment and locked the door. She dropped her case and the package on the bed and went to the kitchen. One last bottle of Aean merlot was in the refrigerator. She eased out of her shoes, loosened her collar, and sat on her small balcony, back against the door, ankles crossed and dangling over the edge. She was calmer now; fear never seemed to cling to her the way it did to the unmodified. She took a mouthful of wine and tried to find a way in which Linder Koeln's interrogation and the man who had followed her had not been a threat.

Her association with Glim Toler, as circumstantial and unwelcome as it had been, threatened her continued life on Aea. She believed that, could see no other way to interpret today's events. Koeln was security—Lunessa as well—and all security dealt in threat and punishment. They were more polite about it here, but she could not see how they could really be different. The unwanted, the inconvenient, suffered here just as they did everywhere; watching the SA tractors tearing down the Nester assemblages confirmed that.

She gazed up at the arch of the world and shuddered at the prospect of leaving it.

She considered her options. There were many mining and manufacturing platforms that formed loose clusters around the L4 and L5 points, several near Aea itself, but almost none of them were independent. She would have to choose a corporation and pledge loyalty to it as if it were a state. She had had enough of that in Lunase. Compdon Orbital was independent, but resource-starved by virtue of being so far from the main traffic routes between the moon, the manufacturing orbitals, and the Belt. It offered too little to trade and had to accept what was left unabsorbed by the rest. It lay out beyond the L2 point, the moon directly between it and Earth. Compdon's population of fifteen thousand lived under constant austerity measures, little more than a military enclave that from time to time stole drone shipments of ore or partially processed material. They made loud noises against the megacorporations and generally shunned everyone else. Better to go back to Lunase than live like that.

Elfor and Brasa both seemed like viable alternatives to Aea, both big orbitals, nearly as old as Aea, neither owned outright by any single corporation. Brasa was the larger of the two, but Elfor was closer, less than eight thousand kilometers from Aea, Brasa much further away, over near the L5 point on the opposite side of the moon. But she had met Brasans and Elfors—loud, brash, eccentric. Elfors constantly criticized Aea, which led her to think that Elfor was less than they claimed; Brasans were arrogant to the point of insufferability, which seemed to have no basis in anything until she learned about the religious foundations of Brasa. Brasans felt they were special, Elfors wanted to feel that way; Brasans saw the universe as one great orbital constructed by even greater hands, Elfors wanted to be those hands; Brasans thought they could learn nothing from anyone else, Elfors seemed incapable of learning anything. The places themselves might be environmentally wonderful, but the thought of sharing them with their inhabitants stifled any desire to visit them, much less live in them.

Mars-Earth Transit was in its first decade of construction at the midpoint between Earth and Mars, intended eventually to replace Midline, which still resisted the idea that it might either merge with the larger platform or become a secondary stop, a sideline, but was still just a glorified shipping transfer station, an immense frame with fuel cells, construction shacks, waldos and dollys, and the rough outline of what might one day be the largest artificial worldlet in the solar system. There would certainly be work for her there and good compensation, probably no more prejudice than she found on Aea. But it would be all struts, beams, environmental pods, and open space. No grass, no open water, no dirt paths, no—

—no pretense of living on the surface of a world. Which left Mars. But Mars was little better than the moon. Sealed domes, underground warrens, containment, and the social conditions born of constant restraint. Burroughs, she heard, had a parkland, Helium a flowing stream. But she imagined it to be more or less like the green sections in Lunase, big rooms with rows of hydroponics troughs burgeoning with plants under bright sunlamps. In time the environment would change—was changing already, the atmosphere thickening from outgassing of factories and the growing human presence, and the expanding network of enclaves that could not help but alter any environment around them— and could one day be better than Aea. In time.

The Belt was out of the question. They had sold her to Lunase in the first place. She knew almost nothing about them except as lists of available materials for cracking, synthesis, and recombination, the needs of the alchemists. Perhaps she misjudged them, but their one act on her behalf—sparing her life only to exile her—deterred any further interest.

The only remaining option would be Ganymede, but that was no more than a toehold, a couple of pressure domes and a few hundred people just beginning to build a home. There was a certain romance to it, a frontier attraction; perhaps being in on it at the start would offer advantages, a sense of daring and accomplishment. But that was not the kind of life Nemily wanted. She like finished places, warm doms, open air, civilization. The seductiveness of frontiers fascinated her the way anything dangerous or horrible fascinates people, cathartic reification of past or future struggles, the details humbling reminders of the cost of safety. People who embraced the risk and pushed the boundaries frightened her just a little, as if were they denied new fields to walk and change they would turn on the things already whole, tear them apart so they could rebuild them once again, just so they might have purpose. She was glad they had somewhere else to go.

Feasibility studies were still being conducted on Venus and exploratory drones buzzed about in Titan's thick atmosphere, but both places were decades from any kind of development and Nemily personally thought Venus was an impossible hope.

A couple of dozen other small stations peppered space between Mars and here, most of them research facilities or shipping transfers that rotated staff. Those seemed less safe after the unexplained destruction of two of them in the past year and a half. Cassidy and Five-Eight, each with populations over a thousand, had broken apart for no apparent reason. The panic and outrage had died down, but their loss had created an undercurrent of fear.

Earth, of course, was utterly out of the question, but for no reason Nemily fully understood. The Exclusion seemed ancient to her, perhaps to most citizens of Signatory Space, but its impact still dominated life. Early in the twenty-first century, the orbital habitats that eventually became Aea, Brasa and the rest declared political independence from Earth. As it was told in Temple, the offworlders turned their backs on the mother world, rejecting the demands Gaia made on them. What little actual history Nemily knew suggested that trade talks broke down and what amounted to a strike was called throughout the offworld habitats. The details were vague, even in the few Aean texts she had read. Not that it mattered—knowing precisely what happened and why changed nothing—but she got the impression that a growing isolationist movement on Earth itself coincided with the rupture, culminating in a global boycott of space. Over a period of several years, the Exclusion shut down all traffic to and from the surface of Earth. For a short time Earth shipped transports full of undesirables offworld to let the overburdened habitats try to cope, but then even that ended. Temple lore blamed the arrogance of the orbitals. This then became Gaia's punishment. Once again, humans were shut out of the garden. Some interaction continued, mostly illegal, and a large black market had developed dealing in contraband—vacuum—purportedly of Earth origin, but the practical result was that the orbitals, including the infant colonies on Mars and the moon, suffered years of hard struggle to secure their long-term survivability. Now people largely ignored Earth—publicly, at least.

No. Out of all the places she could live, Aea and its half million people offered what she wanted. She needed to stay here.

Her eyes stung and she wiped at them. Tears. "That bastard," she murmured, unsure who she meant, Koeln or Toler.

PolyCarb was not Aea. Or maybe it was. Tower, BioSim and Indersoll-Mech owned Lunase and said so and ran it through SetNetComb. Four million people, all working for the company store. "Don't like the rules," the joke ran, "there's the airlock, and leave the pressure suit on your way out, it belongs to the Combine." Aea seemed different. Structural Authority was an independent body, partly elected, partly appointed; perhaps not representative in the mythic sense, but at least something that stood between the megas and the citizenry. But most of the appointed seats were PolyCarb people. PolyCarb was the largest single employer, so the votes tended to reflect company loyalties.

She drained her glass and shuddered.

Her comm chimed. She went inside and slapped the accept.

"Nem? Reese."

The screen remained blank and she saw that she had left on her vid block. She left it on. "Reese, hi."

"Is this a bad time?"

"Depends. What do you want?"

"Oh, I thought you might be interested in attending a party tonight at 5555. But you sound grumpy."

"I am. Is there a special reason you're asking me?"

"Yes. I have a small favor to ask. But mainly I just wanted to invite you. There's a special event I'm hosting and I thought you might like to be one of the chosen few to see it."

"What sort of favor? I don't ghost anymore, Reese."

"I know, but—well, it's up to you, but you might want to hear the details before you say no."

Nemily sighed. She had worked for Reese briefly after she had first arrived on Aea. He owned legitimate businesses, but occasionally he skirted the edge of legality. She hesitated to tell him no, though. Reese had been useful to her—he had helped her get a better apartment and a better job and had given her good advice on getting along in Aea—and he could be a necessary resource in coming days. But the cost of his help might be steeper than the problem.

"I already have plans."

"Maybe you could add this to them."

"What time?"

She could hear the smile in his voice. "Around twenty-four."

"Some of us have to work, Reese."

"I've got some stims you can take home with you if you need them. This really is something you would hate to miss."

"I'll think about it. What's the event?"

"You have to come to find out."

"And the favor?"

"Not over the comm, Nem."

"Ah."

"Is everything all right?"

"Everything's eccentric, Reese."

"Well. Anything I can do to help...."

"Thanks, Reese. I just might take you up on that."

She broke the connection and went to refill her glass.

She checked the time—seventeen-forty—and tried to think about something else, anything other than Koeln and PolyCarb and the possibility of asking Reese for help.

Dinner at nineteen.

She wondered if she should tell Mace Preston what had happened and ask what could he do to help her should it come to expulsion and immediately felt ashamed of the thought. It was a survival response, looking for options, a process that seemed automatic and ungoverned, but she did not want to use Mace.

She stripped out of her clothes and went to the shower.

Of course, if he offered....

NINE

AEA, 2118

"LINDER KOELN IS RETURNING YOUR CALL."

"Ask him to wait, please," Mace told Helen. "Do you have that search protocol ready for me, Helen?"

"Of course. Toler, Glim. Encoding complete, the program is running. Initial results negative."

"Hmm. I didn't expect his name to just pop up on an admission document."

"Of course you didn't."

The search would take time. Getting into Aea was not easy, but once in, disappearing was not so difficult. Structural Authority managed to keep track of residents, but any other agency found impediments in the aversion Aeans had to surveillance for any reason other than safety. Even so, there were ways to make associational connections—purchases were recorded, housing assignments required identification, and of course certain SA records could be accessed by InFlux. As a volunteer, Mace did not officially possess clearance for those files, but he had found ways around the rules.

"Your caller is still waiting," Helen said. "Shall I put Mr. Koeln through now?"

Mace sighed. "Yes."

The screen cleared and a face appeared. Strong cheekbones and wide-set eyes, Linder Koeln appeared otherwise unremarkable.

"Mr. Koeln, what can I do for you?"

"Mr. Preston. I'd hoped to speak with you earlier. I would like to get together with you to ask a few questions."

"Anything you can't ask over the comm?"

"I prefer personal contact. It's a matter of some importance."

"Concerning?"

"Specifically, your wife."

Mace felt himself cool toward the man. "My wife is dead, Mr. Koeln."

"Of course."

"There can't possibly be anything that hasn't been gone over a hundred times in the last few years."

"Lives are complex. Details often remain hidden in spite of the most careful analysis. When they do finally surface, all the rest can change. Does the name Glim Toler mean anything to you?"

Mace hesitated. "Is this an internal PolyCarb matter? You are aware that I'm retired."

"It's perhaps a bit more than that, and yes, I am. Some files do not conveniently close, though, when we walk away from them. I assure you, this will take very little time."

"I doubt that. I have plans for this evening. Perhaps tomorrow."

"This is important, Mr. Preston."

"So are my evening plans. Tomorrow."

"I'll call then."

"Do that." He broke the connection. "Shit. Helen, add a new parameter to the search protocol. See if anything comes up relating Helen to this Glim Toler."

"Done. Do you want me to remind you about his call in the morning?"

"I suppose you better. What time is it?"

"Eighteen-fourteen. Your shower is up to temperature."

He stood. "What would I do without you, Helen?"

"Be consistently late or adapt. By the way, if you're going to be gone more than two days, please let me know so I can forward my findings."

On the shunt, to get his mind off the conversation with Linder Koeln, he tried to recall his last date, the one before Helen, before everything changed. Memory failed. He remembered her face—rounded, small chin, large brown eyes—and the way her head seemed to float on her neck, as if attached by a spring; she had worn...blue? No, periwinkle, which he had found erotic for some reason; her name was Pam...Pamela...no, Pamiel, a Lunase derivation, and yes, it had been in Lunase, during his one and only trip there.

But he could not remember what he had *done.*

The shunt slowed to a stop and the doors opened. There were only three other people in the car with him, two women who seemed to be together, and a man studiously reading *Pen-ching,* the bonsai society newsletter.

One of the women debarked, waving good-bye to the other. The shunt rolled on.

He got off at the first stop in segment three. The man remained on board and Mace stared down the tube as the shunt moved on, the faint slipstream tugging at his sleeves. He realized after a few moments that he had expected to be followed tonight and he was mildly disappointed that he was not.

He climbed the steps to the interior. Corner lights glowed warmly on the cornices of the buildings with the onset of nightcycle. The dirt patch led from the shunt station into the cluster of domiciles that resembled giant toy blocks jumbled together across the landscape. Walkways stretched overhead, connecting balconies. Here and there abstract designs covered walls in bright colors. Mace had only peripherally noticed any of this the other night. He had lived in a place like this during his first months on Aea after Helen's death, having found it impossible to stay in their old dom, waiting for the insurance settlements and his official severance from PolyCarb. He walked among the doms now with a warm sense of nostalgia.

Dom Sixteen stood at the apex of the path's long curve, just as it started to turn back spinward. Mace looked up at the balcony rails on the south-spinward side—that one, yes, Nemily's—and his anticipation increased.

Inside the small foyer, he read the resident list. Dollard, Nemily, third level, apartment G. He touched the icon by the name and proceeded up the stairs.

At her door, he hesitated. For a moment he seemed to experience vertigo, a sensation he had not felt in years. It passed, and in its wake Mace sensed the debris of several emotions. He quickly tried to sort through them—excitement, fear, bewilderment, embarrassment, guilt. He felt briefly that he should be doing something else, somewhere else. He raised his hand to knock on the door.

One emotion emerged very clearly. It did not, as far as he knew, have a name, but he recognized it. A combination of fear and a sense of betrayal, mingled with sharp pleasure. *Nothing will ever be the same again, who you are now you will never be after this.*

He had felt it only twice before. Once when Helen had asked him to marry her. Again when he realized that she was dead. For an instant he considered leaving.

His hand resumed its path, his knuckles struck the door, twice, and he stepped back to wait for Nemily's system to recognize and admit him.

Instead, she opened the door herself.

"Um..."

"Mace." She grinned broadly, the gesture pushing her cheeks up and narrowing her eyes.

"Of course."

She examined him, lower lip caught by her teeth. Self-consciously, Mace clasped his hands behind his back and glanced down the corridor.

"So do I pass?" he asked.

She laughed and moved aside. "Yes, absolutely. Please." She gave a mock bow and waved him inside.

Nemily wore a dark, shimmering blue dress that looked expensive.

"Is this fine?" she asked. "You didn't say where...."

"You look...." Mace wanted to undress her and make love, never mind the rest of the evening's plans. "Yes, that's fine. More than fine."

She stepped close to him. "May I?"

Mace nodded and felt himself tighten as she touched his face, then kissed him. He tried to pay attention to her taste, the feel of her lips moving against his; her tongue stroked along his teeth until he opened his mouth, and the sensations moiled, individual aspects losing distinction. Her hands touched his hair, his neck. She pressed against him.

"It's all right if you touch me," she said.

Mace carefully pressed his palms to her hips as she kissed him again. He pulled away.

"We should eat first," he said thickly. "This time."

"Where?"

Mace cleared his throat. "A surprise." He studied her, then touched two fingers to the back of his own neck and asked, "Sensualist?"

"The best way to have dinner."

"I almost never leave the dom this way," she said as they walked down the path. "There's a direct tunnel to the tube platform."

"We're not taking the tube." Mace checked his watch: nineteen-twenty.

"Another surprise?"

"Well...."

As they started along the stretch to the shunt station, the pad above the entrance came into view. A gondola squatted ponderously on the slab, its twin rotors spinning lazily at either end, creating a wash of air. A small crowd stood nearby; gondolas rarely landed this far down-shaft.

Nemily stared.

"Our carriage awaits," Mace said, gesturing grandly.

The gondola seated twelve. Four other passengers huddled around a table at the rear, laughing and drinking and eating small cakes. Nemily sat by a window, midway down the length of the cabin. When they lifted off, she pressed a hand against the transparency.

The gondola followed the spin of Aea until it approached the core. It lost angular momentum and gravity lessened noticeably. It followed a leisure corkscrew up the length of Aea toward the northern cap, its rotation just enough to keep everyone in their seats and the food from floating off.

Mace watched Nemily watch, her eyes wide and childlike. Her right hand found his thigh and squeezed.

"It's beautiful...."

What would it be like, he wondered, to live with all the receivers on all the time...?

"I made reservations at the Earthview."

"I didn't realize you were wealthy."

Mace brushed the shape of Helen's pendant through his shirt. "I'm not, really, but it's been so long since I indulged myself like this...."

"Am I an indulgence?"

"I'd like to indulge you."

"That's not the same thing."

For an instant she looked intolerably fragile, emotions held suspended by a surface tension of vulnerability. Mace did not breathe, wondering which way she would turn. Then she smiled brightly and kissed him. When she drew back her face was flushed and it seemed as though she had transferred her fragility to Mace. He felt tenuous. Not uncertain, but with such a light grasp on his certainty that it might slip from him with the next full revolution of the gondola, snatched by the stepped gravity of the spinning world.

"I've been asked to a party later tonight," she said. "Some friends...I wondered if you'd like to come with me?"

"I'd hoped to spend the whole night with you."

"Then you'll come."

"I think that's the idea."

She laughed.

Twenty minutes later, the gondola settled onto the landing pad that extended from the cap wall, just antispinward from the top floor of the restaurant. Private balconies extruded from the top and middle floor and a wide shelf from the lower floor supported an "open air" café. A transparency covered the three levels.

The three floors of the Earthview occupied a section of the upshaft cap two-thirds of the way from the core. Two hundred fifty meters above the living surface of Aea substantially lessened g, but not so much as to be a problem for people who had difficulties with food in low gravity.

Mace took Nemily's arm. "Careful on the stairs."

Mace escorted her to the top floor entrance. A maître d' bowed slightly and led them to a table near the other wall, opposite the transparency overlooking Aea's interior.

Nemily almost stopped walking as they approached.

The wall showed stars.

"Is that—?"

"No," Mace said. "Though management wishes it were real."

She sat down in the chair the maître d' held for her.

"But," Mace continued when the man had left, "it is a real-time projection. They have a live feed from the external monitors. I understand that this whole chamber used to extend all the way to the exterior, part of a research facility in the early days of the second ring."

"It sounds mythic, doesn't it?" She deepened her voice, mock dramatic. "'In the days of the second ring, when space was a vacuum and life was lived between punctures.'" She laughed. "When you look at Aea it's hard to imagine when it didn't exist." She looked up at the stars again. "But they say there was a time when none of that existed, either." She sighed and looked back toward the interior. "I suppose it's a required question for someone who hasn't been here before—"

"Why is it called the Earthview when you can't see Earth?"

She nodded.

"'In the days when it was just the second ring,'" he intoned, imitating her melodrama, "Earth was visible." He pointed in the direction of Aea's interior. "That way. Just over the shoulder of the moon. Then the first ring was moved into position to anchor the first segment. The space between the spokes stayed open. As each ring joined itself to the construction to extend Aea, it was still possible to see Earth from here. The view wasn't cut off till the outer wall was complete and the opposite cap closed in the interior space."

Several areas were screened off, giving the place the look of a vast underground chamber with thick ceiling supports. Aural dampers kept the ambient noise low.

"Who's here tonight?" Nemily asked.

"Shareholders," Mace said. He glanced from table to table. He indicated a couple sitting three tables away. "Tyler Dickinson, son of Paul and Vera, potential heir to the Kopernike Cartage Company. Kopernike transports raw material from the Belt to the six major orbitals and Lunase. They own four smaller transport firms. Kopernike is over fifty years old. Along with Tower Enterprises, PolyCarb IntraSolar, and Weber-Schicke-Geston, they're the closest thing we have up here to 'old money.' It might not stay a family-owned firm, though, since Tyler there has no interest in it. But he likes to spend its money. He never uses privacy screens because he likes to be seen spending the family fortune."

"Who's with him?"

"His sister, Prist."

"She's beautiful."

"Tyler thinks so. Now, over there is Lauris San Cove—"

Nemily's head snapped around. "The artist?" She followed Mace's aimed finger. "She's alone."

"Usually. Not many people can place the face and the name together. You know her work?"

"Yes, it's incredible."

"Painting isn't the most widely appreciated form—"

"It's making a comeback, they say."

"Possibly. It may take another decade or two."

"I hope not *that* long! Who are these people coming in just now?"

Mace craned his neck to see toward the entrance. The maître d' led a group of eight through the maze of tables and blanked private areas. Three men and five women. One of them was Oswald Listrom. He had not seen him since the disciplinary hearing after Hellas Planitia. Cambel Guerrera had defended him then, which had cost her. Listrom, Mace recalled, had been unsympathetic: Mace had abandoned him, his assignment.

"PolyCarb," Mace said.

"Is that bad?"

"Hmm? Why would it be bad?"

"The way you said it, as if it hurt."

Mace stared at her until she looked away. "I, uh...my wife and I worked for PolyCarb."

"Oh."

As he tried to sort out his reactions, it occurred to Mace that being sensually amped did not necessarily mean everything experienced would be a joy. He watched Nemily's face as she seemed to fold inward around the knowledge that Mace associated PolyCarb—the company she worked for—with Helen and, presumably, her death. Her eyes disfocussed and her lips hung open slightly, the image of disconsolate empathy. He stabbed the menu icon on the edge of the table.

"It's time to explore new flavors," he said. "There is nothing bad on their entire menu."

Nemily blinked at the glowing square before her. In swift increments, her eyes cleared and the unhappy moue changed to a slight smile. By the time the waiter arrived, she seemed to have completely forgotten her brief depression.

Conversation ceased during the meal. Salad, clam cakes, angel-hair pasta with a fine olive-and-garlic sauce, spring rolls, fresh bread, and a bottle of merlot...watching Nemily eat, each bite inspected, smelled, savored intensely, startled Mace. He considered himself something of an epicurean, but Nemily's evident pleasure made him wonder how much he never tasted.

Before dessert he excused himself and made his way to the rest-room.

Only one other person stood at a urinal. The quiet hum of the siphon was the loudest noise in the room. As Mace stepped up to a stall, the other man finished and left.

Someone else came in. Mace glanced over his shoulder.

A woman leaned over the sink, carefully washing her hands. She met his eyes in the mirror.

"Mace," she said.

The voice sounded familiar. He shook himself and sealed his fly, then stepped up to the basin beside her. She was taller than him, broad-shouldered, thick yellow-white hair. He glanced at her hands—wide, powerful—and then remembered that she had come in with the Poly-Carb party. He knew what she must be—security.

She finished soaping and rinsed, a smile teasing at the corners of her mouth.

"You don't recognize me, do you?" she said.

That voice.... "No, I'm afraid—"

She flicked her hands at the basin, then rubbed her fingertips together in a very familiar gesture.

"Syvestri?"

She grinned. "You must not be paying attention tonight. You must be distracted."

"Uh-huh. The fact that the last time we spoke, you were male has nothing to do with it."

She shrugged and slid her hands into the drying slots next to the basin. "Might."

"When...?"

"Year and a half ago. What do you think?"

"Impressive."

"You're supposed to say 'beautiful' or 'lovely' or something like that. They told me that would be an expected response at the pathic where I had it done."

"Forgive me. Nobody told me."

"Forgiven. 'Impressive' will do just fine. What've you been doing late-ly, Mace?"

"This and that. Retirement stuff. And just in case you haven't heard, PolyCarb and I have settled."

Syvestri looked doubtful. "Really?"

"Yes, really. No more court time, at least not over that. What about you?"

"Still doing personal security for VIPs." Syvestri leaned closer to the mirror, making a show of checking her hair. "Who's your companion?"

Mace felt wary now. Syvestri had never learned how to ask an important question innocuously. He—she—always stressed the nonchalance too much and gave away her interest.

"Her name is Nemily. Is there a reason you want to know?"

Syvestri nodded. "A favor returned, Mace. You got me this job and helped me through the first levels. It paid off, that help. I never had a chance to say thank you." She straightened and turned to face him fully. "Nemily Dollard. She's on a to-be-watched list. So far it's entirely an internal PolyCarb matter and it's very recent. Her name came up in connection to another matter and now she's under scrutiny."

"What 'other matter'?"

"I don't know that. But these trade talks with Lunase have everybody nervous."

"Why would that be? It's just more of the same old who gets to sell what to whom nonsense."

Syvestri shrugged.

"She's just a cyberlink in the actuarial department," Mace said, "working for Piers Hawthorne."

Syvestri frowned. "Odd. She'd hardly be in a threatening position there, would she?"

"I wouldn't think so. Who noticed her?"

"I don't know that either. Ongoing investigation, first-level priority, all those fancy adjectives. I could find out if you want."

"It's got to be a mistake." Mace grunted. "All of a sudden I seem to be in your way. I've got to talk to another agent tomorrow, a man named Koeln."

"Linder Koeln? Who did you piss off?"

"No one. He's good?"

"What he lacks in talent he makes up for in tenacity. He's good. If it's his investigation...."

"I'll be careful."

"When I came in I spotted you right off, then I saw who you were with. I didn't think you were ever going to take a piss."

"That doesn't make much sense. Nemily...what could she possibly—?"

"I'm just bringing the news, Mace. Be clear with me now. You aren't involved in anything that might interest me or my colleagues, are you?"

"Of course not. I told you, I settled with PolyCarb."

Syvestri gave him a skeptical look. "You've stopped trolling for data about Helen?"

"Don't be ridiculous. I'm just giving up on trying to get anything out of PolyCarb."

Syvestri was silent for a time, then shrugged.

"Well, maybe it's nothing. But I wanted to let you know that your companion is on a list usually reserved for assassins, freelance raiders, embezzlers, and political indeterminates—"

Mace laughed. "Political indeterminates? That's new!"

"Came out of Structural Authority about six months ago. But as I was saying, she's on that list. Nothing specified, just if she comes within certain spheres, watch her. If her status goes up, then...."

"That's bizarre. How come all the attention suddenly?"

"You haven't heard about Midline, then?"

Mace felt his scalp go cold. "What about it?"

"Well...." Syvestri gave the room another long look. "You'll find out in a few days along with everybody else anyway. Just like Cassidy and Five-Eight. Midline broke apart about ten days ago, disintegrated. A few ships got out, but no one's taking them in. There's going to be a stink about it, too, since agreements had been signed after Five-Eight about refugees."

"God...."

"Like I said, I owed you." She moved toward the exit. "Be a dear and wait a minute or so before you come out."

They finished the dinner with coffee and a heavy cream liqueur. Nemily gazed around her with a half-lidded expression just past seductive and on its way to drowsy, distracted by the vista of luxury around her. Mace was grateful; she did not seem to notice how distracted he was, his thoughts preoccupied now with the news about Midline.

Besides the shock of so much death, Mace felt personally frustrated by this. Cavery was dead. Cliff Oxmire was now the only one left who might know anything about the debacle at Hellas Planitia and he was completely out of Mace's reach. All his possibilities were dying, one by one, and what accident or mishap had not covered, judicial action compensated on PolyCarb's behalf.

The PolyCarb party had disappeared behind a privacy screen. Mace wanted to talk to Syvestri even more now and the screen taunted his curiosity. The news Syvestri had given him still did not explain what Poly-Carb security wanted with him now and certainly not with Nemily.

Nemily set her cup down with a distinct click. "Now what?"

"Technically, dinner is over."

"Ah. Then technically we should go somewhere else?" She laced her fingers together and leaned her forearms against the table. "Did you have anything in mind or was this part of the evening to be left to luck and gratitude?"

Mace started, then laughed.

"When is this party you wanted to attend?" he asked.

"Oh, now, till first light probably. There's no rush getting there."

"Then...do you have anything in mind?"

"Luck and gratitude."

On the landing platform, Nemily leaned against the railing and looked down the length of Aea, sparkling with light in the duskiness of nightcycle, domiciles and townships glittering like stars caught in the shaft of an improbable telescope.

The gondola was empty when they stepped aboard. It waited a few minutes, then sealed itself and lifted off. Nemily stared out the window during the ascent. "Will we make anymore stops before ours?"

"I don't know. It's late, I doubt it."

"Good."

They sat opposite each other. She turned from the window. Her half-lidded expression was gone, eyes now fully open and focused. Mace felt his ears warm.

She moved to his side, leaned close and kissed his neck, the curve of his jaw, his cheek, then drew his earlobe between her lips and tickled its edge with her tongue.

Mace's sleepy inertia, the pleasant fuzziness from an excess of good food, dissipated. He brought his face around, Nemily's lips sliding over his skin, and kissed her. His breathing sounded loud. She pressed against him, trapping his left arm at his side. Clumsily, he tried to turn toward her without breaking their kiss. Nemily arched herself away from him, propping a knee on the bench, freeing his arm. He brought his hand up, intending to embrace her. It caught against her crotch, lifting her slightly off the bench in the marginal gravity.

Part of him pulled back, amazed at what was happening. His pulse was up and he was fully and uncomfortably erect. His right hand pressed against her face, moved to her neck, her shoulder, down her back—too fast, he wanted to slow down, take more time, but they were on a gondola that could land and take on more passengers—while his left hand pushed against the heat between her legs. He did not remember the last time he had responded so strongly, so quickly. That part that seemed aware of all this wanted to stop. He preferred to be in control, in a familiar environment, moving deliberately, willfully.

Nemily's mouth separated from his with a gush of breath and a low moan. She moved him back against the corner of the booth and began unbuttoning his shirt.

"Wait," he hissed, "wait...."

Nemily stood briefly and pulled her dress off, and tossed it on the opposite bench. It drifted lazily and seemed to splash against the seat. Then she undid his pants and tugged them down over his hips, down around his ankles. She lifted his thighs easily and pulled, sliding him along the upholstery until he half-lay, half-sat in the middle. He wanted to laugh. She grasped his penis and straddled him.

"Nem...."

"Shh. No words."

Then she slid over him and he pushed up, wordless and stunned and embarrassed and desperate. He held her hips, pretending to set the rhythm. He felt himself bob off the bench, eerily disconnected from everything except Nemily. Their breathing shortened, becoming small puffs synchronized to the metered slap of flesh.

Her eyes squeezed shut and she leaned down, her head against his shoulder. Her hair flowed out in an undulous halo, stroking his face, neck, and chest. He felt her shudder, her legs closing against his thighs. She let out a long breath then, straightened up, and smiled at him.

Mace swallowed. She began again, a different pace, slow and long. It took less than a minute. His fingers jammed into her thighs.

"Good god...."

She laughed. "Good goddess?"

"Just...good...."

Gradually, he became aware of small details. Sweat slicked his chest and stomach. His neck, bent at an angle with his head against the back of the bench, hurt dully. He was too warm and slightly dizzy.

Nemily moved off him slowly. Carefully, she retrieved her dress and stood. Her face glistened, her hair bobbed in the near zero g.

"Is there—?"

Mace waved his hand in the direction of the lavatory.

She smiled and bounced a little. She looked momentarily alarmed, then caught the handrail and laughed. She pulled herself toward the front of the cabin, leaving a nearly invisible trail of beaded sweat.

Mace straightened. He pulled his pants up and buttoned his shirt. His thoughts came jumbled and incomplete. Unexpectedly, he felt afraid. He sat very still and tried to figure out why, but the only thing he knew clearly was that he wanted to do it again.

"Take us to spoke forty-five, fifth ring."

Mace hesitated, startled. She nodded emphatically.

"That's the way to the party," she said.

Mace tapped the commands into the gondola control at the rear of the cabin.

NO PAD AVAILABLE AT SPOKE 45, the screen declared. NEAREST AVAILABLE PAD AT ARC 60.

Mace pressed accept and pulled himself back to Nemily. "We'll have to walk a little."

"All right."

"Where is this party?"

"Out in the ring. In the Heavy."

The gondola descended, gaining the rotational speed it had lost in its ascent, returning gravity gradually. At first it felt as if a hand had closed on Mace's belly; then the sensation spread outward, through his legs, up his torso, into his neck.

The pad stood amid a tangle of construction material stacked around the circle. In the dimness of nightcycle it resembled a twisted, colorless stand of trees and shrubs, leafless and angular, winter dead. Mace saw no faces, heard no voices. The stillness teased a shudder from him.

"This way," Nemily said, taking his hand.

They descended the stairs between two mounds of metal and crates and started along the pedistry. It was an empty district, no doms, no shops, no completed facilities of any kind. Work "in progress" to be finished presumably by the time the space became necessary for the slowly expanding population. The pedistry rose half a meter above the plastic underlayment upon which constituted earth would be poured—that, or slabs of plastic with preformed conduit for cable, pipes, air, a substrate for factories, shops, or domiciles. Here, around them, the primal verge, the frozen soup from which life claimed a sanctuary against the dark, the protoshapes and unformed potentials of habitat. The history of Aean evolution, a glimpse of the primitive past when all of Aea awaited development, the equivalent of an areologic stratum.

Rising out of the motionless tangle before them the spoke looked like a vast world tree, stretching to meet its mirror growths in the gravityless center, beacon lights coiling around it, mingled far overhead with ghostly traces of St. Elmo's Fire.

They reached the platform that surrounded the base of the spoke, their footsteps ringing on the metal. Nemily pressed the button for the service elevator.

The doors spread apart noisily. A few people laughed inside the large space. Graffiti covered the walls of the car, garish and complex in the flat white halogen.

The other passengers wore drab coveralls, but no one seemed to react to Mace and Nemily. The elevator custodian wore brilliant crimson, yellow and pale blue wide pants, a swirl of rainbow squares from cuff to crotch, and looked like part of the graffiti.

"Where?" she asked, hand poised over the controls.

"Five," Nemily said.

"They know you in the Heavy?"

"Reese invited me."

The custodian nodded and pressed a button.

The elevator jerked to a stop and the doors opened, admitting a jumbled wash of sound. Nemily flashed a bright smile, grabbed Mace's hand, and pulled him into the ocean of talk and music.

They walked into what had once been an enormous bay for equipment and material, a distribution point in the early days of the ring. Now it was packed with shops and nightclutches, stacked in much the same way as the temporary doms of the segment four interior, though better braced.

Many of the people seemed better braced as well. The myth of the Heavy had become the fashion and the regular inhabitants bought vacuum-distributed adapt treatments in unlicensed pathic centers to build bone and muscle to fit them for the supposedly greater g in the outer rings. Mace picked them out easily, the ones who had bartered five or ten years of life with poorly administered treatments for the presumed advantage of twenty or thirty kilos more mass, deceiving themselves that they were better suited this way to live on a perceived edge. Out here, eighty meters from the interior surface of Aea, g gained less than one and a half percent, roughly equivalent to walking up a noticeable incline; some of the bodies Mace saw seemed adapted for ten or even twenty percent higher g. Paradoxically, one of the few ways for them to regain some of the years lost to bad adapt regimes would be to live in lower g.

Children mingled freely with the crowds. Their presence startled Mace; children were rarely seen in public in the interior. In the Heavy they were simply part of the population, the way they were on Mars and Brasa. A few of them, he saw, already showed signs of adapt treatments—pre-adolescent acne, pronounced bone structure in their young faces, facial hair—already trading a long life to be part of the myth around them.

Nemily gripped his hand and dragged him through the mélange of bright clothes and noise and the smell of open cookeries and a faintly astringent odor of strong cleanser and disinfectant. They crossed the bay and entered a crowded narrow circuit, where the knot of bodies thickened even more near the entrance to 5555. Green and violet neon marked the door before which three overadapted bouncers stood guard. Nemily reached the edge of the throng and touched one of them. The big man glared at her and Mace nearly jerked her back.

The bouncer grinned. "Nem! Good to see you. In."

"This one is mine," Nemily said, patting Mace on the chest.

The bouncer gave a slow nod, examining Mace. "Welcome. In now."

Nemily pulled Mace behind the bouncer and squeezed through a narrow door.

The room that housed 5555 had once been fitted for something else, like almost every other place in the outer rings. From the elevated sections of floor and the peripatetic walkways around the rim, Mace guessed an ops center. Now a forest of people grew from every horizontal surface. On one raised platform, a circle of guests sat crosslegged, a glowing cube the focus of their attention. Overadapted men and women wandered the crowd, conspicuously naked and carrying small trays. Two tubes bisected across the ceiling, slowly, sinuously changing color along their lengths, the only common light source. Mace followed Nemily through the overlap of acoustic shadows from privacy fields and the loud rumble of undamped talk.

"—rumble rumble, and it has stance, so—"

"—right here when she fell and then *claimed* that g had changed. The blood flow was the same anyway. I told Spin, the only constant changed was the one in your head, E-Quil-Librium. Shall I spell it or spill it?"

"She doesn't spell when she's lateral."

"Is that a religious thing?"

"—posted on a public board isn't worth shit, they feed better to the worms in ponic. If you want good equation—"

"—*the moon rises high, tho' it never once moves, in a gaze to the lie, of a*—"

"You never said it rhymed! Damn, waste my time—"

"Listen, you doggerel, find a fuckin' dog—"

"—better interiors in a rock garden, he insists on wielding the brush alone and it's going to be a mess."

"Public?"

"No, of course not, those morons in three-seventy would pound pus out of him. You don't do postcaloteric for brutes, they don't see the way we do."

"—just float, spigot, you have a problem and I don't want it—"

"I heard they shipped up from Earth, upwell, that they have Gaians in custody. Something about a possible exodus—"

"That's static, they can't launch a fistful of rain anymore."

"I wouldn't underestimate them."

"How do you underestimate nothing?"

A waiter stepped into their path, holding her tray back as if prepared to throw it at them. "Something to swallow?"

Nemily craned her neck. "Where's Reese?"

"He hasn't made an appearance yet. Something to swallow? You?"

"Not yet," Mace said.

"Come on," Nemily said, "I know where Reese is."

The waiter scowled and stepped aside. "House rules, you have to swallow."

The snatches of conversation teased Mace. He wanted to stay and listen to some of them; the place seemed filled with the kind of rumor that suggested arcane, hidden and significant knowledge. He had only been here once, a couple years ago. He searched faces now for Cambel. Nemily drew him along, never allowing him to hear more than barely enough to intrigue him.

"—the maximum allowable sentence for that kind of infraction is eighteen months' civic penance, cleaning parks and trimming bushes and trees, washing stains off walls, that kind of grunt. If he opens his mouth to argue, that's contempt, that can get you five years—"

"—Rome managed without a space program for twenty-seven hundred years and in the end they still didn't get anywhere—"

"—wider, wider, then I thought, ooh, if I could do more than watch—"

"—excavations on Mars have turned up nothing of any past civilizations, understand? We're there, we've looked, we've seen, it wasn't true. Lowell was hallucinating."

"But—"

"—doing the whole thing in thirteenths over a whole-tone scale, modulated to ninths in a minor. On the page it's ugly as ugly gets, but when you *hear* it—"

"Didn't Debutante use the whole-tone scale?"

"That's Debussy."

"Yeah, her. I read once—"

Suddenly the press opened up and Mace caught himself at the edge of a big empty space, marked only by a gauzy strand of fiberoptic stretched around it. The floor looked no different than the rest of the clutch surface. Overhead, in the shadows above the light tubes, large shapes hovered darkly, waiting. A projector.

"Slumming tonight, Mace, or did you actually get my message?"

Mace turned. Cambel stood beside him.

"Message...?" he asked.

"I thought not. So this is just coincidence." She gave Nemily a brief glance. "There's a problem."

"Again or still?"

"Either-or. Structural Authority wants to talk to us. Both of us."

"Officer Stat?"

"No, a real live agent contacted me."

"Your Mr. Koeln contacted me this evening. I'm supposed to talk to him tomorrow."

"SA might not wait. Who's your companion, Mace? Are you going to introduce us?"

"Uh...Cambel Guerrera, this is Nemily Dollard."

"Hello," Nemily said, holding out a hand.

For a few moments Mace thought Cambel would ignore the gesture. Then she clasped Nemily's hand and nodded. "Pleased to meet you. I work with Mace."

"I—"

"*Welcome.*"

The word, though spoken in a calm voice, overwhelmed all other sound. The babble that had formed a constant background was now gone, completely damped. A man stood in the center of the empty section, turning slowly, hands clasped behind his back, a grin on his long face. Mace recognized him: Reese Nagel, promoter, vacuum dealer, owner of 5555.

"Welcome, welcome, welcome," Reese repeated, his voice echoing slightly, amplified and deepened. "If everyone would gather closer, we can begin the entertainment. I need your attention for a few minutes, then I'll stop boring you."

Nemily pressed closer to Mace while ranks of people closed, working themselves as close to the edge as possible. Cambel frowned at Nemily, then turned her attention to Reese.

"Good," Reese went on, "good. I'm glad you all could come. Tonight I'm giving a sample of a new event, just a taste to a select audience. I think I know you all, most of you anyway, and I know how you get your thrills. I think you'll want more of this once you see it."

He paused dramatically and did a full turn, smiling indulgently.

"I don't pretend to understand all the technicalities of such a fête. I have people I pay who do, and no, I won't tell you who they are. I don't want a bidding war to start for their services, they work for me." He laughed with the audience. "But we've been told for a long time, so long now that we accept it even if we don't believe it, that direct news from Gaia is impossible. The satellites that would permit access to downwell 'casts are all hardened against tapping, there are treaties preventing us from simple peeking, and the various data organizations down there use particle transcription that simply doesn't bleed, so we must content ourselves with the occasional rumor or bit of sanitized drivel that Structural Authority releases. Now I personally don't care at all for what we may be missing. I don't think Gaia has a thing to say to me anymore. But being shut out is annoying. I'd like to know for myself that there's nothing worthwhile happening downwell and I think you all feel the same."

A murmur cascaded through the crowd.

"I thought so. That's why I've been looking for another way. And because I've been looking, I found one. So that's what I have to show you tonight. Some of our bright technicians have figured out how to tap the signals from certain stations downwell. They tell me that Earth has lost track of its network, that people down there don't always know anymore where the transmissions they're sending are going. A lot of the debris orbiting Earth still functions and we can use it. You might ask, of course, why this hasn't been done before, and I might suggest that in fact it has. But you'd have to ask Structural Authority about that or maybe one of the megacorps why they never told us. In any case, we've liberated a few transmission lines and found a way to eavesdrop on the land of our birth. What you'll be seeing is an actual decoded transmission from Mother Gaia, the cradle of our civilization, the rock that shut us out. Tonight's peek is free, gratis. After that...we'll see."

The light rods winked out, leaving the chamber in near-total darkness. Here and there someone wore luminous jewelry, but it was dark enough that Mace could not see Nemily beside him. She found his hand, though, and squeezed, then traced a circle around the base of his thumb, a sensation he found instantly exciting.

The projectors overhead hummed faintly. Then the volume of air just above the empty area seemed to peel around itself, letting light escape in an unfolding eruption.

The image that formed was disorienting. A wide landscape, grass and trees in the foreground, rising hills, and a mountain range in the distance. A pedistry cut through the middle. Above the mountains, pale to dark, unbroken blue. It took Mace a few seconds to realize what he was seeing. His first thought was Mars. But the pitch and tone of the talk around him gained an anxious quality, fearful and incredulous, and he realized that most of these people had never seen the surface of a world other than in a vid held safely in their lap or displayed across a small screen. They had never stood on a convex plain and gazed up at sky that did not end with the other side of the world, but continued on into void, infinite. And then Mace recognized his mistake. He had assumed it was Mars because that was familiar to him, but this scene was still alien, and he realized: *Earth*.

From the far right, movement disturbed the image. At first it made little sense. A mass of people, on foot, a faint swell of dust floating around their legs. Distance obscured detail, but it was clear that most of them carried burdens on their backs or in their arms. They formed a ragged line advancing on the grass, slowly. No one led, the entire group simply moved forward. Mace estimated quickly that the front rank contained maybe two hundred people. More. Silently, the throng continued its thick pour across the landscape, dust rising into drifting clouds that blew indolently back over those coming up from behind, the entire vast collection growing and growing, until, when the front line reached the edge of the road, halfway into the scene, the numbers clearly reached into the thousands. As if tapping an unused memory, one bequeathed from past generations, a recessive gene coding a specific collection of neurons, dormant till prodded, the reaction came with perfect clarity: this is wrong....

Mace shuddered at the soundless spectacle of the refugees.

The image winked away, superseded by another, at once more familiar and more foreign. In the background rose a squat structure, elegant, straight lines, wide windows, a pleasant pinkish grey and dark blue, standing upon a broad plaza that bore an enormous inlaid emblem that, from this angle, could not be resolved. But the structure was at least ten levels and the top extended out of the image field. A woman in a heavy black suit with green trim stood in the foreground. Her hair, brilliant silver, hemispheric, wrapped around the back of her head. Her mouth moved soundlessly for a few seconds. Then—

"—eterson Institute, Helsinki, threemay, while in-code trans leak solid word about impending fracture in firewall structure. M. Toreggi essayed earlier that further incursions are inevitable without a key to the carrion. In brief, datapools compromised by the in situ assault by a member of the collation staff join other victims of the apparently global dispersion of the destructure plague. Me, Jaomi Kak, GNS—"

Again the image flickered, a new one pushing aside the old one.

Another road, this one wider, more complex, with sidings and dividers, leading to a distant horizon and an improbable collection of towers gleaming in unfiltered sunlight. A city. On the road, people walked, a few rode elaborate pedaled vehicles, all of them moving with a purposeful belligerence away from the towers.

"—outside the city limits," a voice thundered, the speaker invisible, "people believe it's safe, though no one is certain they don't carry the contagion with them. Las Cruces, once the fourth-largest city in this region of the continent, is now an abandoned monument to a past that is devouring itself. From here, it still appears vital, alive, even beautiful. Distance hides the decay that has thus far created six million refugees on a landmass that hasn't seen this kind of desperation for the past seven decades—"

The space turned dark. Then a line of words scrolled raggedly across the air.

THYME?

HERE.

SCARED?

NO. YES. YOU STAYING?

CAN'T LEAVE. DA SAY TOO MUCH TO GIVE UP. HE CAN'T GO TO THE PLANT. INFRA-STRUCTURE COMPROMISED.

GOT FOOD? WATER?

SURE. SPRING-FED STREAM. CHICKENS. GARDEN.

SECURITY?

YES.

Then a final darkness, matched to the stillness in the clutch. For a moment Mace thought the dampers were still on. The light rods ignited, fluoresced from amber to azure, and the nervous chatter of the seriously unsettled filled the silence.

"Thank you all," Reese said, once more in the center of the floor. "I hope you liked—if that's the right word—what you saw and that you'd like to see more. I have the next display scheduled, but this one will be by subscription. I've posted the rates on my usual boards. For the rest of the night, though, there is no charge. Enjoy."

Talk eddied, backed up, flowed. . . .

"—has to be a fake—"

"If not, then we know why SA won't release—"

"—restrictions on external sources, the import regulations are very specific—"

"Float, bag, we all know what Reese thinks of re-gu-la-tions."

"—tapped into the Archive, that's where it's from. Gaia's not like that anymore, you see, not since the early days of the Exclusion—"

"How would you know?"

"—what passes for grammar anymore, if you can believe that actually came from downwell—"

Cambel tugged at Mace's sleeve. "We should go talk to Reese."

"Why?"

"This is relevant to our situation." She smiled at Nemily. "Would you excuse us, Ms. Dollard?"

Nemily gave Mace a confused look, then shook her head. "Wait, please...." She closed her eyes and sighed. "Do you know Reese?"

"We do business with him," Cambel said, frowning. "I know him. Do you?"

"I used to work for him. He asked me here tonight." She pushed past them through the crowd and waved for them to follow.

As they followed Nemily, a tremendous pulse began throbbing in a steady walk-time. By his fifth step, a sinuous doubled bass line threaded around the beat and when he caught up to her, sliding easily through the cracks between people, an airy set of chords were swapping places.

Abruptly, Nemily stopped. He caught her shoulders, almost ramming her. She stood rigidly, muscles tensed, and Mace searched ahead for what she might have seen. But in the next moment she whirled, snatching his hand, and tugged him through the press in a new direction. Mace looked back to see Cambel doggedly following.

Nemily spun around. Her expression startled Mace. The sadness that had suffused it briefly earlier in the evening, that had surprised him, now was matched by a look of terror.

Cambel touched his arm. He looked at her and saw her mouth form the words "What's wrong?" inaudibly through the thunder of music.

Abruptly, Nemily made for the exit, dodging around people with athletic precision. Mace pushed his way after her.

He caught up to her near the door. She stood before a man who was flanked by a pair of overadapted bouncers, one a female who looked on with evident concern. As Mace came up behind Nemily, the man looked up—Reese Nagel. The female bouncer moved to block Mace, but Reese held up a hand and stopped her.

Holding Nemily's arm, Reese stepped closer to Mace. Abruptly, the sound died away to a distant rhythmic hum as Reese's personal acoustic shadow enveloped him.

"You're Nem's friend? I'm Reese. She seems to be in some distress. She's in sensualist, isn't she?"

"Yes."

"How long?"

"It's been hours now. Who—?"

"She needs to swap it out. Come with me." Reese looked past Mace and smiled. "Cambel, so good to see you. Are you with these people?"

Cambel stepped up alongside Mace. "Absolutely."

"Please, all of you. Come to my office. Nemily needs some privacy."

Reese, hand still on Nemily's arm, turned to walk away. Mace reached out to stop him.

The female caught his wrist in a powerful grip and held his hand a few centimeters from Reese's shoulder. Mace relaxed briefly until he felt her grip loosen, then twisted his hand free and closed his fingers around her wrist. He squeezed, enough to get a reaction from her, a brief tremble.

"I believe Nemily is with me, Mr. Nagel," Mace said evenly.

Reese frowned at him, then glanced at his bouncer. She glared steadily at Mace.

"My apologies," Reese said. "By all means. Colf?"

Mace let go and Colf lowered her arm slowly.

"Colf," Reese repeated.

"Yes, sir," she said tightly.

"This way," Reese said and led the way through the crowd.

TEN

AEA, 2118

NEMILY TOOK A SURPRISINGLY LONG TIME to process the memory, all the while staring at herself in the mirror above Reese's sink in his marbled-wall bathroom, trembling and searching for her soul. The time chop in her head told her she had been in active sensualist now going on eight hours. In itself that was not unusual, but seldom in a pool of so much vivid sensory material. The gondola, which she had never ridden before, the Earthview, where she had never been before, and Mace, beneath her, between her thighs, in micro-g, which she had never done before, down to the Heavy, the nightclutch, Reese's new event with all its odd perspectives and language and colors, finally seeing—

Too much, too wonderful, too awful. Collation complete, she exchanged the augment for her synthesist and wanted at once to return to the sensualist, take Mace home, and continue to absorb the night. With an effort, she closed her case and slipped it back into her pouch, just over her left hip. Blinking at her reflection, the colors seeming so ordinary now, she worked herself into a state of composure. The shuddering subsided and the images of the past several hours brought a residue of pleasure which she identified as normal. She washed her face and rested her forehead against the edge of the sink. She recalled every detail, every sensation, felt herself preen inside at the pleasure. The last hour or so, for all its wonderment, still felt like a long, fast fall, the end coming with a face she had never again expected to see.

She smoothed her clothes, moving unnecessarily just to escape the shaking in her hands. She studied her reflection until she found it convincingly calm, then walked back into Reese's office.

Reese wore his Philosopher's Face. He thought the slight pucker of his brow and intent set of his mouth gave him a look of intellectual sophistication. Instead, he only appeared indolently self-impressed. He was by no means a stupid man, but his strengths and talents encompassed far less than he imagined.

Mace sat on the long divan facing Reese's desk, leaning forward, hands folded, elbows on knees. Cambel Guerrera stood at one end of the sofa, back against the wall, arms folded, her expression watchful. Colf leaned against the door; she smiled faintly when she saw Nemily.

Nemily sensed that she had just interrupted a conversation.

"Nem," Reese said, "how are you? Better now?"

"Yes, thank you. Reese, was everyone here tonight by invitation only?"

He looked slightly puzzled by the question. "Well, you were allowed to bring a guest, obviously."

"Everyone else, too?"

"Of course."

"Which," Cambel said, "went against our recommendations."

Reese smiled and looked apologetic. "Risks of the business, Cambel. Sometimes security can be counterproductive. I needed word-of-mouth more than I needed to be safe from infringements."

Cambel shook her head with mild disgust.

Mace watched Nemily with a closed, intent expression.

She did not want to be here anymore. She was tired and mistrusted her ability to make decisions.

"Thanks for the invitation, Reese," she said, closing her eyes. "I know you wanted to discuss something...else...but I'm really—"

"Of course, I understand. Call me tomorrow?"

His abrupt acquiescence surprised her. She had expected him to argue a little, throw a display of mock petulance over being denied a chance to talk.

"Sure...if I'm up for it. Next day at the latest?"

"It's rather important. Don't take too long."

Mace stood. "Thank you for your hospitality, Mr. Nagel. I'm glad we finally got a chance to meet. This was the first time I've been to one of your events. I'm impressed."

"Thank you. Impressing people is one of my passions. Especially when they're people I do business with. I hope to see you again, Mr. Preston."

They shook hands, regarding each other across the desk with false smiles, and Nemily recognized the tableau: cop and felon, security and risk.

"We'll finish later, Reese," Cambel said, moving toward the door.

"You want me to go with them?" Colf asked.

"I'm sure they'll be fine on their own, Colf," Reese said.

Colf opened the door for them and stood aside. As Nemily stepped through, Colf leaned close.

"Be careful," she said.

At the bottom of the stairs, once more within the roar of the clutch, Mace put a hand on her shoulder and guided her toward the exit. Nemily did not look into the room, did not want to risk seeing or being seen, and gratefully moved ahead of Mace and Cambel, directly out of 5555.

"Who did you see?" Mace asked.

She licked her lips. "Someone I never thought I'd ever see again."

"No one good?"

"His name is Glim Toler."

"Toler," Cambel said. "That name keeps coming up."

"He was in there?" Mace asked.

"Yes. I—could we go, please?"

Mace nodded, then looked at Cambel. "What's Reese's connection to him? Did he come up in our security checks?"

"No, he didn't. But like Reese said, he doesn't always follow recommendations. Someone must have brought him. Or just used a different name." Cambel shrugged. "Reese is a magnet for Lunessa activity in the Heavy. If they end up here after passing through InFlux, they eventually come into his sphere."

"So Toler ended up down here? What's the conduit?"

"I—"

"Please," Nemily repeated.

Mace nodded. "Sure. This can wait. I'll talk to you later, Cambel."

"You call me," she said, her tone mildly sarcastic. "I wouldn't want to interrupt."

The Heavy wore all its scars and stains in the calmer view of her synthesist. The restlessness of the circuits distracted attention from the age and abuse. People pushed and darted, aimlessly hurried.

Cambel drifted away from them then and Nemily quickly lost sight of her in the crowds. Mace tucked his hands in his pockets and sauntered toward the lift. They stepped into an empty car.

Mace pressed to stop at level two. "The gondola won't be waiting for us," he said. "We can pick up a shunt."

The doors opened on an empty circuit with almost featureless walls. Their steps crunched delicately and Nemily saw a fine layer of debris, like charcoal and chalk, scattered over the floor. In the dim light the blank walls took on a fine delineation of shading: mold, dirt.

"Ponics," Mace said, quietly as though in a temple or a mortuary. They walked on silently for a time. Nemily felt herself absorbing tension; knowing it was self-created did not alleviate it. When Mace spoke again, she flinched. "The first time I travelled—in space, I mean—it was a maintenance tug heading for Ceres, my first job off Mars. I never could get over the feeling that the ship didn't move. I couldn't feel it move. When I off-loaded at Ceres I imagined that what had moved was space that I had stood still and waited while outside space rearranged itself and instead of Mars now it was Ceres."

"Just a series of rooms," Nemily said, "connected by places where you wait."

"What?"

"Nothing. I—"

Ahead the circuit widened to make room for a two-meter-wide staircase leading up. A poorly effaced graffito at the landing declared "This way to Dreamland," followed by an arrow aimed at the interior.

Mace hesitated on the third step and leaned over the railing to peer down the circuit. Then Nemily heard the sound of many feet walking quickly toward them, punctuated by a few soft-spoken voices. From ahead, then, came a troop of children, a long line, three abreast, led by a woman in a dark blue robe who, upon passing, gave Mace and Nemily a disapproving glare. The children, all in short-legged togs similarly cut but differently colored, looked up at them with expressions ranging from awe to embarrassment. The troop filed by and two more adults brought up the rear, dressed like the leader, who also graced them with clear disapproval.

Mace continued up the stairs, which led onto a tube platform.

"I never get over this," Mace said. "There are nearly half a million people on Aea and you can still find empty space. On Mars the only place you don't find people is out on the sands. Even then...it's against the law to go out alone."

"Two people can be alone."

He only nodded and went to the schedule board. Nemily wanted to change the mood; this one felt too fragile, too easily broken with nothing to replace it. It was difficult to look at him, uncomfortable to look away. It annoyed her like a bruise and attracted her like a deep cut; she did not know what it was and was afraid to imagine what it might be.

"Half a million," he repeated. "Over a million on Mars."

"Two million in Lunase."

He blinked at her. "Really?"

"Not officially. I suppose not all in Lunase, either, but about that on the moon."

"Hmm. Another quarter million maybe spread throughout the system?"

"That many?"

"Maybe. I'm being liberal, I suppose. Three to four million people. Five at the most." He shook his head. "Where did they all come from?"

"I don't know," Nemily said. "Is it enough?"

"For what?"

"To survive."

The question seemed to startle him. The shunt arrived and he broke loose from his brief trance to board with her. He sat down and stared at the opposite bench. Nemily sat beside him.

"I always wondered," she said, "why Aeans put their children in nurseries in the outer rings. In Lunase they're everywhere."

"Mars, too. But that's not the way Aeans want to live."

"I don't understand."

She saw him grin crookedly, as though both amused and disgusted. "Children tend to break things. The interior is full of things they could break."

"Well, sure they do. But...oh."

"Uh-huh. Oh. Have to keep things neat." He shook his head. "Fastidious neuroses."

"Is that why nobody likes immigrants here?"

"Partly," he admitted.

"What else?"

He shrugged.

"What do you think that was we saw?" she asked.

"Hmm? You mean that presentation at Reese's? I don't know. You hear rumors about what's happening on Earth, but...."

"So you really think that was from Earth?"

"From what Cambel has told me, Reese never lies to people about that sort of thing."

"No, he doesn't. So if it's from Earth, that means—it sounds like things are falling apart down there."

"Sounds like it." He frowned thoughtfully.

"You talked to him while I was collating," she said. "What did you ask? What did he say?"

"Business. Cambel and I designed security for him. We were interested in where he got that material. Among other things."

"Oh."

Nemily watched the time internally and after two minutes of silence, she sighed loudly.

"I don't do this," she said.

Mace frowned. "Do what?"

"This. You're being introspective, either because you're upset or because you don't understand. In either case, you sit in silence and what—expect me to think you're profound or that maybe I'm at fault for something and I should realize that you're being more than tolerant for not bringing it up? Or maybe there's something about the fact that I know Reese that you don't like or something else concerned with Glim Toler and you don't trust me? I don't do that. It's a game."

"I don't—"

"There are certain limitations to the way I'm made and one of them is that I don't grasp a lot of subtlety. People play these little attitude shifts off each other all the time and I watch them and when it's done it seems that somebody won and somebody lost or an agreement was made, but I understood none of it. When it's done to me I end up going home feeling completely stupid and angry. You've been...what?...detached ever since we left Reese's and the way you're doing it is making me feel responsible. Am I?"

"...No...."

"You don't sound sure. The evening didn't go the way I expected it to, but most of it was wonderful. If the last hour ruined it for you I'm sorry, but don't work your disappointment out on me by playing stoic and leaving me with the guilt."

"You became upset when you saw this Glim Toler. I didn't change the mood."

"So it *is* my fault? Do you want to know about Glim? You haven't asked yet, I don't know what to expect."

His hand moved absently to his chest where his fingers traced the shape of the pendant beneath his clothes. The gesture infuriated her.

"How do I compare?" she asked.

"I haven't—I don't see women regularly."

"I meant to your wife."

Mace jerked his hand from his chest as if shocked. Color left his face, worsening his injured expression. He leaned forward, elbows on knees, clasped hands dangling, and fixed his attention on the opposite window.

"I don't want to explain any of this," he said.

"Then how am I supposed to know you?"

"Why do you want to?"

"I have no idea."

He glanced sidelong at her, surprise and disbelief livening the abandoned features.

"Want comes as a total package for me," she said. "It doesn't have a reason, there's no why to it." She laughed sharply. "I don't think there is for anybody, but people claim they have reasons to want things all the time, as if they need permission. I *think* they're lying, but I don't know. If I tell the truth am I revealing a big secret everybody knows about?"

The surprise in his face eased into curiosity. "You don't want everything. Something makes you want one thing and not another."

"That's a cause, not a reason." She shook her head impatiently. "Look, I don't want to analyze this. I'm just talking now because I'm afraid, but it's just delay. I want to know you. I think I want more than just that, but I don't know yet. I *do* know that I don't want to negotiate it. And I'm afraid other things could complicate it before I get the chance."

"Glim Toler?"

"Yes."

"You knew him in Lunase?"

"Yes."

"Did he hurt you?"

"No...he tried to."

"You came here to get away from him."

"I came here to get away from Lunase. Glim is a good example of everything that's wrong with it."

He sat back then, nodding slowly. She watched the tip of his tongue trace his lips. His hand shook slightly as it went to his face and methodically massaged his eyes, his cheeks, and came to rest on his jaw.

"All right...." He nodded again, a decision made. "Would you come home with me? Now? I'll show you...."

"Show me what?"

He smiled tentatively. "You have to come and see."

"All right. Yes."

He offered his hand.

"No," she said. "Not yet."

He did not look hurt this time. He nodded and withdrew the hand.

The dom resembled a keep, sort of like those she had seen in the history archives when she had set about constructing her workspace diorama, an ancient fortification. But the walls were smooth and large sections of them were given to transparencies and it glowed pearlescent in the ambient light of nightcycle. A short path through dense shrubs led to the deeply recessed entrance.

"I'm back," Mace said at the door. A moment later it swung open and he waved her through.

Sconces brightened along a spiral stairway up toward the skylight, through which the glitter of the opposite arc shone. Despite its graceful coil and space it seemed austere. A single bonsai stood against one wall, between two of the three doorways that opened from the main floor. The place seemed to be waiting, elegant and empty, for a life to contain.

"Feel free to explore," Mace said. "Then tell me what you think. I'll be just through here." He indicated the door to the right of the bonsai, smiled, and left her alone.

She craned her neck to look at the skylight above, then mounted the stairs to the roof. At each of four landings she found a door and a plant on a waist-high pedestal.

Every keep, she recalled, supported a parapet, and she expected this one to be no different. Even so it surprised her to walk through the last door at the top of the coiled ascent and find open air, a chest-high wall, and an unobstructed view downshaft through Aea.

She had never noticed before just how dark the bottom of the world became....

The opposite direction gave no such perspective. The upshaft cap rose and rose till it appeared to fall away, only to suddenly arch back to join with the interior wall. Lights all across the expanse made it appear as if it sweated, the beads trapping light, holding it against the skin.

For a panicky instant Nemily felt as though she stood on the edge of a great height, about to fall toward the dimmer mirror. She made herself look down at her feet until the vertigo passed and then descended back into the dom.

The next door opened on a bedroom. Plain and nearly impersonal, the partially opaqued window transparency washed it all in spectral, chill light. Nemily backed out after only a few seconds. No one slept here, it seemed to tell her, certainly no one other than Mace. She went down to the next door. Another bedroom; smaller bed, even less disturbed—a guest room? The next one down was an office space, with a large desk supporting a flatscreen and a case full of discs.

One level from the main floor she stepped into a room that differed from the others. He used this place, often and intensely. Benches contained equipment that pulsed with activity, clutter strewn between monitors, half-drunk cups here and there, the disordered signs of time and project. Nemily walked a little way in, drawn by the machines and the sense of his presence. She recognized a lot of the gear, data-cracking equipment, recorders, collators. She saw a row of cyberlink augments in a case before a stack of boxes that she thought might be data scrubbers.

As she stepped back onto the landing she heard faint voices, muffled to incomprehensibility, and remembered that Mace possessed a domestic personality. She wondered if she was being watched, room by room, and reported on.

On the main level, the kitchen led to a transparent-walled breakfast nook. The next door around the circle opened onto a plain-walled room with a single chair in the center—a sensorum? Through the last door she descended a short flight of steps into a utility room. A closet stood open, revealing neatly racked gardening tools. She continued on through the opposite door into a greenhouse.

The air smelled of loam and damp; she felt the humidity on her face and arms. Counters of flowering plants stood to her right, planters of new shrubs to her left, and at the far end she saw Mace, seated by a long bench, working on a small tree. He looked strange, still dressed in his evening clothes, an apron over them, too tall not to hunch over the diminutive plant, large hands performing delicate work with wires and small shears.

"You said earlier that you weren't really rich," she said and immediately wished she had said something else.

"Helen's insurance enabled me to do a lot. I receive a small pension from PolyCarb. I've made a few fortunate investments—nearly lost it all once with a bad one—and I still do work for a few clients." He placed the shears on the table and turned toward her. "I sued PolyCarb two years ago to get them to release Helen's files to me. The official version of her death is a lie and I wanted them to admit it. They started throwing more money at me. At first, they didn't come out and say that it was a bribe for me to go away. Investments Helen had made that turned out to be part of a survivorship trust, another insurance policy they had overlooked, things like that. Then it became explicit and they laid an offer on the table. It has turned out to be a great deal of money. I don't really have to work anymore, at anything. But...."

"What do you do with the augments?"

"Ah. Well, that's...complicated." He looked at the tree he had been tending. Then he stood and removed his apron, brushed bits of dirt from his sleeves.

"I killed my wife. I signed her death certificate and declared her deceased. Her body was never found."

"You don't believe she's dead."

"The first year or so afterward, I kept expecting her to just show up. I tried to put myself in her path by doing volunteer work for InFlux. I still do, but I hardly ever go to the offices anymore. Then I started trying to find out what actually happened. There were...irregularities. Along with the suit against PolyCarb, I started gathering data. The augments...I sift them for anything they might contain relating to several topics in a dynamic search program. When I'm done with them, I clean them out, fix them up, and sell them to Everest or some other place that uses a lot of them."

"Reese?"

"I imagine he's bought some of them, yes. Tonight was the first time I've met him. Most of it goes through an agent; I never deal with it directly."

"You deal with Everest directly."

"Yes, I—yes." He shrugged. "I do security. Mostly just systems now, every once in a while I'll do a job as bodyguard or on-site watchdog. Not often, just enough to stay aware." He hesitated, then added, "Sometimes I do a commission for Structural Authority or the Council."

"Do you still expect your wife to come back?"

"No, I don't."

"But you're still looking?"

"I want very much to know what happened. I want to know why she died. She was on Mars, doing some work—I don't know what kind. I know she was there, I spoke to her. Something happened and a lot of people died. She was with them. But the company—PolyCarb—says she was never there. But they insist she's dead. They've never actually told me where they think she died. I want to know."

"So you deal with Reese because he's a source of vacuum."

"Among others. Not just any kind of vacuum. Information. Like we saw tonight. Information that's very hard to come by."

"You sound like you blame yourself for your wife's death."

"Not her death...." He shook his head. "You like to think that when you love someone that it really means forever, that the causes and feelings will never fade. But they do. I wanted to find out what happened to Helen and why I had to do what PolyCarb made me do—sign off on her death. I thought—I imagined myself—pursuing it until I learned the truth. I didn't think it would take so long or be so hard. When I realized that I was losing interest, I tried to automate the process so I could do other things and not be concerned with the day-to-day grind. But—the fact is, things changed. I feel...guilty...but it's not enough to keep me interested. I don't know anymore what I'd do if she turned up. I don't know what I'd do if I found out what happened. It would be simpler if that day never came."

He looked at her curiously. "Now, though, it seems PolyCarb has recovered its interest. Linder Koeln wants to talk to me about Helen."

"Koeln...."

"You know him?"

"He...interviewed me yesterday."

"What about?"

"Toler."

"Toler again. So tell me about yourself. Why are you on Aea? How do you know Reese?"

"Well. After I came through InFlux I got temporary shelter in one of the barracks in segment five. Every few days, recruiters came through doing interviews for potential employees. Most of the residents went to construction, maintenance, other labor-intensive jobs in the outer shells or even one of the off-station operations. A few more found better positions in various offices and oversight companies. All my experience lay in direct monitoring of particle flow. I worked for the Lunessa alchemists. Here that kind of work is a very special position for people who are citizens. Instead of doing what I was good at, Reese found me. If you know anything about Reese, you know he's not...well, he's diversified, that's how he likes to put it. Partly legitimate, part vacuum. He kept me in legitimate service, but it meant doing a lot of less-than-wonderful jobs. Courier, carrying a node of data in one of my augments; direct-linking with received 'ware to check for traps, viruses, anything that might blow up in his systems; client liaison, which sometimes included sex. He leased me to Everest for a month once, one of Hillary's regulars was in pathic. Then one day I found a position with a small firm that did contract work for PolyCarb on one of their start-up processing lines and I left Reese. We parted on amicable terms, he was satisfied with what he got. Occasionally he'd set me up a job on the side, ask me to do a special service. He always paid me well, always let me go. Compared to regular work in Lunase, it was paradise."

Nemily turned toward the rows of potted plants. "Then PolyCarb absorbed the firm I worked for and integrated the staff. I never dreamed I'd get to work for a mega, not like PolyCarb. Security, good stipend, insurance. I was shifted to an organics department, overseeing forced-growth tanks and sanitation. Comatulids. Then I was moved onto a particle line doing pretty much what I'd done in Lunase. It was alchemist work, teasing molecules apart and recombining them into new arrangements. This one was a metals line, assembling super stable alloys. XM, they call it. Anyway, after a year I was promoted to supervisor of my line, then once more into a quality-control position, and finally, just five months ago, Piers Hawthorne brought me into data collation in his department."

She sighed. "I've been here over two years, almost two and a half. You'd think I'd get used to it by now, but I still wake up occasionally afraid that I'm going to be expelled."

"Tell me about Toler."

"He—my roommate ran with him. He was always trouble. He tried to get me to bring vacuum here when I emigrated."

"What kind?"

"I have no idea. I told him no." She laughed. "This isn't what I had in mind for the rest of the evening."

"Sorry. You said you don't understand a lot of subtlety. Well, neither do I. Not this kind, at least."

"I would have thought—"

"—that someone involved in security would be good at it? After all, I have to know people, anticipate them, understand how they work. As far as it goes, yes. But not...this."

"Interesting problem."

"In what way?" he asked.

"Well, think about it. If we go on from here it means we just might have to tell each other the truth all the time."

"You have to know what the truth is first, don't you?"

"Not all of it," she said.

"A piece at a time?"

"I suppose that depends on how much patience you have."

"I've been sifting for Helen for three years."

"And you gave up."

He frowned. "Your point being?"

"Imagine what it would be like with someone you won't lose interest in."

For a moment his face registered shock. But then he gave her a thoughtful look and nodded.

"Do you have to go to work tomorrow?" he asked. "Actually, today, I suppose."

"I could make arrangements if I want to."

"Do you want to?"

"I don't know yet. Let's find out."

"I'm sorry," Mace said. He stared up at the ceiling. Sweat glistened across his body. "It's been a long night."

"Don't...I left the synthesist in...." Nemily lay on her side and drew her legs up. She felt pleasantly cool now, her own perspiration evaporating. The bed smelled of them, a dense aroma that seemed oddly separate from their abandoned struggle. She rested her fingers on his arm. "I've never used the synthesist for this."

"Why did you this time?"

"I wanted...something else...the sensualist can be overwhelming. Mixes everything together, even when it can pick out one sensation and expand it into...it's hard to keep track of thoughts, reasons. I wanted to know..."

"Know what? If it's worth your time staying?" He closed his eyes.

"Not exactly."

He sighed heavily, shifted lazily. "I left my reserves on the gondola."

Nemily laughed.

A smile reshaped his face. "I suppose I could give you a resumé."

"Complete with references?"

"If you insist. How many would you require?"

"It depends how out of date they are."

He opened one eye at her.

"Maybe," she continued, "we should just stick to having sex in microgravity."

His hand snaked out and clutched at her stomach. Nemily drew herself back and he snatched at her again, making her laugh. She clasped his forearm.

"Are you impugning my physical prowess?" he demanded with mock outrage as he rolled toward her.

"I'm not ticklish in synthesist!" she protested as he straddled her and began poking playfully at her armpits and belly. She tried not to laugh and instead laughed louder. "I'm not ticklish!"

"Maybe on your feet...."

She felt one hand crawling down her left leg. She reached up and grabbed a patch of his chest hair and tugged. He leaned forward, mouth open.

"Do you want these hairs?" she asked soberly.

"Ah...yes, as a matter of fact—*ow*!"

She plucked a few and held them up so he could see them in the pale light. "Here. Don't say I never gave you anything."

"You—"

He tried to seize her wrist but she deftly waved her arm just out of his reach until he began laughing. She shoved him over on his back and sat on his belly. With exaggerated gestures, she began taking one hair at a time and planting each one on his chest.

"Now don't forget to water them," she explained carefully. "Not too much or they'll drown, but with a little care they'll take root and bloom by spring."

He caught her wrist then and pulled her hand to his mouth. He licked the spaces between her knuckles.

"Do you want me to go put in the sensualist?" she asked.

"Yes...no...I don't think I can keep up right now."

"I mean, if I'm already calling in sick I might as well be bedridden."

"That would be...."

"What? Good, bad, indifferent, marvelous, tragic, comic, glorious, disgusting—?"

"Fine. Absolutely fine."

She grasped his hand and kissed it. "I've never been absolutely fine before."

"Neither have I, but I'm willing to learn."

She stretched out along his length and traced the shapes of his face with a fingertip. Silent now, he fought to stay awake, but eventually his eyes closed and his breathing deepened again. Carefully, she slid off him, and sat on the edge of the bed.

Their discarded clothes made the only clutter in the room. A small table on his side of the bed (she was amused that she already thought of it that way, meaning, of course, that where she now sat was *her* side) held a few pieces of jewelry, including his pendant, an antique clock whose large numerals glowed red, and a glass of water. Otherwise, the room revealed nothing of the owner. No art on the walls, nothing scattered on the floor, not even a plant. All Mace did here was sleep.

Until tonight. She wondered if the ungratifying intercourse had to do with that rather than his proclaimed weariness. Perhaps, she mused, she was the first woman to sleep with him in his own place since his wife.

He swallowed air noisily, grunted and rolled onto his side. She watched him dubiously. What would it be like to sleep with him, actually sleep here, every night? She liked her privacy, especially in her own space, and rarely had company. But Mace had been easy to be with in the morning, despite the awkwardness of that first time. Once meant little, she knew, but it had been different from her usual anxieties and growing impatience for the guest to leave.

He did not care that she was a ramhead.

Flattery allowed too much, promised too little. Nemily mistrusted that kind of graciousness, suspecting the agendas it masked. Common decency might explain genuine politeness and tolerance, even honest interest, but decency was not at all common. People lived by masks, even people she judged good, and her own hapteric existence taught that the cost of new attachments, even when beneficial, escalated with importance. The question was never how much do I want—want is cheaper than air—but how much will I trade for what I think I can get. People pretended not to notice the negotiations, claimed that something else was really happening that was finer. Perhaps it became finer in time, after all the initial bartering, and Nemily willingly believed that, but she did not know.

She looked at the pendant containing his dead wife's persona. Helen had been a ramhead, too. Perhaps not wired to the same extent as Nemily, but to make one of those required an interface. . . .

She waited to be sure Mace still slept, then carefully stood. She padded across the room to the toilet, closed the door and peed in the dark.

"And when you finally figure out what they want," she mused aloud, "then you have to figure out what they want."

Day cycle was beginning. The skylight let sufficient illumination to see by, though without color. The lone tree in the atrium looked like a chaotic spill against the grey wall. Nemily went to the study. Even here the neatness seemed absolute, bordering on oppressive.

She sat down behind the desk and touched the keypad. The flatscreen glowed warmly and a menu scrolled up. She selected commlink and the screen switched to another menu. She tapped in the recipient, then selected voice. The screen told her to "Record Now."

"Melissa, this is Nem. I won't be able to make it in"—she glanced at the time chop—"today. Personal stuff. I apologize. If you want, shift anything immediate to my terminal and I'll get to it tonight. Thanks."

She sent it, then cleared the screen. She drummed her fingers along the edge of the desk for a time.

"Are you monitoring?" she asked.

The screen said: YES.

"Good. I wanted to introduce myself. I'm Nemily Dollard."

NOTED.

"I understand you're based on Mace's wife...?"

YES.

"Is this the extent of her personality or are you just being shy?"

WHAT DO YOU REQUIRE?

"I don't know...tell me about her. What's she like?"

WAS. DECEASED. I ALSO DO NOT RECOGNIZE YOUR AUTHORITY TO ACCESS THAT INFORMATION.

"Hmm. Well, that's something anyway. I understand my lack of authorization. I just thought we could talk, one augmented system to another."

NEMILY DOLLARD, CYBERLINK, BORN CERES, DATE UNCERTAIN, TRANSFERRED TO LUNASE SETTLEMENT NETWORK COMBINE A.D. 2102, EMIGRATED TO AEA A.D. 2116, INFLUX PLACEMENT SEGMENT FIVE RING THREE, EMPLOYED BY—

"Stop. Is this an automated function or did Mace request my profile?"

S.O.P.

"All his lovers?"

QUESTION INAPPLICABLE.

"All right. Has Mace accessed your workup on me?"

AFTER A LONG PAUSE: NO.

Nemily thought back over the brief exchange. A few of the responses showed a degree of discretion, though not enough to override a direct prohibition. The d.p. could *act* human without actually functioning with human volition. But from this little she could not tell what limits the chaotic algorithm imposed. Given time she could probably wheedle anything she wanted out of it purely by inference. She felt along the underside of the desk, but found no jack. No doubt there was a connection she could use somewhere, but she already felt uneasy prying.

Odd, she mused, *that even after allowing someone access in the most physically intimate ways such a mundane sensibility could still keep her from invading his privacy: peeking uninvited into the hidden parts of someone's life was bad manners.*

"Are there any physical security systems in place or can I wander the dom freely?"

NO INTERNAL PHYSICAL PROHIBITORS. MACE GRANTED YOU PERMISSION.

Nemily hesitated. In her experience, not even high-order systems could tell a direct lie. They would inform you that such data was inaccessible. But Mace had written the parameters of this one.

It seemed reasonable that he would want to feel safe within the walls of his own space, without the need to guard anything against intruders already inside. They would not get inside.

She hoped she read him correctly.

She descended to the atrium and went out to the greenhouse.

The plants growing in variously sized pots on the three shelves that ran along the right-hand side all looked healthy, lushly green and full. In the far right corner, though, mingling now with a mound of dirt, were piled the discarded carcasses of small trees. The bonsai on the work-bench looked to her like fine-quality work. She knew virtually nothing about bonsai, but it was impossible to live on Aea without coming to recognize good and bad examples.

She flexed her toes on the packed soil, enjoying the cool yielding. With mild reluctance, she went back into the atrium.

She stood in the center of the floor, beneath the skylight, and pivoted slowly, studying the walls. It lacked something, though it seemed a complete enough home for Mace.

She went to the kitchen and drew a glass of water. Leaning against the jamb, she drank and studied.

There was no space for company. A guest room, yes, but she felt certain it had never been used. Beyond that, she saw no area for entertaining, no scattering of sofas and chairs, no area where company might gather except in the kitchen, nothing set aside for the assembly of friends.

She felt suddenly guilty for bringing trouble into this place. Seeing Glim tonight had brought back all the anxiety that had driven her from Lunase in the first place. Mace did not deserve the complications. But she also sensed that he would welcome them on some level, that this was part of what he did. In a way, she felt hopeful that she could add to his life, although it might cost her.

She finished her water and went back upstairs. She wanted to be there when he awoke.

ELEVEN

AEA, 2118

DAY OOZED THROUGH THE SEMI-OPAQUE WINDOW like liquefied ivory. Nemily lay on her side, staring at it as though she had never seen light before.

When she finally rolled over she found herself alone. Her clothes had been picked up, folded neatly, and placed on a chair by the window. She rummaged through them, looking for her augment case.

"Excuse me."

The voice startled her. She spun around. A man dressed in a simple, neatly cut dark suit stood in the doorway, watching her. She did not know him and was about to ask if he was a friend of Mace's when she noticed the bright yellow ID badge hanging from his lapel: Structural Authority security.

"Yes…?"

"Are you a guest of Mr. Preston's?"

"Yes, I am."

"Please get dressed and come downstairs."

He left the doorway and she heard his tread descending the steps.

Nemily quickly put on the evening dress. She felt foolishly overdressed, but Mace was much too large for any of his clothes to fit—besides, she did not know where he kept them.

Downstairs, the floor of the turret seemed filled with security people. The man who had asked her to come down stood on the steps, waiting for her. He motioned for her to come to him. When she reached him, he grasped her arm, took her pouch and led her the rest of the way.

"What's happening?" she asked.

"What is your name?"

"Nemily Dollard."

They reached the floor. Several faces turned to look at her; most of them looked away after a moment. She could not see Mace.

"What is your relationship with Mr. Preston?"

"A ... friend. We—"

"Ms. Dollard."

She looked around. Linder Koeln came toward them. He smiled briefly, then spoke to the SA man.

"I can take her. She works for PolyCarb."

"I'm sorry, sir, but—"

Koeln fished a chit from his jacket and handed it to the man. He released Nemily's arm long enough to pull a reader from his pocket and insert the chit. After a few moments he nodded and returned the chit to Koeln.

"Very well, sir, I give her into your charge."

"Thank you. Ms. Dollard?"

"My augments," she said.

"I'll have to retain these for examination—"

"I need them. They're my personal augments."

"Do you have a warrant for anyone else's property than Mr. Preston's?" Koeln asked.

"The warrant covers what we find on the premises. Once we've examined them she can get them back."

"How long?" Nemily asked.

"Agent"—Koeln leaned forward to read the man's tag—"Rawls. You've remanded Ms. Dollard to my custody. I'm sure such consideration covers her personal belongings as well."

"No, sir, it does not. If you'd care to press the issue, I can retain both the augments and Ms. Dollard and request that you leave the scene."

"I see. Very well. Thank you. Ms. Dollard, please come along."

"But—"

"We'll get them back quickly. Right now, please come with me."

Reluctantly, she let Koeln lead her through the maze of impassive people. Her head swiveled. Finally, she saw Mace, near his front door, sitting on the floor, arms behind him. He looked angry and bitter and did not look up at her as Koeln guided her outside and down the path to the pedistry.

"I wish he had talked to me yesterday," he said. "This might have been avoided."

"What's happening? Is Mace under arrest?"

"It appears that way, yes."

"For what?"

"I only just arrived. I'm not privy to the charges. I had hoped you might enlighten me."

"Me? But I don't—"

He raised a hand sharply, index finger stiffly aimed up. "Not here, not yet."

Baffled and frightened, she let him guide her to the pedistry and out of the enclave. She glanced back and saw more SA people milling about the entrance to the neighborhood. A large, dark blue transport squatted ominously on the grass nearby.

Near the shunt station a smaller vehicle waited, the nose decorated with the PolyCarb emblem.

Koeln ushered her into the car. The hatch sealed quietly and the driver lifted off, heading toward segment one.

"What is going on?" Nemily demanded.

"Mr. Preston is in some trouble with Structural Authority. Isn't that what it looks like to you?"

"Why? And why have you taken me away? Shouldn't I be under arrest, too?"

"Who says you're not?"

Nemily stared at him. Koeln reached over to pat her hand, but she jerked it away from him. He blinked, then shrugged.

"There are questions which need answering," he said. "Simple ones, not difficult at all. You may even know some of the answers. Do you know where Toler is?"

"No. Not now, anyway."

"Explain that."

"He—I saw him last night in the Heavy."

"Where exactly?" When she did not speak, he grabbed her arm tightly. "This is not optional. Answer me or you go back where you came from. Where was he?"

"5555."

"Reese Nagel's clutch?"

"Yes."

"You don't know where he is now?"

"No."

He released her and leaned back in his seat, staring thoughtfully out the window.

"Nemily, do you know who sponsored you?"

"You asked me that the other day. No, I don't."

"And no one ever contacted you? You never spoke with your sponsor?"

"No. I told you—"

"And yet I find you this morning at Macefield Preston's house."

"What do they have to do with each other?"

"You really don't know?"

"At this point what would I gain by lying to you? You already believe I'm guilty of something."

"No, not guilty. No more than the hand is guilty of what the mind directs it to do."

Nemily realized then that Koeln *did* know who had sponsored her.

"I thought my InFlux records were confidential."

"I have a judicial mandate from Structural Authority that grants me certain broad powers. What we're investigating is more than an internal PolyCarb matter and in such cases exceptions are made. In any event, I have your InFlux jacket. What I found there led me to Mr. Preston. Imagine my surprise then when I discover that he's seeing you socially."

"Why should that be a surprise?"

"Because his wife is listed as your sponsor."

"But I was told she was dead."

"Yes. In fact, she died before your sponsorship came through." He glanced at her. "So you see how this looks."

"No, I don't. I met Mace at a party three days ago. Before that I'd never heard of him or his wife. What is it he's suspected of doing?"

"I don't know. Mr. Preston, besides running a rather good security firm, traffics in recovered data and storage media, but that's no distinction, unless he's suspected of possessing a certain kind of data. I said we were looking into data theft. When I found out about your sponsor, I thought perhaps you were a go-between for Mr. Preston and one of his clients. I doubted it, but you were a possibility. But that curious connection wouldn't let me drop it. I thought perhaps Mr. Preston had sponsored you. But why would he use his wife's name on your InFlux jacket and not his own? Besides which, in the event that he was caught at something, that would look even more suspicious, since he might have used a name completely unrelated to him."

"I never knew his wife."

"Nor, really, could you have," Koeln said. "She died on Mars, she was never in Lunase, your paths never crossed. The question is, what purpose could you serve here that someone would import you under an assumed sponsorship?"

"You have my work record, you know what I've been doing."

"And besides some vague work you did for Reese Nagel early on, I have found nothing to indicate that you're involved with anything illegal or dangerous."

"Did his wife's name come up on any other jacket?"

"My mandate is limited, I couldn't go rummaging through all the files InFlux keeps. But as it turns out, yes, it did."

"Who?"

"That's what made this even more interesting. I wondered what possible connection you might have to any of this. If you *are* a go-between, then the question remained, between whom? You haven't done anything remotely illegal since you've been here, so obviously you were either innocent or you were waiting for something. What might that something be? Then I found the connection. You were waiting for some*one*. Now he's here and now SA is interested in Mr. Preston and we are now interested in you."

"Who was I supposed to be waiting for?"

"Glim Toler, of course. He is the other immigrant sponsored by Helen Croslo. Mr. Preston's wife."

Nemily waited the balance of the morning in a small cell in a part of the PolyCarb complex she had never been in before. She was not even sure such a cell was legal, but she could do nothing to challenge it. There was a toilet and a cot, but no commlink, and no one answered her calls through the door.

When someone finally came, it was Koeln, in company with Cambel Guerrera and another woman Nemily did not know. Koeln looked pre-occupied and waited by the door.

"Ms. Dollard?" Cambel addressed her.

"Yes. You're Mace's friend?"

"Cambel Guerrera. We met last night. This is Sonia McCutcheon, an attorney. We've come to take you home."

"Have you talked to Mace?"

"Briefly. Please, save any questions until we're away from here."

The attorney opened her case to reveal a complex reader. She raised the screen and inserted two discs.

"Mr. Koeln," she said. "If you would please enter your ID and ac-knowledge our writ."

Linder Koeln frowned and stared at the screen. "I do so under pro-test, Ms. McCutcheon. This is an ongoing PolyCarb investigation—"

"For which you have no authority to detain anyone unless just cause can be presented to a justice and the appropriate security mandate is issued. You have no such mandate. Ms. Dollard's release is incumbent upon the proper acknowledgement of authority. This is for your protec-tion and PolyCarb's. If you refuse to endorse the release, culpability will be assumed and action will be taken against you in court."

Koeln sighed and slipped his ID chit into another part of the reader. He tapped the keyboard briefly and retrieved his chit.

"There." He looked at Nemily. "Please make yourself available for questioning, Ms. Dollard. I remind you that you are still an employee of PolyCarb IntraSolar and therefore subject to its rules of full disclosure in a security investigation." He glared at the attorney. "I *do* have author-ity for that."

"And Ms. Dollard has the right to have an attorney present when you do." She closed down her reader and snapped the lid shut. "Thank you, Mr. Koeln. Now if you would please allow Ms. Dollard to accompany us."

Koeln stood rigidly aside, not looking at any of them. Hesitantly, Nemily approached the door.

"Come on, Ms. Dollard," Cambel Guerrera said. "We don't need to be here."

She was afraid to speak until she had made her way through the maze of the unfamiliar wing and emerged onto the sward of parkland around the complex. Her legs trembled.

"How—" She cleared her throat. "How did you find me?"

"Mace," Cambel said. "He saw Koeln escorting you out."

"What about Mace?" Nemily asked.

"It's being handled," Cambel said.

"Structural Authority took my augments," she said. "Is there any way I can get them back?"

Cambel looked at the attorney, who nodded. "We can see about that right now. Ms. Dollard, do you empower me as your personal representative?"

"I—" She glanced at Cambel, who gave a brief nod. "Yes."

"Let's go. Do you have the agent's name who impounded them?"

"Um...Rawls."

They took the shunt, antispinward, to the Structural Authority complex, nearly a third of the way around from PolyCarb. In a series of brief, quiet encounters with SA officials, Nemily watched the attorney work efficiently through the rituals surrounding her augments. Finally, an officer brought them the case, wrapped in plastic with an identification seal. Nemily had to sign for it, at the direction of a scowling Sonia McCutcheon.

"Anything else?" Sonia McCutcheon asked as they headed for the exit.

"I—" Nemily clutched her augment case tightly, only now allowing herself to feel the desperation its absence had caused her. "I'm just worried about Mace now."

"He should be out by now," Cambel said.

Outside the SA judicial building, Sonia McCutcheon sighed deeply. "All right," she said. "Something to keep in mind. SA wasn't interested in those augments. It should have been more difficult to get them back if they were actually germane to any investigation. So there are two possibilities. Either SA is entirely concerned with Mr. Preston or they simply didn't get a chance to look at those augments. Someone didn't bring attention to them. It happens. Not often, but it happens. You should be prepared to have them impounded again, just in case the error is caught. Or...."

"Koeln told me he had a judicial mandate from SA," Nemily said.

"Limited. It doesn't extend to isolating people for interrogation, only gives him access to ongoing reports."

"He lied to me, then."

Sonia McCutcheon raised an eyebrow, silent.

"So," Nemily went on, "he can't come and arrest me?"

"No."

"Can you make yourself available on call for the next few days?" Cambel asked.

Sonia McCutcheon raised her eyebrows. "That can get expensive."

"I understand that. Can you?"

"I don't see why not. I can shift anything else over to one of my associates. Consider me available."

"Fine. I'll be in touch."

Somehow, Nemily felt more vulnerable as the attorney walked away. She held her augment case tightly and looked at Cambel.

"Why?"

"Because Mace asked. Let's go."

"Where?"

"Back to his dom. He wanted us to wait there for him."

Cambel pressed the mici and stepped back, waiting. After a few seconds' silence, she began to frown. The door opened then and Mace peered out at them, his expression impassive. He waved them in.

"Something wrong with Helen?" Cambel asked.

"My system's been locked down and tapped," Mace said. "I've taken it offline till I can get a judicial injunction to lift the surveillance."

"Can we talk here?" Cambel asked.

He waved them back into his kitchen. Oil crackled delicately in a pan. Mace went about methodically breaking eggs and slicing sausage. He worked silently, still wearing the same loose sweats that he had been arrested in. Nemily did not know him well enough to read his moods, a skill with which she felt inadequate anyway, but it seemed to her that he was more thoughtful than angry. She glanced at Cambel for some direction. The other woman only shook her head minutely and sat down at the counter.

Mace scooped up platefuls for each of them and poured himself and Cambel coffee. He raised a mug questioningly for Nemily, who nodded, and he poured her a cup.

"I've got us shielded in here," Mace said. "For the time being. We can talk. If I do the whole dom, they'll just be back."

All this took place in a sepulchral stillness, broken only by the small sounds of Mace's cooking. Nemily took a bite of egg, then dropped her fork noisily.

"Should I apologize?" she asked.

Mace looked up. "For what?"

"Getting you involved in something unpleasant."

"How did you do that?" Cambel asked.

"It was my idea to go to the Heavy last night, to Reese's."

"I wasn't aware," Mace said, "that being seen in the Heavy constituted a civil infraction."

"This involves Toler. You were with me, he was there, this morning Structural Authority and PolyCarb security are here."

"Toler. When did his name come up?"

"Koeln asked me about him."

"Really," Mace said.

"I see what she means," Cambel said. "You think they suspect you of being involved with Toler. Therefore anyone you're seen with must also be involved."

"Yes," Nemily said.

"Is that the way it works in Lunase?"

"I'm—"

"If that's the case," Mace said, "then you would have been the primary target of the arrest. So why would Koeln want to remove you from SA custody? For that matter, why would SA just turn you over to Koeln on his request?"

Cambel nodded. "They arrested Mace. You just happened to be here."

"Did they arrest you?" Mace asked Cambel.

"No. They questioned me, but I had already arranged for an attorney. I don't know that they would have refrained from arresting me in any case if I'd been a primary."

"So," Mace said, "the question is, why did Koeln extricate you from SA?"

"He's looking for Toler. He said it was related to a data theft investigation."

"So?" Cambel said. "Wouldn't it have been better to leave you in SA custody? He could easily have gotten interrogation privileges."

"Unless," Mace said, "he didn't want SA knowing anything about his investigation." He shrugged. "Corporate politics."

"This sounds as if you don't think any of this concerned me."

"Does that disappoint you?" Cambel asked.

"No, but—"

Mace set his fork onto his empty plate and took a swallow of coffee. "Koeln is interested in Toler, not me, and you seem to be his link to Toler. SA is also interested in Toler. They're not interested in you, but I'm their link to Toler. At least, they think I am. I don't know why, but the two investigations have one common factor: Glim Toler."

Nemily chewed her lip. She wanted to ask about Helen, Mace's wife, but she was reluctant in front of Cambel.

"For a fact?" Cambel asked.

"They asked only once if I knew Glim Toler. If he hadn't already come up through Koeln, I might have thought the question was only peripherally important."

"What *did* they ask about?" Nemily asked.

"Midline."

"The orbital?" Nemily asked.

Cambel cocked her head to one side. "I don't follow."

"Cassidy. Five-Eight. Now Midline."

Cambel stared at him, her face suddenly paler. "When?"

"I'm not sure. Sometime in the last ten days."

"I don't understand," Nemily said.

"Do you know about what happened to Cassidy and Five-Eight?" Cambel asked. "The transfer stations—"

"They failed," Nemily said. "Catastrophically. Abandoned."

"They broke apart," Cambel snapped. "Dissolved. All the binding materials gave out and the shells just...opened up...."

"Dissolved," Mace mused. "Like the molifiber at Hellas Planitia."

"The thought occurred to me, too," Cambel said. "But the kind of solvent—"

"We saw more last night," Mace said. "Didn't we?"

Cambel frowned. "You mean those pirated transmissions from Earth Reese showed? You think—?"

"Philip said there has been a plague of data destruction on Earth. His sources suggest that whole libraries, whole institutions are disintegrating. Physically. We saw something close to what might have happened to those stations." He shrugged. "It's a stretch. It would mean someone was in touch with forces on Earth."

"That's not that much of a stretch," Cambel said. "Philip gets data upwell and he's relatively small. But—why Midline?"

"That's a very interesting question. Cavery was on Midline. He'd just received a change of status, in fact, which locked him into his position there for at least another year."

"So Cavery's dead. Who does that leave?"

"Oxmire. He's out at Titan."

Cambel blew out a loud breath. "This has gotten very complicated."

"Gotten? It always was."

"Yes, but things never seem complicated until they start to make a little bit of sense. When nothing makes sense, it's just overwhelming, not complicated."

Mace smiled. "Interesting way to look at it."

"So how does Glim Toler fit into this? And Nemily here?"

"I don't know. I had Helen doing a search for him when all this broke. She hadn't reported anything yet. PolyCarb is asking about Toler. Toler is here. Toler knows Nemily, evidently knows Reese or one of Reese's associates. Reese shows us a display he's gotten from a forgotten Earth satellite. And Midline has collapsed." He shook his head. "I don't know."

"It might help to know if Toler has been to Midline," Cambel said.

"Or Cassidy and Five-Eight." He frowned suddenly. "Or Hellas Planitia."

"Everyone on that project was cleared by three security agencies."

"All it would take would be for one of them to look the other way," Mace said. "If one of them had a vested interest in seeing the project fail, maybe?"

"Too much speculation."

"And we still don't have a motive," Mace said, nodding. "After all, no other transport terminal on Mars was hit. In fact, that project has been one of the most sabotage-free of any in Signatory Space. No one seems to object to Mars having a transport system."

"But that was the first leg built by PolyCarb," Cambel said.

"So? The other legs—"

"Martian contractors mainly, but there was a lot of Lunessa input. Materials and so forth."

Mace nodded slowly. "Trade?"

"Nothing you're saying," Nemily said, "makes any sense to me. Who are these people? What's Hellas Planitia?"

"Hellas Planitia is where Mace's wife died," Cambel said.

"It's on Mars? That's what Koeln said."

Mace looked at her narrowly. "What did Koeln say?"

"He told me your wife had died on Mars."

"Why would he bring that up?" Cambel asked.

Nemily looked from one to the other, uncertain. She wanted to talk to Mace, alone. She waited.

Mace stood, scowling. "None of this makes a reasonable connection to me. As far as it goes, Koeln's investigation is completely separate from SA's concerns. What's missing?"

"I can tell you that," Nemily said. She closed her eyes, anxious. "Something Koeln told me. He asked me if I knew who my sponsor was."

"Your sponsor?"

"I came to Aea as a sponsored immigrant. It was the only way I was going to get in. Someone sponsored me. I never knew who until to-day."

"Who—?"

"Your wife. Helen. That's the name on my InFlux jacket. And evidently she sponsored Glim, too."

"Before I left Lunase," Nemily told them, "Glim asked me to bring something here. I told him no. But he must have hidden it in my gear anyway because at InFlux they questioned me about contraband. I didn't know anything about it, I told them that, but it's not possible to be believed under those conditions. I thought they were going to send me back. But something happened—someone else got involved, someone interested in what I'd brought in—and it was all right. They passed me through. Ever since, I've thought that might come out and they'd expel me. Now, if Glim is here—"

"He may be looking for the vacuum you carried for him. It compromises you. I see." He picked up her uneaten food and carried it to the sink.

"What kind of vacuum?" Cambel asked.

"I don't know. Some discs were found in my baggage at customs, so I guess that must have been it. It was two and half years ago—"

Mace's expression startled her.

"Who was your InFlux councilor?" he asked.

"Jeter Malcolm."

"Excuse me," he said. "I'll be right back."

She heard him running up the stairs.

"Funny," Cambel said. "I gave up believing in the power of coincidence a long time ago. Things happen, occasionally they turn out to be serendipitous, but..."

"What do you mean?"

"Mace wanted to find out about Hellas Planitia. The problem was, the company wasn't going to let him. There was a security element way over his level. They wanted him off the investigation. One of the things Poly-Carb does when they don't want to terminate an employee's contract, but want to control him, is move the employee around. They started doing that to Mace, so he resigned. He thought he could tackle the problem from the outside. There was missing data from the accident. He sued PolyCarb for full disclosure, but when all is said and done, they have a lot more clout than a single irate citizen. We've been scrounging for data since we returned, thinking we might stumble on something at the fringes. He did volunteer work for InFlux, hoping Helen might come through under a different name. Her body was never found. For a while, he believed she had gotten away, alive."

"You don't think so?"

"Mars is a big world, with a lot of area to get lost in. Maybe some year they'll find her remains, fifty, a hundred kilometers from Hellas Planitia. No, I don't think she lived. But he started looking. Later, after I resigned from PolyCarb, I helped him. It's turned into a rather comfortable business. The last six months, he really started losing interest. I thought he might...I don't know, normalize, I suppose...and we have our business and things worked out fairly well with the PolyCarb settlement. Then he meets you at a party and all this starts falling out of the air. You're turning out to be the best lead we've ever found. Suddenly everyone is interested in what Mace Preston knows about a particular kind of sabotage. Now this stuff about Helen being your sponsor. Serendipity is a wonderful thing."

"But you don't believe it?"

"No."

"Then—?"

"I think you were put in Mace's path."

"How? Our meeting was an accident."

Cambel shrugged.

"Why are you interested in this? Why did you resign from PolyCarb?"

"Personal reasons."

"And none of my business?"

"I'm glad you're perceptive."

"But—"

She stopped, hearing Mace's footsteps, returning.

"Do you recognize him?" Mace asked, placing an image before her.

It showed a man with thick hair and a heavy beard obscuring the lower half of his face. But the eyes, though narrower than now, were immediately recognizable. She looked up.

"You?"

"Couple of years ago."

"You were there...."

Mace paused. "Yeah."

"You took the discs...."

He nodded. "Would you like to hear them?"

"But—"

"If you're wondering if that's the reason I'm seeing you now, don't. You looked familiar when I saw you at Piers' dom, but only vaguely. I thought maybe I'd seen you at Everest—a ghost—and when I found out that you're a cyberlink I decided that that accounted for it. But two and half years ago? I was doing a lot of things then to—I didn't want to remember certain things. Maybe on some level I made an association, but believe me I did not remember till just now."

Cambel grunted. "Ser-ren-dip-ity."

Mace frowned at her.

"I believe you," Nemily said.

He looked relieved. "As for it giving you trouble, no, it won't. There's no record and I doubt Jeter would remember."

"Unless directly questioned?"

"Maybe. Even then, with no records, he wouldn't tell the truth."

"Why aren't there records?"

"Consistency," Cambel explained. "An arrangement. Mace took the discs. A favor on Jeter's part. He couldn't file any kind of report on them then. He couldn't deny you admission without cause. So it's as if it never happened."

Mace smiled at her. "So there's no threat to your citizenship. Not from that, anyway."

"There's no way for Koeln to know about it, then."

"No."

"But he acts like he knows."

"He's fishing. Helen being listed as both your and Toler's sponsor means that there must be more to the association."

"What did you do with the discs?" Nemily asked.

"Come on. I'll show you."

Part of the left-hand wall of the plain room that contained only a chair slid aside, revealing a floor-to-ceiling rack of shelves filled with discs. She estimated the length of the shelves at three meters, that each shelf, then, contained roughly three hundred discs, and she counted eleven shelves full, a twelfth containing a dozen or so overflow.

"I'm surprised SA didn't find these," Mace said. "I suppose they assumed anything important would simply be on my d.p."

The obsession of Aeans with collecting things fascinated Nemily, both for its manifold expressions and its demands on resource. It unsettled her at times; Lunessa exhibited nothing quite like it, unless their absorption in watching themselves counted. Even in the more cramped confines of the outer rings, Aeans fell into competition over gathering scraps and fragments of a past they barely understood, while others acquired the understanding without the artifacts, and so could impress those with the actual objects with long explanations of provenance and symbolism. Scattered through the labyrinthine matrix of the orbital, in unused niches or spacious sections of the interior, museums proliferated, dedicated to the arcana of misremembered pasts and disconnected remnants, as isolated from their origins as the people who gave their passions to preservation.

Books, music, and images formed the core contents of Aea's reliquaries, but Nemily had seen a host of minor idols filling the sacristy of the necrolater's personal temples. Ancient computer parts, pieces of clothing, small pins designating rank or membership, rectangles of plastic once used for identification or commerce, coins, paper currency, tokens, canceled receipts, manufacturer's logos, stationery letterhead, rubber stamps, place markers bearing the names of emporia or artists or books, small stuffed toy representations of animals, fictional or real, bills of lading from forgotten transport companies, catalogues, brochures, pens and pencils, small figurines cast in plastic, jewelry, utensils, dead flowers pressed in a number of clear media, autographs of people known and unknown, mission patches of ancient spaceflights, various measuring tools, swatches of cloth, food packages, buttons, belts, buckles, videos, samples of material used in forgotten components from unremembered projects, medallions, jars, lids, unopened packets of pharmacopiates, bones, miniature model kits, antique data storage discs, paperclips, thumbtacks, ribbons, cups, coasters, gears, wire, eyeglasses, keys, postcards, game pieces, candles, lists of names of residents of cities, stamps, envelopes, address labels, trademarks, badges, bags, fans, rings, timepieces and pocket knives.

Much, perhaps most, were copies based on drawings, photographs, or descriptions, some taken from authentic artifacts. It did not matter so much that the objects were "originals"—it was recognized that the culture from which they came replicated everything it could as much as it could, rendering the concept of originality itself as fluid and subjective—only that they duplicated as closely as possible the thing copied. Detail mattered more than pedigree.

The Exclusion had driven the dispersed progeny of Gaia in different directions. Some places turned their backs on any heritage that might obligate them to a past that had shut them out, others preserved what they already had and pretended an independence of identity as tenuous as their hold on survival, while Aea embraced recovery of all that might be within the apocryphal Archive short of finding the Archive itself, which in all probability did not exist.

Nemily ran her fingertips along a row of the discs. "Mine are in here?"

"I thought they weren't yours."

"I meant—"

"I know. I'm joking. Yes, they are. In fact, they were the first." He stepped alongside her and pointed at the left-hand corner of the top shelf. "I never bothered to listen to any of them before these. I mean, I'd heard a lot of pre-Exclusion music before, but—I was searching for something else. So I'd analyze them for interlaced data and if I didn't find it, I passed them on through other dealers. These...maybe I was ready to find something else...I kept them for the music."

"Did you analyze them?"

Mace shrugged. "I automated the process to search for key factors. My system alerts me if it finds anything relevant."

"Did they contain anything?"

"I don't know. I never ran a full analysis."

"I don't understand. Were you looking for something or not?"

He scowled and slapped the touchpoint on the wall that closed the doors over the discs.

Nemily followed him out into the atrium. He had started as if he knew where to go, then lost momentum and came to a halt, indecisive, near the center of the floor. She hung back, waiting.

"My wife died on Mars," he said finally. "The company declared it an accident. Her body was never found, but then they claimed she hadn't been there in the first place. The cause of death—well, that's problematic, I suppose, but I never accepted that it was an accident and I don't think PolyCarb did, either. Sometimes it's necessary to put a face on something for the benefit of the shareholders. I—they expected me—demanded—I signed her death certificate."

Nemily glanced at Cambel, who only watched, arms folded. "But you didn't believe she was dead."

"I didn't. And even if I did, the question of why still needed answering. Certain pieces of data went missing from the accident. Never recovered. So I figured they had to relate to Helen in some way. If I could find out what those data are, how they connect with the accident, maybe I could find a starting point to actually begin looking for Helen herself."

"Or explain why she died. If she had lived, wouldn't she have come back here?"

"She couldn't. Not legally and openly, anyway. Part of the death certification. She was barred from access to Aea or Aean holdings. Curious rule, isn't it? If she's really dead, she'll never try. If she isn't, then the rule presumes culpability, fraud, criminal intent."

"People slip past InFlux all the time," Cambel said.

"And if she had, why wouldn't she contact me? So I was left with the same possibilities. Either she couldn't get here or she really was dead. I finally decided she was dead."

"How could she sponsor me, then?"

"Anyone with the right connections with InFlux could falsify those records, use her name as a cover."

"That," Cambel said, "would be a very small pool of people."

"Maybe that's who Koeln is looking for," Mace said.

Cambel shrugged.

"Or maybe she is back in Aea," Nemily said. "You said you didn't believe she was dead. Maybe you were right."

"Maybe...." He shook his head. "She couldn't legally do anything, though. I don't know."

"What about now?"

He breathed out heavily. "Now is complex."

He lapsed into silence, standing in the center of his atrium. Cambel cleared her throat.

"I have some questions to ask of certain people," she said. "So I think I'll get on it. I kept Sonia on retainer for the next few days, just in case."

"Wait," Mace said. "I can't safely access my system. Do you still have the records from Hellas Planitia?"

"Sure. Which ones?"

"Personnel."

"Yes...." She looked at Nemily and nodded. "I'll pull them up, get the images. You want Nemily to go through them?"

"Yes," Mace said.

"Okay," Cambel said. She patted Mace on the shoulder. "I'll call when I have something."

Mace nodded. Cambel gave Nemily a significant look—but what it meant Nemily could not read—and left the dom.

"How do you mean, complex?" Nemily asked.

He shrugged. "Now I'm not sure I would want her to be alive." He turned and gave her a burdened smile. "Maybe I've felt that way for a long time, but...things become habit after so long. I went through the motions of the search for a long time, gathering odd bits of information, collecting—things." He shook his head. "I don't know what I'd do now if I actually found something. I'd been running on momentum for so long and I finally ran out." He coughed. "Then there's you."

"What about me?"

"I don't know yet."

"Do you want to know?"

He laughed. "I don't know yet."

"Well...maybe we can figure it out. If you want."

"Where do we start?"
"Why don't you tell me about Helen."

Listening to Mace, the impression she built of Helen was of headlong pursuit, a bolide in search of a crater yet to be, and that their relationship was largely an accident of trajectory.

Prior to Mace, her encounters had all been brief because the surfaces she impacted lacked substance and, tissue-thin, allowed her to pass through. She never looked back to see the result of her passage. When she reached Mace, he exhibited none of that tenuousness, and Helen came to a momentary halt against him, surprised and intrigued and, in an attempt to extract herself, thoroughly and unexpectedly caught by a perverse unwillingness to go on without him. She found something in him she did not wish to give up, though she often spoke about their relationship as if love had less to do with it than simple compatibility. He never believed her blithe dismissals, believing through it all that she loved him.

For his part, it was the nature of her energy that attracted him and the capacity for achievement that impressed him and the unfettered joy in doing that bound him. They had been shoved together by a job, a project she was supervising which required a local Martian presence, and he was part of the security package, second in authority. At first it seemed unlikely. She was Aean, PolyCarb, management, and he quickly developed a fantasy about her. He had spent a lifetime practicing concealment, so he automatically kept his feelings private and hidden. Part of the process involved denial, and when they did come together, it took Helen the better part of a long night to seduce him, finally abandoning any and all subtlety by simply stripping off her own clothes, matter-of-factly presenting him with an opportunity he could not ignore and a dilemma that overwhelmed his stoic abnegation. When the project ended, she offered him a job and a proposal of marriage, in that order. She had been just as bemused as he, simultaneously dismayed and pleased by an apparent and perversely welcome betrayal of self.

Their respective positions with PolyCarb kept them apart for long periods of time and Mace began to suspect this to be intentional on Helen's part. She did not trust herself to be satisfied with any pretense to domesticity. She played the schedules masterfully to ensure separations that fueled their reunions and still strangled any resentments.

"I like consistency," Mace said. "It was an easy life to grow into. I could have been content for...well, for life. We had just under seven years. I found out she was going to be on Mars again—a last-minute change, she'd been on her way home from Ganymede—so I was able to lever myself onto a security team escorting a PolyCarb board member on a tour of Martian cities. More than that, I ended up in charge of his security. We arrived after Helen had been on the surface for some time. I couldn't get to her, the site was locked in by one of Mars' famous dust storms, but we spoke regularly. The storm was clearing, Listrom was in the final stages of his tour, there would be time for a reunion. Then I stopped hearing anything. Communications went down, and I panicked. I left Listrom in the hands of my second and forced my way onto a transport heading for Hellas Planitia. I got there and took charge of on-site security. I was wrong, it was a violation of procedure, but I couldn't let someone else...anyway, some things went missing, like I said. An augment from a cyberlink and one of the site recorders."

"Were you held responsible?"

"I could have been. That was the threat. But I wasn't, not officially. Something was covered up, I just could never tell what. It's common practice for disasters to be modified for practical reasons. This has all the earmarks of one of those. Still, there wasn't any good reason to deny Helen's presence at the site. Unless...." He shook his head, eyes hard, pained.

"But you aren't really searching anymore. Are you?"

He shrugged. "You'd think I would've found something by now if there were anything to find. But I still have my suspicions, just no way to follow up on them."

Nemily picked up the pendant from the nightstand. "How did you come by this?"

"A gift from Helen."

"Why?"

"Hmm?"

"Why would someone you live with give you a persona encoding of herself?"

"She said she wanted me to keep it, just in case. That last job was a long separation for us, all the way the hell out to Ganymede."

"Did you try analyzing the entire construct?"

"It's layered. I was able to use the top part to model my domestic personality. But the rest...well, you know how complex these things are."

"They require a dynamic interpreter, something that can utilize but is not dependent on algorithmic matrices."

"In other words a conscious mind. I know. Unfortunately, it's against the law."

"Not entirely. Commercial use by any but the owner of the encoding is illegal. So PolyCarb could access it."

"But I don't intend to ask them. This is all I've got of Helen, I'll be damned if I let them take it away."

"Or I could."

"Excuse me?"

She dangled the pendant and let it swing. "I could do this for you. I could become Helen."

TWELVE

AEA, 2118

SOUND THUNDERED THROUGH THE TURRET, the syncopated throb of bass with drum coursing around the walls like electric current seeking ground and, denied a place to sink itself, retracing its path. Mace lay in the center of the atrium, staring at the skylight high above, his hands slapping the beat against the floor as Nemily danced around him, bare feet keeping time with bare hands in syncretic convocation, totemic and umbeset. Sweat sleeked her body, beads fell on him like mistfall; her hair, wet, sent tendrils across her face and neck. A note shrilled above the rest and her head snapped back in response, eyes half-lidded, whited. He glanced at her, brief shifts of attention quickly returned to the darkening dome, and each time felt his own adumbrated hunger, tantrically deferred. He could smell her, which made rest difficult enough without also seeing her. The music helped lull one set of urges by eliciting others, but the trade was temporary, a mask for his wants.

In a flurry of chords, the thunder ended, leaving thickness in his ears and a shuddering sense of release in his arms and legs and neck. He stretched; the floor was oiled with perspiration.

Nemily stepped over him, crotch aimed at his sternum, and grinned around gulps of air. She shook her head, showering him. He could not look away now. Her chest bellowed, light caught against skin contouring muscle and fat. Her nipples appeared the only dry places in all that surface. Mace pushed up on an elbow and reached one finger into the tangle of hair.

"Who was that?" she asked, closing her eyes.

"Santana."

She lowered herself carefully, reaching back to find his legs, moving her hands to the floor, settling her buttocks between his thighs while he kept his finger in place, mindful not to hurt her. He felt her feet slide along his hips, along his sides, then bracing against the small of his back so she could pull herself toward him. She extended a hand to his penis. He added another finger and worked more methodically. Within a minute her breathing, never calmed, changed qualitatively. She pushed herself against his hand. In the next minute she heaved, as if trying from within to exchange herself, one body for another. Mace watched, fascinated.

"Damn...." She laughed. She pushed up, caught an arm around his neck, and pressed against him. She laughed again, then, wriggling into position, she eased around him.

Mace sucked the air through his teeth. He was too tired. His legs trembled and his arms burned, but there was no way to stop except to finish. For a panicked breath he thought his body would fail him, emptied and selfish. When he came, the panic blent with relief and surprise and left him happily immobile, arms outspread, laughing with Nemily.

He dozed and woke with a cramp in his left thigh. His back ached as well from lying on the floor and his groin felt vaguely bruised.

He found her in the bedroom, sitting on the edge of the bed, her face vacant, the case of augments open beside her. She had showered; her hair still let trails of water down her shoulders. Mace sat on the floor to watch her, his back against the wall. All his muscles seemed a gesture away from trembling exhaustion. He wanted sleep.

Her eyes shifted as if seeking focus in fog. She did not see him. Cyberlinks never dreamed, except, occasionally, after ghosting, which most CAPs never did. They had this instead, and their sleep, he had been told, was formless absence.

"You have a call," the flat, emotionless voice of the automated house system said.

Nemily did not react. Mace got to his feet. "Who?"

"Linder Koeln, PolyCarb security."

"Tell him to wait for a moment."

Just then, Nemily took a deep breath and removed her collator. She inserted her synthesist, blinked, then smiled at him. "Sorry, I didn't like leaving you on the floor, but…"

"It's all right. I have to take a call."

"Oh?"

"Do you want to listen? It's Koeln."

She looked uncertain. "Did you know he'd call?"

"I half expected it."

She nodded, still frowning. Mace took her hand and squeezed.

"Accept call and record," he said.

"Mr. Preston?"

"Yes, Mr. Koeln. What can I do for you?"

"Frankly, I thought there might be something we could do for each other. My sympathy for the unfortunate events this morning. Forgive me, but I still need to discuss a matter with you. It seems, though, that things have gotten complicated. I thought perhaps you could use some help."

"What sort of help?"

"Most obviously and immediately, legal help. I'm not sure what that was about this morning, but I could arrange for PolyCarb's legal department to take you into its sphere of protections."

"Do you really think that much help is necessary?"

"I've never known Structural Authority to detain anyone without compelling reasons. It could become necessary."

"This morning may have been a simple misunderstanding."

"I doubt that. Its full complications may have simply not yet been revealed."

"Really. Now that interests me, Mr. Koeln. I would like some help along those lines."

"What lines?"

"The reasons for my arrest. Naturally, they didn't tell me anything. That's one reason they released me. To detain me after petition for release has been filed, they have to give a reason before a justice and my representative."

"Then obviously they didn't want to tell you."

"Or it was a misunderstanding."

"What do you really think, Mr. Preston?"

"I think I would like to know. Perhaps you could make inquiries?"

"SA security isn't in the habit of confiding in corporate security—"

"Don't be coy. I used to work for you people. I know all about your habits and theirs. You have to decide if the questions you want to ask me merit a little personal investment."

"Quid pro quo?"

"More or less."

"Stat check, Mr. Preston. I'll see what I can do for you. In the meantime, could we arrange a meeting?"

"Call me in the morning and let me know what you have for me. We can meet for breakfast and see about clearing up your problems."

"In the morning, then. I look forward to it."

"Thank you, Mr. Koeln. End."

Mace rubbed his eyes, then looked at Nemily. She still wore a disturbed frown.

"What did you just do?" she asked.

"Hopefully, I just got some answers."

"You lied to him, though. Structural Authority did tell you what it was about."

"Not entirely. I'm still not sure why I would be a suspect in the destruction of a station I've never been to."

"Then why—?"

"Why arrest me? Simple. They want to scare me into doing half their work for them. If we're right, Glim Toler is at the center of this and they want me to find him. They think either I already know him or that I can discover where he is. He's gone to ground somewhere and they don't have the time or personnel to find him quickly."

"That's funny. I was starting to think that Mr. Koeln was doing the same thing to me."

"Starting to? You don't now?"

"I'm not sure. When he told me who my sponsor was, it changed everything. Your wife worked for PolyCarb. So did you. I think he wants me to find who's using her name inside the company."

"Why would he think you could?"

"If I were part of the plot, wouldn't I know who my contact is?"

"The problem with that is assuming PolyCarb would hire that many members of a conspiracy. . . ." He stared at her, the faint outline of a pattern teasing at him. "If the person doing the hiring were the one Koeln's looking for, though. . . ."

"But the name of my sponsor is Helen Croslo. Your wife."

"Doesn't help, does it? House, connect to Cambel Guerrera."

"Working," the house responded. "You have an incoming call."

"Who?"

"Philip."

Mace looked at Nemily. "This needs to be private."

She nodded and stretched. Mace watched her body, feeling his own begin to respond. He grunted and went to his closet. He pulled on a robe and went down to his study.

"Morning," he said to Philip's image on the flatscreen.

He cocked his eyebrows. "It's after midcycle, Macefield."

"Afternoon, then. Hello."

"I wondered if you would care to join me for a late lunch."

"Um...I'm entertaining myself, Philip. Is it important?"

"Not particularly."

Mace saw no change in Philip's expression, but he understood that it was important. "I suppose I ought to get out. Who knows when I might be back in detention?"

"Are you in trouble, Macefield?"

"Nothing major. I'll see you in an hour or so, all right?"

"Of course."

The screen went blank. "House, what about my call to Cambel Guerrera?"

"She is not responding."

"Cancel."

Nemily was dressing when he got back to his bedroom.

"I have to go," he said.

"I gathered as much. Who's Philip?"

"Another associate. He hasn't been as involved as Cambel, but he's been irreplaceable." He looked at her and saw her listening attentively. All he wanted to do suddenly was call Philip back and tell him to forget it, that it was over, that he wanted nothing more to do with it. That option no longer seemed possible.

"Your friends are loyal," Nemily said.

"I suppose they are. Sometimes I wonder why. I haven't been the easiest person to get along with. Cambel, for instance—to this day I don't know why she stays with me."

"She's been helping you search for Helen?"

"Partly. At least, do the data search. She set up a collection system, a set of blinds to mask her from her sources, and then she sends what she finds on to me. After several months of it we started doing other things. She acts as an agent for me, finding freelance security work—mostly corporate datasphere security, countersurveillance measures, things like that—and I in turn do recovery work on a lot of the unrelated data she finds. We've made a nice stipend together."

"Do they feel the same way about your search?"

Mace considered the question for a long moment. "I don't know. I always assumed one day I'd wake up and it would be over. Either I'd have found my answers or I wouldn't care. Maybe I just needed something important to happen to let me know that it's over, that it's all right for it to be over. Does that make sense?"

"I don't know. I don't understand people with normal brains all the time. So why aren't you interested anymore?"

"I don't know that I'm not, it's just that it started feeling impossible. With luck, we'd find something. You can't base a life on nothing but luck. The obsession...it burned out...somewhere in the past year or so...and I just kept on out of habit."

"Hobbies are important."

He was startled at the critical tone in her voice. "Do you have a point to make?"

"Something like this—" She swallowed audibly. "Something like this, you either finish it or walk away completely. Anything else and it just lingers."

"Speaking from experience?"

She nodded.

"So what haven't you finished?" The sudden anxiety in her face surprised Mace. "Toler?" he guessed.

"Partly. Lunase, mainly."

"And Toler is Lunase, is that it?" When she nodded again, he said, "I suppose you tried to just walk away."

"And he followed."

"All right. So we finish it."

"Which?"

"All of it. Yours and mine. Toler, Helen, anything else...?"

She looked at him with hopeful uncertainty, a smile challenging the worry that dominated her features. "Why?"

"Because I love you."

Later it occurred to him that Nemily's expression must have mirrored his own and that perhaps the resonance of reflected expectations increased beyond honest response. He was as surprised as she appeared to be and within that frame of artless exposure, just before the complications of assessment damascened their reactions, he thought he saw acceptance and a clean pleasure. Mace did not know why he said it, then did not know if he meant it, although he felt oddly pleased with himself. It occurred to him then that she might not believe him or might not want to believe him. Nothing, though, prepared him for the reply she gave.

"I'm...." she began, then shook her head slightly, as if puzzled. "How?"

"I don't...respond...the way you do," she said.

"You said something about not understanding people with normal brains. I thought that was a joke."

She sighed, desperately uncomfortable. "Why? You said you visited Everest—the ghosts?"

"Yes."

"And you've taken advantage of the possibilities of having different personalities in the same somatotype? I mean, I used to wonder about that myself—why a client couldn't simply choose another companion instead of going to all the trouble to switch persona overlays. But I think people are just...incomprehensible about sex."

Mace smiled. "That's probably the best way to look at it."

"But there's benefit for the ghosts. The overlays set up a psychological buffer."

"I never thought about it that way."

"Most people don't. But by the same token, did you ever ask any of them why they weren't permitted to run full persona encodings?"

"No."

"The augments they use, for different personality types, are very limited, little more than a set of behaviors. Nothing to support them, just...instructions...for an act."

"I figured as much. Anything more and they'd start to develop conflicted personalities themselves."

"That's true, but the reason is a little simpler than just the well-being of the ghost. After a while, they would become incapable of using the surface personas. It wouldn't load. No more empty space for it."

"Wait. The capacity for absorbing information—"

"Intellectual information. Details to supplement information already present. Facts. Numbers. Memories. Not emotions. Did you ever wonder why you have only so many emotional capacities? I mean, the potential for new knowledge seems almost infinite, but you're born with only so many emotions which mature over time, modify, adapt, acquire texture—but you never wake up one day and learn a brand new one. A different way to use what you have, maybe, but you don't find anything beyond what you've always had. Unless it's the result of dysfunction. You know about people who lack one or more emotions—they're considered aberrations—but you don't know anyone with more emotions than what we know about. Do you?"

"I never thought about it."

"Think about it. Love, hate, envy, joy, despair, resentment, like, dislike—a few others. Everything comes out of a combination of these. The spectrum can be nearly infinite, true, but it can always be described within a finite number of simple states. There are only so many hormones, right?"

"And?"

"And. And so there are cyberlinks. Cerebro-Augmented-Persons. CAPs. There are some who have perfectly normal brains. Most of us have some deficit, usually intellectual. Sometimes there's an emotional disorder, sometimes a perceptual breakdown. Often there's an accompanying emotional omission."

"You mean like one or another emotion doesn't develop?"

"I mean like one or another isn't there. Missing hormone, bad wiring, experiential incapacity." Her voice came evenly, without the frustration Mace felt ought to be infusing each word, and her eyes were dry. But she projected a desolation that choked him, made his eyes sting and his fingers close tightly on the arms of the chair. "Quite often it's a matter of access. The emotion is there, somewhere, but because of the way our brains work—don't work, actually—we never know or feel...we don't connect to it... we can be having that feeling somewhere and never know it...until we can learn it through the augment."

"So when you ask me how...."

"I mean it exactly that way. You tell me you love me. Well, that's... good, I guess. But... I like you, Mace. I enjoy being around you, you're fun, I respect you, I want sex with you, I feel good when I'm with you, I'd like it to continue... but I don't know if I love you because I don't know what that is. I can't find that emotion and all the rest don't add up to it."

"Do you hate?"

"No. Maybe. I fear. I resent. But trying to figure something out from its opposites doesn't really work, does it? Not even for a normal."

"When you listen to music in sensualist, you look like someone in love."

"Do I? It's ecstasy, but it's all internal. I can't make music, I can't give it back. I just experience the sensation and when it's done, it's done. It doesn't generate itself. When I'm not listening to music I don't feel that way about it." She scowled, a quick rictus. "It's hard to describe. That's part of the problem. What is love? Can you tell me? You feel it, you say, but—can you describe it for me?"

"No."

"No. I've read a lot about it. People have been trying to for centuries. Even the best... well, I can do all those things, but it never reaches the level they claim."

"How do you know you don't—"

"I know. I don't. At least not where I can get to it."

"Is that why you offered to run Helen?"

"Partly. She loved you, you say. If so, then it's in that encoding. I could learn from it. Find the connections."

"You said partly."

"Yeah. Partly. The rest was a gift. You've been good to me for no reason I understand. I wanted to give you something. You need... completion. You need to talk to her again, if only to say good-bye. I thought...."

"And you claim you don't know how to love."

"I don't."

"Helen used to say that love is a willingness to sacrifice without reservation."

"This isn't much of a sacrifice."

"Every time you offer someone something you make a sacrifice. Time, resource, feelings."

"That's what Helen said?"

"Once or twice."

"I'd really like to know what that's like."

"Well. It will take a day or two to transfer the data into an augment. I'd want to be careful that nothing got jumbled. We wouldn't want you talking upside down."

The small reluctance that had clung to his decision disappeared when he saw her face become hopeful.

"Thank you," she said.

He climbed from the tube station into a crowded plaza. It was well into midcycle, yet the "closed" sign glowed on Philip's door. Mace pressed the mici and waited, casually scanning the throngs.

"Macefield."

Philip stood aside and waved him in. Mace stepped into the shop and waited for Philip to lock the door.

"Please," Philip indicated that Mace should go into the back.

Cambel waited, seated at the low, round table. Philip's tea service waited in the center of the table.

"Sit down, Macefield."

There was a brittleness about them both that Mace found infectious. He welcomed the delay of Philip's tea ceremony. He accepted the cup, turned it, and sipped.

"Very good," he said and set the cup down. "Well?"

"I brought the data about Hellas Planitia," Cambel said, displaying a disc. She set it on the table. "What do you intend doing? Showing it to Ms. Dollard?"

"I thought I'd show her the personnel images," Mace said, reaching for the disc, "see if one of them might be this Glim Toler."

"It seems, Philip," Cambel said dryly, "that our search has finally produced a result. The only problem is, she doesn't know anything."

Mace looked at her. "You don't sound very excited about it."

She shrugged.

"SA," Philip said. "What did they ask you, Macefield?"

"A list of names," Mace said, still watching Cambel. "They wanted to know if I knew any of them."

"Did they monitor your responses?"

"Biomonitoring? As a matter of fact, they did. I believe I passed, even when I lied." He looked at Philip. "Why?"

"*Did* you know any of the names?"

"Three of them. Glim Toler and Nemily Dollard. I got the impression most of the names were Lunessa, probably a lot of them living on Aea."

"But not all?"

"Several were the usual baseline names—entertainers, politicians, artists, public personalities."

"And the third name you knew?"

"Winston Cavery."

Cambel's expression changed then, from somber to surprised. "What about Oxmire?" she asked.

"No."

"So this could be a fluke."

Cambel frowned. "Mace, did you know Cavery was Lunessa?"

"No, but at the time why would it matter?"

"You checked backgrounds," Philip said, "didn't you?"

"Not at the time, but later. I found nothing in his jacket about his being Lunessa."

"So his name might have been included for a different reason," Cambel said. Her surprise turned to suspicion. "What were they looking for?"

"PolyCarb is interested in this Glim Toler," Mace said. "But he may not be the only one. All Koeln has been asking about is Toler, no one else."

"According to your new friend?"

"Nemily?"

"Do you have another new friend?"

Philip frowned at her.

"Anything else?" Mace asked.

"Cambel told me about the show at 5555," Philip said. "Disturbing."

"That's an understatement," Mace said. "If what we saw is true, something is eating away at infrastructure on Earth. You said something the other day about rumors that entire databases were disappearing? This looked like more than data."

"Did it remind you of anything?"

"Of course. Cassidy, Five-Eight."

"Midline," Cambel added.

"Hellas Planitia," Philip said.

"Do you think they're all connected to what's happening on Earth?"

"Directly?" Philip asked. "No. But if Reese Nagel can find out about it, certainly SA knows, and, we can assume, Lunase. It's not exactly secret tech. We've been playing with some form of molecular solvent for a long time. Back in the Twentieth Century there were efforts to make organisms that would eat specific synthetics. Before the Exclusion, we knew about tailored microtech that could dissolve oil spills, reduce plastics content in landfill—"

"What's landfill?" Cambel asked.

"Garbage," Mace said. "There are sites on Mars. It's being reduced in a similar way to promote greenhouse gases, thicken the atmosphere."

"Exactly," Philip continued. "Rumor suggests that it became a viable weapon at one point, especially for industrial sabotage. Some of it, apparently, got away from them."

"But who'd bring it upwell?" Cambel asked.

"Why would they need to?" Mace said. "We'd be able to make it ourselves."

"It's slightly more complex up here," Philip said. "A lot of our materials are quite dense and exotic. Simple microtech wouldn't be sufficient. We proof against failures by layering the different materials."

"Normally," Mace said. "But the molifiber on Mars was just a glorified tarpaulin."

"And even if it had failed through some inherent weakness, its destruction would have impacted the site minimally. Except during a storm."

Mace cleared his throat. "We always knew it was sabotage—"

"You always believed," Cambel said. "I didn't believe until the cover-up. The company couldn't let it get out that someone might be actively sabotaging our sites. Shareholders get very uneasy about that."

Mace stared at her. "Is that why Helen was there?"

"What do you mean, Macefield?" Philip asked.

"The company claimed Helen Croslo was never at Hellas Planitia. But they accepted my signature on her death certificate. They never told me—or anyone—where exactly she was supposed to have died. Cambel was directed to make sure I understood that the matter was closed, that

I wasn't to dig into it anymore. Cover-up. What the shareholders don't know won't make them nervous. The company knew there was a problem and sent Helen to look into it. That's what she did."

"The company couldn't have known what would happen," Cambel said.

"I'm sure they didn't expect her to die. The nature of the sabotage couldn't be known. At least, not the way it was conducted. When Helen failed to prevent it, my presence complicated matters. I suppose if I hadn't managed to get myself to Mars and make contact with her, I would have received a standard notice of death. Accident in space, wherever."

"It's taken you this long to figure that all out?" Cambel asked, her voice strained.

"No. But now I understand that maybe she was chasing someone as well as some*thing*. Was Glim Toler on Mars?"

"Ask your new friend."

"Let's assume he was," Philip interjected. "What would that tell us? That the company knew about him then?"

"They might not have had a name then," Mace said. "Maybe they expected it to be internal. A company employee, higher up the chain. Someone had to get Toler in and cover for him. Toler might be nothing but a gun. Someone else pulled the trigger."

"And that person is still in place?" Cambel asked.

"If we're looking at a pattern," Mace said, "starting at Hellas Planitia, then Cassidy, then Five-Eight...."

"And now Midline," Philip continued, "then perhaps it's become untenable. Getting too close to home, maybe. A name has surfaced. I suspect SA brought you in, Macefield, because of all the senior staff that was at Hellas Planitia, you and Cambel are the only ones on Aea."

"No," Mace said, "Piers Hawthorne was there, too."

"Only as an insurance adjuster," Cambel said. "His involvement was limited. Mine was...."

"Disciplinary," Mace said. "You were there to reprimand me and make sure I hadn't fouled up the investigation. But as soon as you could, you dragged me back to Burroughs, then got the order to bottle me up and keep me out."

"Do either of you know if Piers has been questioned by SA?" Philip asked.

"I haven't spoken to Piers since the day after the party," Mace said. "You?"

"Not since he invited me," Cambel said.

"We need to find out how the microtech is getting in," Mace said.

"How much contraband did you get past InFlux while you worked there?" Cambel asked. "How does Philip acquire his merchandise? How do any of us get vacuum?"

"Of course," Mace snapped, "but you assume then that whatever this destructive agent is, it's coming through as common vacuum."

"Not necessarily," Philip said. "We're talking about a tailored tech that can attack specific materials. Materials that more often than not have no public specifications, which cannot be analyzed outside a very well-equipped lab. So the primary problem is breaking down the molecular stucture to see how to design this presumed solvent. The chief component is going to be the analysis and design coding of the microtech."

"Information," Mace said.

"Exactly."

"It's necessary to know how a given material is put together before you can efficiently take it apart," Mace mused. "If we're looking at a pattern of sabotage—I assume we are now—then we need to know what materials are being attacked."

"That's difficult," Cambel said. "After all, the samples have all been eaten."

"But we can make some guesses," Philip said. "Most of the material that goes into seals and insulation come from Lunase. They've been the primary providers of exotic materials since the Exclusion."

"Glim Toler is Lunessa," Mace said. "We know now that Cavery was also. Did they know each other?"

"Just *being* Lunessa doesn't make someone a criminal," Cambel said. "Unless you think your new friend is part of this."

Mace bit back a sharp reply. Cambel's attitude puzzled him. She was baiting him, but he did not see why. "If she is," he said slowly, "it's not conscious. But, Philip, the molifiber on Mars was Aean, not Lunessa."

Philip smiled thinly. "Aea—specifically, PolyCarb—manufactured it, but the material was a Lunessa design."

"Sold or stolen?" Cambel asked.

"A large use fee was paid several months after the accident, by

PolyCarb, to a Lunessa manufactory. It was larger than it should have been."

"Let me guess," Mace said, "the firm that held the original patent. Damn. PolyCarb pilfered the formula and set up a line to make it."

"So," Cambel said, "the incident at Hellas Planitia was retaliatory? But how could Lunase sanction something like that? It's terrorism."

Philip opened his hands wide. "Publicly, they couldn't. But it would not be the first time in history a government fielded a covert operation that it was prepared to deny once its ends were achieved."

"The trade talks," Mace said. "They'd been suspended the year before Hellas Planitia. They resumed a few months later."

"And they're still going on," Philip said. "I understand Lunase is being intractable over certain manufacturing issues. Their alchemists are demanding monopolies. Of course, the greater system can't sanction that, so we continue, deadlocked."

"Then Cassidy, Five-Eight, and Midline...."

Mace sat back, staring at the ceiling. They had often talked about Hellas Planitia, spun elaborate theories, most of which had gone nowhere because they lacked any real anchor to which the random facts they gathered might attach. Now they had a name, and action by SA and PolyCarb to highlight that name, and—that fast—the theories came together. Mace could not help but think they should have seen this before. Patterns often become meaningful only in hindsight.

Helen had gone to Mars, to Hellas Planitia, looking for Glim Toler. Perhaps she had not even known his name, but something prompted PolyCarb to divert her flight home from Ganymede and send her there. They had known something might happen.

"So what would Ms. Dollard be doing in all this?" Cambel asked.

"Why would she be doing anything?" Mace asked.

"Philip explained to me what you asked him about how cyberlinks are set up. Specifically the way Nemily Dollard is wired. Think about it, Mace. She's the perfect trojan. She could bring something in and not know it. Never know it. Unless someone else has the program to bring it to the surface. If we're talking about data, a recipe, then—"

"The vacuum she brought in would have been a diversion...."

"Or the key to the program."

"I'm not sure I follow you."

Cambel scowled. "When did you get so dense? Think it through,

Mace. Someone—Glim Toler, by her own admission—plants vacuum on her and sends her here with it. She gets searched at Port Authority, the vacuum gets impounded. What then would normally happen to it?"

"Officially, it goes into storage for later analysis and possible inclusion in Aea's public database. But the reality is that the vacuum just gets in by other channels. Favors, private trade among InFlux employees, other means."

"And if it were a prearranged delivery? One person, in the right place, could intercept it."

Mace nodded. "Nemily would get kicked back to Lunase—"

"Or not, depending on what happens at immigration. Say if one of the Port Authority inspectors is also Lunessa and is waiting for her."

"That might be impossible to track down," Mace said. "It doesn't matter at the moment, we have a name. Glim Toler is here. Does that mean it's time to destroy Aea?"

"He needs to be found," Philip said. "The trade negotiations are stalling again. Midline has everyone involved scared and uncooperative."

"We don't even know what he looks like," Cambel said.

Mace held up the disc Cambel had brought. "If he's in here, Nemily can identify him."

"Assuming she's not part and parcel of the whole thing."

"What would you suggest, then? Maybe I should beat it out of her?"

"She might like that."

"What's your problem, Cambel?"

"Mine? What about yours?"

"My problem? I have a problem?"

"Yes, I think you do."

"Please—" Philip raised his hands.

"No, wait," Cambel said. "I need to know something. Are you still interested in seeing this through, Mace? Or would you rather curl up in your dom with Ms. Dollard and just let the rest of us fumble along as best we can? Because all of a sudden now everything we've been poking into for the last couple of years is coming back at us. I think we need to know if you're all the way involved or if you just want to run away. Or if maybe you have a conflict."

"What the hell—? Why are you so pissed at me?"

"Pissed at you. You think I'm pissed at you?" She stared at him for long, furious moment, her mouth working as if trying to dislodge some-thing from her teeth. "Damn you. Nearly three years now you've been all wrapped up inside your own little obsessions and now that you've decided that it's too boring in there you want to know why some other people have some feelings."

"Cambel," Philip said.

"Don't," Cambel snapped at Philip. "This doesn't concern you. Not this part."

"Why is this so important to you?" Mace asked. "Helen was *my* wife."

"This isn't about Helen!" She narrowed her eyes. "You don't know, do you? You really don't know. Well, we never talked about it. You spent so much time drowning your conscience any way you could. Maybe if I'd come right out and—" She pressed her lips shut. "You work with some-one, you get close... I don't know why I'm surprised." She looked down at her hands. "Maybe I'm not." She looked up. "They didn't just fuck you, Mace. When they made you sign Helen's death certificate, they made me take it to you. From then on it wasn't just you. I felt respon-sible. I tried to help. I tried to make it up. I tried to find out why Poly-Carb did that to you and they threatened me with transfer. So I resigned. When you came out of your stupor, I was there. Did you think that was just coincidence? I've spent as much if not more time working on this than you. Did you think that was just because I had nothing better to do? When you started talking about quitting, it hurt, but I couldn't argue with your logic. But it hurt anyway. It matters to me. I didn't want you to settle with PolyCarb, but I understood it. Now things have changed again and maybe there's a chance to see it through. But seeing it through might get your new friend expelled. So I need to know—is this still important to you?"

"Still? No. It is again. I need to finish this."

"How finished?"

"Finished. Over. Finished with Helen, finished with what happened, finished with the search."

"And afterward?"

Mace studied her face for a hint of what she wanted. But Cambel's masks, when she used them, were flawless and unrevealing.

"We have a good partnership," he said. "I don't want to see that change."

"Oh." She nodded slowly. "I see. All right. As long as I know where I stand."

"Cambel, I don't—"

She stood. "You might want to use Philip's system to go over those. Yours is compromised."

Mace watched her wander off toward one of the cabinets. She folded her arms and stared down at the display.

"Macefield?"

Mace looked at Philip. "I don't understand."

"It's difficult sometimes for people who work together to be clear about their feelings."

Mace stared at him. "Oh."

"Can't be helped, I suppose." Philip cleared his throat quietly. "How do you propose to proceed?"

"With the investigation, you mean? We can't overlook the possibility that Toler wasn't the one. At least, not the only one."

"We have an incomplete body count from Hellas Planitia," Philip said. "There was also the murdered cyberlink you found in the tunnel."

"Cyberlink," Mace repeated. "Why murdered? What if she were part of it, why kill her? And the other body, the unaugmented one."

"Witnesses," Philip said. "Especially the cyberlink. What she saw, what she knew, would be part of her augmentation."

"The missing augment?"

"And the missing site recorder. Both may have identified Toler before this."

"He'd still need a way out. He'd need a connection outside the site."

"Cavery?" Philip suggested.

"Security would be logical, but not necessarily the best. You'd look at that first."

"He was on Midline, though. Was he on either of the other two?"

"Cassidy," Cambel said, returning to the table, "but only for a day, transferring to Midline. He was never on Five-Eight."

Mace licked his lips. He wanted to pace, expend the nervous energy being fed by logic. "Any one of them could be it...."

"True, they all had access," Cambel said. "Helen had the most opportunity."

Mace felt himself wince inside. "Do we know if anyone visited and left the site before the incident?"

"No. No, we don't know, but...."

"Why would you say Helen?"

"Helen was ambitious. Maybe they made her an irrefusable offer."

"She loved Aea, though...to hurt it...."

Cambel grunted unsympathetically. "People change. You have."

"Why are you being so—?"

"My career was ruined over this, Mace, and now this search has gotten me threatened with expulsion. I'm not inclined toward kindness concerning anyone who might have done it or been involved in it."

"You believe Helen did it?"

"She was there, she had opportunity, she traveled widely, and she turned up missing. If Glim Toler was there and he's part of this, that connects her to him. We never found her body and Toler got out alive. How does that sum for you?"

"Which also means she might still be alive."

"Not legally. But yes. If Toler was there and he's here now, then he survived. If he did, then she could have. And they killed some people on the way out."

Mace closed his eyes. Instead of revenge or justice for Helen or some kind of memorial by revelation for her, everything turned wrong, and he saw her as criminal. It made no sense, it made every sense.

He sighed. "There still had to be someone who could get people into positions and cover up their records. Helen might have, but she was too distant from that kind of direct management at Hellas Planitia. Besides, someone else is still inside because someone is using Helen's name to import Lunessa through InFlux. We find Toler, we find the trojan."

Mace called his dom to tell Nemily where he was and to ask her to join him. Her voice came back, a recorded message. "Mace, I need to get some of my belongings and take care of some details. I'll be back, I promise." He doubted SA or PolyCarb would pick her up again, but he still felt uneasy about it. He called her dom, but she did not answer. He could have missed her there already.

He scrolled steadily through the files from Hellas Planitia, faces and profiles he had not looked at in years. It amazed him how much data he remembered upon seeing each face—also how much he had forgotten. Birth dates, points of origin, security levels he remembered only imperfectly, but a lot of the personal interests came back to him completely. What sort of collecting they were interested in, if any, their taste in food, pharmocopiates, political opinions—all that came back forcefully. It was the quirks that made for security risks.

He stopped at an image of a man with a slight double chin and pale eyebrows. "Cru Mills" the name read, from Elfor, thirty-six years old. It was an expressionless image, as if the man had been drugged when he had posed for it. He had very few personal quirks—a dull, stable type, with no politics, no real vices, no worthwhile history. Utterly forgettable.

Except that Mace saw familiarity now. He stared at the face and tried to be certain. The lighting made it difficult—the portrait illumination was flat, almost shadowless. Other things...adapt treatments changed faces as much as physiques.

The more he stared, though, the more certain he became. He needed Nemily here to confirm, but he was almost sure that Cru Mills was Glim Toler and that this was the man he had seen at Piers Hawthorne's party, in the hallway, and down the stairs, the house guest Piers denied having.

"Philip," he called. "Cambel."

THIRTEEN

AEA, 2118

MACE MOVED THE FINELY MADE CHESS PIECES around the board, following no particular pattern, watching the light flow around them. He looked up when Philip came out of the back room.

"Cambel is going through the InFlux records you accessed," Philip said.

"Piers isn't answering his comm," Mace said.

Philip sat opposite him, reached out, and moved a piece. "It might be better to wait before confronting him. There could be another explanation."

"Of course there could. I agree, though. I don't want Toler warned or panicked. I want to know where he is first."

"I confess I still don't see the connections."

"What? Between Piers and Toler? Neither do I." Mace moved a bishop, making a mental note to ask Cambel to do a deep background check on Piers.

"It's for sale if you like it," Philip said.

"Tempting. Would you visit me to play a game?"

"If invited, certainly."

Mace picked up one of the kings. The interstellars had left two decades ago. Eleven years afterward, contact ceased. The tentative plans to build more of them now remained tentative.

"It would be something," Philip said, "to be with them. To see what they have seen."

Mace replaced the piece.

"Why would Lunase indulge in mass murder?" he asked.

"SetNetComb emerged out of a harsh beginning. Perhaps they see it as war. A matter of survival."

"Out here, we all survive or none of us do."

"Define 'us.'"

"It's been over seventy years since the Exclusion."

"So, I suppose, we should all have outgrown the trauma of those times? Perhaps. Perhaps most have. But there always seem to be a few who never let go of their fears."

"Like me," Mace said.

"Why would you say that? I've never known you to be fearful."

"I hide it well, don't I? Do you know why I'm here, now, on Aea? Because I was afraid not to be. I signed off on Helen's death—*alleged* death—because I didn't want to be stranded on Mars. Or anywhere else."

"Do you consider that an act of cowardice?"

"Maybe."

"You've continued searching. You've challenged PolyCarb. You've probed—"

"Not very aggressively. I've been waiting for evidence to fall into my lap. And when PolyCarb made it clear that I risked losing everything I'd gained, I backed off."

"Is this fear or prudence?"

"It's hard to tell the difference sometimes. It takes a last act to decide."

"Have you made a last act?"

"I went to Piers' party. I met someone."

Philip frowned. "Meaning?"

"I let go. I gave up."

"On Helen."

"On Helen."

"That was inevitable, though, wasn't it?"

Mace felt a spike of anger and impatience. "I had one goal growing up. Get off Mars. It's hard to explain how much I hated it. The place bored me. Constantly. When it became obvious that the only skill I had was finding holes in systems and closing them, I thought I might be able to use that to finally emigrate. But it wasn't the sort of thing you put on a resumé. I went to security work, thinking at some point I might get a chance to show someone what I could do, someone who could help me. When I met Helen, that was still my main priority. Leave Mars at all cost."

"So you married her to become an Aean."

"That's right."

"Did she understand that?"

"Better than I did, I think."

"So where's the betrayal? If she knew, then she wasn't deceived."

"No, she wasn't. I was."

"I'm not sure I follow."

"Helen . . . knew me better than anyone ever did. Even now. She knew what I wanted and she didn't care. I thought I wanted her, too. I thought I was in love. I couldn't get enough of her. But she was so clear about our relationship, I started thinking the same way. At least partly. She liked me, she said. I thought I was in love with her. But I thought the main reason was because she was getting me off Mars. I was grateful more than anything else. Devoted, loyal. Anything else was extra."

"Like love?"

"It was easy to think that way with Helen. She was away so much for the company. I had duties. It seemed ideal, for both of us. Imagine my surprise when after she died I realized that the main thing had been her all along."

"How did you realize it?"

"After I signed her death certificate. You wouldn't believe the guilt."

Philip nodded. "I think I would."

"A month back on Aea, it all came home. I missed her. I'd betrayed her. I got what I always said I wanted, but it wasn't what I wanted anymore."

"And now?"

Mace shrugged, pressing his lips together.

"So what has been the purpose of the search?" Philip asked after a time. "Such as it's been."

"Moral painkiller."

"Harsh."

"Oh, it gets better. Now I have to wonder if I'd stayed in the company and kept pushing and digging, asking questions, I might not have prevented Cassidy and Five-Eight."

"Don't even imagine that," Philip said sharply. "A person's responsibility is equal to his ability to respond. Taking on blame for things impossible to manage is simple self-pity and a waste of time."

Mace flinched. "Now who's being harsh?"

"Not harsh. Practical. Guilt slows us down, makes us stupid sometimes. We can't get rid of it entirely, but we shouldn't take on extra. Not if you want to resolve anything."

"That's a good question, isn't it? Do I want to resolve anything?"

"Do you?"

Mace opened his mouth to answer, but Cambel leaned into the room. "We have a partial match," she announced. "A place to start, at least. An address."

The address Cambel had found was for an assemblage in segment four, assigned housing for one Kev Eiler. Cambel also found a Kev Eiler listed as an employee of Tower Enterprises—a Lunessa and a CAP, resident of Aea for the last two years. But the Kev Eiler on the InFlux jacket—the one who matched Mace's memory of the man at Piers' party—had just arrived within the last eight days.

No new address was listed for Kev Eiler. Mace found it difficult to believe that he had been unable to secure better quarters in two years, working for a company like Tower. Philip volunteered to make a few inquiries among people he knew at Tower, but it might take time. Mace did not expect Kev Eiler to be found, at least not alive. Someone had stepped into his identity. Toler, he guessed.

Kev Eiler's assemblage seemed deserted when Mace entered. Vacant hallways, quiet and covered by a layer of debris that showed footprints. He walked softly till he came to the correct door....

...Which stood open, wide enough to see that the room was unoccupied. Mace pushed the door wider with one finger and stepped inside.

Two meters by three, with fold-down table, cot and chair, and a toilet in one corner behind a stiff plastic flap, the only details that indicated human presence were the duffle beneath the cot and a jacket draped over the chair. Mace sat down on the cot and pulled the duffle out between his feet. It contained more clothes, a hygiene kit, a portable reader with a number of discs in its cache and a handful of unexchanged credit vouchers, all bearing Lunessa finance logos, all of them different denominations. He found nothing in the jacket.

He found no ID of any kind, nothing to indicate who occupied this space.

He moved to the chair, then, gazing around the room, hoping to recognize something that might give him direction, a hint where to look, how to proceed. Perhaps Toler would come back. But the open door suggested that the unit had either already been searched or had simply been abandoned. Maybe Koeln had already been through it. Except for the vouchers, nothing appeared to be worth coming back for.

Koeln would not have left the door ajar. The vouchers, perfectly useful as vacuum, were still here.

Mace felt slow, like a long unused machine.

He went through the cabinets. Packaged food, cans—picked through. People had been here, taken a few things. But not the jacket?

He pushed the duffle back under the cot and left. He went quietly down the hall, rounded the corner, and stopped. He leaned against the wall and waited.

A few minutes later he heard steps. He eased forward to peer around the corner in time to see a young man slip into the room.

Mace covered the distance in seconds.

The boy looked up in shock, the jacket in his hands.

Mace closed the door.

"I—"

"I'm not SA," Mace said quickly. "Who lives here?"

"No one. I mean—" The boy swallowed hard, looking down at the jacket. "Was a man. He hasn't been back in days."

"That your jacket?"

The boy nodded. Then, looking guilty, he shrugged and shook his head.

Mace pulled a picture of Kev Eiler/Glim Toler from his pocket. "This man?"

The boy blinked at it, then frowned. "No. He came by, though."
"When?"

"Four, five days ago."

"The one who did live here. Have you seen him since?"
"No."

"How long did you wait before you started pilfering?"

"I'm not—!"

"Don't lie. I'm not SA, but I can have them here in minutes. I'm not interested in you or what you're taking; I'm interested in this man." Mace returned the picture to his pocket. "How long?"

"Yesterday."

"And you haven't seen either man in how long?"

"Four, five days."

Mace considered for a few moments. "Did you see both men together?"

"No. That one came."

"How long since you saw the man who's supposed to be here?"

"Seven, eight days. Longer maybe."

"Huh. That's interesting."

"Does it help?"

Mace studied the boy. Tall, thin. Officially, no poverty existed on Aea. The boy did not look undernourished so much as constantly nervous, under stress.

"Yeah," Mace said. "It helps." He pointed. "There are Lunessa credit vouchers in that duffle. Be careful, you can sell them in the Heavy."

The boy glanced at the cot, eyes wide, then back at Mace.

Mace left him in the room, closing the door as he exited.

In the lobby, three men waited. Mace recognized them immediately—not who they were, but what they were: local vigilantes-cum-vacuum dealers-cum-self-appointed protection. Mace was surprised they had waited this long to confront him. He checked how much room he had to move, their sizes and positions. Two of them looked like muscle, which meant the third man made the judgments.

"You," the smallest one said, jabbing a finger at him. "What do you want here?"

"No trouble," Mace said. "I'm looking for someone."

"Do they know?"

One of the larger men moved to Mace's left. Mace pointed at him. "Don't."

The man hesitated.

"I don't work for anyone," Mace said. "Not corporate, not Structural Authority."

"Oh? You just do this sort of thing yourself?"

"This time maybe for you, too." The man on his left began to move again. Mace took a step backward and spoke directly to him. "Powder on steel," he said, using Heavy slang, meaning the man could not take him. "No gain trying."

The other muscle laughed. Their employer smiled.

"SA," he said, "doesn't grace us with security unless they think we're a threat to upshaft. We watch out for each other."

"Good for you."

"Who are you looking for?"

Mace took out the picture. "New arrival," he said extending the print. "Lunessa."

The spokesman stepped closer to study the image. He frowned. "Seen this one. Not much. Why are you looking for him?"

"That's personal."

"Lunessa keep to themselves longer than anybody else. They don't mingle easy. Mostly, they keep to themselves and go to that church they have."

"Where? Is there a Temple chapter near here?"

"No. Outer shell. Arc forty, forty-five maybe."

Mace pocketed the picture. "There was another Lunessa this one was here visiting. Eiler."

"Haven't seen Eiler in days. Seen him, though."

"Did you question him like this?"

The man drew a deep breath. "This is personal, you say?"

"Yes."

"He's armed." He made a shooting gesture with his right hand, two fingers aimed at Mace, thumb angle straight up.

"You're kidding."

The man looked from one bodyguard to the other. "Am I lying?"

Both of the muscle shook their heads.

"I see," Mace said after a pause. "Thank you. May I go now?"

The three stepped back and gave him room. He walked between them, heart racing, his limbs coursing with cool fire, adrenalized. He glanced back once on his way to the shunt station.

No one followed him that he could see.

He caught a shunt antispinward to arc forty-five. There he crossed the platform to the spoke lift and went ring to ring to the outermost, getting off in the Heavy. He asked directions to the Temple of Homo ReImaginoratus. The eighth person he questioned knew roughly where it was.

At the end of a shallow alcove that might once have housed a piece of equipment long dismantled, recycled and forgotten, Mace found the broad entryway to the Temple, marked only by a yellow lemniscate superimposed on a blue triangle. Though clean of the signs of neglect, it looked sadly anachronistic, from a time when mysticism offered a fashionable alternative to the simple imperatives of survival and arcane symbols (especially newly made ones) evoked an æsthetic response all out of proportion to what they symbolized.

Mace pressed the mici at the center of the lemniscate and waited. People passing in the circuit beyond gave him curious looks, a few tolerant smiles and one dedicated scowl of disapproval. He pressed it again. When no one answered, he tried the door. Locked.

"Now what?" he muttered, turning away. Perhaps he could get comm access to it. That in mind, he started back to the circuit.

"Mr. Preston. I didn't think we would actually meet until tomorrow morning."

From a narrow doorway set in the wall to the right of the main entrance Linder Koeln looked out at him.

Mace stood in the center of the sanctuary and surveyed the walls, the icons and emblems, the tall-backed chairs, the pedestals, columns and obelisks etched with signs and ornate lettering, the dais and podium, the painting of Gaia adorning the rear of the sacristy, the sconces, standards and other detritus of ritual. The domed ceiling glittered with constellations; the same symbol adorning the main door covered the floor. The light, the vague scent of soil and cedar, and the chill temperature combined into an æsthetic fog of representative illusion.

The room was slightly disarrayed, chairs moved, a sconce fallen to the floor.

"What do you think?" Koeln asked as he went around straightening chairs.

"It's not what I expected." Mace gestured. "Untidy."

"Someone's been here looking for something," Koeln said, raising the fallen sconce. "There's evidence of searching in the other rooms as well."

"Any idea who?"

Koeln shook his head. "Not a Lunessa. This kind of disrespect, even for a disbeliever, is highly unlikely."

"Are you a believer? Is that why you're contaminating a crime scene?"

"Crime scene?" He smiled thinly. "I'm witness enough. Unless some reason can be found for the vandalism, SA won't take an interest. But no, I'm not a believer anymore. That doesn't mean I'm disrespectful. You've never been inside a ReImaginoratus Temple before?"

"No. There's no chapter on Mars, at least not one I'm aware of."

"That seems strange to me. But then, I grew up with them."

"Do you still attend?"

"Oh, no. I broke with all this when I came here. Many Lunessa do."

"Why is that?"

"In my case, I couldn't seem to maintain the proper frame of mind here, on Aea. In Lunase it's easier. There, this is all a bright place in a hole full of sameness."

"So Aea's not dull enough?"

"Something like that. The religion itself is laced with nostalgia about Earth and how wonderful it was and how somehow we are no longer worthy of that wonderfulness. Then you arrive here and learn that things can be wonderful anyway. The nostalgia remains very strong, though. I think that's really why most people attend. Those who do, at least."

"I thought it was required."

"Socially, at least in Lunase, it has benefits. But there's no law." He pointed at different wall hangings. "You can see by the symbolism that it's an amalgam of other sects. Judaism, Catholicism, Masonry, Islam. All those orders still have small followings, but in the days immediately after the Exclusion, when it seemed that we might all die, I think people wanted to be more together than apart."

"'Man Reimagined'?"

Koeln shrugged. "I don't pretend to understand the mysteries. A new being is necessary for life off the Earth, one that combines nature's evolution with the evolution that is to come. Something like that. But what matters is that it gave us a center, a point of reference. It filled a need."

"Vacuum."

Koeln smiled. "That's very cynical, but yes, in a way. Black-market religion. Borrowed from Earth and redistributed according to different necessities. Just like everything else out here."

"You sound like you miss it."

"I miss the innocence that permitted belief. I miss the purpose of devotion. I miss the thrill of the rituals when they meant something to me. But things pass. We grow. It's sad to think of it all becoming fanatic and desperate." He shook his head and sighed. "So what brings you here, Mr. Preston?"

"Probably the same thing that brought you here. Glim Toler."

"Ah. So you *are* acquainted with him?"

"No. I'd never heard his name until you introduced it to me. Now it seems everything keeps forcing me to pay attention to him. Is that what you wanted to see me about?"

"Partly, yes. I've been investigating an internal PolyCarb problem. His name came up. It attached itself to an employee of ours—"

"Nemily Dollard."

"—yes, her. And when I looked into her past, I found your dead wife's name on both her jacket and Glim Toler's."

"InFlux jackets."

Koeln nodded absently. "And that led me to you. You seemed a natural suspect."

"Suspect for what? Data theft? I don't do that. Any data I traffic in is acquired legitimately."

"That's what you tell your clients anyway, I'm sure."

Mace laughed softly. "*I* don't steal it and neither do my people."

"Hmm. In any event, you're now looking for Toler as well. What about Ms. Dollard?"

"What about her?"

"Where is she?"

"I don't really know right now."

Koeln studied him for a time. "Do you have any idea why your wife's name is being used to sponsor Lunessa immigrants?"

"Is that all it's being used for?"

"As far as I know," Koeln said.

"Someone has a tasteless sense of humor, perhaps."

"I doubt it was an accidental choice."

"Perhaps Glim Toler can tell us," Mace suggested.

"Perhaps."

"Did you search his dom?"

"No, not yet."

"Don't bother. He hasn't been there. This seemed the next most likely place."

"Well," Koeln sighed, "there's no one here, either. Not even the patri."

"Is that unusual?"

"Very. Her office has been searched, too."

"Should we alert SA?"

Koeln shook his head. "If they start running around down here, they could alert whoever may be responsible for her absence. It could prove more troublesome than useful."

"You're not worried that she might be harmed?"

"No Lunessa would hurt a patri of the Temple."

"You're sure about that?"

"Absolutely."

"I'll have to take your word for it, then." Mace watched the man. Koeln was difficult to read. So far their conversation had not gone the way Mace had expected. "What brought you here today? Nostalgia?"

"Related business."

"And none of mine?"

"You don't work for us anymore, Mr. Preston."

"I see. Related to Toler, though, I imagine. Let's see. He's Lunessa. Odds are he might come here to connect with other Lunessa. The patri might know him or know of him."

"The thought did occur to me."

"Is there any history of the Temple being used as a front for terrorists?"

Koeln stared at him. "That's a long leap to a conclusion."

"I'm a Martian. We're used to talking long strides."

Koeln laughed. "No, Mr. Preston, there is no such history. But it's not out of the question."

"How long has PolyCarb known that Helen's name was being used?"

"It only came to my attention when this Toler question came up."

Mace wondered how the Toler question had come up, but doubted Koeln would tell him. "So it may have been in the files for a long time before anyone actually noticed."

"You know how it works."

"I do. Of course, Nemily immigrated two and half years ago, well after Helen's death. She couldn't have done it, then. Not for Nemily Dollard, not for Glim Toler. Ergo, there's a third person involved."

"That's an obvious conclusion," Koeln said.

"And you think I might be that third person?"

"Personally, no. But I have to follow up all possibilities. I am curious why you resigned. I know you didn't believe your wife had died. You made it very clear you thought PolyCarb was hiding something about her death. If it had been me, I would have stayed inside in order to find out what."

"Yeah, well, that wasn't about to work either."

"And now?"

"I settled with PolyCarb."

"But you haven't stopped looking."

"How do you know?"

"You're here."

Mace made a slow survey of the sanctuary. "The patri isn't here. What are you going to do next?"

"I'm not sure. Do you have any suggestions?"

"We're looking for a Lunessa. This is the first logical stop. Time to move on to the next one."

"Reese Nagel?"

Through midcycle, Reese's venue attracted no attention, the plain façade with its unremarkable numbers much the same as any other part of the bulkhead. People flowed by without noticing it. Until the doors opened and the overadapted gatekeepers took their positions, 5555 did not exist.

Mace excused himself before they reached the door. He crossed the circuit to a public commlink and punched in his dom code. Nemily had still not returned, nor did she answer at her own dom. Mace rejoined Koeln at the entrance to 5555.

After the third mici, the smaller access door opened a crack and a face peered out. Mace recognized her, the one who had been Reese's personal muscle—two nights ago?—what was her name...?

"Colf. Is Reese in?"

"What for?" Her voice was startlingly small for her size.

"Talk."

"Then no."

"Now or later," Koeln said. "Later we come with SA."

Colf narrowed her eyes at him, but retreated, opening the door further. She led them down a close passage, three meters, and into a space that once had contained maintenance equipment. The walls still showed the shapes of the cabinets, the holes for retaining bolts, the faded and torn lettering describing tools or procedures. Carpeted now, four chairs lined one wall, and a small monitor filled the corner above and to the left of the inside door.

"Wait," Colf said and left them.

"What interests me—"

Mace casually tapped his ear and gave a small shake of the head.

"I've never been here before," Koeln went on smoothly. "Is it worth the trouble?"

"It's unique. I've only been here once myself."

The door opened again and Colf waved them through into the main area.

Unpeopled, the club space looked smaller. The ringed area in which the projection had been was less than three meters across. The topography of raised platforms cramped it even more and its original design as some sort of control room, now stripped of its consoles and monitors and the energy of its first purpose, gave it an abandoned look, uncompensated by the presence of tables and a long bar and new bright colors on the bulkheads.

Colf took them across the floor, then up to Reese's office.

Reese sat behind his broad desk, eyes on a flatscreen, one hand tapping occasionally on a keyboard. His gaze shifted to his guests, lingering a moment on Mace, who nodded in greeting, and locking on Koeln for the entire time it took to reach the chairs.

"A moment," Reese said and his attention returned to the screen.

Colf stood just inside the door.

Abruptly, Reese drew a sharp breath, stabbed his keyboard dramatically, and the screen disappeared into the desktop. He smiled.

"May I offer you anything to drink? To eat?"

"You may offer us an explanation," Koeln said. "The local Temple has been tossed. Patri Simity, the rector, is missing. What do you know about it?"

"Not on the menu. Anything else?"

"I can bring a Structural Authority mandate and team here later if you like."

"You can and they still wouldn't be on the menu. I don't have them."

"'Them?'" Koeln said.

"You didn't search the Temple?" Mace asked.

"No." Reese smiled thinly. He raised his hands. "What can I tell you? The truth would be best, so I'll tell you the truth. I know nothing about Patri Simity's whereabouts."

"I find that difficult to believe," Koeln said.

"Why?"

"I don't think very much of anything happens in the Heavy that you don't know about," Koeln said. "Consider that a compliment."

Reese tipped his head in mock gratitude. "I still don't know anything about this one. Frankly, Patri Simity's and I don't share much in the way of interests."

"There was someone here the other night," Mace said, "someone who came in the company of an invited guest. Did you invite Patri Simity?"

"I always invite Patri Simity. She rarely comes—"

"But," Mace said, "you have few shared interests."

"It never hurts to be cordial to the important people in your community."

"Did she come two nights ago?" Koeln asked.

"Yes. . . ."

"And she brought a guest. A visitor, someone just arrived through InFlux. Who was it?"

"I don't make a habit of grilling my guests about their guests—"

"Glim Toler. Wasn't it?"

Reese hesitated a few moments too long.

"So," Mace continued, "Toler was staying at the Temple and Patri Simity brought him along to your event. Sometime between then and this morning, the Temple has been searched and Patri Simity has gone missing. Since you're already connected to Toler in other matters, it seems likely that you'd know about this. A moment ago you said you didn't know anything about 'them'—Simity and Toler? Toler was staying at the Temple?"

Reese sighed. "You're making a lot of assumptions."

"And you're not telling me anything to make those assumptions go away," Mace said.

"What is your interest in Toler?" Koeln asked.

"None. He's a low-grade vacuum dealer and a troublemaker. I had intended to talk to him, explain how things are, especially in the Heavy. That's why Patri Simity brought him around. Too many Lunessa come through InFlux with only the guidebook explanation about Aea. Some-one ought to tell them how it really works."

"You're very generous, Reese," Mace observed.

"I am. I'm glad you noticed."

"Is that because PolyCarb signed an agreement with you for your il-licit datafeed?" Koeln asked.

Reese frowned. "That's not public knowledge."

"It's not even knowledge through most of PolyCarb," Koeln said. "My clearance runs high, though."

Mace whistled. "That was fast."

"Yes, it was fast, but I started negotiations that night with a Poly-Carb representative. A very good offer, excellent terms. And it's all le-gitimate."

"There could be complications with that," Koeln said, "if I'm too dis-appointed."

Reese's mood darkened at once. He stared speculatively at Koeln, as if trying to divine his nature. "You know, I have always made it a policy to do business with my own people whenever possible. In your case I would make an exception."

Mace glanced at Koeln to see if he reacted. Koeln maintained a calm demeanor.

"It's very simple," Koeln said. "If you see, hear of, or find either Patri Simity or Glim Toler, I want to know. Immediately. Then—no complica-tions."

"Stat check?"

"Stat check."

"Done. Next time I see you here...well, I'd rather not. As for you, Mr. Preston, you're welcome anytime, even if you do keep bad company." He leaned back. "By the way, how is Nemily? She didn't call me like she promised."

"She was preoccupied. I'll pass on your concerns."

"No concern. I miss her, that's all. She's a good person."

With that he touched a button and the screen rose out of the desk again. The interview was over. Mace stood to leave.

"I'm curious," he said. "The arrangement with PolyCarb—it will be for distribution?"

"Oh, yes. They aren't fools, they know if they tried to buy me to sit on it I'd just vacuum the thing on the side."

"Which you might do anyway, of course."

"That's unfair. You should ask your partner if she thinks I'd do that. I have a reputation to maintain."

"Of course. Forgive me."

"Not at all, Mr. Preston."

Colf let them out the same way. Outside, in the main circuit, Mace leaned against a bulkhead, watching people pass by. Koeln waited.

"What now?" he asked.

"We can't arrest Reese for no cause," Mace said. "Or can we?"

"I would prefer not to risk alerting Toler."

"What did you think of Reese's opinion, that Toler is just a low-grade vacuum dealer?"

"I think he doesn't know the man well."

"What do you think he is, then?"

"I would rather not speculate for your convenience."

"Do you think he had anything to do with Cassidy?"

Koeln frowned. "In what way?"

Mace snorted. "Just speculating. Whoever sponsored him into Aea did it for a reason. I wondered if you had any idea what that reason might be."

"Frankly, I'd hoped you would answer that question."

"Me."

"Your wife—"

"Oh, right; when she was alive she confided everything to me."

Koeln raised his eyebrows skeptically. "I have details to tend to. What will you do now?"

"Now? Go back to my dom. I have some things to take care of, too."

"Then thank you for your time. I wish to talk to you further. Until then. . . ." Koeln bowed and walked away.

Mace watched him head down the circuit, through the shifting crowds, toward the spoke lift. When he was out of sight, Mace scanned the crowds passing before him, as if by glancing quickly some detail previously hidden might be visible for an instant, caught extruded while his back was to it. A face, a shadow, a door that had not been open when he looked before, anything that called attention to itself that might offer direction. In the absence of a clear way, he fell back on the instincts learned early, on Mars, that allowed him to take advantage of chance. It meant waiting for things, watching to catch a glimpse of the important sign, and doing nothing till then because there was nothing to do. Usually, when he looked, there was nothing to find.

Koeln bothered him. After teasing at it for a few minutes, he went back to 5555.

Colf did not question his return, only let him in and took him back to Reese's office.

"It's been so long, Mr. Preston," he said.

"I won't keep you, Mr. Nagel. I wondered how long you've known Koeln."

"Practically since he came here. Four, almost five years ago."

"Has he been here before?"

"Not in some time, but he once frequented my establishment quite often. If you're wondering whether or not to trust him, I can only say that I've never liked him. He's efficient and aloof. He's in many ways a walking cliché—everything a good Lunessa is supposed to be."

"Except for neglecting Temple."

"Most Lunessa give that up after they come here."

"You really don't know where Simity is? Or Toler?"

"No, I really don't. I would appreciate knowing that she's all right. Patri Simity is a good influence in the Heavy. She makes it a better place just by being here."

"Toler came here under a different name. Kev Eiler. Mean anything to you?"

Reese shook his head slowly.

"Eiler is missing, too," Mace said.

Reese frowned. "I really would like to help you, Mr. Preston, but...."

"Things are complicated enough without taking on more?"

"Exactly."

"Thank you again for your time."

"May I ask a personal question?"

"Go ahead."

"Are you involved with Nemily Dollard?"

"What if I am?"

"She worked for me once. She's a kind person, but with certain obvious handicaps. I'd like to know that she's being cared for."

Mace stared at him, startled. It was not the question he had expected.

"She's missing, too," Mace said. "I have to go find her now."
Reese only nodded, but he did not look pleased.
"Thanks again," Mace said. He followed Colf out once more.

FOURTEEN

AEA, 2118

"A NEW CAFÉ OPENED IN THE MALL, Spengler's. We're all going to initiate it for lunch."

Nemily's collation completed and she popped out the augment. The words Tara had just spoken seemed to echo suddenly, sound-shapes without content, repeated aural modulations looking for a place to make sense. Nemily quickly inserted her synthesist and the echoing stopped.

"I'm sorry," she said, "I didn't retain that. You caught me between—"

"A new café," Tara said, with exaggerated care, as if Nemily were unfamiliar with the language. Though she knew that in Tara's case it came out of short-term frustration and not prejudice, it still scraped across her nerves. "In the Mall. Spengler's. Lunch, initiation, us, going. Do you want?"

"No, I don't think so," Nemily said more sharply than she intended. She saw Tara frown. "I've got things to take care of. Maybe another time."

"Can I help?"

Nemily looked up in surprise. She never got used to the occasional failure of her rebuffs on Aea. In Lunase, her words, her tone, her body language would all have been sufficient to turn anyone away. But "leave me alone" did not seem to mean the same thing to Aeans. She knew that, but it still startled her when instead of solitude she received solicitude.

"You never take days off," Tara continued. "I don't remember you taking any personal time. You weren't here yesterday and it was on short notice. Melissa was caught off guard by it and Melissa never gets caught off guard. So...."

Reflexively, Nemily glanced back toward Melissa's office. "So?"

"So now you're acting like this and I wanted to know if there was anything I could do to help. I'm sorry if the offer's unwelcome."

"No, it's not—Tara, thank you, I appreciate that. It's just...."

"Does this have to do with whoever you disappeared with from Piers' party the other night?"

"Guilty," she said.

"If he's hurting you—"

"Just the opposite, actually. And I'm not sure how to take it."

"Ah." Tara smiled as if she understood perfectly and nodded sagely. "Take it as it comes, any way it's offered. Enjoy it while it lasts."

"Lasts?"

"Never expect it to last more than a day, but don't let it go if it doesn't. Let him set the schedule. Unless you get bored." She reached across Nemily's desk and patted her shoulder lightly. "We'll be at Spengler's. If it's as good as I've been hearing from the people in allocations, we may close the place. If you want to talk, you can find me there. Or I'll see you tomorrow."

"Thanks...."

Tara strode across the room with slightly more bounce in her step, as if she had just been given a stipend increase or a merit citation or a genuine compliment. She paused at the door and gave Nemily a coy wave, then disappeared.

While it lasts...?

Nemily believed that dialogue with the unaugmented contained in-built limits that could not be exceeded without prolonged and diligent effort. Meaning came shaded too subtly for easy exchange between two such different forms of wetware, and while she found no problem with the daily level of communication that moved primarily on the surface, when it came to complex interactions she was less confident, convinced that she and they spoke distinct languages with only a coincidentally shared vocabulary and grammar.

Then there was Mace....

There are levels and then there are levels, she thought.

She looked around. She was alone in the office, everyone apparently having gone down to the Mall. She checked her time chop and saw that it was a little past twelve hundred, beginning of midcycle. She had been here a little over four hours already. She had arrived early, deciding to come directly to work from Mace's. She had been a little surprised that security had let her in; she had assumed that her detention would have put her on a list to be kept out, but everthing had gone as it always had and no questions were asked.

She kept a change of clothes in her locker for those occasions when she accepted after-hours invitations from coworkers. The oblique glances she drew as she made her way through the corridors of PolyCarb dressed in her evening wear had added to her anxieties. Her scheduled assignments had been rather full and she realized that no one had done any of her work from the day before. She had linked quickly and been inside the system since.

Now she was finished.

Lunch sounded appealing, but the thought of more of Tara's misdirected concern blunted her appetite. She drummed her fingers idly on the desk, staring at the blank monitor. Before recognizing the decision, Nemily began tapping commands into the keyboard.

Then she was gazing at a sharp-featured woman with a flat chin, wide, thin-lipped mouth, and large blue eyes widely spaced, separated by a long, straight nose. Her hair was short and very blonde and her nostrils very wide. A strong face that seemed to reveal nothing beyond that strength.

"Hello, Helen," Nemily said and began scrolling through the file.

It ended abruptly with a notation of her death, giving a month and year but no day and no location. Beyond that, the file contained little more than a list of dates and places and supervisors, with none of the usual detail found in PolyCarb personnel jackets. All Nemily knew from this was that Helen had been born on Aea, grown up, took employment with PolyCarb IntraSolar, worked her way up from entry-level duties to project management, married Macefield Preston, worked on various projects all through Signatory Space and died of unknown causes in an undisclosed location. Her educational records, merit citations, and promotions flowed by in a smooth, unbroken register of implied substance.

Dismayed, Nemily wondered what to do next. She made a few careful queries until suddenly a prohibition icon came up on the screen.

"So there is more...."

She played with the system for a time, but it quickly became apparent that she needed to be inside to get around the block. It might, she knew, cost her her job...but then if she was being watched anyway, just doing what she had been doing would do that.

Without further thought, she popped out her augment and jacked in.

She made her way almost by instinct. She was outside her diorama, in the system directly, floating among its own virtual iconography—shafts, spheres, cubes, multifaceted constructs with no name. The block resembled a shifting mass of gelatin, roughly spherical, pale green and azure. The moment she connected to it she knew it had a back door. She found it, thrust a feed in, and began loading the contents to a disc. She did not pause to examine any of the data that flowed out. She kept a watch for system securities, but the back door evidently had a protect that shielded access from the system at large. She wondered briefly who had installed it. Nothing responded to her invasion. She felt fragile and invincible at the same time, as if committing suicide in the face of a murderer. *You can't touch me....*

Done, she withdrew and disconnected. She replaced her augment, retrieved the disc, and shut her system down, then left the office and went to her locker. She stuffed the disc in her evening clothes, then packed them into a small bag.

Feeling jittery, she made her way to the Mall in search of Spengler's, vaguely wondering if she would be picked up by security. She glanced up at the balcony, overlooking the patulous arena where she imagined Linder Koeln at his desk, searching for people to question.

She spotted the café near the end of the concourse. Laughter punctuated the din of conversation spilling from it. Nemily veered off, entering another place with fewer people. Self-conscious as she was, she could not cope with solicitous coworkers, who by now probably knew all about her personal dilemma, thanks to Tara.

She took a table near the entrance. No one would notice her sitting alone. Another one of the differences between Aeans and Lunessa in the rules of conduct was that people who sat alone necessarily wanted to be alone. Aeans did not intrude unless they perceived an invitation. Lunessa never left each other alone, despite the nurtured desire of every one of them to be and do exactly that. Watching the easy interactions of the other patrons around her, Nemily saw her transformation from Lunessa to Aean as little more than admitted honesty, a painless abandonment of a lifetime of self-denial. Here she could be what she wanted to be and no one would tell her no. It was easy for them, of course. They risked nothing, because they also did not care. In Lunase, people hid their secret selves for fear of others seeing and disapproving, but here people hid nothing since no one would look anyway unless asked, and then they would only look a little.

Is that what love is? When someone really sees you...?

Hiding in full view, she imagined herself a spy, studying the habits of a community alien to her own. Invisible, she could observe with impunity, search for the public soul of her hosts and steal their valuables while they failed to see her. Unloved, but allowed, she would flee with her spoils and become rich by selling secret tolerance through the vacuum in Lunase.

Lunase? The perversity of her fantasy corrupted its pristine utility, reminding her of what she most feared, that she might have to return to Lunase, where they taught you that mistakes kill and therefore bear the highest penalties.

"Ms. Dollard?"

She flinched involuntarily and looked up at the man standing across from her, his hands resting lightly on the back of the opposite chair.

Not Koeln, she told herself, studying him. He looked familiar. Her heart raced. "Yes?"

He seemed uncertain for a moment, but he smiled. "Piers Hawthorne."

"Piers...oh! I'm sorry, Mr. Hawthorne, I—forgive me, I was...."

"Somewhere else?"

"...daydreaming. I'm sorry. Um...would you care to sit down?"

"Only if I'm not intruding."

"No, not at all. Please."

He pulled the chair out. "Have you eaten yet? I was coming down to see the new place further down and I saw you come in here."

"No, I—if you want to do that instead—"

He waved a hand. "I don't think I'd be able to hear myself eat, from the sound of it." He glanced around until he caught a waiter's eye and motioned him over. "I'd probably just stop in for a drink and leave in five minutes. I can do that after I eat as easily as before."

The waiter arrived and took their orders.

"So," Piers said, "why aren't you at Spengler's with everyone else?"

"I'm not in an especially sociable mood right now."

He nodded. "After Reese's little soireé the other night I can imagine you're thoroughly full of crowds. *I* am, certainly. I was rather surprised to see you there."

"The other night?"

"In the Heavy? 5555? I was more surprised to see Mace. Did you bring him or did he bring you?" He laughed. "I'm sorry, I don't mean to pry, but I'm very curious. Mace isn't usually the most sociable of people. Just getting him to show up at my party was a minor feat. Seeing him in the Heavy was a shock, but a pleasant one."

"I didn't know you were there...We'd been to dinner. Reese had told me about a special event, so—"

"You know Reese personally?"

"He helped me when I first came here."

"Oh, I see."

"Do you know him?"

"Not personally, just by reputation. I was there with an acquaintance. What did you think of his 'special event'?"

"I suppose I wonder if it was real—"

"Oh, it's real. Sly move on his part. As a matter of fact, PolyCarb has just negotiated a distribution deal with him."

"Really? But...why? Wouldn't it be more profitable for him to—?"

"Not really. He would run into problems. What he did wasn't illegal in any strict sense, but it needs better management than it would get in Reese's hands. Everybody's interests will be served by our administration. Tell me, did it frighten you, what you saw?"

"No, I don't think so. Not frighten—disturb, unsettle—but it didn't seem real enough to actually scare me."

"Have you been able to get it out of your head?"

"I'm—" She balked, about to say that she was a CAP and nothing ever left her head. But she had given the event at Reese's almost no thought. The images offered a dramatic effect, certainly, but did she care?

She saw Piers watching her then, his eyes narrowed, waiting. She laughed self-consciously.

"Good question," she said. "I suppose not."

"Did they remind you of anything?"

"Remind me? Of what?"

He shrugged elaborately and seemed about to reply when their lunch arrived.

"Apparently," he continued, "Earth is in a bit of a fix. We've known for some time that a plague was running loose downwell, but this was the first verification of it."

"It sounds like things are falling apart. Literally."

"Yes . . . so you were out to dinner with Mace?"

"Yes."

"Mace is an interesting man," Piers said then. He frowned at his plate. "The broccoli looks small, doesn't it? I wonder if it was a bad season. . . ." He stabbed a forkful of vegetables and ate. "Good, though. I said, 'Mace is an interesting man.'"

"You did. He is, yes."

"Have you been to his dom?"

"I . . . Mr. Hawthorne, I don't mean to be rude—"

"He has, I'm told, the most amazing collection of music. I offered to buy it from him last year, but he said no. I even named a price but he didn't even pause. It must be something."

"It's impressive . . . I'm sorry, Mr. Hawthorne, but I'm not comfortable discussing Mace when he's not here."

"Really? Well, I suppose it would seem to be none of my business. But you *were* at my party, which was *for* Mace. Now ask yourself, why would I throw a party for someone in whom I have no interest? And why would it be a very expensive party if that interest weren't fairly significant? Since you met him there, I only thought that our concerns for him might intersect. You see, after three years as a recluse, it's a surprise and a relief to see Mace doing something other than mourning his wife. My concerns for his well-being are genuine—"

"Did you know her?"

"Know who?"

"Mace's wife. Helen."

"No, I didn't. But I know Mace. We met at the time she died."

"How *did* she die?"

Piers frowned.

"I'm sorry, Mr. Hawthorne, now *I'm* prying—"

"No, it's all right. It was an accident on Mars. Eighty-nine people died; she was one of them. I was the on-site adjuster afterward. That's where I met Mace. He'd been running security on the site. He—well, he didn't cope very well. When he came back here, he became more and more reclusive. Obsessed, really. I think it was significant that he came to his own birthday party."

Nemily watched Hawthorne. He was rambling, as if he had something he wanted to say but could not bring it out. "I'm glad he did," she said.

"So . . . you *are* seeing him?"

"Yes."

"Still?"

"For the foreseeable future."

Piers smiled. "Good. If there's anything you need—advice, information—"

"Mr. Hawthorne—"

"Piers, please. I know you work in my department; I'm your superior in the company, and maybe you find this all a bit awkward, but my concern is primarily for my friend."

"I appreciate that. I'll think about it, Mr.—Piers—all right?"

"Stat check." He ate in silence for a time. Then: "How long have you known Reese? Since you've been here, did you say?"

"Since shortly after I came through InFlux. Too long, I sometimes think."

He laughed. "I know what you mean." He sat back from his half-finished plate. "I'm not as hungry as I thought. I suppose I should go put in an appearance." He gazed reluctantly in the direction of the new café. "It's been pleasant talking with you, Ms. Dollard. I hope we can do it again." He gestured for the waiter. "This is on me."

"Oh, I—"

"I insist. Perhaps sometime we can all go out, then Mace can buy me lunch. Or dinner. See you around, Ms. Dollard."

She watched him sign the bill and hurry out. She watched him head down the Mall toward the new café. She nibbled at her sandwich for a time, then left. She stood in the center of the Mall, undecided, and let herself drift toward Spengler's.

The crowd formed a dense tangle of faces, arms, and glasses, bright against the shadows and colors of clothes and furniture. The features moved, mouths opening and closing, connections made and broken, words gathered in a froth of ritual prattle and spilled over the boundary.

If she could see them she could pluck them from the air around her, one by one, bursting at her touch and leaving her no wiser than when she first reached for them. She raised a foot, moved it forward, preparing to slip through into the jumble at the first sign of a sensible opening—

—and found herself walking away, back toward her office, turned aside by the disordered barrier. On the way, she came to a decision. She wondered briefly if she should let Mace know first, but he might misunderstand and interfere.

Melissa's office was still empty. Nemily left her a message, taking four days of personal time. She transferred the data from the disc to her collator, then erased the disc and tucked it into the stack of blanks in Melissa's office. She went down to her locker and cleaned out her belongings, stripping it bare as if she would not be back, filling a second bag.

She smiled at the security people as she left.

She walked up the steps to the third floor of her dom. She shifted the two bags to her left hand and reached for the lock. The door was already unlocked.

She thought back frantically to the night she had left with Mace. She had worn her synthesist. Had she forgotten to lock up? It seemed unlikely; she had never forgotten that.

Her scalp tingled as she entered her own apartment. Still holding the bags, she went from room to room. She found no one. She stood finally in her bedroom, studying the surfaces for sign that someone had gone through her things. She could not tell.

Quickly, she stuffed the bags in a closet, then pulled out a change of clothes. Grabbing her ID and a credit chit, slipping her augment case in a hip pouch, she left the apartment, making sure to lock the door. Her nerves danced as she descended the stairs to the pedistry and made for the nearest shunt station.

She kept well back in the shadows of the alcove across from Reese's club and waited for Mace and Koeln to emerge. When they did, both relief and fear jolted her. For a few moments she knew Mace would see her. He stood outside the closed club, talking to Koeln as if the two had known each other for years, and all she could think of was that any instant she would do something that would attract their attention. She held herself as rigidly as possible, till it seemed that her skin vibrated.

Koeln walked away, leaving Mace where he leaned back against the wall. He frowned, forehead deeply furrowed. Abruptly, he went back to the entrance to 5555 and banged on it. Colf let him back in. Ten minutes later, he came out once more, and headed in the direction Koeln had gone earlier.

After a time the trembling subsided and she gathered herself to cross the circuit to 5555. Each step recovered confidence till by the time she pressed the mici the shaking was nearly gone.

"What a day," Reese said as she entered his office. He sighed dramatically and laughed. "What else could happen? I'm almost afraid to anticipate."

"I'm doing fine, Reese, thank you for asking," Nemily said.

"Your friend just left."

"I saw." Nemily ignored the urge to ask why Mace had been here; she guessed that it concerned Koeln's visit, and, consequently, Glim Toler. But she did not want Reese to know how deep her interest in Mace ran. She glanced at Colf standing by the exit.

"Is this private?" Reese asked.

"I'd prefer it that way."

Reese nodded and looked at Colf, who turned smartly and left. Reese gestured toward the couch across from his desk and made a sweeping, magnanimous gesture. "So, then, what *can* I do for you? Dare I hope that we can do some business?"

"Probably. I want to trade for it."

"Trade. I gather then that it's not the sort of thing that is readily available to you."

"Yes."

"And you think I can get it for you?"

"Definitely."

"Why do you want it?"

"I have personal reasons, but I think this would be in your best interest as well. So it's not much of a trade since you'll benefit."

Reese's eyes twitched slightly in surprise. "I wouldn't have expected such convolutions from you." He drew a deep breath. "I'm also wondering if this is related to the visit just paid me by Mr. Preston and Mr. Koeln."

"I'd rather not say anything about that."

"What do you need?"

"There's a man on Aea...he was here the other night. I want him off Aea."

"Why not speak to SA? Deportation is more their line—"

"Because I'm sure he can't be deported. If he's here, he's protected. At least from SA."

"But not from me."

"I doubt anyone can be protected from you."

"I'm not *that* dangerous. Who is he and what concern would he be to me?"

"He deals vacuum. Not the light stuff. He could be a direct competitor in time. Also, I think he's here to do damage to Aea itself. I don't know how. But he could certainly do damage to me. I want him gone."

"Dead?"

"I—how you do it is up to you. I suppose that depends on what you want me to do whether or not it's worth that much to you."

"Sensible answer. Who is he?"

"His name is Glim Toler. He's Lunessa, so I'm sure you can find him easily."

Reese was silent for a long time. He sighed then.

"And you'll do my favor in return for this?"

"Yes."

"You don't want to know what the favor is?"

"Do you think I should know?"

"I have an acquaintance with special tastes—"

"Ghosting?"

He spread his hands and nodded.

Nemily swallowed through a tightened throat. "Since your acquaintance evidently can't get it from Everest, I have to assume what's wanted is slightly illegal."

Reese frowned thoughtfully. "No, I don't think so...it's more a matter of confidentiality. Everest is too public. It occurred to me that someone who doesn't ghost at all anymore and wouldn't be likely to ever ghost again would be a perfect solution. I really don't want to do anything to attract SA's attention if I can help it."

"You never used to worry about that."

"Oh, no, I always worried about it, but I never used to have much choice."

"You do now?"

"Most of what I do these days is legitimate, if not entirely respectable. One of the virtues of a frontier economy. Necessity always dictates legality. I'm close enough to complete legitimacy to start to worry about it. But there are loose ends. Always."

"I'll never ask you for anything else."

"Oh, no! Don't make promises both of us may find impossible to keep. I would miss you, Nemily, if you never came around anymore. Just keep in mind the nature of transactions...?"

"When?"

"Tonight."

"That's rather short notice."

"How quickly did you want this...Glim Toler...taken care of?"

Nemily felt herself nod, resigned. She could not truthfully claim to be surprised. "How long do you think this will take? What does your acquaintance expect?"

"As I said, mainly anonymity. You'll be going in as a blank, coming out clean. A few hours at most, I think."

An occluded overlay. Nemily suppressed a shudder. She had done a few of those, and hated them. Often they resulted in days of partial memories and odd emotional reactions. The unmodified thought nothing remained behind after the session, but it did not work that way. What she had explained to Mace was mostly true—deep overlays were shunned by professional ghosts because of the eventual overload, but even mild ones left a residue, and occluded overlays were never light. The occlusions certainly dissipated over time, but in the short term they were simply "hidden" in her brain. There were ways around the blocks, she knew. If she were told exactly what she had ghosted she could find the hidden files and access them, but that never happened. Going in blank and coming out clean meant no one talked about it; it never happened, so no one talked about it.

"I really don't like that, Reese."

"You have my assurances nothing will go wrong."

"Your assurances don't help. If I can't remember, I can't believe you."

"It's terrible not to be trusted."

"I know. It's the whole thinking behind sending someone in blank."

"A point. Still...."

"How soon do you think you can take care of my problem?"

"I can't say. I'll see what I can have for you when you come back to-night, say in four hours?"

Nemily stood. Curiously, all the trembles were gone. "How shall I dress?"

"Nothing was specified. You have good taste, I trust your judgment."

"Four hours."

Nemily left, thinking of the variety of uses to which trust could be put, all of them implying the same thing but few of them overlapping or consequent upon clear intent or thorough understanding.

She took a shunt to a shopping district in segment three, where she drifted from shop to shop. She was on her own time, she should use it rather than use it up. Not until she wandered into a boutique did she understand her own actions. She intended to stay away from her regular spaces until her transaction with Reese was complete. She wanted to view her stolen data, but she wanted to be calmer and more private before she opened the file. After tonight. After her favor for Reese.

She bought an outfit for tonight, a dark green singlepiece that formed itself like skin to her hips and thighs and billowed around her shoulders. Purchase in hand, she found a small coffee shop to idle away the next hour or so before returning to the Heavy.

Her heart picked up speed at odd intervals, as if trying to run away when she was distracted. The effect seemed disconnected from any particular thought, as if her autonomic system were dealing with a separate issue than her consciousness. Sometimes she believed that her unaugmented psyche still functioned apart from her net. If she believed in such things, she might claim to have two souls, one isolated in the unaccessed parts of her damaged brain.

She finished her coffee, picked up her package, and began making her way back to Reese's club. People stopped in small groups and pointed upwell. Against the roseate of the northern cap the bunting and banners and stages for the regatta clustered. Even from here some of the ships were clearly visible, sleek-hulled and broad-winged.

"Have you bet? Have you bet on a ship? It's getting late and the odds are driving up the prices!"

The hawker called from beneath the bright red eaves of a small kiosk.

Nemily came closer. People leaned on the narrow counter, studying the sheets displayed on slates that listed the contestants, their histories and standings, the pilots, and the odds.

"Who's the favorite?" someone asked. With a start Nemily realized it was her voice.

"You mean this hour?" one of the other bettors said and the small crowd laughed.

"*Kazyphon*," the hawker said. "Twenty-to-one at the moment, up from thirty-five-to-one at midcycle."

Nemily looked down the rows of numbers. "I've never bet on a regatta before."

"Then you're not really an Aean," another customer said.

"It's sacrilege not to bet a regatta," said still another.

Nemily wondered resentfully if the speaker even knew what "sacrilege" really meant, but did not respond. The statement stung, especially after the previous remark. She could think of several thousand people in segment four and segment five, probably many more in the outer rings, who had never bet on a regatta simply because they lacked the funds. For that reason alone she thought it would be worthwhile never to bet.

But she felt people watching her now and the perverse homunculus of egoless need to belong took her chit from her pocket and selected a craft and specified an amount. She barely heard the cheers of those around her as she walked away with her ticket, certification of her true status as an Aean.

People jammed together around the doors of 5555 when Nemily returned. The roar of music seemed to seep out of the walls. She squeezed her way through the press until one of the bouncers saw her and in a few seconds Colf tapped her on the shoulder and beckoned her to follow. Epithets and protests followed her through the portal, but no one tried to slip in with her. Colf led her up to Reese's office.

Reese was absent.

"Make yourself comfortable," Colf said.

The monitor, audio off, showed the floor below filled with dancers swept by silent light. Nemily dropped her bag on the couch and began undressing.

"Will it be here?" she asked.

"No."

"Do you—"

"I don't know who, I don't know where. I thought you didn't do this anymore."

"Reese is doing me a favor."

"Hell of a favor."

"It could be."

Nemily spread the green outfit on the couch and began pulling on the undergarments. The motions calmed her, as if she were exchanging one set of concerns for another through a simple change of clothes.

"Do you mind a question?" Colf asked.

"No."

"What's it like?"

"What?"

"Ghosting."

"It's...difficult to describe. Usually—do you understand how the overlays work?"

Colf shrugged.

"Well, they provide a set of inhibitions and proclivities that sort of reroute behavior—like movable walls that change with different needs. I'm sorry if that's too technical—"

"I scan technical. Go on."

"It's like being in a ciné, only full sensory, and there's no dialogue to follow, just a set of responses that you don't know are there until they're triggered. Most of the time a client doesn't care about anonymity, so the overlay is light and you're aware through it. You get to watch."

"This one isn't like that."

"No...it's complete anonymity."

"You don't sound happy."

"I'm not. These scare me. I won't have any memory of what happened while I'm ghosting one of these. The overlay is deep, like a complete persona that just moves in and shoves me out of the way. I don't like them. They're the reason I quit."

"Hell of a favor."

Nemily only nodded and finished dressing in silence. Nemily had never met a ghost whom the experience did not frighten a little, but she had met several who enjoyed the fear. She had found the light overlays—thin ghosts, they called them—bearable, sometimes, depending on the client, even pleasurable. But she could not rid herself of the anxiety each time she loaded one.

So what am I doing offering to run a full encoding for Mace?

She zipped the last zipper and tugged at the suit, ignoring the answer as long as she could. When she sat down to wait for Reese, it came.

You want something...you want to fill the gaps....

"Good choice," Reese said as he came into the room. He stopped in front of her. "Very good choice."

"Did you do what I asked?"

"I've made arrangements." He reached across his desk and picked up an augment. "Load it now."

"Now?"

"Complete anonymity. Colf will take you to the appointment and see that you come back safely."

Nemily held out her hand and Reese dropped the button onto her palm. "How long?"

"As long as it takes. Don't worry, Nem, I've been assured that there's nothing about this that's dangerous."

"You can never tell with the fanatically paranoid."

"That's why I'm sending Colf with you. Now, if you would?"

Nemily drew three deep breaths and exchanged augments.

Vision splintered through a rhythmless headache. She moved her shoulders, twisted her head from side to side to find relief from the pressure, but the pain followed, a shadow across her shoulders and neck and scalp. Her stomach poised on the edge of rejection, as if it contained a poison. She slid her hands along fabric, then tried to push herself up. Dizziness threatened to steal consciousness, but she kept very still until it passed.

"Nem? Here, I have water. Nem? Nemily?"

She blinked at the man kneeling before her, holding out a glass, until she recognized his face.

"Reese?"

"Good. Here, drink it."

She took the glass. Her hand quivered and a little fluid spilled across her thumb. She leaned back against something soft and raised the glass to her mouth. She understood then that she must have exchanged the

overlay augment for her own synthesist. The sharp contrast of the exchange brought on this sort of vertigo. It took time for her wetware to
adjust properly.

The bitter taste nearly gagged her, but she recognized it and made
herself finish all of it. The tension in her neck abated within seconds
and her head soon felt better. She sat still, letting the medicine work
through her system, eyes closed, thoughtless. When she opened her
eyes again she felt familiar to herself.

"Time?" she croaked. She coughed and held the glass out. Someone
took it from her.

"Four-twenty," a voice said—not Reese—and it took a few seconds
for her to place it. Colf.

"...four-twenty...?"

"Long night," Reese said.

The glass touched her hand and she closed her fingers around it.
Plain water filled her mouth this time. The headache was nearly gone.
She noticed then how few other residual sensations remained. No aches,
no scoured sensations. Had anything happened besides a simple persona overlay? The shakes passed quickly.

Colf stood near the exit, arms folded over her chest, one ankle crossed
over the other. The indifference of her pose contrasted sharply with the
angry expression on her face. She kept glaring at Reese, though, and
when she looked at Nemily the anger softened to sympathy. Reese paid
no attention to Colf. He sat on the edge of his desk, idly reading something on his screen.

Nemily decided she wanted a shower. She still wore the green outfit,
but her clothes from the day before lay at the other end of the couch.
She finished the water and began stripping out of the new suit. As she
peeled it off, she thought distantly that Reese was still in the room, but
she did not care, really—he had seen her naked before—she only wanted to get out of these clothes and into her own.

"You owe me for the outfit," she said then, realizing that she did not
consider it her own anymore.

"Of course."

The stiffness faded with movement, but she continued to move slowly, as if attending a ritual that required the respect of time. By the time
she closed the last seal on her own clothes she felt herself again. She left
the green garment on the floor.

"Do you have your ghost back?" she asked.

Reese held up the augment. "I thank you, Nem. I'm told you were more than satisfactory."

Her own set of augments was on the end table by the couch. She sat down and began inserting them. When she had run through all the diagnostics she could, she left the synthesist in and put the case in her pocket.

"What about what I asked for?"

Reese nodded. "Not an easy thing to obtain, either. It took some favors. But I'm assured that he'll be gone from Aea in the very near future. You don't need to know details."

"No...thank you...do I owe you anything?"

He seemed to think about it for a few seconds, but shook his head with a faint smile. "No. We're more than squared."

"I won't do this again. Ever."

Reese pursed his lips.

"I'll be back," Colf said. Reese frowned at her but said nothing as she left the office.

"Did I make a bad exchange?" Nemily asked.

"That depends. I still don't see why you couldn't go to SA. He doesn't seem as well connected as you suspect. What's your association with him?"

"That's personal."

"Then only you can judge if it was worth it. If it helps any, what you did has given me the opportunity to take one more step toward complete legitimacy." He grinned when she looked at him. "I've been working toward it since I got here. Most of my interests are completely approved by SA. I'm converting the rest a little at a time."

"Next thing you'll tell me is you're a member of the council."

"Not yet."

The humor in his face failed to hide the complete seriousness underlying the remark. Reese occasionally ran on about his plans, his ambitions, but until now Nemily had thought of him as a thoroughly sensible man, well aware of his limitations and his capabilities.

The door opened then and Colf stepped back inside. Nemily took it as an opportunity to leave.

"Good luck," she said.

"You, too, Nem."

Nemily went to the exit. Colf opened it for her, then followed her out.

"I recommend," Colf said then, "that you not go back to your dom."

Nemily paused, looking at the big woman. Colf shrugged.

"Why?" Nemily asked.

"Can't say here. If you need a place for a while, just to clean up, maybe run a better diagnostic. . . ."

"I'd appreciate that," she said.

Colf nodded. "I'll take you, then."

Colf's dom was three levels up, a knot of small rooms centered on a kitchen, and sparsely furnished. It seemed too small for Colf, whose overadapted bulk seemed to fill any space in which she stood.

One room contained a sleeping mat and hundreds of brilliantly colored scarves hung from the walls, organically thick and variegated. Nemily stared, caught by the inseparability of pattern and texture.

"My. . . ."

"I collect them," Colf said, her voice small now with modest pride. "A couple are from the last century."

"From Gaia?"

"No! On my stipend? No, reproductions. But the patterns are all Gaian. Except this section here, that's Martian."

"You sleep here?"

Colf nodded. "First thing I see every morning. Lights come up, 'minder screams at me, and *poof!* This."

"It's beautiful."

Colf reddened slightly and backed out of the room. "You can stay as long as you like," she said, retreating. "Hour, a day, whatever. I have to get back to Reese."

"If it's all right," Nemily said, following, "I'll just clean up and view my data. I have another place I can go, but I need to do this in private."

Colf nodded. "Whatever. If you go out, just press the mici three times, real fast, it sets the security."

"Thank you. Really."

Colf gave her one more self-conscious nod and ducked out of the dom.

Nemily sat on the sleeping mat for a time, gazing at the collection of scarves, letting her thoughts drift. It helped sometimes to pay as little attention to her own processes as possible.

Colf's water came colder than Nemily liked, but she stood in the stinging spray of the shower until the goosebumps faded, then soaped up as thoroughly as she could. She toweled off and stretched out on Colf's mat.

She thought this job for Reese would be easier, since it revisited the familiar. In the first months after being cleared through InFlux, work came easily, but none of it provided sufficiently for any kind of advancement. Cramped as it was, her dom in Lunase had been far better than the assemblages of GHs in segment four she had lived in for nearly a year. Step by step, in justifiable increments difficult to retrace later, she found Reese and Reese provided work with a higher stipend. For a long time ghosting did not bother her. It was too like everything else she had ever done, only combined in ways she had never thought to combine them. But over time the anxieties increased and a sense of grime began to intrude in her apprehension of sex. Reese, never unreasonable, found other things for her to do. By then she had acquired legitimate work with a better stipend and began the move upshaft, and less than a year after her association with Reese began it ended.

For the most part, at least. From time to time Reese had asked a small favor, and since none of it involved ghosting or seemed in any way illegal, she had responded. *This would be the last,* she thought.

Colf's terminal lacked a direct interface. Running a pathic on herself would have to wait, along with a complete net diagnostic. It was too early still to call Mace, though she doubted he would mind. Instead she downloaded the stolen file from her collator onto a disc and slipped it into Colf's reader.

Reading about someone's life in the form of a corporate profile felt like ghosting without the sensations. It dismayed Nemily that so much could be reduced to a format. Born, raised, educated, worked, died, and in these ways at these levels, a set of specifications on the off chance one might wish to bet on the life's performance or recreate it or relive it.

Which is exactly what I've offered to do, she thought.

Helen had been a few years older than Mace, which turned out to be a complicated detail to determine given her birth on Aea and his on Mars. Nemily had never considered the problem till now, that "local time" required a difficult operation to bring into conformity with a different "local time" which, in view of everything else implied by the term "local," ended up meaning almost nothing. Earth years still dictated standard chronology, but it was only a convenience that could easily be discarded for some other, more relevant system, and probably would be when reverence for Gaia finally burned itself down to the cinder of historical relic.

Helen's father had died in an accident on a construction site.

She had originally wanted to become a commercial pilot.

Her mother had remarried when Helen was twelve. The new parent figure had been a woman. Helen had sued for legal autonomy. Instead, her mother had signed her into a corporate college that offered several career vectors.

At thirteen Helen had attempted suicide.

At fifteen she had graduated with honors. It was the last recorded time she had seen her mother. A year after that her mother emigrated to Brasa and all contact ceased.

It did not say, in the typically judgmental objectivity of such reports, if the estrangement resulted from her mother's remarriage or from her mother's choice of partners or some other, unrelated issue, the timing of which gave a false impression.

Helen's first recorded lover came into her life at seventeen. A woman.

Her next partner was a male and so was the one after that. The list scrolled on, names and dates and places, durations and separations, all related to her psychological profile and job performance, a matter that became relevant at eighteen when she took a position with PolyCarb. Only a very few of her partners had been from within the company. At twenty-two she had been required to attend counceling on the matter, though the report did not specifically state that as the reason.

At twenty-three she had herself sterilized. Nemily wondered if Mace knew about that.

She became a project assistant on a platform development in Mars orbit at twenty-five. Over the course of the eighteen-month-long job, it came to corporate attention that *she* was actually running the program, due to her supervisor's lack of involvement. He was transferred and Helen was given the position. Despite the delays already accrued, she brought the project in only a few weeks behind schedule and slightly overbudget. In all other regards she had performed better than profile and she was brought into the regular management pool.

By thirty she had reached the top of her classification. The following year PolyCarb brought her into Executive.

The next several years saw her bounce from one interest to another, as if she were exploring all the possibilities within the corporate structure. For five years there were no recorded lovers. Nemily weighed that against the workload Helen had taken on and decided that, simply, there had been no time.

She settled finally on outer system project development and began working on the Titan project. Titan looked like an impossible objective, in some ways more daunting than Venus, but it was still a world of acceptable size with an atmosphere that could be modified over time. A new human settlement, another world, one more anchor to guarantee survival. It said more than the numbers about how much PolyCarb thought of Helen that they gave it to her.

After three years, though, she was recalled. No reason was given. She took several small assignments, most of them on Mars. During this period she met Macefield Preston. After a fast courtship, they married. Given her history, this event came as a surprise. Seven years after the marriage she died on Hellas Planitia.

More details followed, medical records mostly, and organizational charts from all her projects. Two details startled Nemily.

First, she *had* worked with Piers Hawthorne, on two separate projects, one of which had been Titan. Piers had lied about that at lunch. The other project had been Mars, on the Trans Ares underground.

Second, Helen had been a CAP.

Nemily stared at the notation. Helen had had a net installed when she turned thirty-five. A very late date for the modification, a high risk of rejection or maladaption. According to her pathic profile she had not needed it. It was an elective augmentation. She had wanted it for her career. Not uncommon.

But Mace did not know. At least, she thought he did not know. The fact was not so much surprising as it was a verification. Nemily had suspected—people who had their personas downloaded to ROMs tended to be CAPs; there were other ways to do it, but none as simple or as reliable.

Nemily rubbed her eyes. The time chop said six-fifty. She decided to try to sleep for a while before doing anything more. She closed the file and tucked the disc in with her augments, then lay on Colf's mat.

She stared at the wall of color, frightened all over again.

FIFTEEN

AEA, 2118

NEMILY SAT UP IN SEMIDARKNESS, a hazy memory of dust and wind just out of reach behind her eyes, receding now even as she groped for it. She hated dreaming and had forgotten, among so many other reasons, about this unpleasant aftereffect of ghosting. Dissociated images drifted through her net, randomly assembling into bizarre set pieces until collation—sometimes more than one, sometimes only after a very deep collation and a complete diagnostic—cleared them out. It was the only time a CAP dreamed and it frightened her. The occluded overlaps were the worst because she had no way of knowing from which side of the augment the images emerged—the assumed persona or the encounter with the client. She could not imagine the lives of the unmodifieds, living with these incoherent dramas waiting in the shadows of sleep every night.

Usually erotic dreams followed ghosting, but this one offered nothing sexual. She had never been in a storm, but she understood the concept. Storms happened on Gaia, on Mars, in the atmospheres of worlds. Sometimes a brief one occurred as the result of a blowout, a sealed habitat violently releasing its air and life. She looked around for a panicked instant at the walls for signs of a breach.

She blinked again at the muted colors hanging all about. Colf's dom. She had offered sanctuary, a place to sleep, to recover, and had warned her not to return to her own dom. . . .

She rolled off the mat and found her shoes in the half-light. At the comm terminal she slipped them on, then quickly inventoried her augments. She was tempted to collate, but she wanted to be gone from here. She wanted to do a full net diagnostic and purge whatever remnants from the overlay might still be lingering. Supposedly that could not happen, but often tantalizing fragments continued to drift through her wetware for days after a deep overlay. She used to dream about particles combining and splitting apart when she worked for the alchemists. Everything she did for them had been classified and occluded, but the barriers were never complete.

Colf had told her how to set the alarm. Doubting now, she wondered what else it might trigger.

Never mind what you leave behind, just get out, now....

Nemily flinched at the clarity of the thought—almost audible, it seemed, with the kind of visceral reality dreams possessed—and pressed the button. She stepped into the corridor outside and let the door slide shut. Her hand hovered over the mici, unconsciously moving to set the alarm, responsibly, like a conscientious guest, until she made her fingers close and pulled away. Self-conscious paranoia made her aware of all the sounds around her, the taste of the air, and her own fallibility.

Now....

Colf's dom was at the end of a short alcove off a main circuit. She walked out as if going somewhere, though she had nowhere in mind other than away. The circuit ran unobstructed in both directions, disappearing in the upward curve of the ring, the walls broken by alcoves. A section of flooring was torn up to her right, revealing the old tram railing. She saw no people, then remembered the time and the fact most of the people living here would be on-shift somewhere, and immediately realized that she was confusing Lunase with Aea and had thought of this space as worker area. Workers did not live segregated on Aea, at least not as a class.

What do you call segment four? Could you live in segment two?

She stumbled at the voice. Her heart rate increased. How deep the overlay had gone now became a matter of importance. She needed to run that diagnostic. The residuals ought to have faded by now to random images. The thoughts might have been her own—in fact, the observation was nothing new—but for the sour edge to them, the bitterness and spent rage. Her own opinions and beliefs, channeled through this persona, would come back twisted and darkened, recognizably her own, but stolen and despoiled. She caught her stride in the next step and concentrated on escape, ignoring the way the walls seemed for a moment to be stone.

She walked on, uncertain of her location, but confident that eventually she would find a lift or another corridor intersecting this one. A group of men burst from an alcove, startling her, and hurried in the opposite direction, showing no sign that they had even seen her. She noticed more people now, withdrawn into shadow, squatting in small huddles or sitting alone, some staring at nothing, others studying a handheld reader. Her nerves danced as she darted looks at faces, expecting to find familiarity and unwelcome recognition. Instead, she saw only a vague suggestion of commonality and the dull reserve of mistrust not formed sufficiently for open complaint.

She came to one of the big elevators. The spoke at arc ninety.

Which way?

Get lost....

The voice irritated her, frightened her a little, but right now it made sense. When the doors opened, she stepped into the car, joining the half dozen others already aboard, and pressed the button for ring three. No one spoke to her or, as far as she could tell, even looked at her. The doors opened again and she exited alone.

The rich odor of humus and chlorophyll and pulp enveloped her. It reminded her of the comatulid lines she had worked during her first months with PolyCarb, densely organic and curiously relaxing. A narrow corridor ran straight ahead between transparent walls through which Nemily saw tier upon tier of hydroponics platforms filled with green. Ring three, she remembered then, contained almost nothing but farms. The real farms, that fed Aea and produced the excess for export. Only one of the original tori farming rings had been changed to something else, and that was the endcap ring upshaft that bounded segment one. The Interior farms were mostly experimental and produced a significant fraction of Aea's total output, but far from enough to feed the resident population.

Nemily hurried along, hoping she looked as if she belonged here, unsure what she would say if anyone asked her where she was going. She glanced back. No one had followed from the lift.

The transparency ran unbroken for nearly a hundred meters and ended at a wall with a door across the corridor. Anxiously, she pressed the access button. She exhaled heavily when the door opened.

The chamber beyond contained banks of equipment. Cable and conduit flowed across the ceiling. Nemily recognized several components from the comatulid lines—monitors, sample analyzers, atmospheric regulators, nutrient processors—and many more she knew nothing about. She hesitated only a moment before crossing the chamber to the opposite door and stabbing the button. Again, the door opened and she walked through.

She stopped. The ragged tops of plants stretched to the close horizon, shifting gently in an artificial breeze, beneath banks of bright lights. She did not recognize the crop, but it seemed familiar. She pushed her way in among the stalks. They brushed against her face lightly and their aroma came sharp. Her feet sank a few centimeters in the earth and she knew this had to be an experimental plot and that her presence here might distort the results, damage the effort. But if that were the case, why no security code on the entrance? Typical Aean arrogance, she decided. Why would anyone who did not belong here enter in the first place? Good manners in lieu of locked doors. Knowing she should not be here ought to be enough to make her leave. In that case it made a good place to hide for a short while.

When she could no longer see the door through which she had entered, she sat down and pulled out her case. She wanted to go to her dom and use her terminal for a full external diagnostic, but for the time being this would have to do.

She pried open the cover on her collator to reveal three tiny buttons and a jack. From beneath the lining of her case she took a cable, then opened the back of her mathematics augment and linked it to the collator. The combination allowed a deeper probe than the collator alone. The math augment read the coding in her system faster, as machine code, and passed it to the collator in a decipherable form. She rarely used it because of the ease of jacking through a full terminal and the fact that, powerful as the combination of the two was, this method still had limits. She exchanged her synthesist for the collator and closed her eyes, initiating the probe. She disliked going through these—the external diagnostic made them unnecessary—but it was the only way to find out if something had been buried so far down in her implants that a standard collation would not discover it. The last time she had done one had been a year before leaving Lunase.

Her internal sensorem built an image for her....

Walls formed, odors and textures filling in quickly. The differences were small, almost unnoticeable, but nagging, like a paper cut. Reddish sand gathered at the angles of the passage. Nemily felt as if she had just come inside out of a harsh wind, even though the air had moved barely enough to shift the stalks of the plants. The details completed themselves and she started along the coil.

Near the bottom, wan amber light filtered up through dust-laden air. Sand piled deeper along the last coil, spilled across the floor, and shifted slightly as if stirred by a breeze. She came round the last turn to find the door standing open, the light coming from within the room.

The shelves had been torn from the walls and all the packages ripped open. Contents slewed across the floor, jumbling together in a morass of facet bits and sludge. Sand and light poured through a jagged gap in the opposite wall. Nemily stepped over the debris to the crack and peered out across a landscape that could only be Mars.

The ground sloped uphill gradually, the horizon no more than a line to mark the separation of land and sky. Nemily eased through the opening and set her foot into the yielding soil. Off to the left she saw a shape on the crest of the rise against a background of anemic cloud.

She looked back into the room and ordered it to sort itself. The mess began to shift to the urging of faint puffs of light and Nemily started up the slope toward the form that waited.

Within ten paces she knew it was a person. Ten more and she saw that it sat crosslegged, leaning slightly forward with wrists on knees, hands dangling, head cocked as if contemplating a distant object or an intimate thought. Air pushed at her, but the silence persisted, reminding her that this was all inside. That provided no comfort now. Her buffers, doors, walls, labyrinths, pits and mirrors had failed and something had managed to work its way here. Not the ghost, no. Overlays normally did not possess the complexity to get this deep. None she had ever encountered. But she did not remember this one, so she could not know what else might have been done during her time with the client. The collator kept her fear at bay; otherwise she might be incapacitated by terror. Instead, she saw the figure on the hill as a problem to be solved.

The person did not look up when Nemily stopped alongside. The compact body wore an environ suit, dark, oil-sheened fabric and a breather mask. Yellow-orange hair shifted in tangles around the straps. Nemily walked all the way around the intruder, but provoked no response. She crouched directly before the reflecting eyepieces and waited for a sign of recognition.

She grabbed the edges of the mask and ripped it up and off.

The woman could only be dead. Lifeless black eyes, mouth slack and partly open, all tension gone from the jaw. Nemily did not recognize her, even though this whole scene seemed familiar. Perhaps it came from the overlay, a leftover like the dreams. But how did it get here? Was it a trojan or the shell of one? She looked back toward the damaged wall.

The building that housed her sensora rose up from the red sand. She had never seen it from the outside before. She had never expected it to have a shape, really. But it resembled Mace's dom. Higher, but the same basic structure. Perhaps the system assembled it from the most relevant iconography within her net. The last time she had come here, the place resembled the mazes of Lunase and she had not gone "outside."

She followed the corpse's gaze. In the middle distance stretched a long, straight trench in the otherwise homogeneous aresian landscape.

She crossed the intervening distance through the soundless shift of thin air and stood on the edge of the hole. Sand partially filled the bottom, drifting up the sides, incompletely hiding the bodies. Arms and legs extruded at macabre angles. Along the rim at even intervals pylons jutted up, shards of material limply clinging to them. Nemily crouched at the nearest and tried to lift the fabric, but it dissolved and drifted away at a touch, electrons flying off in a swift chain reaction that undid the covalent bonding in the material.

She retreated to the sentinel corpse and sat down beside it. The fluttering hair drew her attention. The way it shifted, she realized, repeated itself every few seconds. Nemily pushed it up from the neck, revealing an empty augment socket. She felt around in the sand in the unlikely event that the button had fallen out. Finding nothing, she scooted around to peer more closely into the socket. It seemed too small for a normal implant, but she had no idea how death might effect the muscles around a CAP socket. She ran a finger around its rim to see if it stretched—

—and it closed around the tip. Nemily yanked back reflexively and nearly toppled the corpse onto her. She grabbed its shoulder with her free hand to support it and scooted around onto her knees for balance.

The corpse's arms flew out from the sides and it tried to pull away from Nemily's attached finger. The body convulsed, shoved itself backward, then swung its legs out to the left, twisting onto Nemily's lap. The face grinned up at her.

"One piece still missing," it said inside Nemily's skull. "Who put me here?"

The face began to desiccate, the skin drying rapidly, cracking, revealing bone coated with a faint tinge of blood. The black eyes became empty sockets and the clothes sagged. For all its melodrama, Nemily admitted that it was effective.

The augment socket reopened and let her finger go.

Nemily scrambled back and watched every trace of the corpse dissolve to nothing. In the middle distance the trench sealed itself, puckering up like a wound healing. She got to her feet and ran back to the tower. The breached wall was beginning to repair itself as she squeezed through. Within seconds the wall was smooth, without a sign of the break.

The floor had been cleaned up, the opened boxes all repacked and stored on their shelves.

She opened her eyes and stared at the overhead lights. She sat up. She had knocked several stalks over and her case lay tangled among them a meter away. With exaggerated care she retrieved it and slowly switched collator for synthesist, then disconnected the collator from the math augment.

The thrill of recent fear rippled through her, chilling her, tightening her muscles, followed quickly by a sudden rage. She did not move and tried to concentrate on a point in midair, but the serpentine quality of her reactions pulled her away from possible calm. Her hand trembled. Her carefully constructed sense of self-determination was in shambles, but she at least understood now. Glim Toler had used her as a mule and now the delivery had been made. Whatever overlay she had experienced last night, its purpose was recovery and verification. Her sensorem had been ransacked for whatever Toler had hidden there. She had thought for a long time that the discs hidden in her luggage, discovered at InFlux, removed by Mace unreported, had been the contraband data Toler wanted smuggled in. But they had been something else—an announcement to someone that she had arrived, decoys, she was uncertain—and she had been the package. Somehow she had missed her contact upon entering Aea. A mistake which Toler had now come to correct.

She was partly amazed at her logic. For three years she had been working all this out, in the cracks of her mind where it could be contemplated safely, hidden from daily consciousness. It happened sometimes to CAPs: a wetware analog to the unconscious, especially in the presence of overlays and the coincidental architectures they created, supposedly temporary structures that nevertheless persisted under certain conditions; good places to hide things, especially one's own secrets. If collation missed them, the absence of dreaming allowed them to exist, segregated, until they completed themselves and dissolved, like code run to a conclusion. Occasionally, they reintegrated whole, as now, and it was like finding a forgotten year or a friend or another life.

So whose overlay did I run last night? she wondered.

In the distance the door opened. Nemily tucked her case away and started crawling through the stalks.

After several meters she became aware of a low hum somewhere behind her. She paused and listened and decided it was only agro equipment, maybe a seeder or possibly a reaper. She crawled on until the sound grew louder. As she listened now, the source of the noise seemed to shift from left to right and back again. Slowly, she stood.

A small shape crossed the field about a meter above the tips of the stalks, moving at a brisk speed, perhaps fifty meters away. Nemily dropped back to the ground, her pulse quicker now, and began scrambling in the opposite direction as fast as she could without knocking over plants. Several people had seen her get off the lift, but none of them had seemed to pay her much attention. Still, she no longer expected to be followed and her skills at recognizing a shadow had atrophied on Aea. Being innocuous was necessary to the task. Even so, there were other ways to trace her, and Reese of all people seemed now to be involved with the people who knew of her hidden vacuum—

The sound grew closer and no longer seemed to be moving from side to side. She did not want to stop to look, did not want to risk being spotted. She had no idea how big this section was, or if there would be an exit when she reached the far wall.

The hum roared directly above her and she felt the wind from the rotors in the searcher's belly across her back and hair. She dropped flat and waited and it came back and stopped. She rolled over and looked up at the disc, maybe fifty centimeters in diameter, a central hole that funneled the lifting force of blown air, surrounded by a rim set with optical jewels.

Nemily snatched her augment case from her pouch, stood, and shoved it into the fan cowl. The blades jerked it from her hand with a hideous grinding and spit it back out immediately. The searcher slewed off the side, its motor laboring, and began slicing through stalks.

Nemily retrieved her case. One end was scarred and bent, the smooth surface torn. She tucked it away and broke into a run toward the nearest wall. She imagined she heard shouts, but it was hard to tell over the angry buzzing of the damaged searcher. She did not look back. She collided with the wall, lungs heaving from fear, and looked right, then left, and found the exit. She sprinted for it, stabbed at the control panel, and the heavy door slid aside.

A group of people stood in a small gallery on the other side. They looked like a tour, one man standing before the rest, an arm raised in mid-gesture. They all froze in place as she hurried through, faces locked in startled expressions.

"Sorry," she said as she reached the far side. "Go on. It's all right."

She plunged through the next door into a corridor and ran, dimly aware that on the other side of her stretched, behind transparency, more hydroponics. A few people worked amid all the green and watched her passage curiously, but none moved to stop her or report her that she could tell. They were all good Aeans and minded their own business.

She came to a small elevator and waited anxiously for it to open. When it did, more people emerged, and she weathered the flood stoically. Finally, she fell into the box, alone, and the doors closed. She stabbed a button without looking and pressed back against the wall and worked on controlling her breathing.

The elevator stopped and the doors opened. She stepped out into the Heavy.

She drifted through the throngs crowding the Heavy, trying to imitate the look of intense ambiguity, ambivalent concentration and casual urgency around her. It seemed they had nowhere to go and a powerful need to arrive. Another ghost would help. The one aspect of ghosting that seemed a benefit even in the midst of the less salutary uses of the tech had been the negation of self. Worries, concerns—they disappeared with the adoption of certain aspects of a persona unaffected by her own problems, giving her time and room to breathe. Not a deep ghost, just a light overlay that would give the patina of difference, enough to obscure her own self, but she did not know where in the Heavy to acquire one discreetly. Reese's influence suffused the Heavy like metastasized cancer. Even if he was sincere about legitimizing his interests, those cells would not simply evaporate, but would reach for autonomy. They would know. The afterimages from the ghost had all disintegrated, eaten away by her own defenses and any self-destruct commands imbedded within the overlay itself. She could not pretend that the dreams and the diorama on the hill had been errors from a too-complex overlay. At best, with all the optimism in the world, she might question that it had been intended for her, but under inspection even that faint hope dissolved. It had been left inside her sensorem, triggered by her "touch," and given directly to her in terms she recognized. Reese had delivered her to people who knew her and had used her.

Glim, probably. Or Glim's contact, who had been here all along, waiting for whatever it was she had been intended to deliver. That suggested another Lunessa.

"One piece is still missing…" she mused. What besides vacuum might connect Glim to a trojan on Aea? "Who put me here?" the ghost had asked. Who was running Toler? Who had gotten Toler onto Aea? That was the missing piece.…

Glim had been a devoted attendee of the Temple, a fact that had lessened her respect for the Temple. Lunessa, with a few exceptions, started at the Temple of Homo ReImaginoratus when they first arrived on Aea.

Nemily continued along the circuit until she saw a restaurant that offered public terminals. Few people occupied the small tables within; one man sat at the far end of a long, chromed bar. She leaned between two stools midway along its length and gestured for the tender.

"Terminals?" she asked.

He pointed toward the back. "Sorry, the light's out. The lock works, though."

"Thanks."

She settled within the booth and pulled the door shut, thumbing the latch to lock it. The only light came from the display itself. She tapped a request for a schema and scrolled until she found the Temple. She was surprised how close she was.

She tapped Mace's number.

"Macefield Preston's dom," the d.p. answered.

"Is Mace available?"

"Who is calling, please?"

"Nemily Dollard."

"He's out. I am instructed to tell you to come directly here if you can."

"Right now I better not. There's been a little difficulty. Tell him I'll try to call him later if I can."

"Do you wish to be more specific?"

"I can't. It's . . . I'll explain later."

"Very well."

She left the restaurant and made her way to the Temple, only four arcs away along the circuit. Traffic thinned as she neared it.

She went past the broad, austere façade with its lemniscate in fading paint, and drifted across the circuit to the opposite wall. She kept to the shallow impressions and worked her way back, scanning the few people who she passed to see if any looked at her too closely or ignored her too diligently.

When she felt certain that no one was watching the Temple, she made her way up to the entrance, trying to act as if she did this often, a normal routine. She rapped on the door three times and entered.

The sanctuary, empty, threatened nothing, and Nemily found it oddly comic. Like a broad play area for children, with pictures on the walls, and a raised space from which the tutor could oversee them, it looked almost carnival.

She remembered coming to Temple as a child, moving with the enforced slowness of large groups, the monitors constantly reminding them to keep their heads bowed and their mouths shut. The incantations had appealed to her. Latin, she later learned, mixed with other languages, distorted by time and separation from the mother tongues on Gaia into unique shapes, and used only for ritual purposes. Just that struck her as worth a small loyalty, to come and hear those words, remnants of days of connection to Gaia, to Earth. The rest of it might have impressed her if it had not been used to intimidate and frighten, hand in gauntlet with SetNetComb maintaining the ubiquitous darkness of Lunase. The Temple domes offered light, relief from the austerity of the warrens, but it was forbidden to look up. The images on the walls told stories, but it was forbidden to interpret them for herself. The music inherent in the litany offered solace, but it was forbidden to sing along. She did not so much lose faith as leave it. She knew where it was, she had simply chosen not to bring it with her.

Then there was confession. Her first patri became angry when she offered nothing in the confessional. She had not understood what it was she was supposed to tell him. Later she tried to talk about how unhappy she was working for the alchemists but she was told she was disloyal, sinful, corrupt for thinking such things. Did she not have guilts, errors, or transgressions to confess? Did she not wish to offer atonement for these small violations against her nature and against her neighbors? Did she not steal, deal vacuum, take illicit pharmacopiates, lie, spread false rumor, fuck indiscriminately, resent the rules, hate, fear, fail?

When Patri Collum had learned that she was a CAP he had refused to confess her anymore and soon after she had been transferred to another Temple. The unexplained banishment stripped away the caul of illusion and broke her connectedness with the larger community. From then on, she lived in Lunase because she could go nowhere else.

This Temple occupied much less area than those in Lunase. The auxiliary chambers huddled around the perimeter of the sanctuary, compact, almost cramped rooms. The confessional was one booth instead of a row of them; the kitchen was an automated processor with a counter and three tables close together; Patri Simity's office was a cubicle with a small desk and a terminal.

The stacks of discs had been searched and left strewn over the floor. Someone had gone through the office in a hurry. Perhaps the search had been interrupted.

Where was Patri Simity?

She sat down before the terminal, examined it until she found the direct link, then removed her synthesist and made the connections.

The system possessed no diorama, only stacked tallies of files that riffled through her awareness. Nemily made an adjustment and imported them into her own sensora, sat down amid piles of documents, and began going through Temple records.

She located Patri Simity's personal correspondence and requested a match with the words "Glim Toler" and waited. A sheaf of mail rose to the top of the stack.

The most recent one read: "I am sending an acolyte of questionable ethics to Aea to deliver a package. He will no doubt seek the Temple. His name is Glim Toler."

Nemily skimmed through the pile. The dates ran back nearly two years and many of them referred to other letters in other files. She set loose a collation program that gathered all the related correspondence together, and began a search for the start of the chain, which seemed to trail throughout Simity's large body of communications.

She found one finally from a rector named Vin that began "Simity: It has come to my attention that our people are engaging in a program not in keeping with the principles of Gaia or common sense. It is not, of course, an 'official' program, but it has support among the more extreme members of SetNetComb."

Nemily sat back to read.

When she finished, she downloaded Simity's correspondence into a single file which she forwarded, after a few moments' thought, to Cambel Guerrera. She hesitated, feeling she should do more. Reluctantly, she sent a copy directly to Structural Authority, selecting three separate departments.

She had told herself then that she needed to leave, but she was tired and worn from the last several hours. Nemily wandered from room to room, uncertain what to look for, scanning the walls and furniture and floors—

In the kitchen she noticed that several pots and pans had been stacked on a countertop near the large double sink. She picked a few of them up. All clean. She went back to the office. The floor to the right of the desk was wet. She squatted over the small puddle and dipped her fingers in it. Coffee perhaps, or tea. Then she saw the cup, halfway under the desk. She returned to the kitchen.

From the third cabinet she opened, a small, folded body fell out onto the floor. The head cracked against the tile. Blood pooled beneath the skull.

Nemily backed away, pulse racing. It was Patri Simity, though it was a far different face than the smiling icon that kept appearing on her home comm with polite invitations to come back to the Temple. Her immediate impulse was to run. But she stood still, trying to force calm on herself and be rational.

She noticed, then, a faint pinkish trail that ran across the floor to the entrance. It had been wiped up, but traces of the blood still remained. The floor was cleanest right before the cabinet where the assassin had hidden Simity. The entire attempt had been hasty, interrupted. Which suggested that the killer would possibly be back, given a chance, to clean up better. But more likely not. The possibility that Simity had already been found would be greater the more time passed.

She needed to call pathic, get Simity medical attention. She could not tell if the old woman was alive.

Before she could reach the door, it opened.

Glim Toler glared at her. Then, slowly, he smiled.

"Surprise," he said. "Tell me you're glad to see me, Nem."

She lunged, thrusting her left arm out to catch him in the sternum with the heel of her hand. He stepped aside, caught her wrist, and sent her flying through the door, across the narrow hallway, into the wall. She collapsed on the floor, her wrist in bright, sharp pain.

"Shit," he hissed when he saw Simity. He let Nemily go and crossed the floor to kneel beside Simity. He began examining her carefully, looking for life. "This fouls everything up. I *needed* her."

"You didn't do this?" Nemily asked.

"No. Patri Simity was my way off Aea. Some of my other exits have been closed off." He looked up. "How long ago did you find her?"

"Just now. I—"

"She's still alive." He went to the sink and found a towel. He soaked it in water, then carefully placed it beneath Simity's head. "Come on."

He took her back to the office. He tapped in a call to the local pathic.

"Why are you doing this?" Nemily asked.

"What did you expect? She's a patri. She's old. We have to leave."

"We? I'm not going with you."

"For now you are," he said, reaching for her.

She tried to knock the hand aside, but her wrist erupted in sickening pain when she struck him. Glim took hold of her right arm and steered her out into the sanctuary.

"We're going back to your dom, Nem. Least, till I figure a way off this can."

He opened the doors and pushed her through, then left them open. Out in the main circuit, the pain subsiding slightly, she looked around for someone who might notice them, recognize that the situation was not normal and help. But this was the Heavy, more like Lunase than Aea, and all the faces seemed to turn away just as she found them.

She looked at Glim. He seemed thinner than she remembered, even though he had obviously gone through adapt treatments. The bones in his face protruded more sharply. His face was tight, his eyes wide and too alert. He surveyed the crowds with barely concealed fear.

A loud whine approached—the emergency pathic team, on its way to the Temple—and Glim tightened his grip for an instant. Then he relaxed. Too much.

Nemily stepped forward onto her left foot, stopped, and deftly jammed her right foot into Glim's knee and jerked her arm free at the same time.

He screamed, both hands reaching reflexively for the knee. Nemily braced herself and threw her elbow into his cheek. He spun away and she ran.

The pathic team was twenty meters away. People moved aside at the sound of their siren and Nemily squeezed between the medtechs and the crowd.

She made the elevator. As the doors closed, she saw no sign of Glim.

SIXTEEN

AEA, 2118

MACE PRESSED NEMILY'S MICI, then knocked on the door. The hallway was intensely quiet otherwise. He leaned against the door to listen, but heard no sounds from within the apartment. The silence stretched and he knew she was not inside.

He backed up against the opposite wall and slid to the floor. Possibilities ran through his mind.

She had more errands to run and he had simply missed her.

Perhaps she had gone in to work to personally request a leave of absence.

She had decided not to see him anymore and was staying with a friend till she could move or make sure he would not bother her.

Glim Toler had found her.

The last possibility unsettled him the most, but it seemed the least likely. Mace was sure Koeln had surveillance on Nemily in case of exactly that eventuality. Besides, InFlux records were damnably difficult to access, even for an insider like Mace; how would Toler find her address? Privacy was an Aean obsession, even though it seemed most Aeans could care less what they revealed about themselves. But that was just it—the choice to reveal details was personal, no one else could take that away. At least, not easily. Consequently, it was unlikely a newcomer like this Toler could track her down easily, certainly not quickly.

So was it possible she had changed her mind about him?

No. Maybe he was simply unwilling to accept that possibility, but it made no sense.

The first two were the most likely but he believed she would have let him know. She was an ordered person, she would take care of small details like that, especially when something important was at stake. If she had had more to do than simply come home to get a change of clothes, she would have let him know.

Unless it concerned something she did not want him to know about.

Toler?

Or Reese....

Koeln had lied to him about knowing Reese. He probably thought Reese was his agent, but Mace doubted Reese had ever been so dedicated. The fact that Reese was one of Cambel's sources attested to his adaptability. It was more likely that Reese worked both sides. Toler had been at his club. That in itself meant nothing, but Mace got the impression that Koeln believed there was a connection.

He was overlooking something, he could feel it. Probably because he was distracted. Where was Nemily?

If anyone would know, it would be Reese.

Would Reese tell Toler where he could find Nemily?

Mace pushed himself to his feet and headed for the stairs.

He hesitated at the sound of footsteps coming from below. Mace glanced back down the hallway, but there was no other exit. He started down the steps.

A man came around the landing, carrying a package. He looked up at Mace, momentarily startled, then smiled and nodded. He was completely unfamiliar to Mace. Tall, broadshouldered, with a slightly rounded face...Mace did not know him. Mace turned aside to let him pass and watched him continue up. He heard him start up the next flight.

Mace continued on down, relieved.

He strolled back to the shunt station, half hoping to see her walking toward him, returned from her errand. The more he imagined it the less likely it seemed. By the time he reached the station he felt certain that something had gone wrong, but he could not logically figure out how or what. Nemily was missing.

He tapped in his number at the public comm.

"Macefield Preston's domicile," the d.p. answered. He could not wait to get the lock off his system so Helen could function again.

"It's me. Did Nemily call?"

"Yes."

He suppressed his irritation. The house system did not have the autonomy to assume Mace would want more. He missed the Helen d.p.

"What did she say?"

"Would you like me to play it back?"

"Yes."

He listened to the message, relayed verbatim by the house system.

"There's been a little difficulty," he heard Nemily say. "Tell him I'll try
to call him later if I can."

"Do you wish to be more specific?"

"I can't. It's . . . I'll explain later."

"End message," the system said.

"Damn. That's . . . any other messages?"

"Yes. From Philip Huxley. Do you wish to hear it?"

"Yes."

"Tell Macefield to meet me as soon as he can at the pathic in ring five,
near arc ninety. You want to ask to see Patri Simity. It's important."

"If he calls again," Mace told the house system, "tell him I'm on my
way."

The pathic ward was two arcs antispinward from the arc ninety elevator.
Mace waited at the reception desk until the attendant noticed him.

"Visiting?" she asked.

"Patri Simity."

"Just a moment." She tapped a keyboard and watched a screen.
"Someone is already with her. Would you mind—"

"What room, please?"

"Uh, six . . . but—"

"Thank you."

Mace strode down the hall before she had a chance to deny him access. He wrinkled his nose at the faint but pervasive smell, a combination, he had always thought, of gin and aloe. He walked down the row
of private rooms till he reached number six. There, he glanced back to
see if anyone was coming to eject him. No one. He pushed through into
the quietly lit chamber.

Philip looked up from the opposite side of the bed. He began to rise, but Mace gestured for him to remain seated. Faintly, Mace could hear the whir of Philip's exoskeleton. Mace stopped at the foot of the bed.

Patri Simity was a small woman who seemed tiny in the bed surrounded by monitors. Across her lap was a tray with a bottle of water and half-eaten bowl of broth. Her face was pale and lined where it was not bruised; her mouth hung open slightly, a trickle of drool trailing down her chin into the pillow.

"Macefield," Philip said quietly. "Thank you."

"What happened?"

Philip's lips puckered distastefully. "Obviously she's been beaten. From the damage it's clear someone tried to kill her." He gestured at Simity with his right hand. "Broken bones, ruptured capillaries...she needs a new kidney. They're growing one for her, but it will be a few days." He shook his head. "The worst part is the skull fracture. She lost a lot of blood, too. There may be brain damage."

"I don't understand. What purpose could this serve?"

"I wouldn't have thought any. But—"

"I have always believed...."

Mace started at the sound of Simity's thin voice. Her head shifted on the massive pillow, mouth working as if chewing something, and her eyes blinked open. She squinted up at Philip, her left eye puffy and purple.

"Philip."

"Patri."

"Where am I?" Her eyes drifted left to right, moist and fearful.

"Pathic. You've been hurt."

"I know. It—I don't understand...thank you for coming. I wasn't sure anyone..." She noticed Mace then and frowned.

"Not at all," Philip said. "You're a friend. How can I help?"

She looked back at him briefly. "You just did. I haven't heard such simple sentences in months. If you're being insincere, don't tell me."

"Never. But you know I mean it. So. What happened?"

"Do you expect me to be indiscreet in front of strangers?"

"Ah. Patri Simity, this is my friend, Macefield Preston."

"How do you do, Macefield Preston," Simity said. "A friend of a friend and so forth...why are you here?"

"I'm looking for another friend," Mace said.

"Mmm. I didn't realize there were so many friends left in the world. That's encouraging."

"Patri—" Philip said.

"Did you check on the Temple?"

"Yes, I did."

"And it was all right?"

"It's been ransacked, I'm afraid. Nothing broken, just...disrespected. Now can you tell me what happened?"

She drifted back to sleep then. Philip glanced anxiously at the monitors above her, but they seemed normal enough. He looked up at Mace.

"Pathic was called anonymously two hours ago," he said. "They aren't sure exactly how long she's been like this—much easier to tell such things from a corpse than from a survivor—but they believe it was sometime in the last twenty to twenty-two hours."

"That's a long time to be left alone like this. She's tough. Toler?"

"That would, of course, be the easy assumption, but it doesn't make sense. She would be one of his best resources if he got into trouble. The Temple acts as a transition hospice for Lunessa, both immigrants and emigrants. Killing the patri would draw a lot of unnecessary attention and close one of his avenues off Aea. It would accomplish nothing."

"How did you get here?"

"Ah. Now that *is* interesting. Cambel received a data transfer from Simity to her dom system a little over two hours ago."

"I didn't know Cambel knew Simity."

"She didn't. Not well enough to be receiving comms from her. And this was an enormous file. When she opened it, she found Simity's entire correspondence with a patri in Lunase named Vin. Vin, it seems, is quite displeased with current Lunessa policy. There is detailed information concerning the use of the Temple and its acolytes by SetNetComb in various covert operations, mostly trade sabotage. It suggests an organized attempt to undermine trade among the Signatory stations."

"The war you were talking about."

Philip nodded. "Toler is a soldier in that war."

"You say this was sent two hours ago. But if Simity was beaten yesterday—"

"Then who sent us the file? Exactly. It was sent shortly before the anonymous call to pathic. I called Simity when we opened the documents to find out what she wanted us to do with them and found pathic already there. So here I am."

"These documents—"

Simity opened her eyes again.

"I'd like you to continue checking on it while I'm here, Philip," she said. "A place can be like a person; it needs to feel cared for or it can die."

"It's in the Heavy, Patri."

She scowled. "I don't want you to conduct services. No one comes anyway. I just want you to go there and see that nothing is out of order. Check on it. Remind it that people still know it's there. The Temple hasn't been left empty since it opened. Just because I'm stuck in pathic is no excuse."

Mace found himself liking this old rector even while she tested his patience. Philip gave him a sympathetic look.

"All right," Philip said. "I can do that. Now. What happened?"

"Are you being kind or are you genuinely interested?"

"Both. Now stop testing me and tell me."

"Did you hear," Simity said weakly, "that Lunase is at war?"

"I'd heard something like that," Philip said. "With whom? Why?"

"Oh, everyone, for everything. No one is happy there."

"It would help to know who did this to you, Patri."

"Mmm. You probably already know. You're just confirming."

"Perhaps," Philip said. "What we do not know is why or how he did this or what your Temple has to do with it."

She drifted to sleep again. Philip sighed wearily. "This could take a long time."

"These correspondences," Mace said. "Any names in them?"

"Oh, yes. Toler figures prominently. SetNetComb comes up a great deal. The impression I have, though, is not an overall effort. It sounds more like one department in the larger government that has gotten out of hand. Vin mentions attempts to shut the program down, but suspects it has continued covertly."

"As if that's never happened before."

"Exactly. Toler, according to Vin, was sent here to initiate this phase of the operation. He was supposed to meet his contact and begin."

"And that contact would be—?"

"That name isn't mentioned. Toler was supposed to meet, start the program, spend a week or so here, then return to Lunase. Evidently, Toler is a well-travelled Lunessa. Some of his other destinations are interesting—Cassidy, Five-Eight, and Midline."

Mace took a few moments to think about that. "So what happened? How did they meet?"

"We don't know. Vin sent Toler to Simity instead of to his contact."

"Reese should know."

"Probably, but we can't ask him anymore. I am hoping Simity—"

"Yes? Philip, are you still here?"

"Yes, I am. Can I help you with anything?"

"I doubt it. I'm beyond help."

"Don't be cynical on me."

"You must wonder," she said quietly, "what I believe anymore, Philip. We've had many talks about the nature of faith and the objects of reverence, but all that was mostly theoretical. Enjoyable. I look forward to many more. But I always knew you never accepted the tenets I'm supposed to represent." She drew a deep breath, swallowed loudly. "Fair enough. Tenets change. But there's something at the base of it all that drives us and keeps us bound to the forms even when they seem to have lost their meaning."

"Possibly—"

"No. Definitely." She looked around as if gathering her thoughts. "You see, many of my peers in the Temple have lost their faith, but they continue in it. They go through the motions because people depend on structure. They know they fulfill a purpose even if the original meaning is gone for them. But they misunderstand faith. You see, they placed their faith in something outside, something they expected to direct them or give them anchor or let them measure themselves against. Faith isn't static. Faith is...." She closed her eyes and fell silent for several seconds. Mace glanced at the monitors reflexively. "You don't have faith in something," Simity continued suddenly. "You simply have faith. Like truth, it's a process. It is always the same and it is never the same. If you expect it to remain unchanged it will pass you by. It follows you where it leads you. People who do the inexplicable in the name of their faith have misplaced it. Of course, they're looking in the wrong place, in the wrong way. I have never lost my faith, Philip, because I have never mistaken faith for property."

"What does all that have to do with what Lunase is doing?" Mace asked.

"Nothing. Everything. They're trying to turn the future into the past by pretending that nothing changes, that faith is eternal and therefore always the same."

Mace tried to match her words to circumstances, but it seemed that she was only rambling. She was old and frail and badly injured. She might live, but the fear, the brush with mortality, had certainly distorted her sense of priority, her perception of relevance.

"Do you know where is Glim Toler?" he asked.

"I don't know."

"Who would know?"

"Gaia. It revolves, you see, around the central nature of causality. I wrote a paper once. It helps to remember." She winced. "Thank you for coming, Philip. I seem to remember you told me stories...."

A pathologist came in then and leaned close to one of the monitors. He made a quick adjustment and Patri Simity slipped instantly into sleep.

"That's all for now," he said. "Thanks for talking to her for so long. It gave us a real good baseline to map the damage."

Philip glowered at the man as he stood. For a moment, Mace thought he might see Philip erupt in rage. But Philip drew a deep breath and walked out of the room.

"I'm sorry for your friend," Mace said.

"They seem to have some expectation that she'll recover," Philip said, glancing back at the pathic facility.

"It doesn't make sense that Toler would do that."

"No, it doesn't. But it doesn't make sense for anyone to do it. She's not—she's been rector here for forty years. This branch has been losing importance for all that time, till now...."

"Till now the rector can lie bleeding in her own Temple for hours before anyone finds her."

"Yes. Which is sad, but it is also a contradiction. What motive?"

"Did you say twenty hours ago?"

"That is their best guess."

"I was in the Temple nearly that long ago, with Koeln."

Philip frowned. "What was he doing there?"

"The same thing I was. Looking for Toler. We both had the idea of asking the patri."

"And?"

"And she wasn't there. Or if she was, she was hidden."

"They said they found her on the floor in the kitchen."

"Wouldn't make sense that Koeln could miss her, then."

Philip shook his head. "But he's an even less likely suspect. Why would a member of PolyCarb security try to kill Simity?"

"He's Lunessa. Maybe he hates the Temple. Who else does that leave? Reese Nagel?"

"Again, why?"

"So no one we can think of would have a motive to kill Patri Simity?"

"I can't think who."

"Then it's someone we don't know."

"Toler's contact, our trojan. Koeln?"

Philip shook his head slowly. "Why would he be looking for Toler if he was the contact?"

"Koeln has lied to me already. He found Nemily and questioned her about Toler. Did I tell you that Helen's name is on both their InFlux jackets as sponsor?"

"I looked into that, Macefield. The dates go back before Hellas Planitia. Those sponsorships were made prior to Helen's death."

Mace stared at his friend, absorbing the information. "How is that—? Toler was on Mars, at the site. We know that. If she sponsored him...."

"It's doubtful she did. Someone in PolyCarb used her name to do this. The trojan, we can assume, since Helen was out at Ganymede when these were filed."

"The trojan set this up that long ago?"

"We can assume this operation has been going on for several years."

"What operation? Lunase?"

"Yes. Trade talks have broken down repeatedly over the last few years on PolyCarb's—and by extension Aea's—entry into the manufacture and distribution of exotics, materials Lunase insists are theirs to make and sell by right. The current talks are supposed to reach an accommodation between the orbitals—specifically Aea—and Lunase regarding who gets to make and sell what. It's that simple. When the issue first came up, Lunase made several unfortunate statements suggesting they would make us suffer for encroaching on their rightful purview. We suspect they developed a very efficient process for breaking down exotics at the molecular level. The first trial was Hellas Planitia."

"A threat to boost their side at the talks."

"Exactly. When that failed to get them what they wanted, they destroyed Cassidy and Five-Eight."

"And now Midline. But—"

"The word I have is that the operation has gone rogue. The talks are currently proving successful. Agreements are being reached. But someone within SetNetComb has decided to continue the war."

"Lunase can claim that it was a rogue operation all along."

"Of course."

Mace thought it through silently. Then: "If Lunase wants to shut it down, then Toler arrived here with no contact. He's still here because whatever he's supposed to do, he can't do it. He may be stuck here, with no way off."

Philip nodded. "So he went to Patri Simity to get back home and she told him no. He flew into a rage and beat her. That would make sense, in a way. But he would have to go somewhere else then to get off Aea."

"Nagel?"

"Possibly. We may never know now. Nagel is dead."

Mace stared at him, his ears warming. "What? When?"

"Several hours ago."

"I didn't—he—" Mace grunted. "Maybe he told him no, too. That sounds desperate. I—"

Something in the timbre of conversation around them changed. Mace caught Philip's frown and then looked away as the sound grew louder. People were huddling close to one another, the thickest gatherings around the public terminals.

Philip crossed the circuit toward the nearest terminal. He stood head and shoulders above most of the crowd. He came back a moment later.

"SA has made Midline public," he said.

"Hell."

"Perhaps. I'm going back to my shop. This is getting tiring, being here. What are you going to do?"

"I'm still trying to find Nemily. I might have another talk with Koeln. Assuming he's still alive."

Philip smiled grimly. "Be careful, Macefield."

Blue-uniformed SA security hovered around the entrance to 5555. A crowd stood at a wide yellow marker strip, watching. Other people came in and out of the nightclutch as Mace looked on. A pathic gurney came out then, surrounded by half a dozen medics. All Mace saw was a patch of skin and gauze where a face should have been.

Koeln stepped out of the entrance. Behind him came Colf, Reese's muscle. They stopped briefly and Koeln spoke to her. Colf nodded and walked away. Mace squeezed between the people in front of him to stand at the edge of the marker and stare at Koeln. Koeln glanced back toward the door, then did a quick survey of the crowds gathered. It seemed to Mace that he lingered briefly on him, then let his gaze sweep past. He spoke to a pair of SA security people, then pushed his way through the crowd.

Mace backed away from the line and worked his way out into the open circuit.

He spotted Koeln heading toward the spoke elevator. Mace hung back, watching to see if anyone else trailed along after Koeln. He hurried to close the distance as Koeln reached the spoke and slipped onto the elevator as the doors slid shut.

More than a dozen people rode up with them. At each ring, a few left, one or two got on, until at the final stop, the interior, everyone got out.

Koeln stood against the opposite wall of the car, watching Mace. The doors closed again and they were alone. Koeln punched in a code and the car locked in place.

"Is there a problem, Mr. Preston?"

"Reese is dead, I take it?"

"Yes. Someone crushed his skull."

"Toler?"

"That's my first guess."

"Where's Nemily Dollard?"

"I don't know. I'm beginning to suspect that she's made contact with Toler and if so she's either in the same condition as Reese and Patri Simity or they're working together."

Mace felt his scalp tingle. "That's a stretch, don't you think? Why one or the other?"

"Ms. Dollard has been central to this, as are you," Koeln said. "She came here sponsored by your wife. So did Toler. Now that both of them are here, people are dying. I can only assume that these murders are being committed to keep people silent."

"Silent about what?"

Koeln shrugged. "We'll learn that when we have Toler. Perhaps there are others here who are part of it, but none of them were sponsored here by a dead PolyCarb employee. One who, herself, might have been culpable. One who, I'm sure, was at least acquainted with whoever is now running the operation."

"What operation?"

Koeln smiled. "Some things are still confidential." He reached for the button. "We've held the lift up long enough, I think. Other citizens need to get places."

"I don't think Toler killed Reese."

Koeln's finger paused. "Why not?"

"Because it keeps him on Aea and he has to know that if he stays, he'll die."

"Perhaps. Perhaps he doesn't care anymore." Koeln dropped his hand. "Last night, Ms. Dollard went to see Reese. She was escorted to ring one by Colf, to perform an illegal ghost for someone. This wasn't the first time she'd done work like this for Reese."

"Who was the client?"

"I don't know. Colf didn't see. My guess would be Toler. He had approached her to carry vacuum here from Lunase when she emigrated. She claims she refused. Perhaps she did. But then why would Toler bother to try to contact her now? And why, afterward, would Toler kill Reese unless Ms. Dollard had confirmed something about Reese?"

"Maybe something just went wrong. You're not even sure if the client was Toler."

"No, I'm not. But I suspect that whatever Ms. Dollard knows or did, it was compromising to the trojan. Loose ends like Reese would have to be tidied up."

"And Patri Simity?"

Koeln shrugged. "Who knows?"

"So you don't know where Nemily is?"

"No. We had her shadowed, but we lost her."

"And you don't know where Toler is?"

"No."

"Why not? All you have to do is follow the bodies. If you're right."

Koeln punched the release button. "There is another possibility," he said. "Your wife could be alive, could be working for Lunase, could well be the trojan." He grinned at Mace.

"Well. You work for PolyCarb. Find out."

The doors opened on ring four and Mace stepped out before Koeln could answer.

He was missing something and it made him feel slow and stupid.

He had wandered the rings until he found a 'ponics farm. He sat on the loam just inside the door. Soybean grew as far as he could see, the green carpet sweeping up at the horizon to disappear around the curve of the ring.

"Where are you?" he asked in a whisper, then realized that he did not know about whom he asked.

He had played the last couple years so low-keyed, so subtly, so distantly, that he had lost touch with nearly everything. He had lost touch with the reason for doing any of it. Fine, he had known that for some time, but now that he had found a new reason to take up the effort again he practically had to start from scratch.

All the pieces were still there, though. He just could not see how they wove together to form the pattern he needed. And his feelings were getting in the way.

If Nemily had come to hurt him, to use him to hurt Aea, then she was a most perfect weapon. She was naïve, ignorant, and desperate not to be someone bad, and she was convincing. She was a cyberlink, so all that could be a shell around a truth she did not even know she possessed. She might have been used as a mule throughout, a carrier with no conscious knowledge of her role or mission.

If she had struck at Reese, did that mean she now knew?

But Mace mistrusted the appearance of perfection. He could not, ultimately, accept that she had been all that and aimed at him, too. The chances of him taking the bait...perhaps he was being naïve himself, but the odds were too high.

Why had she ghosted for Reese, though? And who had been the client? If that was the reason for Reese's death, then perhaps he needed to reevaluate all his assumptions. And if it *was* the reason for his death, then why had they let Nemily live?

If they had....

He rubbed his face roughly. "Start somewhere else," he said.

The trojan, if there was one, might possibly even be Linder Koeln and could be presumed to be running any Lunessa agents. Who would they be and how would they operate? Assuming CAPs had been used by this rogue operation out of SetNetComb to smuggle in data, maybe even components with which to construct the sabotage material, Philip's explanation of the isolating architecture of Nemily's augment net meant that they were designed for keeping the secrets of their operators. If they all worked the same way, all of them could contain hidden data usable at the discretion of a single operator with the correct code.

Or she was just an observer. Recording everything she saw, storing the data until someone came along to use what she knew....

To what end?

Any end. Reese sent Nemily to do an illicit ghost. Could her hidden programming, if any, now be in use? Or was she simply passing along what she had learned about Aea? Not knowing where she was or if she was alive, he could not ask.

But she had called his dom. Something had gone wrong and she could not tell him about it over the tapped line.

And someone had sent those files from Patri Simity to Cambel. Why? Who would know to do that? Assuming that they were ultimately intended to reach him, it had to be someone who knew that his domestic personality, his home system, was compromised, and that he and Cambel worked together.

Nemily or Koeln?

Koeln would have no real reason to send such a cryptic message. Nemily, on the other hand, might be trying to prove her innocence of any sabotage.

All right, the trojan had brought her here, using Helen's name as sponsor. It would be interesting to see if others had come in under the same sponsorship. But the important ones were Nemily and Toler. Why would the trojan use Helen's name when he could have used any other deceased Aean in the same way?

Of course, she had not been deceased when the sponsorships had been made.

Koeln?

No, not likely. Because whoever had used her name knew Helen, knew a lot about her, could answer the requisite questions on the In-Flux sponsorship forms. Mace doubted Koeln knew the first thing about Helen.

It would be someone who had been with PolyCarb before the Hellas Planitia incident, with a high enough security clearance. If the trojan was good enough to successfully use Helen as a fake sponsor, then probably the trojan was good enough to hide a Lunessa origin. Koeln openly admitted his.

The murders could only be to protect exactly that. Someone else knew.

Perhaps that was what Nemily's ghost had been about. Verification of associations. Who might know the trojan and where were they now?

Mace stared at the field of green and the close roof of the world, a mild throbbing behind his eyes, and tried to match the pieces of the puzzles. It amazed him how quickly it had all become so complicated and he had not yet asked himself how it all related to Helen's death.

"All because Nemily Dollard took me home after a party," he mused.

He closed his eyes and imagined the faces of the players drifting across each others' paths, like bodies in space, just missing each other because the trajectories were just right. He did not believe in coincidence. Unpredictable results, yes, but coincidence was an after-the-event imposition of pattern to try to make sense of randomness. If Nemily had been put in his path as bait, it had to have been with the assumption that he would take it. There was no way to guarantee that.

The only other face that seemed connected to both Nemily and Toler. . . .

He hated being set up.

Slowly, he opened his eyes. The pieces orbited a common center. He had avoided this conclusion, wanting first to rule out all other possibilities.

First, though, he had to do one more check.

He wondered who would be in the InFlux offices at this hour.

SEVENTEEN

AEA, 2118

NEMILY HESITATED TO APPROACH MACE'S DOM. She rode the spinward shunt all the way around three times before she made herself get off at the station.

She walked up the pathway with palpable reluctance. There was no way Mace could know that she had read Helen's jacket, that she probably knew more about her than Mace did. But all her instincts made her afraid to confront him, as if the certainty of her intellect meant nothing to the emotional weight of her betrayal. If he did not now know, he would soon enough, because she would tell him. And he might hate her for it.

How do I expect to stay on Aea, she wondered, *when I've already made sure they won't want me?*

She walked up to the door, glancing nervously around to see if anyone watched. The other doms were almost invisible through the thick stands of dwarf trees. The upshaft end of Aea was thick with genetically altered trees and shrubs. She had looked them up once and saw photographs of their originals on Earth, giant things that towered over their landscapes. These barely reached three and four meters, but they were rich with leaves and heavy bark, green and lush and, for her, emblematic of all that she wanted.

She pressed the mici.

"Yes?" Helen's voice said.

"Hello. This is Nemily Dollard. Is Mace home?"

"No."

She waited, but the door did not open. She realized then that she expected it to open for her until it remained closed. "Helen?"

"I am the basic house logic system. 'Helen' is the domestic personality currently offline."

"I see. May I come in?"

"Given the present circumstances, I don't think it prudent to make that decision. If you want you may wait there till Mace returns."

"How long?"

"I don't know where he is. He checked in two hours ago."

"Where was he then?"

"He had just left your domicile."

"He's looking for me?"

"Yes."

Nemily looked back up the path as if she might see Mace walking toward her. "Two hours ago?"

"Yes."

"Then where...?"

She had left her augments at the Temple. She did not want to risk returning for them, although after SA finished searching the place they would find them and know she had been there. She had another set at her dom. She needed a few other things from there as well, even though it now seemed impossible to hope that she could remain on Aea.

"Tell him I was here and tell him I'm going back to my dom. If I'm not back here in an hour, then that's where I'll be. Will you tell him?"

"Yes."

She felt mildly guilty at the half-truth. She *did* intend to go to her dom eventually—she had to—but not at first. She did not know if SA was monitoring Mace's house system. Perhaps she would not have to explain this small lie; it seemed insignificant compared to the trouble she expected to be in.

She strode up the path to the pedistry, anxious and worried that at any moment she would see either Structural Authority security or Glim Toler coming to seize her.

What surprised her most was that the address was in segment three. She had been certain when she looked it up that Cambel Guerrera lived in segment two, a neighbor perhaps to Mace.

That Cambel let her in was another surprise.

Cambel wore a short silk robe of deep blue and pale green. Her apartment, spacious and high-ceilinged, seemed crowded with small objects: lamps, end tables, curios, frames, small figures on shelves, one long sofa, chairs and a display on one wall of ornate fans.

Nemily stood near the center of the room, looking around, nervous and uncomfortable. She watched Cambel empty a chair of a stack of folders. Cambel waved at the chair, then sat down on the sofa opposite, one leg tucked casually beneath her.

"I'm guessing," Cambel said, "that you sent us that file from the Temple rector."

Nemily sat down. "Yes. I thought Mace should see it, but I didn't know if his comm was being monitored."

"By SA? It's not, not anymore, but I suppose you couldn't know that. So you sent it to me and thought I'd pass it on."

"Yes. Did you?"

"I haven't seen Mace in the last several hours. He's out looking for you." She nodded then. "It was a fascinating read, that file. How did you know about it?"

"I didn't. I mean, I went to the Temple to see if I could stay there for a time." Nemily felt herself scowl. "No, that's not true. I went there looking for Glim Toler. I thought the rector might know."

"And you went through her files while you were there?"

"I—she wasn't—no one was there. The place had already been searched. Whoever had done it had missed her protected files. Or just couldn't get to them."

"But you could."

"I'm a CAP, Ms. Guerrera. We're very good at getting around systems like that."

"I see. What do you want now?"

"I've been to Mace's dom, he's not there—"

"I told you—"

"—so I came here. You're his friend, you work with him. If I can't trust you, then...."

Cambel leaned forward. "Then?"

"Then Mace has no friends."

Cambel Guerrera's face remained impassive. She stared at Nemily a long time. The only sign of tension came through her hands; the tendons stood out sharply.

Finally she sat back. "He has better friends than he knows."

Nemily's sense of relief came in a rush. She swallowed thickly and let herself lean back in the chair.

"Toler was at the Temple," she said.

"What? When?"

"It's been a little over two hours. I was getting ready to leave and he came in. The patri—she had been beaten and someone had left her in the rectory kitchen. I thought Glim had done it, but he called pathic. Then he wanted me to go with him. I got away from him. I've been wandering since."

"Why didn't you call SA?"

"I—" She sighed and closed her eyes. "No reason. I *did* send them the same files I sent you, but...I thought I might not see Mace again if I called them. I didn't know if they'd believe me that I had nothing to do with Patri Simity's injuries. I was afraid Glim would tell them we were together." She looked at Cambel. "I didn't want to be expelled."

Cambel seemed to be weighing information. Her fingers tapped arrhythmically on the back of the sofa.

"Do you love Mace?"

"I can't answer that."

"Oh? Is it a secret?"

"No, it's—Mace knows, we talked about it. I can't. I've never experienced it, so I have no way to know. I need to—it's the nature of my augmentation."

"For a person who doesn't know, you act like you love him. Or at least want him."

"I want to be with him. Is that the same?"

"It is for me."

"Oh. I see."

Cambel waved a hand dismissively. "Don't worry. Mace and I have come to an understanding. I won't interfere. I can't. But if you don't know, how do you intend to find out?"

"I offered to run Helen."

Cambel blinked. "As a ghost?"

"Yes."

"That wouldn't be a very good idea."

"Why? Didn't she love him?"

"I don't know. But for me, it would always be a question as to who it is I'm loving."

"I don't—I'm not sure I understand what you mean."

"Secondhand emotion. Mace loved Helen. Whether or not she returned it, we may never know. Unless you ghost her. What if you find out that she didn't? What if she was only with Mace because it was convenient? And what if she did love him? Would Mace be returning *that* love or loving you for yourself?" She shook her head. "That's too many possible ways to mess it up. If I understand what you're telling me, there are treatments for it. You don't have to become a ghost to fix your problems."

"I see. Why are you interested?"

"Mace is . . . I don't want to see him hurt again. Not the same way. You become Helen for him, someday you'll have to bury her all over."

"What about Helen? I could settle the question of her complicity."

Cambel nodded thoughtfully. "Possibly. But does Mace really need to know? If she was innocent, then it confirms what he already believes. If not, if just adds to the hurt."

This was not what Nemily had come here for, but it was accidental wealth. She had not considered the possible impact on Mace when she had made the offer. One more problem with the way her brain worked— sometimes the obvious was the hardest thing to see.

"Now," Cambel said. "Why don't you tell me all about Glim Toler. Then maybe we can decide what to do."

"Mace wasn't even supposed to be there," Cambel said. "He got himself assigned to head security for one of the Directors, Listrom, if I recall. Helen was on her way back to Aea, but had been diverted to Mars to do something at the Hellas Planitia site. No one knows what, because the company decided to seal everything and pretend she'd died somewhere else."

"Why would they do that?"

"They do that in cases where someone is doing high-level, special work and it's not supposed to be public. In other words, it's kept from the shareholders. Helen Croslo, among other things, was a spy for Poly-Carb."

Nemily thought for a moment. "That makes sense."

"Does it? In any case, Mace found out she would be there, and arranged to be there, too. Then the accident happened and he abandoned his assignment to run out there. He took over security on the recovery mission, then got in over his head. I believe—and the company believed at the time—that Macefield Preston would not be a team player and let it drop. He had too much personal investment. He would dig and make scenes and embarrass PolyCarb. Couldn't have that. So I was given the thankless job of removing him permanently from the investigation. I didn't know either one of them before that, Helen or Mace, but PolyCarb handed me the assignment of convincing Mace to sign off on Helen's death certificate. I can't tell you how that felt." She stared at her hands for a few seconds. "Maybe I can. I felt like a first-rate Judas. The arguments were so logical, so sensible, and I believed Helen was dead. There's no way she could have made it across that desert without transport. Which made the second tier of logic work—if she had transport, she was culpable. But I could see the logic work on Mace and it was ugly. PolyCarb made me hurt him. Badly. They shouldn't have done that."

"You didn't have to do it."

"You aren't management. You can't imagine the pressure."

"You've never lived in Lunase. Would you care to compare?"

Cambel's eyebrows went up. "Touché. Anyway, I had to accompany him back to Aea and get him settled into a new position. The trip back...well, he didn't settle. He kept asking questions and poking into places he had no authority for. I was given another assignment. Get him to stop or he'd be expelled."

"Would they have done that?"

"There was a window of opportunity, but once Mace accepted the insurance settlement and resigned from the company, it would have required an SA judicial action to do it. The company missed its chance. But once he was outside, his avenues of research became very limited. He still wasn't going to quit and he kept bothering me to help him. There were...inconsistencies...with the PolyCarb official version, so I started giving him small things on the side. PolyCarb must have found out. They reassigned me. I recognized the pattern. They were about to ship me all over the system to keep me out of the way. They'd done that to a lot of the personnel at Hellas Planitia. I told them to go to hell this time and handed in my resignation."

"Whose idea was it to go into business together?"

"Mine. Mace would have done it by himself. He would have tried to, anyway. As much as he wanted to be an Aean, he was more Martian. He really didn't know his way around, not like he does now. PolyCarb had granted him citizenship but the job had kept him moving around Signatory Space most of the time."

"You wanted more."

Cambel nodded. "Maybe it was guilt. Certainly I felt responsible. I *did* literally take care of him for that first year. So, yes. I thought—I hoped—it would become more."

"You're very good friends."

She grunted. "Very good friends. Like brother and sister." She shook herself as if suddenly cold. "So now we find out that one of the survivors from Hellas Planitia, possibly the only one, was Toler. That makes it look even worse for Helen, especially with her name on Toler's immigration petition as sponsor. Working with Lunase."

"Do you think she was?"

"No. I think she was *hunting* Toler. Maybe not him specifically, but the thing that he was—is: a saboteur, if our guess is right."

"You said one of the survivors. There are others?"

"It's not clear. A few people got into the tunnel on Hellas Planitia. We found two, dead. One was a CAP, by the way. There were enough footprints to suggest more people, possibly two or three. But we couldn't be certain. Still, before that, someone had to clear Toler to get him on the site to begin with. He had an accomplice. We just don't know who. The trail is covered too well."

"You don't even have a possibility?"

"Oh, we have a very good one, as it happens, but we're going to be very, very certain before—"

The comm chimed. Cambel excused herself and left the room. A minute later, she hurried back in, carrying a change of clothes in her left hand.

"Time for you to go home."

"What—?"

"That was Mace. He wants me to meet him. But he wants me to escort you back to his dom."

Nemily stood. "He didn't want to talk to me?"

"In the worst way. But it'll wait. His words." Cambel peeled off her robe and pulled on the loose singlepiece. "Come on."

"I need to go by my dom first. There are things I need."

"It can wait."

"No, it can't. I left my augments in the Temple. I need my spare set. Please. It's actually not far from here, just a dozen arcs."

"Fine. But in and out and don't bring the whole wardrobe."

Cambel refused to tell her where she was to meet Mace. After the third attempt, Cambel simply stopped talking. Nemily now stood before her door feeling suddenly exhausted. She had, she realized, been on the run for almost a day. The collations had been insufficient time for recovery, especially when they released her back into a feeling of being pursued and watched. It would be good to simply lock her own door and go to sleep.

"I used to live in one of these," Cambel said as Nemily tapped in her personal code. "Not as nice a one, though. Segment four."

"Yes, well—"

She pushed open the door and led the way in to her apartment. It seemed as if she had not been here in a week. She stood in the middle of the small living room and tried to think what she needed to take.

The sound of a dull thud and the impact of a weight hitting the floor brought her around.

"Imagine my surprise that you could live in a place like this."

Nemily stared at Toler's grinning face, marred now by a bruise on his left cheek. On the floor at his feet sprawled Cambel, her face hidden by her hair. Toler held a thick, black handgun.

"Let's talk, Nem."

He stepped forward and shoved her toward the couch. She caught herself before she sat down.

"I expect I'll be taken into custody soon enough," he said. "But I wanted to see you again. I wanted to tell you a few things. I wanted you to know what's happening." He sat down in the chair opposite the couch. "Sit, please." He glanced back at the door. "The security measures here are pathetic, you know."

She continued to stand. After a few seconds, Toler rose smoothly to his feet, stepped up to her, and shoved her hard in the chest. She stumbled back against the sofa and sat.

"I've had adapt treatments, too," he said. "Otherwise I couldn't even walk here. Good thing, too, or that little maneuver you pulled on me might have left me in pathic for a month. That was good, you know. I always thought you had a good head for a crisis."

Nemily looked toward Cambel. "You hurt her."

"Not bad. She'll come around." He rubbed his bruise gingerly. "This isn't my first treatment, though. I've been through adapt before. Just never for a full Gaian gravity." He rolled his shoulders. "Now that I'm getting used to it, I can see the appeal. There's something...natural...to the way it feels. I can't wait to get home. Six times stronger than everybody else. The possibilities are staggering."

"What do you want to talk to me about?"

"Aren't you glad to see me?" he asked wryly. He shook his head. "Never mind. Things have gone all wrong. I'm trying to get off this thing now and someone keeps closing exits on me. You wouldn't happen to know who, would you?"

"No."

He frowned. "I'm not here to hurt you—"

"You hurt me just showing up. You hurt Patri Simity. You hurt Cambel. My life was good before you came here. Why?"

"Your life was never yours. If it was good it was because we didn't need you." He glanced back at Cambel. "I never hurt Patri Simity. I liked her. She was going to help me get back to Lunase. Why would I hurt her?"

"Because you don't know any better. It's what you do."

"You wouldn't even be living here if it weren't for me, Nem, haven't you figured that out by now?"

"You damn near got me expelled before I even had a chance!"

Toler looked confused for a moment, then grinned. "The vacuum? That went wrong, didn't it? All that was supposed to do was introduce you to your operator, but you ended up losing it before he made contact."

"What did you do to me?"

"On Lunase? Nothing much. A little block to keep you from finding the vacuum before you got here. Another little bit of code to make you useful. Eventually."

"Am I...am I a weapon?"

Toler laughed. "Hardly. You're just an observer. Not even consciously. You did just what you were supposed to do. Snoop, look, record. If we'd needed it...well, no matter. We didn't need it. Nothing I did compromised your life here."

"You show up and suddenly I'm being questioned by security and my friends are in trouble and now—"

"Who questioned you?"

"PolyCarb security."

"PolyCarb? Not SA?"

"I'm sure they're about to get around to it."

"Nem, I didn't come here to mess up your life. At least, that's not why I came here in the first place. Things have gone wrong, do you understand? None of this was supposed to happen."

"What *was* supposed to happen?"

"I can't tell you."

"You thought you'd come in, drop off a package, set things in motion and leave before Aea fell apart."

He looked surprised and Nemily felt an instant of gratification.

"Were you the one I ghosted for the other night?" she asked.

"No. I was there, but I didn't need that information."

"Who was it?"

Glim shook his head absently. "I need to get out. I have one more way. I want you to take me there."

"Why? If it's your contact—"

"Things have gotten complex. Believe me, if I could go there alone, I would." He grinned. "Of course, I could do worse in travelling companions."

"Where is it?"

"I'll come to that. I need to explain, though, that none of what's happened was my fault."

"How would you define 'fault'? You set me up when I came here to get rejected and sent back to Lunase. You hid vacuum in my gear, you planted something in my head, you—"

"I'm not talking about that! I'm talking about everything that has happened since I got here! Damnit, Nem, someone's trying to kill me!"

"I'd kill you myself if I thought I could."

She had said it calmly, with almost no inflection. The effect on Glim was startling. Color leached from his face and his expression went slack. For several seconds he stared at her blankly.

"You don't understand," he said. "I'm a soldier. That's all. I do what I'm told, for a cause. I work toward a purpose. I've been a good soldier. Now my own people—*our* people—are trying to kill me. Policy has changed. Do you understand? I've been betrayed."

"I understand betrayal."

Glim Toler looked away from her, afraid.

"What do you want, Glim?"

"I want to get out of here. I do not want to be picked up by SA, although the only thing they can really do to me is expel me. They don't have the juice for anything more. But if they arrest me, then my usefulness is over. I'll be known. I'll be a file in a Signatory database. Worthless."

"You don't think you are already?"

His eyes narrowed. "What do you know?"

"Nothing. But if someone's trying to kill you—one of *your* people—how much worth are you to them? They must think you've already been compromised."

"I can clear that up when I get back. But I have to get back. Once I'm back they can't deny me. If they kill me here...."

"Why come to me? I can't get you out."

"No, but you can get me to someone who can."

"Why should I?"

"Oh, because I'll kill you if you don't." He waved his blockish, black handgun. "Or I'll kill your friend here. Nothing personal. It's war."

"War?"

"Yes. That's what *you* were. A missile, sent to hit a target. Something went wrong, though, so they sent me to fix it. Now it's fixed. Now I get to go home."

"It doesn't sound like they want you."

"It's not Lunase that set me up. It's the people here. They turned. Especially that gutless wonder who's going to get me out. He *likes* it here. He doesn't agree with the program anymore. That's why I had to come here." He nodded, desperation infusing his voice. "It makes sense now. He set me up. He's the one trying to kill me before I go back and report. Thank you, Nem. You've helped me think it through."

"I'm not going to help you, Glim. I have a life here."

"Maybe you don't understand. You're going to be expelled anyway. Or die. You take me to my contact and there may be a way to save your precious citizenship. He's the only one likely to be able to do it for you."

"Not if you kill him."

"How can I? I need him to get me off Aea."

Nemily could see no way around it. She felt more trapped than when he had grabbed her in the Temple. She knew he held out false hope, but when there is no other, even false hope convinced her.

"All right," she said finally. "Where?"

No one paid them any special attention while they waited for a shunt. Glim guided her to a rear seat on the nearly empty car; he sat on the aisle side. The nearest passenger was several seats away.

"So what was it I ran the other night?" she asked.

At first, she did not think he heard her. Then he glanced at her and shrugged. "A dead woman's persona."

Nemily felt a crawling sensation over her scalp and down her back. "Helen Croslo?"

Glim frowned. "How—?" His lips pressed into a thin line and he stared the length of the car. "As a matter of fact, yes."

"You killed her on Mars."

"I killed a lot of people on Mars. You're full of surprises today. That ghost was supposed to be fully occluded. Reese promised."

"You never know about CAPs. Sometimes the damnedest things refuse to erase." When he said nothing for a time, she pressed. "So did you?"

"What?"

"Kill her on Mars?"

He nodded. "Out on the sands. She was one tenacious bitch. But it wasn't murder. She was trying to kill me. But...be quiet, Nem. This is much too public a place for this talk."

"So who was I ghosting it for? Where did it come from?"

"Shut up."

"I have to assume you took it from her after you killed her, so it went back to Lunase with you. But you could have run it there, then. Unless you didn't take it back to Lunase. Unless you delivered it to someone on Mars—"

Glim closed his hand around Nemily's knee and squeezed, hard. Pain lanced up from her old surgery scar and she nearly doubled over. "I said enough. It's time to shut up."

"I haven't collated in a long time, Glim. It's like my brain is too busy, trying to sort things out. I can't get calm."

He gave her a thoughtful look and released her knee. "How long do they take?"

"A couple of minutes . . . but I don't have my augments. . . ."

He reached into his jacket and pulled out her battered case. "These? You left them behind at the Temple."

She snatched the case from his hands and he chuckled. The few other people in the car glanced their way, one or two of them frowning, but no one moved. In a few seconds everyone had lost interest.

"And you thought I didn't care," Glim said.

She pried open the case, her hands shaking. She nearly dropped the collator-recorder, then fumbled at the back of her neck and swapped augments.

"Now if you aren't done by the time we stop, I'll rip that out of you," Glim said, but the words jumbled together, lost in the opening of her mind—

—and her entry into the sensorem. She descended the stairs to the storeroom and opened the door. The shelves were all still neatly stacked, the packages in undisturbed rows. She began going from one to the next, looking for a particular label. She knew it when she found it because she could not read it. The occlusion from the overlay masked it. The masking itself was like a beacon.

She pulled the package down and peeled the lid off.

"Something I can help you find?"

A woman stood beside her. Tall, very blonde, smiling quizzically as if she had never before seen such a thing as Nemily was doing. Nemily straightened.

"I just found it."

"Oh?"

"You."

"Me. You were looking for me in a box?"

"Silly idea, isn't it? But you see, that's where the occlusion put you. I would only have known to look for you there if I had known exactly who it was I had ghosted. It required outside verification—I couldn't just guess—someone had to tell me before I could find you—"

"Whoa, wait, you're going too fast. You're saying I'm a ghost?"

"Yes. This is my sensorem. I'm Nemily Dollard."

"I don't know you."

"We have a mutual acquaintance," Nemily said. "Mace."

Helen's ghost frowned. "And how do you know Mace?"

"We just met."

"Just met."

"We're seeing each other."

"Uh-huh. My husband—"

"Helen, you've been dead for nearly three years."

It took the ghost a moment to absorb that. She nodded. "Then it would be time. I hope you're not the first. Three years is quite a dry spell."

"A what?"

"A dry spell—old Earth metaphor—long time to go without water—a weather thing."

"Oh."

"All right, then," Helen said, folding her arms. "You're seeing my husband—my former husband—and you ghosted me? But it was an occluded ghost, so you wouldn't have remembered. Did Mace—?"

"No. Do you know Glim Toler?"

"I don't think so."

Nemily thought for a moment, then produced a reconstructed image of Toler. "Him," she said.

Helen's face hardened. "Cru Mills. Yes. Not well, but we've met. What do you have to do with him?"

"He ran you through me."

"What in hell for?"

"I don't know. Someone he knows wanted him to. I hoped—"

"Those bastards. So you're telling me that I died three years ago, but that they're still alive?"

"Yes."

"Then I failed." Suddenly, she sat down on the floor beside her box. "They never found the data packet I left..." She shook her head. "I hate failing."

"Maybe you didn't, not entirely," Nemily said. "If you can help me."

Helen looked up at her. "What do you need?"

Nemily laughed sharply. "What do I need? Oh, everything. Answers to start. What data packet? Where did you leave it?"

"It was an augment. When the storm began tearing the cover off the site, I was chasing Cru Mills. I followed him into the tunnel. He'd killed his accomplice, a CAP, and removed her augment. I never figured out what he needed a CAP for, but I left my update recorder/collator in her jack. I figure the company would run it and find my report, if I didn't survive."

"I see. It disappeared."

"Then there *was* another. Inside." She looked up at Nemily. "You want answers?"

"Yes."

"Fine. Give me your hand."

Hesitantly, Nemily reached for Helen's outstretched hand. Then she stopped.

"I need one straight answer first," Nemily said.

"To . . . ?"

"Do you love Mace?"

Helen smiled. "What do you think?"

Nemily nodded once and grasped Helen's hand—

—and removed the collator. She quickly inserted the synthesist and blinked.

"Feel better?" Glim asked.

She licked her lips and nodded.

A few minutes later, Glim grabbed her hand.

"Come on. We're here."

Nemily managed to get the augment back into its slot in the case and the lid snapped shut before Glim dragged her from the seat. He held her close as they ascended the stairs to the interior.

She looked around at the stop. Not far away was a secured entry. Club Standard.

"We're going to see Piers Hawthorne," she said.

"The one and only," Glim said.

"He's your contact. He's the one you ran the overlay through me for."

Glim grinned at her. "Exactly so. Shall we pay him a visit? I'm not welcome anymore, but I'm sure you can get us in without a bit of trouble."

EIGHTEEN

AEA, 2118

MACE PRESSED THE MICI and stepped back from the oversized door. It was impossible to see the size of the dom from here—the entry portico was practically a small room in itself—but he could feel it, it seemed, a vastness just beyond. There were larger doms in Aea but not many and most of them reduced the impact of size by architectural tricks. This one had simply been added to until it was a sprawl.

The door opened. Piers blinked at him, then grinned.

"Mace! Twice in one week, this is a record. Come in, come in."

Mace followed Piers down the hallway and into the wide living room.

"What can I blame for this?" Piers called over his shoulder. "Or have you changed your mind about Delia?"

"We need to talk, Piers."

Piers glanced at him. "Of course. I was just about to go up to my garden."

Mace waved his hand as if giving permission and Piers smiled.

"Something wet?" Piers asked. "You're not smiling, Mace, which means you're thirsty or you have something on your mind."

"Stat check."

"Excuse me...?"

"Let's sit down."

Piers' grin faded, but he led the way to his kitchen where he picked up a tray with a pitcher of amber liquid and a glass. He hesitated, frowned, and set the tray on the counter. He took another glass from the cabinet, then smiled at Mace.

"I tried to find out who has been bothering you from PolyCarb, Mace," he said as he went out a rear door and started up a set of ornate metal steps. "There's some security thing going on, something to do with pension fraud. The agent in charge—"

"Linder Koeln?"

"Yes, as a matter of fact."

They emerged on a broad patio. The walls were rimmed with flower boxes abloom with tulip, vinca, carnation and iris. Around a filigreed table and chairs, trees grew from heavy tubs. Piers placed the tray on the table and gestured Mace to a chair.

"I don't know anything about him, though," Piers continued, "and I got slapped in the face with a stern 'Confidential' icon when I dug around. Sorry."

"It's not important." Mace sat across from Piers. "Except that you're lying."

Piers poured without glancing at Mace. He set a glass before his guest and took his own. "Of course I am. What about?"

"Not knowing what the investigation concerns. You know."

"Do I?"

"I stopped by InFlux before coming here. I had some questions." Mace pulled a disc from his shirt pocket and dropped it on the table. "That is an InFlux record. Instead of detailing immigrations, though, this one is a record of sponsorships. It took some doing to get around the confidentiality protocols, but I managed to ask the right questions."

"Sponsorships. I don't understand."

"You know about sponsorships, Piers. Most immigrants to Aea are sponsored, they can't just come in here on a whim and live. Corporations do a lot of it for workers of one kind or another, and people who travel make friends they want to help immigrate. Once in a while there's a marriage involved, like me. From time to time it's political and I understand that there's a genealogical group that specializes in reuniting families. Nemily Dollard was sponsored."

"Really. I didn't know that."

"She works for you, Piers, of course you knew that."

Piers shrugged. "I'll take your word for it."

"It was brought to my attention that there was a peculiarity in her sponsorship."

"And that would be?"

"Helen sponsored her."

Piers frowned. "Helen...? As in—"

"My wife."

Piers looked at the disc. "How—?"

"I'd appreciate it if you'd stop lying to me, Piers."

"How could Helen have sponsored Nemily Dollard? Nemily didn't come here till—"

"The same way she sponsored Glim Toler."

Piers' eyes shifted toward the stairs, then up at Mace.

"Or," Mace went on, "do you know him better as Cru Mills? After all, you worked together on Mars for a short while."

"We did?"

"Yes. And Helen. At least, it was the same issue. I also found out you'd been to the Hellas Planitia site before the storm. Just a few days. You got back to Burroughs a couple days before the storm hit."

"Routine matters, Mace. Doesn't mean anything."

"Except that you never told me. In all this time, you never told me you knew Helen. See, your signature turns up on a number of her reports as adjuster of record. It never occurred to me to look before. Silly me. But once I realized that Cru Mills and Glim Toler were one and the same and that you'd had Toler as a guest in your house, well...."

A series of expressions passed over Piers' face in the next few seconds—shock, fear, panic, resentment, resignation, returning finally to shock. Piers lurched to his feet and staggered away from the table.

Mace rushed at him. Piers looked again toward the stairs but did not move. Mace grabbed his shirt, high at the collar, and snapped his fist into Piers' nose. Blood sprayed, forming a red mustache on Piers' lip. Mace spun him around and dropped him back in the chair.

Piers raised his hands to fend Mace off, but his gestures were uncoordinated. His eyes closed as the blood ran down his chin. Mace tightened his grip on the shirt and drew back to punch Piers again.

"I didn't know—! Mace, stop! I didn't—it wasn't supposed to happen—"

"What wasn't? Killing Helen?"

"I wasn't there when it happened! She—"

"You and Cru Mills worked for SetNetComb. You were there to destroy the project. Helen got in the way, didn't she?"

"I don't know! I'm telling the truth!"

Mace hit him again. Piers barked sharply in pain and would have fallen out of the chair if Mace had let him go.

"Stop! Damn, Mace, I *didn't do it!*" His voice was plagued with a strong lisp, the result of a now-broken nose.

"You know who did! Why was Toler in your house?"

"Please...."

"Why was Glim Toler in your house? Why did you have Nemily Dollard here?"

"Mace, Mace, it isn't what you think—damn, you broke my nose—"

Mace pulled him to his feet and brought his face close.

"I'll break a lot more than that if you don't start talking to me!"

"Yes, for the—all right! Now don't hit me again!"

Mace shoved him at the chair, hard, and Piers toppled over it. He rolled on his shoulder and tried to get to his feet. Mace stepped up to him and swung his right foot up into Piers' stomach, sending Piers sprawling with a loud shout.

"Why?" Mace asked.

Piers looked at him resentfully. He tried to talk, but winced and held his stomach. He breathed deeply and finally managed a breathy "Which part?"

"Start somewhere."

Piers prodded gingerly at his nose. Mace could hear cartilage crackle delicately. Suddenly he leaned down and took Piers' nose between both hands and jerked. Piers yelled and sneezed violently and more blood sprayed.

Piers slowly rolled into a sitting position and wrapped his arms around his waist. He gulped air for a minute, then said, "It—we were supposed to undermine the Hellas project. Aea was making XMs...exotic materials, molifiber definitely, but other material, too...we were only going to damage the sheeting, the cover, not...." His eyes reddened. "All those people, Mace...it wasn't...that was never...."

Piers sobbed loudly, once.

"Toler intended to kill. He said it was the only way to make the point—that SetNetComb had decided that any attempt to manufacture XMs off the moon had to be blocked. You do that by attacking the credibility of the material. You make it stick by causing deaths. A war, he said. It was a war. That's not what SetNetComb said, but the department deploying Toler did. I didn't want any part of that. I left."

"You, Toler—who else? Cavery?"

"No, he didn't know—he was paid, that's all. He just looked the other way for a fee, fixed records."

"And Oxmire?"

"I think he might have been with Toler. I don't know."

"Tell me about Helen."

Piers moaned, shaking his head. "She...knew. She knew Toler, she knew me." He sniffed and winced. "She figured it out soon after she arrived. Toler commed me to let me know. I think she'd been investigating us, I don't know for sure, but Toler—when she showed up that's when he decided to go for maximum impact."

"You *think* she knew?"

"Well. Yes. She knew. I only confirmed that recently. Yes, she'd been investigating suspected industrial sabotage for a long time. That's why she was brought back in from Ganymede, because she had been out of the loop all that time and corporate knew she could be trusted. Her method—typical Helen—was to join us."

"She knew you."

Piers nodded. "We'd worked together before. At Hellas I'd heard she was coming and I told Toler I had to leave, that my presence would compromise the operation. I didn't know then that she already suspected me. He agreed with the proviso that I pick him up afterward. I didn't know exactly what afterward he meant, but he said it would be obvious. As it turned out, it was. We had a tractor stashed near one of the service bores. We'd planned to set a booby trap at that shaft, just in case. I *did* set it up."

"Before Toler could get out?"

"I never intended to get him out. The man was insane."

"What about Helen?"

Piers shook his head.

"What about the sponsorships?" Mace insisted.

"That was...Lunase needed people in place. When Helen was away, I used her ID to sponsor trojans. Only a few. Most of them left Aea soon after arriving."

"To where? Cassidy? Five-Eight? Midline?"

Piers nodded.

"Why?" Mace asked. "Loyalty to Lunase? Why? Why Helen?"

Mace reached for him. Piers slapped his hand away and scooted back.

"What do you want? I've tried to make it up to you! I made sure you retained your citizenship, I pushed through your insurance claims, I even got you work! I never intended Helen to die! When I came back with Cambel and I saw what had happened, I was sick! I quit then! I turned my back on Lunase and retired from the so-called war! I've done what I could to make it up to you—"

"Short of telling me the truth."

"And what would you have done? *I* have a life, too!"

"I might have understood."

"Of course you would have. When? After you'd killed me? Or would you just have turned me in and seen me deported, back to Lunase where I'm considered a traitor? Don't try to tell me you have the capacity to be more than human, Mace Preston."

Mace took a step back. Piers was right, he knew. Anytime in the last three years he might have gone for revenge without any thought to circumstance.

"Nothing justifies what you did on Mars," he said.

"No. Nothing. But it's done."

"What about Toler? Why'd you bring him here?"

"I didn't."

"You sponsored him!"

"Before Mars! I never sent for him, he just showed up. Why would I? He's insane."

"That's a hell of an excuse. What's yours?"

"I didn't—I never wanted—"

"Damnit, Piers, Helen sponsored you." He bounced the disc off Piers' forehead.

"Of course she did, years back, when I needed help to get off Lunase. That was legitimate."

"Why? What did she get from you?"

"I was—" He swallowed, looking away. "I was a double agent. I did freelance work for PolyCarb. Helen was my operator. Lunase found out. Helen got me out before they arrested me."

"She helped you hide the trail?"

"Yes. It was necessary, then. Lunessa were even less trusted than they are now. And besides, it was possible Lunase would come after me. Turns out, they did."

"So you started working for Lunase again. What was that, habit?"

"Money. All right? Money. It was all harmless anyway, just information. Lunase felt it could never get a fair chance with Aea—"

"They're not exactly doing anything to earn our trust, are they? Like you! She sponsored you, helped you, and you betrayed her!"

"No! I didn't—it wasn't supposed to happen that way! The storm made it worse than it should've been!"

"She died, Piers! You helped kill her! Was that harmless?"

Piers writhed, refused to look at Mace.

"What about Cassidy and the others since?" Mace asked.

"I didn't know anything about those. I told you, I quit, I didn't have anything—"

"Toler came here, to see you, though. I saw him."

"Bad timing, I swear. I was visiting Reese when Simity brought him to Reese's clutch. Then he just showed up."

Mace picked up the disc from the floor and sat down. "Death came here with Toler. He had the key to activate the molecular solvent, didn't he? What did Nemily have to do with it?"

"Nothing, she was just a carrier. She had the algorithms embedded, deep. As she worked here, she discovered the weaknesses in Aea that the molecular solvent could attack. Toler could download the algorithms and the specifications, which were combined through a CAP's collator. She was analyzing everything without ever knowing it."

"You needed a CAP for the whole thing to work, then?"

"Yes."

"The dead CAP's missing augment on Mars."

"Yes. I'm sorry, Mace, but she had seen us both, she knew, she contained the initiation protocols. If you'd gotten a chance to look at it—"

Mace raised his hand. "So any one of dozens of Lunessa emigrés could have been mules, carrying the same occluded instructions, all waiting."

Piers nodded.

"Nemily never would have been sent back," Mace said. "Those discs in her baggage were just an introduction, a way to get her listed with the right people...so who are the right people?"

Piers stood carefully, holding his ribs. He righted the overturned chair and sat down. "I always thought there was another trojan in the company. I have no idea who."

"The same person who killed Reese Nagel and tried to kill Patri Simity."

"Patri—why would anyone try to kill her?"

"Because she was betraying your little war."

Piers scowled painfully and slammed his hand on the table. "It is *not* my little war. I retired from the field. Hellas was enough. Too much."

Mace studied Piers for a time. The man was in shambles, his face and shirt front covered in blood, tears streaming from his eyes, his breathing shallow and labored. Piers shuddered a couple of times. He picked a napkin off the drink tray and started carefully cleaning his face. Abruptly, Mace lost any desire to hurt Piers further.

"Toler contacted Simity before anyone else," Mace said. "She sent him to Reese with the data with a note that Reese ought to turn it over to SA. But Reese was working a deal with PolyCarb for his new illicit datafeed from Earth. If he got SA involved then, it might have ruined the whole thing for him. He wanted that deal done first, so he took the problem to PolyCarb security."

Piers looked up, frowning. "Through whom?"

"Linder Koeln."

"You have a guest at the front door," the house system announced, causing both of them to jerk.

"Who?"

"Nemily Dollard and an unidentified man."

Mace headed for the stairs.

"Mace, wait; this is still my dom."

Piers descended the metal stairs carefully.

"I don't think anything is actually broken," he said at the bottom, "but you certainly bent something."

They approached the door and Piers waved Mace aside, into the living room.

"I'll take care of it. I won't run off, I promise."

"I don't think you can."

Piers nodded. "You're right." He stepped into the bathroom along the hall. Mace heard water running, then Piers emerged with a damp rag with which he wiped off the rest of the blood on his chin. He shrugged. "So I walked into a door, if anyone asks," he said and continued on.

Mace stepped out of the hallway and leaned against the wall just inside the living room, and watched Piers.

"Open," Piers said.

The door obeyed. Mace glimpsed Nemily and someone else right behind her.

"Ms. Dollard, what an—oh, hell."

Mace saw Piers suddenly drop limply to the floor. The man behind Nemily shoved her forward and started to turn. His head jerked to one side and he collapsed against the door.

Nemily staggered over Piers and tried to catch her balance. Mace leapt for her. She looked up, eyes wide, and opened her mouth to shout—

—Mace collided with the wall, his left leg suddenly useless beneath him. The pain came a few seconds later—along with the instant realization that he had been shot. He rolled. Nemily crawled toward him. He caught her hand and pulled. He tried to push himself to his feet, but could not manage it with a shattered kneecap. Nausea crept through him.

Linder Koeln stood in the doorway to the kitchen, a pistol fitted with a silencer in his hand.

"Very neat," he said. "I never imagined that I'd be able to finish it all in one place."

Mace pulled the disc from his shirt pocket and sailed it at Koeln. It caught him across the forehead and he pulled back. Mace started lurching toward the living room. Nemily took his arm and dragged him the rest of the way.

"Damn," Koeln said. "You've complicated matters, Mr. Preston. Now I have to kill you, too. Don't think I'll miss a second time."

"I don't."

"Mace...." Nemily whispered.

He put a finger to her lips, then pointed at the dining room entrance. She nodded and crawled away.

"Good, Glim has his own weapon," Koeln said. Another muffled shot went off, a heavy, suppressed sound that was obvious now. "That was very cooperative of him."

"Why are you doing this?" Mace asked.

"Evidence."

"You killed Reese."

"Yes. And Simity. And this unfortunate at my feet is Toler."

"You didn't finish with Simity."

"Really? She's tougher than I thought. She should have bled to death."

"That's what you were doing in the Temple when I found you there."

"You interrupted things then, too. I was interrogating the good Patri first. She was reluctant. I didn't have time to clean up as well as I like. Talking is fine, Mr. Preston, but I won't humor you for long." Koeln's voice sounded closer.

"Interrogating her for what?"

"I needed to find all the players," Koeln said. "I even had Ms. Dollard under surveillance in her workspace when she was linked in, hoping to trace any messages she might send to confederates. But it turned out she didn't have any, she was just a mule."

The pain was overwhelming. Mace's entire left leg felt as though it had been crushed, and beneath the agony he felt dampness spreading.

"You've been in the house all along?" Mace asked.

"I overheard your interrogation of Mr. Hawthorne."

Then Koeln stood above him, aiming at him, but then suddenly frowned and spun around.

"I'll find Ms. Dollard before the end of the day," he said, turning back to Mace. "So you've only postponed her death."

"Why?"

"She's a witness."

Mace shivered. That was bad, he knew that, but he could not think what it meant. "I don't—"

"No, of course not. I'm closing down the program. Those are my instructions. Midline, in case you're wondering, never should have happened."

"Rogue operation?" Mace asked, remembering what Philip had told him. He wondered then how Philip knew so much, but he felt cold and knew he was beginning to go into shock. His memory might just be tricking him.

"That's exactly right," Koeln said. "Originally, I was supposed to oversee implementation of the program. Aea was a target. But politics change all the time, often very quickly. It's been called off. Except a few overly dedicated zealots refused to stand down. So now I'm to eliminate all trace of what we were doing. Piers, Glim, and regrettably Ms. Dollard now, were the last components of a very complex program. Piers was the one party I couldn't trace at first, he'd covered his trail very well. When Toler showed up—contrary to orders, by the way—he flushed Piers for me. After that it was simple to find all the connections."

"You said . . . closing down? Aea—"

"Will not be destroyed, no. An agreement has been reached and Lunase-Aean relations are moving to a new phase. This . . . program . . . is an embarrassing leftover. Time to bury the remains. And of course, you are part of those now. I have to ask, though, if there's anyone else. Do you know?"

The shivering was becoming uncontrollable now. The pain had diminished slightly, but he knew he was in trouble.

"You're in shock, Mr. Preston. Too bad. I suppose I'll have to bury your associates, too, just to be sure."

"PolyCarb—you got inside?"

Koeln laughed. "Of course. It's easy when you're invited in. Now, enough. You should think about something pleasant. I'm going to kill you now."

"That's . . . pleasant. . . ."

"Yes, well."

Mace braced himself as best he could, though the shivering persisted and grew stronger. He wondered what death would sound like, if he would hear the shot. Probably not. Too close, too immediate. He waited.

He heard . . . something . . . clattering, a thud, grunting. Furniture was being moved. That was odd. Why would Koeln move the furniture before killing him? The man was Lunessa, who knew what rituals they practiced in extremes?

Toler was dead, Reese was dead, he would kill Nemily. Mace felt intensely sad and angry at that. Nemily deserved better.

It was quiet now. Death would come silently, he knew, a quick passing from apprehension to nothing. He tried to imagine nothing. The dreams of a cyberlink? So he had heard. So he had heard. . . .

Mace opened his eyes and saw Philip leaning over him. Philip looked very concerned.

"Macefield? Can you hear me?"

Mace opened his mouth, but a garbled croak was all he could manage.

"Pathic is on its way. I've given you something to stabilize you, but you're going to pathic for a time. Do you understand?"

Mace made himself nod.

Philip looked up. "He's all right."

"You're SA," he heard Cambel say. "I should have known."

"Are you certain you didn't?" Philip asked wryly. "You went along with a great many coincidences on my part."

Mace strained to see who else was around. He wanted to see Nemily, but all he saw was Cambel, standing against the opposite wall, scowling, and beside her a woman with broad shoulders: Colf.

"Pathic is here," Cambel said.

Mace reached up to grab Philip's arm. "Nemily...?"

"She's fine." He leaned close to whisper. "There should be no problems." He straightened. "It's time for you to go be healed, Macefield." He patted Mace's hand.

Philip had answered the wrong question. Mace wanted to know if Nemily would be expelled. What would happen next? But Philip was gone and suddenly strangers in coveralls were around him, prodding him and hooking him up to their devices. And then he was asleep.

Cambel sat by his bedside. Mace blinked; his eyes felt gummy. He coughed and she looked up.

"Thirsty?" she asked. She moved a tube to his mouth and he sucked. "Welcome back to the world of the living."

"Thanks. How long?"

"Oh, less than two days. I told them you prefer to be awake and they finally decided that you weren't hurt badly enough to keep you under."

"That was considerate of you."

"I thought so."

The door to his room opened and Philip stepped in. He carried two packages under his arm.

"Macefield."

"Philip."

"How are you feeling?"

"I don't know yet. Cambel says I'm alive."

"A hole in your leg. They're regrowing your kneecap. Painful, I'm sure, but not fatal." He looked uncomfortable for a moment, then held up the packages. "I considered just sending these to your dom, but I thought you might prefer a more personal delivery." He set the larger package beside Mace.

It was actually a metal case. Mace fingered the latch and the lid

popped open. Within, set in padding, were three ranks of the miniatures Philip had promised him. The colors, even in the flat lighting of
the pathic room, glowed brightly.

"Thank you. Thank you very much." He looked up. "What's that?"

Philip set the smaller box beside the larger. "Your friend Ms. Dollard's
augments. We confiscated them to vet them of anything... classifiable.
But they're clean."

Mace opened the case. "I see. What am I going to do with them?"

"I imagine you could give them back to her."

Mace looked up at Philip. "I remember someone saying that you're SA."
Philip nodded.

"Why were you there?"

"Cambel. Glim—"

"Slugged me from behind at Nemily's apartment," Cambel said.
"There's no way to put a decent spin on it."

Philip pursed his lips in an almost-smile. "I was about to confront
Piers anyway. I finally had enough evidence."

"What evidence was that?"

"One of my people witnessed him present during a private ghosting
session—with Nemily Dollard. He was there with Toler."

"Ghost...?"

"Something Piers had from Hellas, evidently. An augment. The one I
believe was missing from the site."

"Piers took it."

"That and the recorder," Cambel said.

"Where is it now?"

"We have the recorder—it was in his dom—but the augment is missing again. I suppose we could do a deep probe on Ms. Dollard to find
out—my agent tells me it was an occluded overlay, Nemily would have
no conscious memory of it—"

"Your agent. Colf?"

"Yes."

"She was also working with Koeln."

"No. Colf took over Reese's operation when he was killed. Koeln had
to deal with her then."

They were silent together for a time. Mace felt certain that he was not
being told everything, but now it did not bother him. He knew Helen
had been innocent.

"Piers was the first trojan. Koeln was the one you needed to find."

"Yes," Philip said sourly. "Piers never really did anything, so we couldn't be sure. He just did his job and acted his part and waited. I think he actually changed his mind about the situation and wanted just to live here. Likely as not he had simply grown too comfortable. His position here would never be matched in Lunase."

"You didn't know about Koeln, though."

"I had begun to suspect." He looked mildly embarrassed. "Your arrest was a rather heavy-handed ploy to get him to make a move. It worked better than we had hoped thanks to Ms. Dollard's presence. He showed up and removed Ms. Dollard. He had no legitimate reason to do that. But then he offered you PolyCarb assistance to deal with what he thought we had arrested you for."

"You mentioned evidence. What evidence?"

"Evidence Helen had accrued. She'd been looking into some irregularities in the Ganymede project, which was being supplied by the first generation of Aean exotic materials to come off the new lines. Some of the same materials that had gone into the Hellas Planitia project. No one outside PolyCarb was supposed to know about that, but as soon as they shipped, Lunase began making demands in the Signatory trade talks to limit any and all potential manufacture of XMs outside the Lunase labs. The timing was suspect. PolyCarb brought her back in to find the source of the leaked data. She hadn't gotten far, but there was a body of evidence. Someone inside PolyCarb was not only passing information but beginning to undermine the projects. Small things, things that might have been coincidences, but—Helen never believed in coincidence and neither do I."

"Helen was security, wasn't she?"

"Among other things. She really was an excellent engineer. But her talents were unique."

Mace swallowed thickly and cleared his throat. "Did you know her?" he asked.

"Not personally. But I'm familiar with her work. Remarkable person."

"I never knew."

"She gave you her persona encoding," Cambel said. "She probably thought you'd access it. Then you'd have known all of it. I think she'd be pretty pissed off if she knew you never did."

"I'm beginning to think she married me just to have a backup in case something went wrong."

"I don't think that's the case," Cambel said.

"Mmm. Maybe." He looked at Philip. "What happens now?"

"About what?"

"Don't do that, Philip. We've been friends too long."

Philip pursed his lips. "And the question is, are we still?"

"Partly."

"I would like to think so, Macefield."

"Then tell me what happens now. What is SA going to do to Nemily?"

"I don't know. Nothing much, I imagine. I've already vouched for her."

"And me?"

"I don't understand. Why would anything happen to you?"

"I—" He glanced at Cambel. "I probably obstructed your investigation."

"Nonsense. Without you, it might never have been resolved. If anyone is going to have to answer for anything, I imagine it will be Lunase and PolyCarb. They colluded over eradicating evidence. A number of people are dead."

"PolyCarb could have prevented Midline," Cambel said. "If I understand what this new agreement is all about."

"No," Philip said. "Lunase had ordered the program terminated after Cassidy. Even Five-Eight was an unauthorized strike. The people responsible had stopped taking orders." He looked troubled, a deeply conflicted expression Mace had never seen on his face before. "I don't know what will happen. If anything."

"If anything," Mace echoed.

"If anything." He leaned over and rapped his forefinger on the augment case. "But you can return these to Ms. Dollard personally."

"Is SA going to expel her?"

Philip frowned. "Not on my recommendation, certainly. There will be a hearing. What they'll decide...."

"What about me?"

"That was never a question."

"Not for you."

"It was never a question."

Mace picked up the augment case. "Thank you."

"Macefield. I would like to know."

Mace studied Philip's dark face for a long time. Then he nodded. "We're still friends, Philip."

Philip nodded. "I have details to attend."

He left the room and it seemed that a heaviness remained. Mace wondered if he could live up to his answer. He hoped so.

"Will we still be doing business?" Cambel asked.

"If you want to continue a partnership with an unobservant, insensitive idiot."

"No, I don't think so. But with you—I think we can work something out."

"Thank you."

"Oh, don't thank me. You may live to regret this."

Mace reinitiated his domestic personality.

"How long am I going to be online?" Helen asked immediately.

"As long as you want," Mace said.

"Not if you're going to put me in a closet every time something happens that makes you nervous. I could probably have kept SA out. You should trust me a little more."

"Sorry."

"But that's not the reason you closed me down, is it?"

"What do you mean?"

"Nemily Dollard is in the building. This is highly suggestive, Mace."

Mace was silent for a time.

"Mace?" the d.p. prompted.

"I think I want her to stay with me."

"I think that might be a good thing. What about me?"

"What about you?"

"Don't you think I'll get in the way?"

"You know the answer to that better than I do."

"You're right."

"So I'll leave the choice up to you."

"I think you need someone watching your back door."

"I take that as a yes, then."

"Yes. Now let me go through all the backlog that's stacked up since you took me offline. Go see Nemily. It's your turn to make a decision."

Nemily sat on the floor of the greenhouse. Mace breathed in the rich odors of mulch and loam and green life and ached to touch her. She held another augment in her hands, turning it over and over. Finally, she handed it to him.

"Mace, I—" She seemed conflicted, but he did not push. She sighed heavily. "I talked to Cambel about this while you were in pathic," she said. "She recommended I not run it. I agreed with her reasons."

"What did she say?"

"That you should be with me if you love me. That my becoming Helen, even a small part, would only complicate things for you. That you should choose and that I should be myself only. It could be unhealthy for you to carry on a sometime relationship with your dead wife."

Mace winced, but he could not fault the logic. He had the faint suspicion she was withholding something, but if it involved Cambel it might be best left unexamined.

"What about—?" He hesitated.

"Love? How will I know?" She smiled sadly. "I don't want to be anywhere else—with anyone else. Maybe that's enough. But I don't want to complicate what we have with...." She waved at the augment now in Mace's hand.

"Ghosts?"

"Yes." She shrugged again. "I've had more than my fill of them. Maybe there's another way to learn it. I'd like to find that out first. If you want to try."

Mace looked down at the augment for a time. "I never accessed the ROM and I never knew why. Maybe I should just always wonder." He walked over to a tree on the workbench and screwed the augment into the dirt at its base. It resembled a dull metal mushroom, but then gradually took on the coloring of the earth. "At least we've got the time."

"Maybe. That depends on what SA decides. If they—"

"It will be fine. Philip vouched for you. So did I, as if it'll do any good."

She shrugged. "We'll see. If they decide to expel me...will you come with me?"

"I—"

"No, don't answer now. Wait till their decision." She smiled quickly. "Maybe some things are better left unanswered. But for us...yes, I would like to try."

He descended to the kitchen deep into nightcycle. His body felt tight, almost vibrating from the physical exhaustion. His leg still ached from the bullet wound, but it was passing. Nemily slept.

Will you go with me?

Mace wished she had not asked him that. He believed he would, but he could not say it with absolute certainty. He had always wanted to live on Aea. Even now, tainted as it was, he could not think of another place he wanted to spend his life.

Would he have gone elsewhere with Helen?

Fortunately, the question was moot.

Philip would intercede with Structural Authority on Nemily's behalf. She was, for the moment, still a citizen. The SA lock had been taken off his personal accounts, his d.p. was back up and functioning smoothly, and Cambel still wanted them to work together, although, she said, she needed some time. He thought he understood that. Time was not enough by itself, but without it nothing else could heal.

He poured himself a glass of orange juice and drank it in the semi-dark of the touret.

That Philip worked for SA no longer surprised Mace. He understood, or thought he did. Colf had been a surprise—she had infiltrated both Reese's organization and PolyCarb security. Koeln had thought she was working for him because of the connection to Reese. Thinking about it, Mace felt like an amateur.

"Mace?" Helen said. "You know you still never opened your presents."

"I forgot all about them." He laughed. "Cart them out. I hope there weren't any perishables."

"My scans didn't indicate so."

The closet door slid open, allowing the dolly to roll forward, still laden with his presents from Hawthorne's party.

The wrapping paper varied from shimmery silver and blue to plain white to dark red. Most of the packages were small, less than twenty-five centimeters on a side. One thin rectangle looked to be about a hundred by eighty.

Careful of his still-healing knee, Mace sat down on the floor by his gifts. He took a package at random—mauve paper—and carefully pried up the edges and uncovered the hinged box. Inside he found a stack of discs. He lifted the first and felt a thrill at the faded label. It was old, very old—Shostakovich, Symphony 11, a full-sized CD from the last century. He looked through the others quickly. All Shostakovich, all vintage recordings, no two from the same manufacturer or conductor or orchestra. This had cost someone a great deal. He did not even want to do the math for the freight. Eight discs, almost half a kilogram, and they *had* to have come up the well from Earth. Possibly from Lunase, but....

Unexpectedly, he felt warmly sentimental. He wondered who had gone to the expense. He could think of at least ten people who had been at the party who could afford it, but he would never have expected it. Who would have known that he had no Shostakovich? For once he wished custom permitted him to ask.

He set the box aside and opened another. Handmade earrings, small silvered pearls with a spark of corundum. Mace knew who had made them, he already owned some of her work. They were delicate things and he might wear them only once and then put them in the display case in his sensora room with her other gifts.

The next contained three handpainted kerchiefs, soft expanses of translucent fabric swirled in colors. No, he did not know who might have given him these.

Four of them had software packets, two revealed polished geodes—probably from the Belt—and five of them held rings, all of them purchased from one of the jewelers in Segment Three Mall, downshaft near Tsiolkovsky Park. The workmanship was impeccable. Mace slipped on a cobalt blue circle that held a gold plat with intricate carvings. It reminded him of old chip patterns, but it might as easily be a map of some city on the moon, or even a section of one of the old cities on Earth. The ring fit nicely.

He opened a heavy box and stared at the plastic wrapping for several seconds before realizing what it contained. He lifted it out and held it in his lap. Topsoil. Dark, loamy. He turned the bag over and a small printed label said "Idaho" and nothing else. It took an effort to put it back in the box and set it aside. Earth soil. Never mind the expense, he thought, just getting it through customs would require...he could imagine what Structural Authority would say.

A small package contained a cube that held, suspended and possibly still alive, a dragonfly.

The large one was, as he had thought, a painting. Tiny triangular flakes of color combined across the board to form impressions of clouds, blotches of light, fragmented spectra. Mace recognized the work. He decided to have it framed. He would hang it and invite the artist to dinner.

The envelopes all contained cards with birthday wishes and redeemables for various shops and artisans. One held five shares of stock in a new ore-cracking company.

One contained a letter. He unfolded the sheaf of pages and started to read. At the top the date indicated that it had been written over three years earlier, before Mars. He sat very still for a long time, staring at the opening line, unable to read further.

"My darling Mace, I have a feeling this will be my last opportunity to tell you how much you mean to me...."